NEW GEPT
新制全民英檢
初級 閱讀測驗必考題型

U0035168

許秀芬／著

國際語言中心委員會 ＆

Part 1
詞彙

◎ 意義辨析

|常|考|詞|彙|題|型|

TYPE 1 意義辨析

P art 1 共有 10 題，每題各有一個空格，要考慮整個句子表達的意思，從選項中選出意義上最恰當的答案。原本在舊制的初級閱讀測驗中，Part 1 也包括文法考題，但新制的 Part 1 已經改為以測試詞彙能力為主，而不會考單複數、動詞時態、助動詞用法之類的問題。不過，了解句子的結構並掌握句中的連接詞，對於理解語意、找出正確答案也會有幫助。

Study 1 意義辨析：名詞

Q1 **Become a _____ and enjoy special offers in our store.**
（A）friend （B）member
（C）visitor （D）officer

Q2 **This is my _____ card. Contact me if you need to.**
（A）birthday （B）business
（C）credit （D）memory

Q3 **Is your birthday in this _____ or the next?**
（A）case （B）moment
（C）month （D）year

Q4 **Have you read the _____ in the morning paper?**
（A）meaning （B）novel
（C）article （D）picture

Q5 Most teenagers are interested in popular _____, especially pop music.
(A) classic
(B) comic
(C) career
(D) culture

Q6 The _____ of paper is too heavy for me to lift.
(A) piece
(B) sheet
(C) pile
(D) number

Q7 Everyone should follow the _____ when playing a game, or it won't be fair.
(A) rules
(B) leaders
(C) guides
(D) fashion

Q8 Because of complaints about the problem, the team had to find a _____.
(A) solution
(B) standard
(C) skill
(D) secret

Q9 John was late for work this morning because of heavy _____.
(A) accident
(B) crowd
(C) traffic
(D) damage

Q10 _____ must report truth when they write a news story.
(A) Artists
(B) Dentists
(C) Journalists
(D) Scientists

Q11 This _____ of the textbook is difficult, so our teacher taught us twice.
(A) decision
(B) education
(C) operation
(D) section

Q12 Many wild animals will be in _____ if we don't protect the environment.

(A) doubt
(B) trouble
(C) question
(D) relation

Q13 Doctors agree that good sleep can improve one's _____.

(A) health
(B) breath
(C) illness
(D) stress

Q14 I don't know how to solve this problem. I need to ask for some _____.

(A) advice
(B) concern
(C) space
(D) progress

Q15 The _____ of the study is to find out the causes of the crisis.

(A) result
(B) problem
(C) influence
(D) purpose

Q16 Cold and flu are more common when the _____ change.

(A) seasons
(B) years
(C) days
(D) feelings

Q17 The debate between them was a _____ of time. They were just arguing.

(A) matter
(B) waste
(C) lot
(D) length

Q18 To save money, you need to compare _____ before buying.

(A) sales
(B) qualities
(C) functions
(D) prices

Q19 I made a _____ of tasks to do, or I may forget later.

（A）list　　　　　　　　　（B）post

（C）number　　　　　　　（D）system

Q20 This cake has fruits on top and chocolate at the _____.

（A）base　　　　　　　　　（B）end

（C）beginning　　　　　　（D）time

Study 2　意義辨析：形容詞

Q1 The teacher was _____ that half of the students were late for school.

（A）surprised　　　　　　（B）surprising

（C）interested　　　　　　（D）interesting

Q2 It was _____ of him to leave the umbrella in the train.

（A）careful　　　　　　　（B）careless

（C）helpful　　　　　　　（D）helpless

Q3 The cats look very _____. I can't tell their difference.

（A）same　　　　　　　　（B）different

（C）alike　　　　　　　　（D）unique

Q4 Not _____ fast foods are bad. Some can be good for your health.

（A）some　　　　　　　　（B）all

（C）few　　　　　　　　　（D）several

Q5 Peter feels lonely because he has _____ friends in the company.

（A）few　　　　　　　　　（B）a few

（C）some　　　　　　　　（D）lots of

Q6 **We have** _____ **time to waste. We have to leave right now.**

(A) all   (B) some

(C) no   (D) a little

Q7 **The sentence is not** _____ **. It lacks a verb.**

(A) true   (B) full

(C) complete   (D) necessary

Q8 **A greedy person is never** _____ **with what he has.**

(A) concerned   (B) careful

(C) upset   (D) satisfied

Q9 **People wear** _____ **clothes now since the weather is warmer.**

(A) lighter   (B) tighter

(C) brighter   (D) broader

Q10 **Thank you for the delicious food, but I'm** _____ **now.**

(A) full   (B) fine

(C) enough   (D) afraid

Q11 **How could he be so** _____ **to kill the lovely dog?**

(A) scared   (B) painful

(C) jealous   (D) cruel

Q12 **Joseph is a** _____ **person. He doesn't share anything with his friends.**

(A) confident   (B) diligent

(C) selfish   (D) ordinary

Q13 **I thought it was a** _____ **problem, but it turned out to be quite serious.**

(A) major   (B) minor

(C) general   (D) generous

Q14 **It was a _____ trip. We enjoyed it very much.**

（A）used （B）usual

（C）pleased （D）pleasant

Q15 **Most people use _____ media sites to stay in touch with their friends.**

（A）official （B）social

（C）special （D）mass

Q16 **After one week's search, their child is still _____.**

（A）missing （B）missed

（C）alive （D）absent

Q17 **As a beginner, you have to learn _____ grammar first.**

（A）basic （B）classic

（C）difficult （D）serious

Q18 **I am _____ to hear that your father passed away.**

（A）glad （B）able

（C）sorry （D）interested

Q19 **Susan is really _____. She can't stay quiet for a moment.**

（A）active （B）positive

（C）effective （D）talkative

Q20 **Mr. Smith is not _____ right now. Would you like to leave a message?**

（A）possible （B）available

（C）responsible （D）comfortable

Study 3 意義辨析：副詞

Q1 **You came _____. He has already left.**

（A）early （B）late

（C）beforehand （D）afterward

Q2 She keeps singing that song _____. She's really crazy about it.

（A）every now and then　　（B）over and over again

（C）once in a while　　（D）from time to time

Q3 Mary isn't _____ early for school. Sometimes she comes late.

（A）never　　（B）seldom

（C）sometimes　　（D）always

Q4 Just wait for a moment. He will be here _____.

（A）fast　　（B）soon

（C）once　　（D）nearly

Q5 The cakes are _____ the same. There isn't any difference.

（A）nearly　　（B）exactly

（C）likely　　（D）hardly

Q6 He didn't have enough money. _____, he gave up buying that book.

（A）Therefore　　（B）However

（C）Even so　　（D）In other words

Q7 There was a car accident this morning. _____, no one was hurt.

（A）Painfully　　（B）Luckily

（C）Recently　　（D）Suddenly

Q8 I found that famous shop _____ when I was taking a walk.

（A）by accident　　（B）on foot

（C）at times　　（D）at once

Q9 **By practicing every day, his English is improving** _____.

（A）one by one   （B）side by side

（C）little by little   （D）back to back

Q10 **We have to leave** _____, **or we will be late for the party.**

（A）for good   （B）on purpose

（C）at times   （D）right away

Q11 **My leg ached so much that I could** _____ **stand.**

（A）badly   （B）hardly

（C）even   （D）ever

Q12 **I don't know why he didn't call me after we first met.** _____ **he doesn't like me.**

（A）Therefore   （B）Finally

（C）Sometimes   （D）Perhaps

Q13 **I can't see the words** _____. **I need my glasses.**

（A）patiently   （B）fairly

（C）clearly   （D）quickly

Q14 **Helen feels very happy because her husband loves her** _____.

（A）dearly   （B）fairly

（C）silently   （D）calmly

Q15 **As a team, we should work** _____ **and help each other.**

（A）around   （B）alone

（C）alike   （D）together

Q16 **Among the seasons, Sylvia likes winter the** _____ **because she usually catches a cold.**

（A）best   （B）least

（C）last   （D）most

Q17 **I don't understand this chapter very well. I'll go _____ and read it again.**

（A）back
（B）away
（C）down
（D）along

Q18 **My report is _____ done. I just need to write the last sentence.**

（A）all
（B）almost
（C）half
（D）never

Q19 **Even though we can't travel _____, we still have many places to visit in Taiwan.**

（A）abroad
（B）alone
（C）recently
（D）yet

Q20 **Can you go _____ and take out the trash for me?**

（A）further
（B）anywhere
（C）downtown
（D）downstairs

Study 4　意義辨析：連接詞

TIP

that, if, whether 等從屬連接詞，可引導名詞子句（在整個句子裡扮演名詞的角色）。

when, while, after, before, till, since, as soon as 等從屬連接詞，引導副詞子句（在整個句子裡扮演副詞的角色）。when 表示時間，where 表示地方，because 表示理由、原因，so, so that 表示結果，if, unless 表示條件，although 表示讓步。

Q1 **Ken is a teacher, _____ he likes his students.**

（A）and
（B）or
（C）but
（D）so

Q2 **She likes cooking, _____ she hates to do the dishes.**

　（A）and　　　　　　　　　　（B）or

　（C）but　　　　　　　　　　（D）so

Q3 **Study hard, _____ you will fail the exam.**

　（A）and　　　　　　　　　　（B）or

　（C）but　　　　　　　　　　（D）so

Q4 **It may rain today, _____ don't forget to bring an umbrella.**

　（A）and　　　　　　　　　　（B）or

　（C）but　　　　　　　　　　（D）so

Q5 **_____ the package arrives, I'll let you know right away.**

　（A）Once　　　　　　　　　　（B）Before

　（C）Except　　　　　　　　　（D）Until

Q6 **The gangsters ran away _____ they saw the police officer.**

　（A）although　　　　　　　　（B）where

　（C）when　　　　　　　　　　（D）unless

Q7 **I wonder _____ he will show up. He didn't really promise to come.**

　（A）if　　　　　　　　　　　（B）how

　（C）what　　　　　　　　　　（D）while

Q8 **We will leave early, _____ we can get there before sunset.**

　（A）till　　　　　　　　　　（B）before

　（C）except　　　　　　　　　（D）so that

Q9 **He was absent _____ he didn't feel well.**

　（A）although　　　　　　　　（B）whether

　（C）because　　　　　　　　（D）unless

13

Q10 **What places have you visited _____ you arrived in New York?**

（A）until 　　　　　　　（B）till
（C）if 　　　　　　　　（D）since

Q11 **I won't give her a rose on the first date because I don't know _____ she likes it.**

（A）that 　　　　　　　（B）whether
（C）why 　　　　　　　（D）where

Q12 **_____ my grandfather is 73 years old, he is strong and healthy.**

（A）If 　　　　　　　　（B）That
（C）Unless 　　　　　　（D）Although

Q13 **People do not know the value of health _____ they lose it.**

（A）because 　　　　　　（B）if
（C）till 　　　　　　　　（D）although

Q14 **_____ we came into the house, it began to rain.**

（A）Now that 　　　　　（B）Even if
（C）As soon as 　　　　（D）As long as

Q15 **_____ you give up smoking, I will not marry you.**

（A）While 　　　　　　（B）Whether
（C）Unless 　　　　　　（D）That

Q16 **I won't stop searching _____ I find my lost wallet.**

（A）as 　　　　　　　　（B）when
（C）since 　　　　　　　（D）until

Q17 **_____ we have finished our homework, we can play video games.**

（A）Now that 　　　　　（B）Even though
（C）In case 　　　　　　（D）No matter how

Q18 He didn't know _____ he could buy some flowers, so he checked the map.

(A) why   (B) how

(C) when   (D) where

Q19 Someone knocked the door _____ David was making dinner.

(A) if   (B) while

(C) before   (D) because

Q20 _____ you have any question, you can call Miss Jones for help.

(A) If   (B) Unless

(C) Though   (D) Because

Study 5 意義辨析：動詞

Q1 Can you _____ me this book? I'll return it to you tomorrow.

(A) give   (B) show

(C) lend   (D) borrow

Q2 I can't find my gold necklace! It must have been _____.

(A) bitten   (B) broken

(C) chosen   (D) stolen

Q3 I have to _____ my clothes so I can bring them to Korea.

(A) pack   (B) change

(C) compare   (D) decorate

Q4 The ship hit the rocks and started to _____.

(A) sink   (B) flow

(C) drown   (D) swing

Q5 He _____ to go on a picnic even though no one was interested.

（A）forced　　　　　　　　（B）allowed

（C）insisted　　　　　　　（D）promised

Q6 When everyone was looking at him, Alex _____ he was wearing two different shoes.

（A）accepted　　　　　　　（B）believed

（C）complained　　　　　　（D）realized

Q7 You should _____ the water glasses before the guests arrive at the restaurant.

（A）fill　　　　　　　　　（B）lift

（C）share　　　　　　　　（D）return

Q8 The first step of baking a cake is to _____ the flour and eggs.

（A）put　　　　　　　　　（B）mix

（C）enter　　　　　　　　（D）steam

Q9 Please _____ these chairs so we can sit in a circle.

（A）count　　　　　　　　（B）arrange

（C）receive　　　　　　　（D）treasure

Q10 The team _____ every day before the soccer match.

（A）trained　　　　　　　（B）behaved

（C）expected　　　　　　　（D）increased

Q11 Joanne's three-year-old son likes to _____ that he is a train driver.

（A）ignore　　　　　　　　（B）confirm

（C）imagine　　　　　　　（D）apologize

Q12 I _____ my jacket in the hotel room, but the workers say they haven't seen it.

（A）left　　　　　　　　　（B）held

（C）threw　　　　　　　　（D）bought

Q13 The teacher _____ the word to show that it is important.

(A) compared (B) determined

(C) investigated (D) underlined

Q14 We can _____ the environment by recycling as much as possible.

(A) achieve (B) damage

(C) pollute (D) protect

Q15 The printers work well because the company _____ them regularly.

(A) designs (B) maintains

(C) prepares (D) supplies

Q16 I _____ your hard work. We couldn't succeed without your help.

(A) consider (B) expect

(C) encourage (D) appreciate

Q17 A recent study _____ that women are usually healthier than men.

(A) blames (B) organizes

(C) produces (D) indicates

Q18 If you _____ your ticket a month before your trip, you can get a better price.

(A) pay (B) book

(C) need (D) examine

Q19 Steve _____ his daughter for getting good grades in math.

(A) adopted (B) charged

(C) praised (D) rejected

Q20 Most students _____ Miss Wang as the best teacher in the school.

（A）regard   （B）prefer

（C）follow   （D）discover

Study 6　意義辨析：片語動詞

Q1 Please _____ for a moment. I'll get Mr. Johnson on the line for you.

（A）call up   （B）hang up

（C）hold on   （D）go on

Q2 Look at all the mess! You really should _____ your room.

（A）put away   （B）tidy up

（C）see off   （D）look after

Q3 You may _____ the jeans before you decide to buy them.

（A）pack up   （B）send off

（C）pay back   （D）try on

Q4 I haven't _____ Jerry since he went to America last month.

（A）heard from   （B）listened to

（C）fallen for   （D）smiled at

Q5 _____ your shoes before your step on the carpet.

（A）Take off   （B）Take out

（C）Give away   （D）Give back

Q6 I don't know how this machine works, but I want to _____.

（A）look up   （B）catch up

（C）figure out   （D）watch out

Q7 The sofa is on fire! We have to _____ before it spreads to the kitchen.

（A）turn it off 　　　　　（B）put it out

（C）calm it down 　　　　（D）give it away

Q8 The baseball game was _____ because of heavy rain.

（A）called off 　　　　　（B）shown off

（C）filled out 　　　　　（D）handed out

Q9 Karen walked slowly so that her younger sister could _____.

（A）follow up 　　　　　（B）make up

（C）grab up 　　　　　　（D）catch up

Q10 I _____ Tom by accident when I was shopping in a mall.

（A）ran into 　　　　　　（B）went after

（C）looked for 　　　　　（D）stopped by

Q11 I don't believe him. I think the story was _____.

（A）made up 　　　　　　（B）spoken up

（C）read out 　　　　　　（D）crossed out

Q12 Time's up. _____ your test papers, please.

（A）Hand in 　　　　　　（B）Hand out

（C）Take in 　　　　　　（D）Take out

Q13 We're running out of gas. We need to _____ the tank.

（A）turn in 　　　　　　（B）turn up

（C）fill in 　　　　　　（D）fill up

Q14 When you don't know the meaning of a new word, _____ in the dictionary.

（A）get into it 　　　　　（B）look it up

（C）look at it 　　　　　（D）pick it out

Q15 When I took the bus for the first time, I felt sick and
_____.

(A) flew up   (B) flew away

(C) threw up   (D) threw away

Q16 As a single parent, he _____ his children all by
himself.

(A) brought up   (B) pointed out

(C) escaped from   (D) thought about

Q17 To sign up for the basketball team, please _____ this
form.

(A) fill out   (B) show off

(C) look into   (D) put together

Q18 I _____ the invitation to the party because I have to
work on my report.

(A) got over   (B) gave away

(C) turned down   (D) checked out

Q19 I don't _____ my brother. I'm always fighting with
him.

(A) get along with   (B) look down on

(C) do away with   (D) keep away from

Q20 I can't _____ the heat any longer. Let's get some ice
cream to cool down.

(A) put up with   (B) come down with

(C) look up to   (D) look forward to

Study 7　意義辨析：wh- 疑問句

Q1 _____ are you talking about? The one wearing the black hat or blue hat?
（A）What
（B）Who
（C）When
（D）Where

Q2 You look tired. _____ did you go to bed last night?
（A）Why
（B）How
（C）Where
（D）When

Q3 _____ are you going to buy at the department store?
（A）How
（B）What
（C）Where
（D）When

Q4 _____ would you like to pay, by cash or by card?
（A）How
（B）How much
（C）What
（D）What else

Q5 _____ did Betty beat her son? What did he do wrong?
（A）Where
（B）When
（C）Why
（D）How

Q6 _____ people are more likely to have a successful career?
（A）How come
（B）How about
（C）What time do
（D）What kind of

Q7 I have "The Sleeping Beauty" and "The Little Prince". _____ book do you want to borrow?
（A）Whose
（B）Which
（C）How many
（D）What kind of

Q8 _____ pen case is this? There's no name on it.
（A）What
（B）Whose
（C）Which
（D）In which

Q9 _____ did they pay for their new house? It looks very expensive.

（A）How soon
（B）How much
（C）How well
（D）How often

Q10 _____ do you swim, once a week or every day?

（A）How far
（B）How long
（C）How well
（D）How often

Q11 I feel so bored. _____ we listen to some good music?

（A）Why do
（B）How come
（C）How about
（D）What's the point

Q12 _____ is your daughter? Does she go to elementary school now?

（A）How big
（B）How old
（C）How tall
（D）How heavy

Q13 _____ is the cartoon on? I thought it's on weekends.

（A）Where
（B）When
（C）What time
（D）What day

Q14 I'm afraid you've got the wrong number. _____ number are you calling?

（A）What
（B）Which
（C）How many
（D）What kind of

Q15 _____ do you wear, medium or large?

（A）What kind
（B）What size
（C）What color
（D）What number

ANSWER 詞彙（解答）

Study **1** 意義辨析：名詞

Q1 Become a ＿＿＿_B_＿＿ and enjoy special offers in our store.

（成為會員並享受本店的特別優惠。）

（A）friend（朋友）　　　　　▶（B）member（會員）

（C）visitor（訪客）　　　　　（D）officer（警官）

▶**解析**　special offer 是商店的「特別優惠」，選項中能夠享有優惠資格的是 member（會員）。

Q2 This is my ＿＿＿_B_＿＿ card. Contact me if you need to.

（這是我的名片。如果有需要就聯絡我。）

（A）birthday（生日）　　　　▶（B）business（商務）

（C）credit（信用）　　　　　（D）memory（記憶）

▶**解析**　business card = name card =「名片」。

birthday card：生日卡

credit card：信用卡

memory card：記憶卡

Q3 Is your birthday in this ＿＿＿_C_＿＿ or the next?

（你的生日是這個月還是下個月？）

（A）case（情況）　　　　　　（B）moment（片刻）

▶（C）month（月份）　　　　　（D）year（年）

▶**解析**　句子是問生日在哪時候，所以 month（月份）是最恰當的答案。生日每年都會過，所以 year（年）不是正確答案。

in this case：在這種情況下，這樣的話

Q4 Have you read the ___C___ in the morning paper?

（你讀了早報的那篇文章嗎？）

（A）meaning（意思）　　（B）novel（小說）

▶（C）article（文章）　　（D）picture（照片）

▶解析 因為是 morning paper（早報）裡面的東西，而且是可以 read（閱讀）的，所以 article 是最恰當的答案。

Q5 Most teenagers are interested in popular ___D___, especially pop music.

（大部分的青少年對流行文化有興趣，尤其是流行音樂。）

（A）classic（經典）　　（B）comic（漫畫）

（C）career（職業）　　▶（D）culture（文化）

▶解析 空格後面接的 especially...（尤其…）是舉出最具代表性的例子，也就是屬於空格所指事物的其中一種，所以 culture（文化）是正確答案。pop music（流行音樂）並不是 comic（漫畫）的一種例子，所以 comic 不是正確答案。

Q6 The ___C___ of paper is too heavy for me to lift.

（這疊紙太重了，我抬不起來。）

（A）piece（片）　　（B）sheet（張）

▶（C）pile（疊）　　（D）number（數目）

▶解析 因為句子表示紙很重的意思，所以 pile（疊）是最恰當的答案。a piece/sheet of paper（一片／張紙）不可能重得抬不起來。「number of...」表示「…的數目」，表示數目的抽象概念，所以不能當成 lift（抬）的對象。

too... to...：太…而不能…

a sheet of paper：一張紙

two sheets of paper：兩張紙

Q7 Everyone should follow the ___A___ when playing a game, or it won't be fair.

（每個人在玩遊戲的時候都應該遵守規則，不然就不公平了。）

► （A）rules（規則） 　　　　（B）leaders（領導人）

（C）guides（導遊） 　　　　（D）fashion（流行）

▶ 解析　遵守規則和遊戲的公平性直接相關，所以 rules（規則）是正確答案。follow 的基本意義是「跟隨」，在這裡則是「遵守」的意思。

Q8 Because of complaints about the problem, the team had to find a ___*A*___.

（因為對於問題的抱怨，那個團隊當時必須找到解決方式。）

► （A）solution（解決方式）　　（B）standard（標準）

（C）skill（技術） 　　　　（D）secret（祕密）

▶ 解析　空格表示對於問題所做的處理，所以 solution（解決方式）是最恰當的答案。

solution to a problem：問題的解決方式

Q9 John was late for work this morning because of heavy ___*C*___.

（約翰今天上午因為交通擁擠而上班遲到。）

（A）accident（意外事故）　　（B）crowd（人群）

► （C）traffic（交通） 　　　　（D）damage（損害）

▶ 解析　注意空格前有 because of（因為…），所以空格表示上班遲到的原因。heavy traffic 表示「擁擠的交通」，所以 traffic（交通）是正確答案。accident（意外事故）和 crowd（人群）都不會用 heavy 來形容。damage（損害）在這裡不能明確表示造成遲到的原因是什麼，所以不是恰當的答案。

Q10 ___*C*___ must report the truth when they write a news story.

（記者寫新聞報導時必須報告真相。）

（A）Artists（藝術家）　　　　（B）Dentists（牙醫）

► （C）Journalists（記者）　　　（D）Scientists（科學家）

解析 會寫 news story（新聞報導）的人是 journalist，journalist 是指撰寫文字稿的記者。

Q11 This ___D___ of the textbook is difficult, so our teacher taught us twice.

（課本的這個部分很難，所以老師教了我們兩次。）

（A）decision（決定）　　　　（B）education（教育）

（C）operation（操作）　　▶（D）section（部分）

解析 空格後面有介系詞 of，表示 textbook（教科書）裡面的東西，所以 section（部分）是正確答案。考慮到空格是老師所教的東西，（A）、（B）、（C）都不是恰當的答案。

Q12 Many wild animals will be in ___B___ if we don't protect the environment.

（如果我們不保護環境的話，許多野生動物會有麻煩。）

（A）doubt（懷疑）　　　　▶（B）trouble（麻煩）

（C）question（問題）　　　　（D）relation（關係）

解析 in doubt：不確定的

in trouble：遇到麻煩的

in question：（議題等）正在談論的，要考慮的

in relation to：關於⋯

Q13 Doctors agree that good sleep can improve one's ___A___.

（醫師們同意好的睡眠能促進一個人的健康。）

▶（A）health（健康）　　　　（B）breath（呼吸）

（C）illness（疾病）　　　　（D）stress（壓力）

解析 improve 是「改善，促進」的意思，所以 health（健康）是最恰當的答案。illness（疾病）和 stress（壓力）都表示負面的結果，和文意不符。

Q14 I don't know how to solve this problem. I need to ask for some ___*A*___ .

（我不知道怎麼決解這個問題。我需要尋求建議。）

► （A） advice（建議）　　　　（B） concern（擔心）

（C） space（空間）　　　　　（D） progress（進步）

▶️ 解析 ask for advice：尋求建議

Q15 The ___*D*___ of the study is to find out the causes of the crisis.

（這項研究的目的是找出造成那個危機的原因。）

（A） result（結果）　　　　　（B） problem（問題）

（C） influence（影響）　　► （D） purpose（目的）

▶️ 解析 to 不定詞表示目的，所以 purpose（目的）是最恰當的答案。其他選項的名詞，後面基本上都不會接「is to do…」表示內容。

Q16 Cold and flu are more common when the ___*A*___ change.

（感冒和流行性感冒在季節變換的時候比較常見。）

► （A） seasons（季節）　　　（B） years（年）

（C） days（日子）　　　　　（D） feelings（情感）

▶️ 解析 seasons change 表示「兩個季節變換」，也就是從一個季節變成另一個季節。

Q17 The debate between them was a ___*B*___ of time. They were just arguing.

（他們之間的辯論是浪費時間。他們只是在爭吵而已。）

（A） matter（問題）　　　► （B） waste（浪費）

（C） lot（很多）　　　　　（D） length（長度）

▶️ 解析 …is a matter of time：…只是時間的問題（遲早會發生的意思）

a waste of time：浪費時間

length of time：時間長度

Q18 To save money, you need to compare ____*D*____ before buying.

（為了省錢，在購買前必須比較價格。）

（A）sales（銷售額）　　　　（B）qualities（性質）

（C）functions（功能）　▶（D）prices（價格）

◐解析 和 save money（省錢）直接相關的 prices（價格）是最恰當的答案。另外，quality 雖然通常是「品質」的意思，但如果當可數名詞的話，則是指某個人事物的各種「性質，特性」。

Q19 I made a ____*A*____ of tasks to do, or I may forget later.

（我做了一份待辦工作清單，不然之後我可能會忘記。）

▶（A）list（清單）　　　　（B）post（貼文）

（C）number（數目）　　　（D）system（系統）

◐解析 選項中，可以用來提醒人不要忘記一系列工作的 list（清單）是正確答案。task to do 表示「要做的工作」。

Q20 This cake has fruits on top and chocolate at the ____*A*____.

（這個蛋糕上面有水果，底部有巧克力。）

▶（A）base（底部）　　　　（B）end（盡頭）

（C）beginning（開始）　　（D）time（時間）

◐解析 這是在描述蛋糕的特徵，和 top（頂部）相對的 base（底部）是正確答案。at the end 則是指在某個有長度的東西的「盡頭」或「末端」。

Study 2　意義辨析：形容詞

Q1 The teacher was ____*A*____ that half of the students were late for school.

（老師對於一半的學生上學遲到感到驚訝。）

► （A）surprised（感到驚訝的）　　（B）surprising（令人驚訝的）

（C）interested（有興趣的）　　（D）interesting（有趣的）

▶ 解析　這是分辨情緒形容詞 -ed 形與 -ing 形的題目。-ed 表示「感到…」，-ing 則是「讓人有…的感覺」。因為題目要表達的是「老師感到驚訝」，所以答案是 surprised（感到驚訝的），而不是 surprising（令人驚訝的）。

Q2　It was ___*B*___ of him to leave the umbrella in the train.

（他很粗心，把傘留在列車上了。）

（A）careful（小心的）　　► （B）careless（粗心的）

（C）helpful（有幫助的）　　（D）helpless（無助的）

▶ 解析　「It was 形容詞 of 人 to do…」是一個固定句型，表示「某人做…這件事很…」。空格描述做出「把傘留在列車上」這個行為的人，所以 careless（粗心的）是正確答案。helpless 是「無助，無能為力」的意思，不適合描述句中的情況。

Q3　The cats look very ___*C*___. I can't tell their difference.

（這些貓看起來很像。我分不出他們的不同。）

（A）same（相同的）　　（B）different（不同的）

► （C）alike（相像的）　　（D）unique（獨特的）

▶ 解析　look + 形容詞表示「看起來…」，tell the difference 表示「分辨不同的地方」。無法分辨不同之處，表示長得很像，所以 alike（相像的）是正確答案。如果要使用 same 的話，應該加 the，也就是 look the same（看起來一樣），而且不能用程度副詞 very 修飾 same，而要用 quite：look quite the same（看起來很相同）。

Q4　Not ___*B*___ fast foods are bad. Some can be good for your health.

（並非所有速食都是壞的。某些速食可能有益於你的健康。）

（A）some（一些）　　► （B）all（所有）

（C）few（少數）　　（D）several（幾種）

解析 否定詞 not 和 all 同時使用的時候，表示「部分否定」，也就是「有一部分不是」，而不是「全部都不是」的意思。在這一題裡，就是先表達「有一部分的速食不是壞的」，然後再表達「某些速食有益健康」的意見。在 not all 的句子之後，經常會用 some（一些，某些）表示部分否定的那群對象。

Q5 Peter feels lonely because he has ____*A*____ friends in the company.

（彼得覺得寂寞，因為他在公司的朋友很少。）

► （A）few（很少）　　　　　（B）a few（幾個，一些）

　（C）some（一些）　　　　　（D）lots of（很多）

解析 few 表示「很少」，有負面的意味，a few 則是「幾個，一些」的意思，而不是表達「很少」的負面意義，所以 few 才是正確答案。

Q6 We have ____*C*____ time to waste. We have to leave right now.

（我們沒有時間可以浪費。我們必須立刻出發。）

　（A）all（所有）　　　　　（B）some（一些）

► （C）no（沒有）　　　　　（D）a little（一些）

解析 因為要「立刻出發」，表示很急、不能浪費時間，所以 no（沒有）是正確答案。雖然這句話也可以說成 We have little time to waste（我們可以浪費的時間很少→我們沒什麼時間可以浪費），但不能把 little 換成 a little，因為 a little 沒有「很少」的負面意義，這和 few – a few 的對比是相同的。另外，few – a few 用於可數名詞，little – a little 用於不可數名詞。

Q7 The sentence is not ____*C*____. It lacks a verb.

（這個句子不完整。它缺少一個動詞。）

　（A）true（真的）　　　　　（B）full（滿的）

► （C）complete（完整的）　　（D）necessary（必要的）

解析 lack 表示「缺少」。因為有缺少，所以是不完整的，

complete（完整的）是正確答案。另外，例如考是非題的時候，說 the sentence is true 是指「句子敘述正確」，而「不正確」是用 false 來表達。

Q8 **A greedy person is never _____*D*_____ with what he has.**
（貪心的人從來不會對自己擁有的感到滿足。）
（A）concerned（有關的）　　（B）careful（小心的）
（C）upset（生氣的）　　▶（D）satisfied（感到滿足的）

解析 be satisfied with 是「對…感到滿意」的意思。另外，be careful with 表示「小心處理…」，be concerned with 表示「和…有關」，be concerned about 則是「擔心」的意思（請注意介系詞的不同）。

Q9 **People wear _____*A*_____ clothes now since the weather is warmer.**
（人們現在穿比較輕薄的衣服，因為天氣比較暖。）
▶（A）lighter（比較輕的）　　（B）tighter（比較緊的）
（C）brighter（比較亮的）　　（D）broader（比較寬廣的）

解析 因應天氣變暖，穿 lighter（比較輕的）的衣服是最恰當的答案。另外，形容詞 broad 通常是形容空間很寬，或者事物的種類範圍很廣。如果要說衣服很寬鬆的話，通常會用 loose-fitting 來形容。

Q10 **Thank you for the delicious food, but I'm _____*A*_____ now.**
（謝謝你美味的食物，但我現在很飽。）
▶（A）full（飽的）　　（B）fine（好的）
（C）enough（足夠的）　　（D）afraid（害怕的）

解析 第一個子句說謝謝對方的食物，但後面接了對等連接詞 but，可見後面的子句是表達自己並不想吃的意思。full 基本上表示「滿的」，但也可以形容人「完全吃飽了」。fine 表示事物「還不錯」，或者人「身體狀況健康」。如果要用 enough 的話，應該說 I've had enough.（我已經吃得夠多了）。

31

Q11 How could he be so ___D___ to kill the lovely dog?

（他怎麼可以那麼殘忍，把那隻可愛的狗殺了？）

（A）scared（害怕的） 　　　　（B）painful（痛苦的）

（C）jealous（嫉妒的） 　　► （D）cruel（殘忍的）

▶解析　How could he be so...? 並不是問「他是怎麼做到的」，而是很驚訝地表達「他怎麼會那樣」。這裡最適合描述殺狗行為的形容詞是 cruel（殘忍的）。另外，雖然 scared 是從 scare（驚嚇）衍生的形容詞，但不一定是「被嚇到」的意思，也可以單純表示對某事物感到「害怕」。

Q12 Joseph is a ___C___ person. He doesn't share anything with his friends.

（喬瑟夫是個自私的人。他不跟朋友分享任何東西。）

（A）confident（有自信的） 　　（B）diligent（勤奮的）

► （C）selfish（自私的） 　　　　（D）ordinary（普通的）

▶解析　第一個句子形容喬瑟夫是怎樣的人，第二個句子則是舉出實際的例子。能夠表達「不分享東西」的 selfish（自私的）是正確答案。

Q13 I thought it was a ___B___ problem, but it turned out to be quite serious.

（我以為那是輕微的問題，但結果是很嚴重的問題。）

（A）major（重大的） 　　► （B）minor（輕微的）

（C）general（普遍的） 　　　（D）generous（慷慨的）

▶解析　turn out to be 表示「（後來發現）結果是…」。因為中間有連接詞 but，表示「結果很嚴重」的事實和自己一開始的想法相反，所以 serious（嚴重的）的反義詞 minor（輕微的）是正確答案。

Q14 It was a ___D___ trip. We enjoyed it very much.

（那是趟愉快的旅行。我們非常享受那趟旅行。）

（A）used（二手的） 　　　　（B）usual（通常的）

（C）pleased（感到滿意的） ► （D）pleasant（令人愉快的）

▶ 解析　因為非常享受旅行，所以 pleasant（令人愉快的）是正確答案。pleased 表示人「感到滿意」，不能用來形容事物。另外，從動詞 use 衍生的 used 字面意義是「用過的」，也就是「二手的」。

Q15 Most people use ___*B*___ media sites to stay in touch with their friends.
（大部分的人用社群媒體網站和朋友保持聯絡。）

（A）official（正式的）　　▶（B）social（社會的）

（C）special（特別的）　　（D）mass（大眾的）

▶ 解析　stay in touch with 表示「和…保持聯絡」。
social media site：社群媒體網站（例如 Facebook、Twitter）
mass media：大眾媒體（電視、廣播等等）

Q16 After one week's search, their child is still ___*A*___.
（在一個禮拜的尋找之後，他們的孩子仍然失蹤中。）

▶（A）missing（失蹤的）　　（B）missed（被想念的）

（C）alive（活著的）　　（D）absent（缺席的）

▶ 解析　後面的子句出現了 still（仍然），表示 search（尋找）的原因還沒有解決，所以 missing（失蹤的）是正確答案。當形容詞用的 missing 和 missed，意思完全不一樣，missing 形容事物時表示「遺失的」，形容人時表示「失蹤的」；missed 則是「被想念的」。

Q17 As a beginner, you have to learn ___*A*___ grammar first.
（身為初學者，你必須先學習基本的文法。）

▶（A）basic（基本的）　　（B）classic（經典的）

（C）difficult（困難的）　　（D）serious（嚴肅的）

▶ 解析　As a... 表示「身為…」。因為是 beginner（初學者），所以剛開始學的當然是 basic（基本的）的文法。另外，請注意 serious 可以表示「嚴重的」或「嚴肅的」。

Q18 I am ___*C*___ to hear that your father passed away.
（我很遺憾聽到你父親過世的消息。）

（A）glad（高興的）　　　　　　　（B）able（有能力的）

► （C）sorry（感到遺憾的）　　　（D）interested（有興趣的）

▶解析　pass away 是「過世」的意思，也就是 die（死亡）比較委婉的說法。sorry 雖然通常表示「感到抱歉的」，但在聽到不幸的消息時，會用 sorry 表示「遺憾的，難過的」。

Q19 Susan is really _____*D*_____. She can't stay quiet for a moment.

（蘇珊真的很愛講話。她一刻都無法保持安靜。）

（A）active（活躍的）　　　　　　（B）positive（積極的）

（C）effective（有效的）　　► （D）talkative（愛說話的）

▶解析　第一個句子形容蘇珊是怎樣的人，第二個句子則是詳細說明。連短短的 moment（片刻）都不能保持安靜，就表示很 talkative（愛說話的）。effective 表示事物「有效」，通常不會用來形容人。另外，active 形容人的時候，也有「經常運動」的意思。

Q20 Mr. Smith is not _____*B*_____ right now. Would you like to leave a message?

（史密斯先生現在沒空。您想要留言嗎？）

（A）possible（可能的）　　► （B）available（有空的）

（C）responsible（負責任的）　　（D）comfortable（感到自在的）

▶解析　這是電話交談的內容，因為問對方要不要留言，由此可知 Smith 先生不能接電話，所以 available（有空的）是正確答案。雖然 available 通常表示事物「可以取得，買得到」，但用來形容人的時候，則是表示「沒有其他正在忙的事」。另外，comfortable 形容人的時候，並不是指身體的健康狀態，而是指心理上「感到自在」，所以「他身體不舒服」不能說成 he is not comfortable，而應該說 he is not well。

Study 3 意義辨析：副詞

Q1 You came _____*B*_____. He has already left.

（你來晚了。他已經離開了。）

（A）early（早早地）　　　　► （B）late（晚地）

（C）beforehand（預先）　　　（D）afterward（之後）

▶解析　第二個句子說他已經離開，可見說話對象抵達的時間太晚而不能見到他，late（晚地）是正確答案。注意 late 本身就可以當副詞用，如果改成 lately 反而會變成「最近」的意思。beforehand 表示在某件事之前「預先」做某種準備的意思。使用 afterward（之後）的時候，需要先提到之前發生的某件事，然後才能用 afterward 表示「在那之後」。

Q2 She keeps singing that song _____*B*_____. She's really crazy about it.

（她一直反覆唱那首歌。她真的為那首歌瘋狂。）

（A）every now and then（偶爾）

► （B）over and over again（一再，反覆）

（C）once in a while（偶爾）

（D）from time to time（偶爾）

▶解析　選項中唯一適合表達「一直唱」的行為的副詞片語是 over and over again（一再，反覆）。其他三個選項都是「偶爾（但不是很常）」的意思，意義上都不恰當。

Q3 Mary isn't _____*D*_____ early for school. Sometimes she comes late.

（瑪莉並不總是早到學校。有時候她會晚來。）

（A）never（從不）　　　　（B）seldom（很少）

（C）sometimes（有時候）　► （D）always（總是）

▶解析　not always 也是一種部分否定的表達方式，Mary is not always early 就等於 Sometimes Mary is not early。

Q4 Just wait for a moment. He will be here _____*B*_____.

（只要等一下就好。他不久就會到這裡。）

（A）fast（快速地）　　　▶（B）soon（不久）

（C）once（一次）　　　　（D）nearly（接近地）

▶**解析**　第二句呼應第一句「只要等一下」，所以要選擇表示「很快」的答案。這裡要注意的是，副詞 fast 表示「移動速度很快」，所以會修飾 walk、run 等移動動詞，而不能修飾這個句子裡表示存在的 be here（在這裡）。soon 則是表示時刻「很早，不久」的意思。

Q5 The cakes are _____*B*_____ the same. There isn't any difference.

（這些蛋糕完全一樣。沒有任何不同。）

（A）nearly（幾乎）　　　▶（B）exactly（確切地）

（C）likely（很有可能）　　（D）hardly（幾乎不）

▶**解析**　因為沒有任何不同，所以能修飾 the same 表示「完全一樣」的 exactly（確切地）是正確答案。nearly the same 則是「幾乎一樣」，表示彼此還是會有些微不同。

Q6 He didn't have enough money. _____*A*_____, he gave up buying that book.

（他當時沒有足夠的錢。所以，他放棄買那本書。）

▶（A）Therefore（所以）　　（B）However（然而）

（C）Even so（儘管如此）　　（D）In other words（換句話說）

▶**解析**　空格是表示前後兩句邏輯關係的連接副詞。「沒有錢」和「放棄買書」屬於因果關係，所以 Therefore（所以）是正確答案。However（然而）和 Even so（儘管如此）表示語意上的轉折。In other words（換句話說）表示前後兩句基本上是相同的意思。

Q7 There was a car accident this morning. _____*B*_____, no one was hurt.

（今天上午有一場車禍。幸好沒有人受傷。）

（A）Painfully（痛苦地）　　▶（B）Luckily（幸運地）

（C）Recently（最近）　　　　（D）Suddenly（突然）

▶解析 空格中的副詞修飾「沒有人受傷」的事實，所以 Luckily（幸運地）是正確答案。如果只看第二句的話，Recently（最近）也說得通，但意義沒辦法和第一句連貫，所以不對。

Q8 I found that famous shop ___*A*___ when I was taking a walk.

（我在散步的時候偶然發現那家有名的店。）

▶（A）by accident（偶然）　　（B）on foot（用走路的方式）

（C）at times（有時候）　　　（D）at once（馬上）

▶解析 句子表示在散步途中發現一家店，所以 by accident（偶然）是最恰當的答案。如果選擇 on foot（用走路的方式）的話，意義上和 taking a walk（散步）重複，所以不是恰當的表達方式。

Q9 By practicing every day, his English is improving ___*C*___.

（靠著每天練習，他的英語一點一點地進步。）

（A）one by one（一個一個地）　（B）side by side（肩並肩）

▶（C）little by little（一點一點地）　（D）back to back（背對背）

▶解析 空格修飾 is improving（正在改善），唯一恰當的答案是表示程度逐漸增加的 little by little（一點一點地）。one by one 則是「一個一個進行、一個一個處理」的意思，但英語進步程度不能區分成「一個一個」，所以不對。

Q10 We have to leave ___*D*___, or we will be late for the party.

（我們必須馬上出發，不然我們參加派對會遲到。）

（A）for good（永遠）　　　　（B）on purpose（故意）

（C）at times（有時候）　　▶（D）right away（馬上）

▶解析 or 連接兩個子句時，表示「不做 A 的話，就會 B」。為了不要遲到，應該馬上出發，所以 right away（馬上）是正確答案。for good（永遠）通常用來修飾 leave（離開）、give up（放棄）之類的動詞，表示再也不回到原來的狀態，所以 leave for good 就是「離開之後再也不回去」的意思。

Q11 My leg ached so much that I could ___*B*___ stand.

（當時我的腿很痛，幾乎沒辦法站。）

（A）badly（很差地）　　　　▶（B）hardly（幾乎不）

（C）even（甚至）　　　　　（D）ever（曾經）

▶**解析**　hardly（幾乎不）是帶有否定意味的副詞，意思相當於「almost not」，所以使用時不需要再加否定詞 not。

Q12 I don't know why he didn't call me after we first met. ___*D*___ he doesn't like me.

（我不知道他在我們第一次見面後為什麼沒打電話給我。或許他不喜歡我。）

（A）Therefore（所以）　　　（B）Finally（最後）

（C）Sometimes（有時候）　▶（D）Perhaps（或許）

▶**解析**　第一個句子說「不知道他為什麼沒打電話」，第二個句子說「他不喜歡我」，第二個句子是針對說話者所不知道的理由加以推測，所以表示推測的 Perhaps（或許）是正確答案。因為第一個句子表示自己不明白對方的想法，兩個句子之間並沒有必然的因果關係，所以 Therefore（所以）不是適當的答案。

Q13 I can't see the words ___*C*___. I need my glasses.

（我不能清楚看見那些字。我需要眼鏡。）

（A）patiently（有耐心地）　（B）fairly（公平地）

▶（C）clearly（清楚地）　　（D）quickly（動作快地）

▶**解析**　需要眼鏡表示看不清楚，所以 clearly（清楚地）是正確答案。

Q14 Helen feels very happy because her husband loves her ___*A*___.

（海倫覺得非常幸福，因為她的丈夫非常愛她。）

► （A）dearly（非常）　　　　　　（B）fairly（公平地）

（C）silently（沉默地）　　　　　　（D）calmly（冷靜地）

▶️解析　最適合表達「愛得讓人感到幸福」的副詞是 dearly，雖然字典上的解釋是「非常」，但實際上通常用來修飾 love、miss 等表示關愛的動詞，有「十分珍惜」的感覺。

Q15 As a team, we should work ___*D*___ and help each other.

（身為一個團隊，我們應該合作並且幫助彼此。）

（A）around（到處）　　　　　　（B）alone（獨自）

（C）alike（同樣地）　　► （D）together（一起）

▶️解析　動詞 work 和副詞 together 一起使用，可以表示「合作」的意思。其他選項雖然文法上沒有錯誤，但不符合整個句子的意義。

Q16 Among the seasons, Sylvia likes winter the ___*B*___ because she usually catches a cold.

（在季節當中，席維亞最不喜歡冬天，因為她通常會感冒。）

（A）best（最高程度地）　　► （B）least（最低程度地）

（C）last（最後）　　　　　　（D）most（最多地）

▶️解析　表示原因的 because 後面接的是負面敘述，可知席維亞不喜歡冬天，所以 least（最低程度地）是正確答案。like the best/most 都表示「最喜歡」的意思。last 修飾動詞的時候，是表示做事的先後順序在「最後」，而不能表示「最不喜歡」的意思。

Q17 I don't understand this chapter very well. I'll go ___*A*___ and read it again.

（我不是很懂這一章。我會回頭再讀一次。）

► （A）back（往回）　　　　　　（B）away（離開）

（C）down（往下）　　　　　　（D）along（沿著，向前）

▶️解析　因為空格後面提到 read it again（再讀一次），所以 go back

是正確答案。go back 在這裡並不是「行走」的意思，而是表示「回到這一章的開頭重來」。另外，go along 是「繼續進行下去」的意思。

Q18 My report is _____ *B* _____ done. I just need to write the last sentence.

（我的報告幾乎完成了。我只需要寫最後一個句子。）

（A）all（全部） ► （B）almost（幾乎）

（C）half（一半） （D）never（從不）

▶ **解析** 因為只需要寫最後一個句子就完成了，所以表示接近 100% 的程度副詞 almost（幾乎）是正確答案。

Q19 Even though we can't travel _____ *A* _____, we still have many places to visit in Taiwan.

（雖然我們不能出國旅遊，在台灣我們還是有很多地方可以造訪。）

► （A）abroad（在國外） （B）alone（獨自）

（C）recently（最近） （D）yet（仍然（不））

▶ **解析** 後半說可以造訪台灣的很多地方，所以前半應該是說不能在台灣以外的地方旅遊，abroad（在國外）是正確答案。因為我們可以造訪台灣的許多地方，並不是在任何地方都不能旅遊，所以 recently 和 yet 都不對。

Q20 Can you go _____ *D* _____ and take out the trash for me?

（你可以下樓幫我丟垃圾嗎？）

（A）further（更遠地） （B）anywhere（到任何地方）

（C）downtown（到市中心） ► （D）downstairs（到樓下）

▶ **解析** 丟垃圾這件事在家附近就能完成，所以 further（更遠地）和 downtown（到市中心）不是恰當的答案，表示非特定地點的 anywhere（到任何地方）也不合適。downstairs（到樓下）是正確答案。

Study 4　意義辨析：連接詞

Q1 Ken is a teacher, ____*A*____ he likes his students.

（肯是老師，而且他喜歡他的學生。）

▶（A）and　　　　　　　　　　（B）or

（C）but　　　　　　　　　　　（D）so

▶解析 第一個子句說「肯是老師」，第二個子句補充說「他喜歡他的學生」，所以單純表示並列兩項資訊的 and（而且⋯）是正確答案。

Q2 She likes cooking, ____*C*____ she hates to do the dishes.

（她喜歡烹飪，但她討厭洗碗盤。）

（A）and　　　　　　　　　　（B）or

▶（C）but　　　　　　　　　　（D）so

▶解析 第一個子句敘述喜歡的事，但第二個子句提到不喜歡的點，所以表示語意轉折的 but（但是⋯）是正確答案。

Q3 Study hard, ____*B*____ you will fail the exam.

（要努力讀書，不然你考試會不及格。）

（A）and　　　　　　　　▶（B）or

（C）but　　　　　　　　　　（D）so

▶解析 or（不然⋯）連接兩個子句的時候，表示可能的因果關係：如果不做 A 的話，就會發生 B 的情況。

Q4 It may rain today, ____*D*____ don't forget to bring an umbrella.

（今天可能會下雨，所以不要忘記帶傘。）

（A）and　　　　　　　　　　（B）or

（C）but　　　　　　　　▶（D）so

▶解析 第一個子句說可能會下雨，第二個子句告知應該採取的行動，所以能表示「因為⋯所以⋯」的因果關係的 so（所以⋯）是正確答案。

41

Q5 _____A_____ the package arrives, I'll let you know right away.

（一旦包裹送到了，我就會立刻讓你知道。）

► （A）Once 　　　　　　（B）Before

　（C）Except 　　　　　　（D）Until

▶解析　第二個子句的「讓你知道」是指「告訴你包裹送到了」，兩個子句有時間上的前後關係，所以 once（一旦…就）是正確答案。另外，except 是「除了…」或者「要不是…」的意思。

Q6 The gangsters ran away _____C_____ they saw the police officer.

（當匪徒們看到警察，他們就跑走了。）

　（A）although 　　　　　（B）where

► （C）when 　　　　　　（D）unless

▶解析　when + 子句 = 副詞子句，表示時間，意思是「當…的時候」。

Q7 I wonder _____A_____ he will show up. He didn't really promise to come.

（我不知道他會不會出現。他並不是真的答應了要來。）

► （A）if 　　　　　　　　（B）how

　（C）what 　　　　　　（D）while

▶解析　wonder + if 子句 = 不確定、想知道是否…。wonder 後面也可以接疑問詞，例如 wonder how 表示「想知道如何…」，wonder what 表示「想知道什麼…」。這裡要表達的是「不知道他來還是不來」，所以 if 是正確答案。

Q8 We will leave early, _____D_____ we can get there before sunset.

（我們會很早出發，好讓我們能在日落前到那裡。）

　（A）till 　　　　　　　（B）before

（C）except ►（D）so that

►解析 so that 表示「好讓…，以便…」，後面接表示目的的子句，前面的子句則表示為了達到目的而做的事。

Q9 He was absent ___*C*___ he didn't feel well.

（他沒出席，因為他覺得不舒服。）

（A）although （B）whether

►（C）because （D）unless

►解析 「覺得不舒服」是「他沒出席」的原因，所以後面接表原因、理由子句的 because（因為）是正確答案。

Q10 What places have you visited ___*D*___ you arrived in New York?

（自從你到紐約後，你已經參觀過哪些地方？）

（A）until （B）till

（C）if ►（D）since

►解析 因為主要子句是完成式（have visited），所以能表示「從過去某個時間點到現在為止」的 since 是正確答案。其他三個選項的主要子句通常會使用簡單式。

Q11 I won't give her a rose on the first date because I don't know ___*B*___ she likes it.

（我不會在第一次約會時送她玫瑰花，因為我不知道她喜不喜歡。）

（A）that ►（B）whether

（C）why （D）where

►解析 選項都可以當成名詞子句連接詞，但意義各有不同。

that she likes a rose：她喜歡玫瑰花的事實

whether she likes a rose：她喜歡玫瑰花還是不喜歡

why/where：她為什麼／在哪裡喜歡玫瑰花

Q12 ___*D*___ my grandfather is 73 years old, he is strong and healthy.

43

（雖然我祖父已經 73 歲，但他強壯而且健康。）

（A）If
（B）That
（C）Unless
►（D）Although

▶解析 因為「已經 73 歲」和「強壯而且健康」對一般人而言是兩項對立的事實，所以表示前後語氣轉折的 although（雖然）是正確答案。

Q13 People do not know the value of health ____*C*____ they lose it.

（人到了失去健康時，才知道它的價值。）

（A）because
（B）if
►（C）till
（D）although

▶解析 till 本來是做某件事「直到…為止」的意思，但「not... till + 子句」則是表示「直到（子句）的時候，才…」，表示從這個時間點才開始做某事。

Q14 ____*C*____ we came into the house, it began to rain.

（我們一進到屋裡，就開始下雨了。）

（A）Now that
（B）Even if
►（C）As soon as
（D）As long as

▶解析 now that：既然…（後面接既成的事實，表示理由）
even if：即使…（表示假設）
as soon as：一…就（表示時間點）
as long as：只要…（表示條件）

Q15 ____*C*____ you give up smoking, I will not marry you.

（除非你戒煙，否則我不會跟你結婚。）

（A）While
（B）Whether
►（C）Unless
（D）That

▶解析 unless + 子句的意思是「除非…」，表示條件。

Q16 I won't stop searching ____*D*____ I find my lost wallet.

（直到找到我遺失的皮夾之前，我不會停止尋找。）

（A）as （B）when

（C）since ►（D）until

▶解析 因為要等到找到皮夾，才會停止尋找，所以表示「直到…」的 until 是正確答案。從屬連接詞 until 有兩種使用情況，當主要子句是肯定句時，從屬子句表示持續行為結束的時間點；當主要子句是否定句時，表示保持不做某事的狀態到哪時候才結束，也就是「直到…才做某事」。另外，since 表示「自從…」的時候，主要子句通常會是完成式或過去簡單式，而不會用未來式。

Q17 _____*A*_____ we have finished our homework, we can play video games.

（既然我們已經做完作業了，我們就能打電玩了。）

►（A）Now that （B）Even though

（C）In case （D）No matter how

▶解析 Now that（既然…）表示理由，而且有強調「現在這件事已經是既定事實了」的意味。

even though：儘管…

in case：萬一…，假如…

no matter how：不管如何…（都會～）

Q18 He didn't know _____*D*_____ he could buy some flowers, so he checked the map.

（他不知道哪裡可以買花，所以他看了地圖。）

（A）why （B）how

（C）when ►（D）where

▶解析 選項中的疑問詞都可以當成名詞子句連接詞使用，不過句子後半部說他看了地圖，表示他查看的是地點，所以表示地點的 where（哪裡）是正確答案。

Q19 Someone knocked the door _____*B*_____ David was making dinner.

（當大衛正在做晚餐的時候，有人敲門。）

（A）if　　　　　　　►（B）while
（C）before　　　　　　（D）because

▶解析　前後兩個子句並沒有條件或因果關係，所以 if（如果…）和 because（因為…）不對。注意從屬子句是進行式，所以能表示「正當在做…的時候」的 while 是正確答案。before（在…之前）表示時間點，所以後面通常不會接表示持續狀態的進行式。

Q20　_____*A*_____ you have any question, you can call Miss Jones for help.

（如果你有任何問題，可以打電話請瓊斯小姐幫忙。）

►（A）If　　　　　　　（B）Unless
（C）Though　　　　　　（D）Because

▶解析　第一個子句使用了 any（任何），並不是說你已經有問題了，而是假設「如果你有任何問題的話」，所以 If（如果…）是正確答案。

Study 5　意義辨析：動詞

Q1　Can you _____*C*_____ me this book? I'll return it to you tomorrow.

（你可以借我這本書嗎？我明天會還你。）

（A）give（給）　　　　（B）show（讓人看）
►（C）lend（借出）　　　（D）borrow（借入）

▶解析　lend 表示把自己擁有的東西借給別人，borrow 則是借別人的東西。give（給）表示東西不再屬於自己，也就不需要 return（歸還），所以 give 不是正確答案。

A lend B something（A 借給 B 某物）

= A lend something to B（A 將某物借給 B）

= B borrow something from A（B 從 A 那裡借了某物）

Q2　I can't find my gold necklace! It must have been _____*D*_____.

（我找不到我的金項鍊！一定是被偷走了。）

（A）bitten（咬）   （B）broken（弄壞）

（C）chosen（選擇）   ► （D）stolen（偷）

▶ 解析 選項都是不規則形的過去分詞，看起來可能有點陌生，但如果記得原形動詞是什麼，就不難選擇了。

bite → bitten

break → broken

choose → chosen

steal → stolen

Q3 I have to _____ *A* _____ my clothes so I can bring them to Korea.

（我必須打包我的衣服，好讓我能帶到韓國。）

► （A）pack（打包）   （B）change（換）

（C）compare（比較）   （D）decorate（裝飾）

▶ 解析 說這句話的人正在為出國做準備，所以 pack（打包）是正確答案。change clothes 的意思是「換衣服」（例如出門前打理服裝，或者晚上換睡衣準備睡覺的時候）。

Q4 The ship hit the rocks and started to _____ *A* _____ .

（那艘船撞上岩石，然後開始下沉。）

► （A）sink（下沉）   （B）flow（流動）

（C）drown（溺水）   （D）swing（擺動）

▶ 解析 人或事物都有可能 sink（下沉），但只有人或動物才會 drown（溺水），所以 sink 才是正確答案。

Q5 He _____ *C* _____ to go on a picnic even though no one was interested.

（他堅持要去野餐，儘管沒人有興趣。）

（A）forced（強迫）   （B）allowed（允許）

► （C）insisted（堅持）   （D）promised（承諾）

解析 insist（堅持）表示即使情況很困難，或者遭到許多人反對，仍然堅持做某事的意思。forced（強迫）的意思看起來是恰當的，但 force 必須接人當受詞，例如 he forced them to go on a picnic（他強迫他們去野餐），在這個題目裡則是缺少了人物受詞，所以不對。

Q6 When everyone was looking at him, Alex ___*D*___ he was wearing two different shoes.

（當每個人都在看他的時候，艾力克斯意識到自己穿著兩隻不一樣的鞋子。）

（A）accepted（接受）　　　（B）believed（相信）

（C）complained（抱怨）　▶（D）realized（意識到）

解析 四個選項中的動詞，後面都可以接 that 子句，並且可以省略 that，所以只能從單字的意義來判斷答案。realize（明白，意識到）可以表示察覺到原本不知道的事情，在這個題目裡是因為大家的注視才讓他有所察覺。

Q7 You should ___*A*___ the water glasses before the guests arrive at the restaurant.

（你應該在客人抵達餐廳之前把水杯裝滿。）

▶（A）fill（裝滿）　　　　（B）lift（舉起）

（C）share（分享）　　　　（D）return（歸還）

解析 空格表示在客人抵達之前所做的準備行為，所以 fill（裝滿）是最恰當的答案。

Q8 The first step of baking a cake is to ___*B*___ the flour and eggs.

（烤蛋糕的第一步是混合麵粉和蛋。）

（A）put（放）　　　　　▶（B）mix（混合）

（C）enter（進入）　　　　（D）steam（蒸）

解析 要表示混合兩種物質，可以說 mix A and B 或 mix A with B。雖然 put（放）看起來有可能是正確答案，但這個動詞使用時必須要能確定「放在什麼地方」，而題目中並沒有關於位置的資訊，所以不對。

Q9 Please _____*B*_____ these chairs so we can sit in a circle.

（請排列這些椅子，讓我們能坐成一圈。）

（A）count（數）　　　　　▶（B）arrange（排列）

（C）receive（接收）　　　（D）treasure（珍惜）

▶**解析**　中間的連接詞 so 是 so that（好讓…）的意思，表示目的。因為目的是要讓大家坐成一圈，所以應該要排列椅子的位置，arrange（排列）是正確答案。

Q10 The team _____*A*_____ every day before the soccer match.

（那個球隊在足球比賽之前每天訓練。）

▶（A）trained（訓練）　　　（B）behaved（行為舉止良好）

（C）expected（期待）　　　（D）increased（增加）

▶**解析**　train（訓練）可以當及物動詞，表示「訓練某人」，也可以像這個句子一樣當成不及物動詞，表示「接受訓練，進行鍛鍊」。expected（期待）的意思似乎正確，但這個動詞後面必須要有受詞（名詞或名詞子句），表示期待的對象，而在題目中並沒有受詞，所以不對。

Q11 Joanne's three-year-old son likes to _____*C*_____ that he is a train driver.

（喬安的三歲兒子喜歡想像自己是火車駕駛員。）

（A）ignore（忽視）　　　　（B）confirm（確認）

▶（C）imagine（想像）　　　（D）apologize（道歉）

▶**解析**　對於三歲小孩而言，he is a train driver（他是火車駕駛員）顯然不是事實，所以能表示並非事實的動詞 imagine（想像）是正確答案。ignore（忽視）和 confirm（確認）後面接的 that 子句都表示事實，apologize 後面接的 that 子句則表示道歉時說的話，例如 he apologized that he didn't mean it（他道歉說他不是那個意思）。

Q12 I _____*A*_____ my jacket in the hotel room, but the workers say they haven't seen it.

（我把外套留在飯店房間裡了，但是員工說他們沒看到。）

► （A）left（留下）　　　　（B）held（握著）

（C）threw（丟擲）　　　　（D）bought（買）

解析　這同樣是測試動詞不規則變化的題目，請把動詞原形和變化形一起記下來。

leave → left

hold → held

throw → threw

buy → bought

Q13 The teacher _____*D*_____ the word to show that it is important.

（老師把那個字畫了底線，以顯示它很重要。）

（A）compared（比較）　　　（B）determined（決定）

（C）investigated（調查）　► （D）underlined（畫底線）

解析　句子後半部是表示目的的不定詞片語，因為目的是「顯示它（= the word）很重要」，所以 underlined（畫底線）是最適當的答案。另外，compare（比較）應該要有兩個比較對象，例如 compare A and B 或 compare A with B；determine 則通常會以 determine to do（決定做…）或 determine that 子句（判定…）的句型使用。

Q14 We can _____*D*_____ the environment by recycling as much as possible.

（我們可以藉由儘量回收資源來保護環境。）

（A）achieve（達成）　　　　（B）damage（損害）

（C）pollute（污染）　　　► （D）protect（保護）

解析　as much as possible 是「儘量多」的意思。多回收資源可能對環境有益，所以 protect（保護）是正確答案。

Q15 The printers work well because the company _____*B*_____ them regularly.

（印表機運作很正常，因為公司定期維護它們。）

（A）designs（設計）　　► （B）maintains（維護）

（C）prepares（準備）　　（D）supplies（供應）

▶ 解析　maintain 除了「維持」以外，也有「維護」物品以免故障、老舊的意思，所以是最恰當的答案。

Q16 I ＿＿＿ *D* ＿＿＿ your hard work. We couldn't succeed without your help.

（我很感謝你的努力。沒有你的幫忙，我們就沒辦法成功。）

（A）consider（考慮）　　（B）expect（期待）

（C）encourage（鼓勵）　► （D）appreciate（感謝）

▶ 解析　因為第二個句子是過去式，所以這是在對某個人過去的努力表達意見。正確答案是 appreciate，除了「欣賞」以外，也有「感謝」的意思，後面通常接事物名詞當受詞。encourage（鼓勵）表示期待之後的行為，而不是對以前的行為表達意見。

Q17 A recent study ＿＿＿ *D* ＿＿＿ that women are usually healthier than men.

（最近的一項研究指出，女人通常比男人健康。）

（A）blames（責怪）　　（B）organizes（組織）

（C）produces（生產）　► （D）indicates（指出）

▶ 解析　要表示研究提出的論點，可以用 indicate（指出）、show（顯示）、claim（主張）等動詞來表達。

Q18 If you ＿＿＿ *B* ＿＿＿ your ticket a month before your trip, you can get a better price.

（如果你在旅行的一個月之前訂票，就可以得到比較好的價格。）

（A）pay（支付）　　► （B）book（預訂）

（C）need（需要）　　（D）examine（檢視）

▶ 解析　在旅行一個月之前會做的事情是「預訂」，所以 book 是正確答案。book 雖然當名詞時是「書」的意思，但也可以當動詞「預訂」使用，請特別注意。pay（支付）雖然看起來好像是對的，但如果要表

達「付錢買票」的話，應該說 pay for your ticket 才對。

Q19 Steve _____*C*_____ his daughter for getting good grades in math.

（史蒂夫稱讚他的女兒數學得到了好成績。）

（A）adopted（收養）　　　　（B）charged（向⋯收費）

► （C）praised（稱讚）　　　　（D）rejected（拒絕）

▶ 解析　praise someone for doing...：因為某人做了⋯而稱讚他

charge someone for something：向某人收取某事物的費用

Q20 Most students _____*A*_____ Miss Wang as the best teacher in the school.

（大部分的學生認為王老師是學校最好的老師。）

► （A）regard（認為）　　　　（B）prefer（偏好）

（C）follow（跟隨）　　　　（D）discover（發現）

▶ 解析　請注意空格之後有 as 所引導的介系詞片語，選項中唯一適合使用 V someone as... 句型的動詞是 regarded（認為）。regard someone as... 是「認為某人是⋯」的意思。

Study 6　意義辨析：片語動詞

Q1 Please _____*C*_____ for a moment. I'll get Mr. Johnson on the line for you.

（請暫時不要掛斷。我會幫您轉接強森先生。）

（A）call up（打電話給⋯）　　　（B）hang up（掛電話）

► （C）hold on（不掛電話）　　　（D）go on（繼續（做某事））

▶ 解析　get someone on the line for you 是電話用語，表示「把某人轉到電話線上和你交談」，所以表示在電話線上暫時等候的 hold on（不掛電話）是正確答案。call up（打電話給⋯）要接人當受詞。

Q2 **Look at all the mess! You really should _____*B*_____ your room.**

（看看這一團亂！你真的該把你的房間整理一下了。）

（A）put away（收好（東西）） ▶（B）tidy up（整理）

（C）see off（送別（某人）） （D）look after（照顧）

▶ 解析 因為是對於房間很亂所提出的勸告，所以 tidy up（整理）是正確答案。put away（收好）是指「把拿出來使用的東西放回原來的地方」，受詞是物品，而不是表示空間的名詞。

Q3 **You may _____*D*_____ the jeans before you decide to buy them.**

（在你決定買牛仔褲之前可以試穿。）

（A）pack up（打包） （B）send off（寄出）

（C）pay back（償還） ▶（D）try on（試穿）

▶ 解析 不管是上衣、褲子或者帽子、鞋子等等，都可以用 try on 表示「試穿」或「試戴」。

Q4 **I haven't _____*A*_____ Jerry since he went to America last month.**

（自從傑瑞上個月去了美國，我就沒接到他的聯絡了。）

▶（A）heard from（接到…的聯絡）

（B）listened to（傾聽）

（C）fallen for（愛上…）

（D）smiled at（對…微笑）

▶ 解析 hear from 表示別人用寫信、寄 e-mail、打電話等方式聯絡自己，也就是「接到…的聯絡」。動詞 listen 有「主動、專注聆聽」的意味，用在這個句子裡會變成「我刻意不去聽 Jerry 說話」的意思，所以不恰當。fall for 後面接人物名詞的時候，表示「愛上…」，接其他名詞時則可以表示「被騙」，例如 I fell for the story he made up.（我被他編造的敘述給騙了）。

Q5 _____ ___A___ _____ your shoes before your step on the carpet.

（踏上地毯之前，先把你的鞋子脫掉。）

▶（A）Take off（脫掉）　　　　（B）Take out（拿出來）

（C）Give away（分送）　　　　（D）Give back（歸還）

▶️解析　step on 是「踏上…」的意思。take off 除了表示「脫掉…」的意思以外，也可以當不及物動詞使用，表示飛機「起飛」。

Q6 I don't know how this machine works, but I want to _____ _C_ _____.

（我不知道這部機器是怎麼運作的，但我想要弄清楚。）

（A）look up（往上看）　　　　（B）catch up（趕上）

▶（C）figure out（弄清楚）　　（D）watch out（小心）

▶️解析　句子後半部省略了受詞，也就是 I want to figure out how this machine works（我想要弄清楚這部機器怎麼運作）的意思。figure out 是「設法了解某件事」的意思，和 know、understand 比起來，帶有比較強的主動意味。

Q7 The sofa is on fire! We have to _____ _B_ _____ before it spreads to the kitchen.

（沙發著火了！我們必須在火蔓延到廚房之前把火撲滅。）

（A）turn it off（關掉電源）

▶（B）put it out（撲滅（火））

（C）calm it down（使冷靜下來）

（D）give it away（分送出去）

▶️解析　spread 的基本意義是「展開」，在這裡則是「擴散，蔓延」的意思。turn down（關掉電源）的受詞是燈或者電器用品，calm down（使冷靜下來）的受詞則通常是人。

Q8 The baseball game was _____ _A_ _____ because of heavy rain.

（那場棒球比賽因為大雨而被取消了。）

▶（A）called off（取消）　　　　（B）shown off（炫耀）

（C）filled out（填好）　　　　　　（D）handed out（分發）

意義辨析

解答篇

▶️**解析** 句子後半部提到原因 because of heavy rain（因為大雨），所以 called off（取消）是最恰當的答案。fill out（填好）的受詞通常是 form（表單）。hand out（分發）是指把一些東西發放給一群人。

Q9 Karen walked slowly so that her younger sister could _____ *D* _____.

（凱倫慢慢地走，好讓她的妹妹可以趕上。）

（A）follow up（（對某事）採取進一步行動）

（B）make up（和好）

（C）grab up（（把東西）抓起來）

▶（D）catch up（趕上）

▶️**解析** so that 後面的子句表示「慢慢走」的目的，所以 catch up（趕上）是正確答案。另外，如果要表示「趕上誰」的話，則會用 catch up with someone 的形式表達。也請注意 follow up（採取進一步行動）的意思和 follow（跟隨）完全不同，例如 follow up the customer's complaint 是表示「對那位顧客的投訴做進一步的處理（例如詢問問題是否已經解決等）」。

Q10 I _____ *A* _____ Tom by accident when I was shopping in a mall.

（我在購物中心購物的時候偶然碰到湯姆。）

▶（A）ran into（偶然碰到）　　　（B）went after（跟在後面）

（C）looked for（尋找）　　　　（D）stopped by（短暫拜訪）

▶️**解析** 因為句中提到 by accident（偶然），所以表示「偶然碰到」的 ran into 是正確答案。go after（跟在後面）和 look for（尋找）都是主動、有意去做的事，和 by accident 的意義會產生矛盾。stop by（短暫拜訪）則是接地點當受詞，例如 stop by Tom's house（短暫拜訪湯姆的家）。

Q11 I don't believe him. I think the story was _____ *A* _____.

（我不相信他。我認為他的說法是編造出來的。）

► （A）made up（編造） （B）spoken up（大聲說）

（C）read out（朗讀） （D）crossed out（劃掉，刪除）

解析 story 在這裡並不是「故事」的意思，而是「對過去發生的事所做的敘述」。make up 在這裡的用法是「編造與事實不同的說法」。

其他選項用法如下：

Speak up. I can't hear you.（大聲說。我聽不見。）

Read out the sentences on the page.（朗讀這一頁的句子。）

Cross out his name from the list.（把他的名字從名單上劃掉。）

Q12 **Time's up. _____A_____ your test papers, please.**

（時間到了。請交出你們的考卷。）

► （A）Hand in（交出）

（B）Hand out（分發）

（C）Take in（接受）

（D）Take out（（從裡面）拿出來）

解析 hand in 是指「交出自己負責的東西」，例如 hand in the homework（交作業）、hand in the report（交報告）。hand out（分發）應該用在 the teacher handed out the test papers（老師發考卷）的情況才對。take in（接受）可以用在 take in the fact（接受事實）的情況。

Q13 **We're running out of gas. We need to _____D_____ the tank.**

（我們（的車）快沒油了。我們必須把油加滿。）

（A）turn in（交還） （B）turn up（調高）

（C）fill in（（填入（空格）） ► （D）fill up（裝滿）

解析 題目裡的 gas 是 gasoline（汽油）的意思，tank 則是指「油箱」，所以 fill up（裝滿）是正確答案。

其他選項用法如下：

turn up the volume（調高音量）

fill in the blank（填入空格）

Q14 **When you don't know the meaning of a new word,**

_____*B*_____ in the dictionary.

（當你不知道某個新字的意義時，就查閱字典。）

（A）get into it（進入） ► （B）look it up（查閱）

（C）look at it（看著） （D）pick it out（選出）

▶ 解析 在字典、百科全書之類的書裡尋找一個條目，要用 look up（查閱）來表達。

Q15 When I took the bus for the first time, I felt sick and _____*C*_____.

（我第一次搭公車時，覺得噁心而且吐了。）

（A）flew up（往上飛） （B）flew away（飛走）

► （C）threw up（嘔吐） （D）threw away（丟掉）

▶ 解析 sick 在這裡不是生病的意思，而是「噁心想吐」，所以 threw up（嘔吐）是正確答案。

Q16 As a single parent, he _____*A*_____ his children all by himself.

（身為單親爸爸，他完全靠自己把孩子養育長大。）

► （A）brought up（養育） （B）pointed out（指出）

（C）escaped from（逃離） （D）thought about（考慮到）

▶ 解析 single parent 指「單親家庭的父親或母親」，all by himself 是「完全靠他自己」的意思。bring up（養育）也可以用動詞 raise（養育）來表達。thought about（考慮到）雖然看起來也是合理的答案，但 think about 的行為本來就是獨自進行的，並不是合作進行的行為，所以用 all by himself 來強調「不需要別人協助」是不合理的說法。

Q17 To sign up for the basketball team, please _____*A*_____ this form.

（要報名籃球隊，請填好這張表單。）

► （A）fill out（填好） （B）show off（炫耀）

（C）look into（調查） （D）put together（組裝）

解析 看到 sign up（報名）、form（表單）等詞彙，就可以判斷答案是 fill out（填好）。另外，選項中的 look into 就是 investigate（調查）的意思。

Q18 I _____*C*_____ the invitation to the party because I have to work on my report.

（我拒絕了派對的邀請，因為我必須做我的報告。）

（A）got over（克服）　　　　　（B）gave away（分送）

▶（C）turned down（拒絕）　　（D）checked out（查看）

解析 invitation to... 表示「⋯場合的邀請」，work on 表示「從事某個工作」。because 後面陳述的原因是「必須做報告」，所以 turned down（拒絕）是正確答案。get over（克服）可以用在 get over the difficulties（克服困難）等情況。

Q19 I don't _____*A*_____ my brother. I'm always fighting with him.

（我和我哥哥相處得不好。我總是和他吵架。）

▶（A）get along with（和⋯相處良好）

（B）look down on（藐視）

（C）do away with（廢除，消除）

（D）keep away from（遠離）

解析 因為總是在 fighting（吵架）的狀態，所以兩人 don't get along（相處得不好）。要表示相處不好，可以說 A and B don't get along，或者 A doesn't get along with B。

Q20 I can't _____*A*_____ the heat any longer. Let's get some ice cream to cool down.

（我再也受不了這炎熱了。我們買些冰淇淋涼快一下吧。）

▶（A）put up with（忍受）

（B）come down with（得⋯這種病）

（C）look up to（尊敬）

（D）look forward to（期待）

▶ 解析　can't... any longer 表示「再也不能…」的意思。在這個題目裡，get 表示「買」，cool down 則是「感覺變涼」的意思。come down with 用在 come down with a cold（得了感冒）之類的情況。look forward to 後面可以接名詞或動名詞，例如 look forward to the party（期待派對）、look forward to seeing you（期待見到你）。

Study 7　意義辨析：wh-（疑問句）

Q1 _____*B*_____ are you talking about? The one wearing the black hat or blue hat?

（你在說的是誰？是戴黑色帽子還是藍色帽子的人？）

（A）What　　　　　　　　▶（B）Who

（C）When　　　　　　　　（D）Where

▶ 解析　talk about 是「談論…」的意思。題目先是問對方談論的對象，然後舉出兩個選項。因為戴著帽子的是人，所以表示人物的疑問詞 Who 是正確答案。

Q2 You look tired. _____*D*_____ did you go to bed last night?

（你看起來很累。你昨晚什麼時候上床睡覺的？）

（A）Why　　　　　　　　（B）How

（C）Where　　　　　　　▶（D）When

▶ 解析　第一句提到對方很累，所以第二句應該和疲勞的理由有關，所以問上床睡覺時間的 When 是正確答案。如果要問對方睡眠品質如何，應該用 How well did you sleep? 來表達才對，注意 go to bed 是指上床睡覺這個時間點的動作，sleep 才是表達整個睡眠期間的狀態。

Q3 _____*B*_____ are you going to buy at the department store?

（你打算在百貨公司買什麼？）

（A）How　　　　　　　　▶（B）What

（C）Where　　　　　　　（D）When

解析 句中的動詞 buy（買）需要有表示購買物品的受詞，所以能表示物品的 What 是正確答案。

Q4 ___*A*___ would you like to pay, by cash or by card?
（您想要怎麼付款，用現金還是信用卡？）
► （A）How   （B）How much
（C）What   （D）What else

解析 句子後半部提到 by cash or by card（用現金還是信用卡），所以能詢問「方法」的 How 是正確答案。
What else（其他的什麼）的用法：
What else do you need to buy?（你還需要買什麼？）

Q5 ___*C*___ did Betty beat her son? What did he do wrong?
（為什麼貝蒂打她的小孩？他做錯了什麼？）
（A）Where   （B）When
► （C）Why   （D）How

解析 第二個句子 What did he do wrong?（他做錯了什麼？）是想詢問貝蒂打小孩的可能理由，所以能詢問理由的 Why 是正確答案。

Q6 ___*D*___ people are more likely to have a successful career?
（哪種人比較可能擁有成功的職業生涯？）
（A）How come   （B）How about
（C）What time do   ► （D）What kind of

解析 選項中只有 What kind of 能和 people 結合成一個名詞片語，表示「什麼類型的人」。
How come：為什麼（= Why）
How about：…怎麼樣（後面接名詞、動名詞或子句，表示提議）
What time：幾點（詢問時刻）

Q7 I have "The Sleeping Beauty" and "The Little Prince".
___*B*___ book do you want to borrow?

（我有《睡美人》和《小王子》。你想要借哪本書？）

（A）Whose ►（B）Which
（C）How many （D）What kind of

▶解析 第一句話提出了兩本書供對方選擇，所以表示在特定範圍內選擇「哪一個」的 Which 是正確答案。另外，請注意 How many 後面必須接複數名詞。

Q8 _____*B*_____ pen case is this? There's no name on it.

（這是誰的筆盒？上面沒有名字。）

（A）What ►（B）Whose
（C）Which （D）In which

▶解析 不要看到後面接物品就直接選擇 What。因為第二句提到筆盒沒有名字，所以詢問的應該是物主身分，表示「誰的」的 Whose 是正確答案。另外，In which pen case is this? 的意思會是「這個東西在哪個筆盒裡面？」。

Q9 _____*B*_____ did they pay for their new house? It looks very expensive.

（他們為了新房子付了多少錢？（房子）看起來非常貴。）

（A）How soon ►（B）How much
（C）How well （D）How often

▶解析 因為第二句提到房子非常貴，考慮兩個句子之間的關係，問價錢的 How much 是最恰當的答案。
How soon：多快（詢問時間點）
How well：（做某事做得）多好
How often：多常（詢問頻率）

Q10 _____*D*_____ do you swim, once a week or every day?

（你多常游泳，是一週一次還是每天？）

（A）How far （B）How long
（C）How well ►（D）How often

解析 once a week or every day（一週一次還是每天）表示頻率，所以詢問頻率的 How often 是正確答案。

How far：多遠

How long：多長，多久（詢問物理上或時間上的長度）

How well：（做某事做得）多好

Q11 I feel so bored. ___C___ we listen to some good music?

（我覺得好無聊。我們聽些好音樂怎麼樣？）

（A）Why do　　　　　　　　（B）How come

►（C）How about　　　　　　（D）What's the point

解析「聽音樂」是排解無聊的建議，所以答案是表示建議的 How about（…怎麼樣？），後面可以接名詞、動名詞或子句。

How come：為什麼（= Why）

What's the point?：重點是什麼？有什麼用？（也就是沒用的意思）

Q12 ___B___ is your daughter? Does she go to elementary school now?

（你的女兒年紀多大？她現在在上小學嗎？）

（A）How big

►（B）How old

（C）How tall

（D）How heavy

解析 選項中只有 How old（年紀多大）和是否上小學有關。注意 How big 表示事物的尺寸大小，而不能表達年齡的大小。

Q13 ___D___ is the cartoon on? I thought it's on weekends.

（那部卡通是星期幾播出？我還以為是週末。）

（A）Where　　　　　　　　（B）When

（C）What time　　　　　　►（D）What day

解析 I thought 表示「我以為…」，但實際上並非如此，所以要問的是「不是週末播出，那麼是星期幾」，表示「星期幾」的 What day 是正確答案。另外，如果要問的是「幾月幾日」，則應該說 What date。What time 問的是時刻，也就是「幾點」。

Q14 I'm afraid you've got the wrong number. _____*A*_____ number are you calling?

（您恐怕打錯電話了。您打的是幾號？）

► （A）What　　　　　　　　　（B）Which

（C）How many　　　　　　　（D）What kind of

▶️**解析**　I'm afraid... 是用來委婉地表達自己的推測。電話號碼「幾號」用 what number 表達，而不是 which number，是因為這裡並不是表達「從幾個號碼裡面選擇」的意思。

Q15 _____*B*_____ do you wear, medium or large?

（你穿什麼尺寸，中等尺寸還是大尺寸？）

（A）What kind　　　　　　► （B）What size

（C）What color　　　　　　（D）What number

▶️**解析**　句子後面的 medium 和 large 表示尺寸，所以問尺寸的 What size 是正確答案。

Part 2 是段落填空（即所謂「克漏字」），分為 2 個題組，共 8 題，必須選擇最恰當的詞語或句子填入文章段落的空格中。在 8 個題目中，有 2 題是填入整句或長段文字，另外大約有 4 題是詞彙題，2 題是考文法概念。雖然文法題的比重不高，但對於掌握文章意義而言，正確理解文法概念仍然很重要。以下就讓我們透過分門別類的練習，掌握英檢初級考生必須具備的基本文法知識。

Part 2
文法練習篇

◎ 「一致性」問題   ◎ 句型結構分析

◎ 時態判斷   ◎ ANSWER 解答篇

|常|考|文|法|題|型|

「一致性」問題

在這類題目中，主要是藉由文法概念的前後一致性來判斷答案，例如第三人稱單數主詞的動詞形式是 is, was, does、代名詞 I 的所有格是 my、附加問句的時態必須和主要子句相同等等。

Study 1 單數名詞＋單數動詞

TIP

第三人稱單數主詞必須使用動詞單數形（is, was, does 等等）。同樣地，如果動詞是單數形，則可以判斷主詞是第三人稱單數。

Q1 Among the baseball teams, the one based in Taichung _____ the most fans.

（A）are （B）is
（C）have （D）has

Q2 My American friends think that Chinese _____ hard for foreigners to learn.

（A）are （B）is
（C）were （D）was

Q3 There _____ nobody who loves me like my mother.

（A）is （B）are
（C）see （D）sees

Q4 He told me everything _____ fine, but I didn't believe him.

（A）is （B）are
（C）was （D）were

Q5 **When I saw his face, I knew _____ was wrong.**
（A）anything　　　　　　（B）any things
（C）something　　　　　 （D）some things

Q6 **_____ is knocking at the door.**
（A）Anyone　　　　　　 （B）Someone
（C）Person　　　　　　　（D）People

Q7 **I guess nobody _____ that idea at all.**
（A）is　　　　　　　　　（B）are
（C）like　　　　　　　　（D）likes

Q8 **There wasn't _____ I could do for her.**
（A）things　　　　　　　（B）nothing
（C）anything　　　　　　（D）some things

Q9 **Writing letters _____ not as difficult as you may think.**
（A）is　　　　　　　　　（B）are
（C）which is　　　　　　（D）which are

Q10 **What they say _____ not true.**
（A）does　　　　　　　　（B）do
（C）is　　　　　　　　　（D）are

Study 2　複數名詞＋複數動詞

TIP

複數主詞必須使用動詞複數形（are, were, do 等等）。同樣地，如果動詞是複數形，則可以判斷主詞是複數。

Q1 **The members of my family _____ all well.**
（A）is　　　　　　　　　（B）was
（C）are　　　　　　　　 （D）did

67

Q2 There are three _____ in the meadow.

（A）goat   （B）cow

（C）sheep   （D）ox

Q3 _____ live in New York City now.

（A）Mr. Wilson   （B）Ms. Wilson

（C）The Wilson's   （D）Wilson's

Q4 Three loaves of bread _____ one hundred dollars.

（A）cost   （B）costs

（C）spend   （D）spends

Q5 Both Tom and Ann _____ late for school yesterday.

（A）is   （B）are

（C）was   （D）were

Q6 Over half of the class _____ boys.

（A）do   （B）does

（C）is   （D）are

Q7 _____ of us were tired after the long trip.

（A）Each   （B）Most

（C）Everyone   （D）One

Q8 Do _____ of your friends have bad eating habits?

（A）one   （B）each

（C）any   （D）anyone

Q9 Each of the _____ in the hotel has its own bathroom.

（A）room   （B）rooms

（C）person   （D）people

Q10 There _____ a couple of things you can do.

（A）has   （B）have

（C）is   （D）are

Study **3** 代名詞

Q1 **She always does _____ own homework.**
（A）her （B）his
（C）its （D）my

Q2 **They call _____ a silly boy.**
（A）it （B）her
（C）him （D）himself

Q3 **The boy doesn't like _____ parents.**
（A）his （B）her
（C）its （D）whose

Q4 **The teacher told us to find the answer by _____.**
（A）himself （B）itself
（C）herself （D）ourselves

Q5 **George and Mary both like _____ math teacher the most.**
（A）his （B）her
（C）their （D）whose

Q6 **I have seen Mrs. Green wearing this ring. It must be _____.**
（A）them （B）theirs
（C）her （D）hers

Q7 **I met Mr. Smith and _____ family for the first time at the party.**
（A）his （B）my
（C）our （D）their

Q8 **Heaven helps those who help _____.**
（A）himself （B）ourselves
（C）yourselves （D）themselves

Q9 **Sally moved to a new apartment. _____ is three blocks away from her office.**

（A）It   （B）She

（C）There   （D）Either

Q10 **There are trees on _____ sides of the road.**

（A）either   （B）both

（C）all   （D）neither

Study 4 連接詞

Q1 **I bought some fruits and some _____ at the supermarket.**

（A）things   （B）foods

（C）apples   （D）vegetables

Q2 **Alice is friendly and _____.**

（A）kind   （B）kindly

（C）kidney   （D）kindness

Q3 **She got up and _____ on the light.**

（A）turn   （B）turns

（C）turned   （D）has turned

Q4 **They are poor but _____.**

（A）honest   （B）honesty

（C）weak   （D）weakness

Q5 **She is not beautiful, but she is _____.**

（A）stupid   （B）smart

（C）lazy   （D）handsome

Q6 **She is not a high school student, but _____.**

（A）a university   （B）a student

（C）a university student   （D）a girl

Q7 He as well as _____ is guilty.

（A）her
（B）she
（C）hers
（D）herself

Q8 Professor Liang is well-known not only in Taiwan but also _____.

（A）Dr. Wang
（B）heard
（C）the world
（D）all over the world

Q9 Nothing is as important as _____.

（A）health
（B）healthy
（C）ill
（D）illness

Q10 The teacher liked _____ better than his.

（A）I
（B）me
（C）my
（D）mine

TYPE 2 時態判斷

在英文中，動詞及助動詞會顯現出句子的時態。如果是需要選擇時態的題目，應該先看看句子裡是否有時間副詞。例如句子裡有 yesterday，表示時間在過去。

Study 1 助動詞

TIP

＊時態與助動詞

主詞	We / I / You	She / He / It
現在式	Do / Don't	Does / Doesn't
過去式	Did / Didn't	
未來式	Will / Won't	
現在完成式	Have + p.p.	Has + p.p.

Q1 He _____ not have any brothers or sisters – he is an only child.

（A）does
（B）did
（C）has
（D）will

Q2 I _____ write my own name until I was in grade three.

（A）can
（B）can't
（C）could
（D）couldn't

Q3 My boyfriend is going to study in France next month, but I'm not sure if I _____ with him.

（A）go
（B）should go
（C）have gone
（D）have been going

Q4 Sharon just told me that she _____ not come to the party tomorrow night.

（A）has （B）did

（C）is （D）will

Q5 I can't tell him now, but I _____ him about it some day.

（A）tell （B）have told

（C）will tell （D）would tell

Q6 My brother is very picky. I hope he _____ say anything bad about this birthday present.

（A）will （B）would

（C）won't （D）wouldn't

Q7 Kevin _____ in public before, so he was very nervous.

（A）doesn't speak （B）didn't speak

（C）hasn't spoken （D）hadn't spoken

Q8 With his experience in the past ten years, he _____ a great teacher.

（A）becomes （B）has become

（C）hasn't become （D）has to become

Q9 We _____ the dog for ten years. He's become a member of my family.

（A）keep （B）kept

（C）have kept （D）are keeping

Q10 I should _____ the letter on that day, but I forgot to.

（A）mailed （B）mailed to

（C）be mailing （D）have mailed

Study 2 時間副詞

TIP

*時間副詞與時態的搭配

現在式	過去式	未來式	現在完成式
today 今天	yesterday 昨天 one day 某一天 the other day 幾天前	tomorrow 明天 some day 總有一天	lately 最近
this ~ : this year 今年	last ~ : last Monday 上星期一 last month 上個月 ago : three months ago 三個月前	next ~ : next week 下星期 next year 明年	since + 過去時間點 : since last week 從上星期開始 since three months ago 從三個月前開始
			for + 期間 : for three months 在三個月的期間

Q1 Mr. Wang lives in Taoyuan, but he drives to Taipei for work _____.

（A）every day　　　　　（B）the other day

（C）some day　　　　　（D）one day

Q2 I couldn't get a ticket when Jolin had a concert _____.

（A）now　　　　　（B）until now

（C）last time　　　　　（D）next time

Q3 It was her first time when she went to London for vacation _____.

（A）a month ago　　　　　（B）in a month

（C）during a month　　　　　（D）every other month

Q4 I met Amanda on the train _____ when I was going to visit my uncle in Tainan.

（A）some day　　　　　（B）every day

（C）other day　　　　　（D）the other day

Q5 **I am late because I was caught in the traffic _____.**

（A）that morning　　　　（B）this morning

（C）every morning　　　　（D）early morning

Q6 **Jason's son is going to be two years old _____.**

（A）next month　　　　（B）the next day

（C）next time　　　　（D）last time

Q7 **I will travel around the world _____. It's been my dream since I was in high school.**

（A）some day　　　　（B）a day

（C）the other day　　　　（D）every other day

Q8 **Bill has been ill _____, and I hope he'll get well soon.**

（A）one day　　　　（B）sometimes

（C）some day　　　　（D）for some days

Q9 **I haven't heard from Lucy _____, and no one seems to know where she is now.**

（A）lately　　　　（B）later

（C）further　　　　（D）sooner or later

Q10 **My family has lived in Taichung _____ I was ten years old.**

（A）for　　　　（B）when

（C）since　　　　（D）from

Study 3　一般動詞變化

TIP

第三人稱單數現在式：

→動詞字尾加 -s。如果字尾是 s, x, ch, sh，則加 -es。

規則動詞過去式：

→動詞字尾加 -ed。如果字尾是 e，則只加 -d。

規則動詞過去分詞：

→動詞字尾加 -ed 或 -en，需要個別記憶。如果字尾是 e，則只加 -d 或 -n。

不規則動詞的變化，也需要個別記憶。

Q1 **My father _____ his car every week, and my mother complains that for him the car is more important than her.**

（A）washed   （B）washes

（C）watered   （D）waters

Q2 **The first bus _____ at 5:50 in the morning, and I always get up early to catch it.**

（A）leave   （B）leaves

（C）left   （D）is leaving

Q3 **I got off in a hurry and _____ my bag on the bus.**

（A）let   （B）led

（C）left   （D）leaved

Q4 **Julia _____ her teacher when she was about to leave the movie theater.**

（A）see   （B）sees

（C）saw   （D）seen

Q5 **She _____ in love with the man when he came to Taiwan for business last summer.**

（A）falls   （B）fell

（C）felt   （D）fallen

Q6 **They were late for school because they _____ the bus.**

（A）miss   （B）missed

（C）take   （D）took

Q7 **Peter usually _____ in the library before an exam when he was in school.**

（A）study （B）studies

（C）studied （D）has studied

Q8 **His parents _____ him to a boarding school when he was only ten.**

（A）send （B）sent

（C）bring （D）brought

Q9 **It is the most beautiful scene I've ever _____ .**

（A）see （B）seen

（C）saw （D）seed

Q10 **I _____ to see polar bears, and I finally saw real ones.**

（A）always want （B）was always wanting

（C）had always wanted （D）will always want

Study 4 be 動詞

TIP

	第一人稱	第二人稱	第三人稱
現在式	I am We are	You are	He/She/It is They are
過去式	I was We were	You were	He/She/It was They were

進行式：be 動詞 + V-ing

進行式表達未來：be 動詞 + going to + V

Q1 **Even three-year-olds know that the Earth _____ round.**

（A）becomes （B）became

（C）is （D）was

Q2 **Marilyn and her sister _____ twins. They look just the same.**

（A）are （B）were

（C）had （D）have been

Q3 It is a lovely day. The sun _____ and the birds are singing.

（A）shine （B）shines
（C）shone （D）is shining

Q4 She _____ a shower when the doorbell rang.

（A）took （B）takes
（C）has taken （D）was taking

Q5 He got hurt _____ he was playing football.

（A）so （B）and
（C）while （D）that

Q6 They _____ begin the new work until they finish the current one.

（A）will （B）go to
（C）are going to （D）are not going to

Q7 When I looked inside, the doctor _____ the boy's arm to see whether the bone was broken.

（A）is feeling （B）is going to feel
（C）was feeling （D）will feel

Q8 The perfume _____ good, but I didn't buy it.

（A）will smell （B）smelled
（C）is smelling （D）was smelling

Q9 I _____ a strange sound and woke up suddenly.

（A）hear （B）heard
（C）am hearing （D）was hearing

Q10 We all _____ Tom plays an important role in our team.

（A）think （B）thought
（C）are thinking （D）were thinking

Study 5 直接引述 vs. 間接引述

TIP

直接引述時，引用的句子放在引號裡面，和主要子句以逗號分隔。

間接引述時，注意以下兩點：

1. 間接引述句的時態和主要子句一致。

2. 不過，如果間接引述句的內容是永久不變的事實、習慣性的行為，則使用現在簡單式。

Q1 He said, "Debbie _____ gone out. Why not come later?"

（A）is （B）has

（C）was （D）had

Q2 "I _____ succeed in the examination if I study hard," he thought.

（A）can （B）could

（C）have to （D）had to

Q3 James asked the boy how old he _____.

（A）is （B）was

（C）has been （D）had been

Q4 The teacher said that if I _____ not feel well, I might go home early.

（A）do （B）did

（C）may （D）might

Q5 Tom said that he _____ there the next day.

（A）goes （B）could go

（C）comes （D）could come

Q6 The manager said that he _____ too busy to attend the meeting.

（A）is （B）was

（C）was being （D）will be

Q7 The man asked his wife from whom she _____ the news.

(A) hears   (B) heard

(C) has heard   (D) will hear

Q8 Mr. Brown said he _____ in Taipei for seven years.

(A) lives   (B) lived

(C) has lived   (D) had lived

Q9 She said that she _____ jogging every morning.

(A) goes   (B) is

(C) has gone   (D) will go

Q10 Jimmy asked why an airplane _____ fly in the air.

(A) can   (B) could

(C) will   (D) would

TYPE 3　句型結構分析

這 類題目測試的是對於整體句子結構的觀念，例如每個子句只有一個主要動詞，如果有其他動詞，則有可能是 to V 或 V-ing 的形式，除非像是後面可以接原形動詞的 help 這種特例。

Study 1　代名詞

TIP

■人稱代名詞

		主格	所有格	受格
第一人稱	我	I	my	me
	我們	we	our	us
第二人稱	你	you	your	you
	你們	you	your	you
第三人稱	他	he	his	him
	她	she	her	her
	它	it	its	it
	他們	they	their	them

■所有／反身代名詞

		所有代名詞	反身代名詞
第一人稱	我	mine	myself
	我們	ours	ourselves
第二人稱	你	yours	yourself
	你們	yours	yourselves
第三人稱	他	his	himself
	她	hers	herself
	它	its	itself
	他們	theirs	themselves

Q1 Everyone knows Betty. No one doesn't know _____.

    （A）she   （B）her

    （C）hers   （D）herself

Q2 Jane said, "Between you and _____. I don't think he's an honest man."

    （A）he   （B）him

    （C）me   （D）them

Q3 Sally is a good friend of _____. We often have a chat over coffee.

    （A）mine   （B）her

    （C）hers   （D）ours

Q4 No matter where David goes, I always go with _____.

    （A）he   （B）him

    （C）himself   （D）myself

Q5 The baby is only five months old, and he can't stand by _____.

    （A）he   （B）him

    （C）his   （D）himself

Q6 They look at _____ in the mirror while they're dancing.

    （A）their   （B）theirs

    （C）them   （D）themselves

Q7 I didn't bring my umbrella, so I had to buy _____.

    （A）one   （B）ones

    （C）some   （D）any

Q8 The black cat likes to play, but the white _____ don't.

    （A）one   （B）ones

    （C）other   （D）others

Q9 My uncle bought his mother a house last month. _____ is five-year-old.

（A）He （B）She
（C）It （D）One

Q10 The wet clothes were still in the washing machine, so I had to hang _____ up.

（A）it （B）ones
（C）some （D）them

Study **2** 名詞性質的成分

TIP

在主詞、受詞的位置，或者一部分的主詞／受詞補語，需要填入名詞性的成分。名詞性的成分有：

1. 一般名詞
2. 動名詞（動詞原形加 -ing）
3. 不定詞（to + 動詞原形）

不過，在介系詞後面只能接一般名詞或動名詞當受詞，而不能接不定詞。

Q1 Jamie is fond of _____ basketball. He plays basketball for more than two hours every day.

（A）plays （B）playing
（C）to play （D）the play of

Q2 I like to swim in the morning. _____ really wakes me up.

（A）Swim （B）Swam
（C）Swimming （D）Swimmer

Q3 Daisy's dream is _____ an astronaut. Therefore, she reads a lot of books on the space.

(A) just
(B) likely
(C) to be
(D) in itself

Q4 To see is _____. I only believe something when I see it with my own eyes.

(A) believe
(B) belief
(C) believable
(D) to believe

Q5 It's no use _____ over spilt milk. We have to accept it and move on.

(A) cry
(B) cries
(C) cried
(D) crying

Q6 Spending money is much easier than _____ it.

(A) make
(B) makes
(C) making
(D) to make

Q7 Writing English is not as easy as _____ it.

(A) speak
(B) speaking
(C) to speak
(D) to speaking

Q8 I did not know how _____ her the truth.

(A) tell
(B) telling
(C) to tell
(D) told

Q9 The problem is where _____ so much money.

(A) to be
(B) will be
(C) to get
(D) will get

Q10 Smoking will do _____ a lot of harm.

(A) you
(B) to you
(C) on you
(D) for you

Study 3 修飾語

TIP

1. 形容詞除了修飾名詞以外，也可以當主詞補語或受詞補語，表示主詞或受詞的狀態。例如「someone is getting + 形容詞」表示「某人越來越⋯」，「make someone + 形容詞」表示「使某人變得⋯」。

2. 副詞可以修飾動詞、形容詞或副詞。副詞通常是「形容詞-ly」的形態，但也有不規則變化的情況，或者副詞會變成不一樣的意思。

形容詞	副詞	副詞
good 好	well 好（當形容詞時，表示「健康的」）	
fast 快	fast 快	
late 晚	late 晚	lately 最近
hard 困難	hard 努力	hardly 幾乎不

Q1 Susie's _____ subject is music.

（A）favor
（B）flavor
（C）favorite
（D）favorable

Q2 I can't forget how _____ she danced.

（A）ugly
（B）friendly
（C）pretty
（D）wonderfully

Q3 Riding a bus is not as _____ as riding a train.

（A）late
（B）lately
（C）fast
（D）soon

Q4 My wife drives the car more _____ than I do.

（A）often
（B）sometimes
（C）careful
（D）quick

Q5 Ken can jump _____ than Kylie does.

（A）high
（B）highly
（C）higher
（D）highest

Q6 **Everyone wants to know who will be _____ actor of the year.**

（A）best
（B）better
（C）the best
（D）the better

Q7 **Tom is a naughty boy and often makes his parents _____.**

（A）angry
（B）angrily
（C）anger
（D）with anger

Q8 **We got _____, so we took a rest.**

（A）tire
（B）tired
（C）tiring
（D）tiresome

Q9 **If you want to play the guitar _____, you have to practice every day.**

（A）good
（B）great
（C）well
（D）hard

Q10 **Don't speak so _____. I can't understand what you're saying.**

（A）nice
（B）hard
（C）fast
（D）slow

Study 4 假設句型

TIP

1. 表示條件的句型，一般最常用的形式是「if... + 現在式，現在式/未來式/祈使句」，表示現在或未來可能發生但不確定的事。

2. had better（最好…）和 would rather... than（寧願…也不）也帶有假設的意味，後面都接原形動詞，中間不加 to。

Q1 **If you don't try your best, you _____ what you want.**

（A）get
（B）are
（C）will not get
（D）are to get

Q2 **If you _____ something, change it. If you can't change it, change yourself.**

（A）are like （B）don't like

（C）will like （D）haven't liked

Q3 **If I must choose, I _____ die than lie.**

（A）shall （B）had better

（C）would rather （D）have to

Q4 **In order to pass the exam, I had better _____ preparing.**

（A）start （B）starting

（C）to start （D）not start

Q5 **If you don't have enough money, you'd better _____ a car.**

（A）buy （B）to buy

（C）not buy （D）not to buy

Study 5 倒裝句型

TIP

1. so, neither 用於句首時，會發生倒裝，也就是把 be 動詞／助動詞移到主詞的前面。

2. never, nor, hardly, seldom, rarely 等否定詞移到子句的開頭強調時，也會發生倒裝。

Q1 **He is a great astronaut, _____ was his father.**

（A）and （B）and so

（C）and that （D）as well as

Q2 **Donald is my friend, and so _____. I like both of them.**

（A）Joe is （B）is Joe

（C）Joe does （D）does Joe

Q3 **Wendy didn't lend him money, and _____ did I.**

(A) so
(B) nor
(C) either
(D) neither

Q4 **He can't say no to Mary, and neither _____.**

(A) I do
(B) do I
(C) I can
(D) can I

Q5 **_____ have I imagined that I would be able to talk with a foreigner.**

(A) Never
(B) Sometimes
(C) Always
(D) Often

Study 6 被動語態

TIP

1. 被動語態的句型是「主詞 + be/get + 過去分詞 + by someone」。在不需要表達行為者是誰的情況下，會省略「by someone」的部分。

2. 過去分詞經常當成形容詞單獨使用，這時候可以說「be/get + 過去分詞」的文法結構和「be/get + 形容詞」相同。過去分詞當形容詞的用法，經常和特定的介系詞搭配使用。

Q1 **The class will _____ by Ms. Lee. She really knows how to deal with young kids.**

(A) teach
(B) be teaching
(C) taught
(D) be taught

Q2 **Coffee, tea and wine _____ on the plane.**

(A) serve
(B) are serving
(C) are served
(D) be served

Q3 The morning paper _____ over 200,000 people every day.

(A) reads

(B) is reading

(C) is read by

(D) is about to read

Q4 When Janice heard about Margaret's death, she _____ and couldn't stop crying.

(A) shocked

(B) was shocking

(C) was shocked

(D) was shocked by

Q5 English is not only _____ in England.

(A) talking

(B) speaking

(C) talked

(D) spoken

Q6 I was very _____ when I spilled my drink on the man's shirt.

(A) hurt

(B) excited

(C) pleased

(D) embarrassed

Q7 Our dog was _____ thunder and hid under the bed.

(A) close to

(B) frightened by

(C) finished with

(D) made of

Q8 I didn't do well on the exams. I am _____ my grades.

(A) excited about

(B) worried about

(C) interested in

(D) pleased with

Q9 My parents _____ thirty years ago. After all these years, they still love each other very much.

(A) were married

(B) got married

(C) had to marry

(D) would like to marry

Q10 Jake _____ for stealing things from the shop.

(A) arrested

(B) was arresting

(C) got arrested

(D) was going to arrest

TIP

■形容詞子句：

用來修飾名詞的子句，稱為形容詞子句。因為這類子句是由關係代名詞引導，所以也稱為關係子句，而關係子句前面被修飾的名詞稱為「先行詞」。

關係代名詞的格	先行詞為"人"	先行詞為"物"
主格	who	which
受格	who/whom	which
所有格	whose	—

另外，which, who, whom 也可以用 that 代替，但直接接在介系詞後面的關係代名詞不能改為 that。

■名詞子句：

在句中扮演名詞角色的子句，稱為名詞子句，可以是句子裡的主詞、補語、受詞等。名詞子句可以由 that 引導，表示「…這件事」，或者由 if, whether 引導，表示「是否…」。

■副詞子句

用來修飾句子裡的動詞、形容詞、副詞，或者修飾整個主要子句的，稱為副詞子句。副詞子句可以由 when, because, although, before, than 等從屬連接詞引導。

Q1 **The building in _____ the American President works is called White House.**

（A）whom
（B）which
（C）where
（D）that

Q2 **Mr. Gates is a mechanic _____ you can trust.**

（A）which
（B）whose
（C）who
（D）for whom

Q3 **He has a horse _____ runs faster than any other in the world.**

（A）who
（B）whom
（C）whose
（D）that

Q4 **The boy _____ had ran away from home was finally found.**
（A）that （B）which
（C）whose （D）whom

Q5 **I understand _____ he was too tired to wake up early.**
（A）who （B）that
（C）if （D）whether

Q6 **We don't know _____ our grandfather will recover from the illness.**
（A）what （B）whose
（C）whether （D）either

Q7 **_____ we were in Sydney, we went to the opera house every month.**
（A）If （B）Though
（C）When （D）Whether

Q8 **He didn't tell the truth _____ he was afraid of being punished.**
（A）so （B）when
（C）after （D）because

Q9 **_____ the farmers work from morning till night, they are still poor.**
（A）If （B）Since
（C）Until （D）Although

Q10 **Sean was surprised that he got better grades _____ he had expected.**
（A）as （B）to
（C）than （D）with

TIP

1. 在同一個子句裡面，只能有一個主要動詞。如果在主要動詞以外還有其他的動詞，則會變成不定詞、動名詞或分詞。

2. 有些動詞後面接動名詞或不定詞，意思差不多。

   例：start, begin, continue, hate, love, prefer 等

3. 有些動詞後面接動名詞或不定詞，意思不同。動名詞表示之前做過的事，不定詞表示之後要做的事。

   例：stop, remember, forget

Q1 The child _____ crying when he couldn't find his mother.

（A）begins   （B）began

（C）wants   （D）wanted

Q2 Margaret _____ exercising so much that she goes to the gym every day.

（A）likes   （B）hates

（C）hopes   （D）prefers

Q3 In winter, Europeans _____ sitting in the sun to staying at home.

（A）prefer   （B）continue

（C）remember   （D）regret

Q4 They continued _____ after a short break.

（A）run   （B）running

（C）rest   （D）resting

Q5 Jason asked his brother _____ making noise.

（A）don't   （B）not to

（C）stopping   （D）to stop

Q6 Tracy is an easy-going person. She wouldn't _____ sharing a house with someone.

　（A）keep　　　　　　　　（B）mind

　（C）agree　　　　　　　（D）refuse

Q7 Mr. Brown gave up _____ when his first child was born.

　（A）smoke　　　　　　　（B）smoking

　（C）to smoke　　　　　　（D）and smoke

Q8 I enjoy _____ alone once in a while, but not always.

　（A）being　　　　　　　（B）to be

　（C）becoming　　　　　　（D）to become

Q9 After playing the online game for four hours, he finally stopped _____.

　（A）going sleeping　　　（B）to go sleeping

　（C）going to bed　　　　（D）to go to bed

Q10 My parents are used to _____ early.

　（A）get up　　　　　　　（B）getting up

　（C）be getting up　　　　（D）having got up

 **ANSWER** 文法練習篇（解答）

TYPE 1 | Study | 1 單數名詞＋單數動詞

Q1 Among the baseball teams, the one based in Taichung
_____*D*_____ the most fans.

（在棒球隊之中，以台中為基地的那一隊有最多球迷。）

（A）are　　　　　　　　　（B）is

（C）have　　　　　　　► （D）has

▶**解析** based in... 表示「以…為基地的」。the one 表示「某一個」，是單數名詞，在這裡是指「the baseball team」，所以動詞單數形 is 和 has 是可能的答案。因為 the most fans（最多的球迷）是球隊所擁有的對象，所以表示「擁有」的 has 是正確答案。

Q2 My American friends think that Chinese _____*B*_____ hard
for foreigners to learn.

（我的美國朋友們認為華語對外國人而言很難學。）

（A）are　　　　　　　► （B）is

（C）were　　　　　　　（D）was

▶**解析** 句型是 think + that 子句（S + V）。空格是 that 子句的動詞，而 that 子句的主詞 Chinese 表示「華語」，是不可數名詞，所以是單數，is 和 was 是可能的答案。因為「華語對外國人而言很難學」是對一般事實的敘述，而不是對過去的敘述，所以表示一般事實的現在簡單式 is 是正確答案。

Q3 There _____*A*_____ nobody who loves me like my mother.

（沒有人像我媽媽一樣愛我。）

▶（A）is （B）are

（C）see （D）sees

▶解析　關係子句 who loves me like my mother（像我媽媽一樣愛我的〔人〕）修飾前面的 nobody（沒有人）。There 是虛主詞，後面接 be 動詞和真主詞時表示「有…（存在）」的意思，而 nobody 是單數名詞，所以單數動詞 is 是正確答案。

Q4 He told me everything ____*C*____ fine, but I didn't believe him.

（他告訴我一切都很好，但我不相信他。）

（A）is （B）are

▶（C）was （D）were

▶解析　空格部分要填入 be 動詞，而主詞是 everything（每件事，一切）。everything、everyone、everybody 雖然表示「每件事、每個人」的意思，但文法上都當成單數名詞，所以 is、was 是可能的答案。這個句子其他的動詞都使用過去式，所以時態一致的過去式 was 是正確答案。

Q5 When I saw his face, I knew ____*C*____ was wrong.

（當我看到他的臉（表情）的時候，我就知道出了點問題。）

（A）anything （B）any things

▶（C）something （D）some things

▶解析　句子後半部的句型是 know + (that) 子句，表示「知道…這件事」。因為動詞是單數形 was，所以單數名詞 anything 和 something 是可能的答案，而從語意來看，something（某件事）是最恰當的答案。anything（任何事）經常用在疑問句和否定句，在這個句子如果要表示「一切都有問題」的話，應該用 everything 而不是 anything。

Q6 ____*B*____ is knocking at the door.

（有人在敲門。）

（A）Anyone ▶（B）Someone

（C）Person　　　　　　　　　（D）People

解析 動詞 is 是單數形，所以先排除複數的選項 People。剩下的選項中，表示「某個人」的 someone 是最恰當的答案。Anyone（任何人）用在這裡的話，意思不恰當。如果要使用 Person 的話，應該加上冠詞：A person is knocking at the door.（有個人在敲門）。

Q7 **I guess nobody _____ _D_ _____ that idea at all.**

（我猜根本沒人喜歡那個主意。）

（A）is　　　　　　　　　　　（B）are

（C）like　　　　　　►（D）likes

解析 句型是 guess + (that) 子句。從屬子句的主詞是 nobody（沒有人），屬於單數名詞，所以動詞單數形 is 和 likes 是可能的答案。如果選擇 be 動詞 is 的話，後面的名詞變成主詞的補語，表示「沒有人是那個主意」，意思說不通，所以 likes（喜歡）才是正確答案。

Q8 **There wasn't _____ _C_ _____ I could do for her.**

（當時沒有什麼是我能為她做的。）

（A）things　　　　　　　　（B）nothing

►（C）anything　　　　　　（D）some things

解析 空格後面的子句修飾前面的名詞，表示「我能為她做的…」。前面的 be 動詞 was 是單數，所以 nothing 和 anything 是可能的答案。因為句中有否定詞 not，選擇 nothing 會造成雙重否定，所以 anything 是正確答案。not anything 表示「沒有任何事物」，也就是全部否定的意思。

以下 -one、-body、-thing 的名詞都是單數名詞：

someone, anyone, everyone

somebody, anybody, nobody, everybody

something, anything, nothing, everything

Q9 **Writing letters _____ _A_ _____ not as difficult as you may think.**

（寫信沒有你可能想像的那麼難。）

► （A）is   （B）are

（C）which is   （D）which are

▶解析 Writing letters 是句子的主詞，表示「寫信這件事」，而動名詞視為單數，所以動詞單數形 is 是正確答案。如果使用有關係代名詞的 which is，會把空格後面的部分都變成修飾前面的內容，使得整段內容變成一個名詞片語，而不是完整的句子。

Q10 **What they say** _____ *C* _____ **not true.**

（他們說的不是真的。）

（A）does   （B）do

► （C）is   （D）are

▶解析 主詞是 What they say，表示「他們所說的事情」，視為單數；空格後面的 true 是形容詞，所以能接形容詞當補語的 be 動詞 is 是正確答案。

TYPE 1　Study　2　複數名詞＋複數動詞

Q1 **The members of my family** _____ *C* _____ **all well.**

（我家裡的人都很好。）

（A）is   （B）was

► （C）are   （D）did

▶解析 主詞 members（成員）是複數，所以 be 動詞複數形 are 是正確答案。注意這裡的 well 是形容詞「健康的，過得好的」而不是副詞。

Q2 **There are three** _____ *C* _____ **in the meadow.**

（草地上有三隻綿羊。）

（A）goat（山羊）   （B）cow（乳牛）

► （C）sheep（綿羊）   （D）ox（公牛）

▶解析 選項中只有 sheep 是單複數同形，可以當成複數使用。

goat, cow 的複數：加 -s

ox 的複數：oxen（不規則變化）

Q3 _____*C*_____ **live in New York City now.**

（威爾森一家現在住在紐約市。）

（A）Mr. Wilson（威爾森先生）　　（B）Ms. Wilson（威爾森小姐）

▶（C）The Wilson's（威爾森一家）　（D）Wilson's（威爾森的）

▶解析 動詞 live 是複數形，「the + 姓氏's」表示「姓…的一家人」，當成複數名詞使用。

Q4 **Three loaves of bread** _____*A*_____ **one hundred dollars.**

（三條麵包要價一百元。）

▶（A）cost　　　　　　　　　　　（B）costs

（C）spend　　　　　　　　　　　（D）spends

▶解析 主詞使用了單位詞 three loaves（三條），所以視為複數，cost 和 spend 是可能的答案。cost 和 spend 的用法分別是「物品 cost 價錢」和「人 spend 金錢」，所以答案是 cost。

Q5 **Both Tom and Ann** _____*D*_____ **late for school yesterday.**

（湯姆和安昨天上學都遲到了。）

（A）is　　　　　　　　　　　　（B）are

（C）was　　　　　　　　▶（D）were

▶解析 主詞 Both Tom and Ann（湯姆和安）是複數，而且時間 yesterday（昨天）是過去，所以複數的過去式 were 是正確答案。

Q6 **Over half of the class** _____*D*_____ **boys.**

（班上超過一半的人是男生。）

（A）do　　　　　　　　　　　　（B）does

（C）is　　　　　　　　　▶（D）are

▶解析 Over half of the class（班上超過一半的人）是複數，而且空格後面的 boys（男孩）是表示主詞的補語，所以 be 動詞複數形 are 是

正確答案。

Q7 ____*B*____ of us were tired after the long trip.

（我們大部分的人在那次長途旅行之後都很累。）

（A）Each ► （B）Most

（C）Everyone （D）One

▶解析 動詞 were 是複數形，所以能表示複數的 most（大部分）是正確答案。each（每個）、everyone（每個人）、one（其中一個）都是單數。

Q8 Do ____*C*____ of your friends have bad eating habits?

你有任何朋友有不好的飲食習慣嗎？

（A）one （B）each

► （C）any （D）anyone

▶解析 助動詞 Do 是複數形，所以能夠表示複數的不定代名詞 any 是正確答案。雖然 any 可以表示單數或複數，但 anyone 只能表示單數。

Q9 Each of the ____*B*____ in the hotel has its own bathroom.

（飯店內每一間房間都附有浴室。）

（A）room ► （B）rooms

（C）person （D）people

▶解析 Each of...（…之中的每一個）後面一定是接複數名詞，而後面出現的所有格 its（它的）表示事物，所以複數的事物名詞 rooms 是正確答案。

Q10 There ____*D*____ a couple of things you can do.

（有幾件你可以做的事。）

（A）has （B）have

（C）is ► （D）are

▶解析 表示存在的「有…」是以 There is/are 表達，而不能說成 There has/have。因為句中真正的主詞 a couple of things（幾件事）是複數，所以複數形的 are 是正確答案。a couple of... 表示「兩個」或

「（不多的）幾個」。

TYPE 1 Study 3 代名詞

Q1 She always does ___*A*___ own homework.

（她總是做她自己的功課。）

▶（A）her　　　　　　　　（B）his

（C）its　　　　　　　　　（D）my

▶解析 主詞是 she，所以答案是同樣表示女性的所有格 her。
one's own... ：自己的…

Q2 They call ___*C*___ a silly boy.

（他們叫他傻男孩。）

（A）it　　　　　　　　　（B）her

▶（C）him　　　　　　　　（D）himself

▶解析 空格是動詞 call（叫）的受詞，a silly boy（傻男孩）是受詞
補語，所以人稱、性別符合的 him 是正確答案。反身代名詞必須和主詞
的人稱、性別相同，所以不能選 himself。

Q3 The boy doesn't like ___*A*___ parents.

（那個男孩子不喜歡他的父母。）

▶（A）his　　　　　　　　（B）her

（C）its　　　　　　　　　（D）whose

▶解析 空格填入的所有格，應該和句子的主詞 The boy（那個男孩
子）相符，所以 his 是正確答案。

Q4 The teacher told us to find the answer by ___*D*___.

（老師叫我們自己找答案。）

（A）himself　　　　　　　（B）itself

（C）herself　　　　　　▶（D）ourselves

> **▶解析** by oneself 表示「自己做…」的意思。因為找答案的人是「我們」，所以表示「我們自己」的 ourselves 是正確答案。

Q5 George and Mary both like _____*C*_____ math teacher the most.

（喬治和瑪莉都最喜歡他們的數學老師。）

（A）his   （B）her

▶（C）their   （D）whose

> **▶解析** 主詞 George and Mary 是第三人稱複數，所以 their（他們的）是正確答案。

Q6 I have seen Mrs. Green wearing this ring. It must be _____*D*_____.

（我看過格林太太戴這只戒指。這一定是她的。）

（A）them   （B）theirs

（C）her   ▶（D）hers

> **▶解析** 第二句的 It 代表上一句的 ring（戒指）。第二句是推測戒指是誰的，所以表示「她的（東西）」的所有代名詞 hers 是正確答案。如果使用受格 her，意思會變成「戒指就是她」，所以不對。

Q7 I met Mr. Smith and _____*A*_____ family for the first time at the party.

（我在派對上和史密斯先生與他的家人初次見面。）

▶（A）his   （B）my

（C）our   （D）their

> **▶解析** 因為要表達「史密斯先生的家人」，所以人稱符合的 his 是正確答案。

Q8 Heaven helps those who help _____*D*_____.

（天助自助者。）

（A）himself   （B）ourselves

（C）yourselves   ▶（D）themselves

(▶)解析 這是一句諺語。those who... 表示「…的人」，是指非特定的多數，所以第三人稱複數的 themselves 是正確答案。

Q9 Sally moved to a new apartment. ___*A*___ is three blocks away from her office.

（莎莉搬到新的公寓了。它在距離她辦公室三個街區的地方。）

▶（A）It   （B）She
（C）There   （D）Either

(▶)解析 空格代表 new apartment，所以 It 是正確答案。There is...「有…」是表示某個人事物存在的意思，和題目不符合，所以不能選 there。Either（兩者之中的任何一個）必須在有兩個已知對象的情況下才能使用。

Q10 There are trees on ___*B*___ sides of the road.

（道路兩旁都有樹。）

（A）either   ▶（B）both
（C）all   （D）neither

(▶)解析 因為道路只有兩側，所以答案是 both，而不是表示三者以上的 all。either（兩者之中的任何一個）和 neither（兩者都不是）後面要接單數名詞。

TYPE 1 〔Study〕 4 連接詞

Q1 I bought some fruits and some ___*D*___ at the supermarket.

（我在超市買了一些水果和蔬菜。）

（A）things（東西）   （B）foods（食物）
（C）apples（蘋果）   ▶（D）vegetables（蔬菜）

(▶)解析 and 連接兩個或兩個以上同屬性的單位，因為前面是 fruits，

所以 vegetables 是正確答案。things、foods 的範圍包含了 fruits，而 apples 是 fruits 的其中一種，都不適合和 fruits 並列。

Q2 **Alice is friendly and ＿＿＿ _A_ ＿＿＿.**

（艾莉絲既友善又親切。）

▶（A）kind（adj. 親切的）　　　（B）kindly（adv. 親切地）

　　（C）kidney（n. 腎臟）　　　（D）kindness（n. 親切）

▶解析　對等連接詞 and 前後應該連接相同的詞性，所以和 friendly（友善的）同樣是形容詞的 kind（親切的）是正確答案。注意 friendly 不是副詞，而是形容詞。

Q3 **She got up and ＿＿＿ _C_ ＿＿＿ on the light.**

（她起床並且開燈。）

　　（A）turn　　　　　　　　　（B）turns

▶（C）turned　　　　　　　　（D）has turned

▶解析　對等連接詞 and 前後應該連接相同的動詞時態，表示連續或同時的動作。got 是過去式，所以同樣是過去式的 turned 是正確答案。

Q4 **They are poor but ＿＿＿ _A_ ＿＿＿.**

（他們貧窮但誠實。）

▶（A）honest（adj. 誠實的）　　（B）honesty（n. 誠實）

　　（C）weak（adj. 虛弱的）　　（D）weakness（n. 虛弱）

▶解析　對等連接詞 but 前後應該連接詞性相同、意義互相對立的成分，所以相對於負面形容詞 poor 的正面形容詞 honest 是正確答案。

Q5 **She is not beautiful, but she is ＿＿＿ _B_ ＿＿＿.**

（她不美，但她很聰明。）

　　（A）stupid（笨的）　　　▶（B）smart（聰明的）

　　（C）lazy（懶惰的）　　　　（D）handsome（帥的）

▶解析　對等連接詞 but 前後連接的子句意義互相對立，因為第一個子句是負面的意思，所以正面的連接詞 smart（聰明的）是正確答案。handsome（帥的）通常只用來形容男性。

103

Q6 **She is not a high school student, but _____C_____.**

（她不是高中生，是大學生。）

（A）a university（大學）

（B）a student（學生）

► （C）a university student（大學生）

（D）a girl（女生）

▶解析 對等連接詞 but 前後應該連接相同屬性的詞彙，所以和 a high school student（高中生）同樣屬於學生類型的 a university student（大學生）是正確答案。

Q7 **He as well as _____B_____ is guilty.**

（他和她都有罪。）

（A）her   ► （B）she

（C）hers   （D）herself

▶解析 相關連接詞 as well as 前後要連接相同屬性的詞彙，所以和 he 同樣是主格代名詞的 she 是正確答案。

Q8 **Professor Liang is well-known not only in Taiwan but also _____D_____.**

（梁教授不止聞名台灣，也聞名全世界。）

（A）Dr. Wang   （B）heard

（C）the world   ► （D）all over the world

▶解析 相關連接詞 not only... but (also) 要連接相同屬性的成分。題目中的 not only 後面接副詞片語 in Taiwan（在台灣），所以 but also 後面也要接副詞片語，能當副詞片語的 all over the world（在全世界）是正確答案。

Q9 **Nothing is as important as _____A_____.**

（沒有什麼跟健康一樣重要。）

► （A）health（n. 健康）   （B）healthy（adj. 健康的）

（C）ill（adj. 生病的）   （D）illness（n. 疾病）

▶ 解析 　as + 形容詞 + as + 名詞：像…一樣…。因為空格要填入「重要」的事物，所以 health（健康）是正確答案。

Q10 **The teacher liked ____*D*____ better than his.**
（老師喜歡我的勝過他的。）

（A）I （B）me

（C）my ▶（D）mine

▶ 解析 　than 後面接的 his 是所有代名詞，表示「他的東西」，所以空格也要填入所有代名詞，也就是 mine（我的東西）。

TYPE 2 Study 1 助動詞

Q1 He _____*A*_____ not have any brothers or sisters – he is an only child.

（他沒有任何兄弟姊妹—他是獨生子。）

▶（A）does　　　　　　　　（B）did
（C）has　　　　　　　　　（D）will

▶解析 因為第二句使用現在式 is，所以現在式的 does 是正確答案。

only child：獨生小孩

only son：獨生兒子

Q2 I _____*D*_____ write my own name until I was in grade three.

（我直到三年級前都不會寫自己的名字。）

（A）can　　　　　　　　　（B）can't
（C）could　　　　　　▶（D）couldn't

▶解析 until 表示某個持續狀態結束的時間點。因為 until 後面接的子句是過去式，所以主要子句的時間也是過去，couldn't 是正確答案。

肯定句 + until...：保持某個狀態到…為止

否定句 + until...：保持不做某事的狀態到…為止 → 到…才開始做某事

Q3 My boyfriend is going to study in France next month, but I'm not sure if I _____*B*_____ with him.

（我的男朋友下個月會去法國念書，但我不確定我是否應該跟他一起去。）

（A）go　　　　　　　▶（B）should go
（C）have gone　　　　　（D）have been going

▶解析 現在式 go：一般的事實、習慣等等

should go：「應該去」（表示責任、義務）

現在完成式 have gone：已經做了

現在完成進行式 have been going：從過去到現在一直進行中的事

Q4 Sharon just told me that she _____*D*_____ not come to the party tomorrow night.

（雪倫剛剛告訴我她明天晚上不會來參加派對。）

（A）has （B）did

（C）is ► （D）will

▶**解析** tomorrow night（明天晚上）是未來時間，所以未來式的助動詞 will 是正確答案。

Q5 I can't tell him now, but I _____*C*_____ him about it some day.

（我現在不能告訴他，但我總有一天會告訴他的。）

（A）tell （B）have told

► （C）will tell （D）would tell

▶**解析** 時間副詞 some day 表示「在未來的某一天」，所以未來式 will tell 是正確答案。另外，one day（有一天，某一天）可以表示過去或未來的某一天。

Q6 My brother is very picky. I hope he _____*C*_____ say anything bad about this birthday present.

（我弟弟很挑剔。我希望他不會批評這份生日禮物。）

（A）will （B）would

► （C）won't （D）wouldn't

▶**解析** 主要子句的動詞 hope（希望）是現在式，而希望的是之後發生的事情，所以表示以現在為基準的未來的 won't 是正確答案。助動詞 would 則是以過去為基準的未來，或者用在假設語氣的句子裡。

Q7 Kevin _____*D*_____ in public before, so he was very nervous.

（凱文以前沒有公開演講過，所以當時他非常緊張。）

（A）doesn't speak （B）didn't speak

（C）hasn't spoken ► （D）hadn't spoken

解析 從句子的後半部得知這是描述過去的情況，而前半部的時間副詞 before（以前）又表示比當時更早的過去時間，所以表示過去時間點所擁有經驗的過去完成式 hadn't spoken 是正確答案。

Q8 With his experience in the past ten years, he ___*B*___ a great teacher.

（靠著他過去十年的經驗，他成為了很棒的老師。）

（A）becomes   ► （B）has become

（C）hasn't become   （D）has to become

解析 現在簡單式表示不會隨著時間改變的狀態，而 become（成為）是一次性、非持續性的動作，也不能反覆進行，所以先排除 becomes。剩下的選項中，表示「成為了」的現在完成式 has become 是語意上最恰當的答案。has to become（必須成為）則是表示因為所處情況的關係，被迫、不得不做這件事的意思。

Q9 We ___*C*___ the dog for ten years. He's become a member of my family.

（我們已經養這隻狗十年了。他已經成為這個家庭的一份子。）

（A）keep   （B）kept

► （C）have kept   （D）are keeping

解析 因為句中有表示持續時間長度的 for ten years（為期十年），所以能表示某個狀態持續多久的完成式 have kept 是正確答案。進行式 be doing 是指某個時間點正在做什麼事，所以不會和表示期間的時間副詞一起使用。

Q10 I should ___*D*___ the letter on that day, but I forgot to.

（我那天應該把信寄出去的，但我忘了。）

（A）mailed   （B）mail to

（C）be mailing   ► （D）have mailed

解析 should have p.p. 表示「在過去某個時間點應該已經做完某事了」。

TYPE 2 **Study** 2 時間副詞

Q1 Mr. Wang lives in Taoyuan, but he drives to Taipei for work _____*A*_____.

（王先生住在桃園，但是他每天開車到台北上班。）

▶（A）every day（每天）　　　（B）the other day（幾天前）

（C）some day（總有一天）　　（D）one day（某一天）

▶解析 lives、drives 都是現在簡單式，表示一種常態，所以 every day（每天）是正確答案。

Q2 I couldn't get a ticket when Jolin had a concert _____*C*_____.

（Jolin 上次開演唱會的時候，我買不到票。）

（A）now（現在）　　　　　　（B）until now（直到現在為止）

▶（C）last time（上次）　　　　（D）next time（下次）

▶解析 助動詞 could 顯示這是關於過去的敘述，所以表示過去時間點的 last time（上次）是正確答案。until now（直到現在為止）雖然也是過去時間，但是指從過去某個時間點到現在為止的整段期間，所以通常是搭配現在完成式使用。

Q3 It was her first time when she went to London for vacation _____*A*_____.

（她上個月是第一次到倫敦度假。）

▶（A）a month ago（一個月前）

（B）in a month（一個月後）

（C）during a month（在一個月的期間）

（D）every other month（每隔一個月（兩個月一次））

▶解析 動詞 went 是過去式，所以表示過去時間點的 a month ago（一個月前）是正確答案。

Q4 I met Amanda on the train _____*D*_____ when I was going to

visit my uncle in Tainan.

（幾天前我在要去拜訪台南的叔叔的時候，在火車上遇到亞曼達。）

（A）some day（總有一天）

（B）every day（每天）

（C）other day（缺少冠詞 the）

► （D）the other day（幾天前）

▶ 解析 主要子句的動詞 met 是過去式，所以表示過去時間的 the other day（幾天前）是正確答案。

Q5 **I am late because I was caught in the traffic ___*B*___.**

（我遲到了，因為我今天上午困在塞車車陣裡。）

（A）that morning（那個早上）

► （B）this morning（今天早上）

（C）every morning（每天早上）

（D）early morning（早上很早的時候）

▶ 解析 句中的「遲到」用現在式表達，「困在塞車車陣裡」則是過去式，表示過去遇到塞車，造成現在遲到的結果，this morning（今天早上）是最恰當的答案。that morning 表示今天以外的某天早上。如果填入名詞片語 early morning（早上很早的時候），則缺少了介系詞，應該改為 in the early morning 才對。

Q6 **Jason's son is going to be two years old ___*A*___.**

（傑森的兒子下個月就滿兩歲了。）

► （A）next month（下個月）　　（B）the next day（隔天）

（C）next time（下次）　　（D）last time（上次）

▶ 解析 動詞部分 is going to be 表示「即將成為…」，所以表示未來時間的 next month 是正確答案。注意 the next day 是指發生某件事之後的第二天，例如：We went to Alishan, and on the next day we went to see the sunrise.（我們去了阿里山，然後隔天我們去看日出）。

Q7 **I will travel around the world ___*A*___. It's been my dream since I was in high school.**

（總有一天我要環遊世界。這是我從高中開始的夢想。）

► （A）some day（總有一天）

（B）a day（一天）

（C）the other day（幾天前）

（D）every other day（每隔一天（每兩天一次））

▶️解析 助動詞 will 表示這是未來的行為，所以表示未來時間的 some day（總有一天）是正確答案。a day（一天）只能當名詞，不能當副詞使用。

Q8 Bill has been ill _____*D*_____, and I hope he'll get well soon.

（比爾已經病了幾天，我希望他能趕快好起來。）

（A）one day（某一天）　　（B）sometimes（有時候）

（C）some day（總有一天）　► （D）for some days（為期幾天）

▶️解析 has been 是現在完成式，表示從過去到現在的狀態，所以表示期間的 for some days（為期幾天）是正確答案。

Q9 I haven't heard from Lucy _____*A*_____, and no one seems to know where she is now.

（我最近都沒收到露西的聯絡，似乎也沒人知道她現在在哪裡。）

► （A）lately（最近）　　（B）later（稍後）

（C）further（更遠地）　　（D）sooner or later（遲早）

▶️解析 have heard 是現在完成式，所以表示到現在為止的近期時間的 lately（最近）是正確答案。later（稍後）表示未來，sooner or later（遲早）表示對未來的推測。

Q10 My family has lived in Taichung _____*C*_____ I was ten years old.

（從我十歲的時候開始，我家就住在台中了。）

（A）for　　　　　　　（B）when

► （C）since　　　　　　（D）from

▶️解析 空格前後都是完整的子句，所以空格要填入連接詞。have

lived 是現在完成式，所以能表示從過去時間點開始的持續期間的 since（自從…）是正確答案。for 連接子句的時候表示理由，當介系詞並且接時間名詞時（例如 for ten years）才是表示期間。from 是介系詞，後面不能接子句。

TYPE 2 | Study | 3 一般動詞變化

Q1 My father _____*B*_____ his car every week, and my mother complains that for him the car is more important than her.

（我爸爸每個禮拜洗他的車，而我媽媽抱怨對他而言車子比她還重要。）

（A）washed（洗（過去式））

► （B）washes（洗（現在式））

（C）watered（澆水（過去式））

（D）waters（澆水（現在式））

▶**解析** 只看時間副詞 every week（每個禮拜）不能判斷時態，因為它可以搭配現在簡單式或過去簡單式使用，表示現在或過去反覆發生的事。第二個子句的動詞 complains 是現在簡單式，所以同樣是現在簡單式的 washes 是正確答案。

Q2 The first bus _____*B*_____ at 5:50 in the morning, and I always get up early to catch it.

（第一班公車早上 5 點 50 分出發，而我總是為了趕上它而早起。）

（A）leave

► （B）leaves

（C）left

（D）is leaving

▶**解析** 如果不看第二個子句的話，leaves（現在簡單式）、left（過去簡單式）、is leaving（現在進行式：可以表示「即將…」）都是可能的答案，但因為第二個子句是現在簡單式，表示一般的情況，所以同樣是現在簡單式的 leaves 是正確答案。

Q3 I got off in a hurry and _____*C*_____ my bag on the bus.

（我匆忙下車，把包包留在公車上了。）

（A）let（讓）　　　　　　　　（B）led（帶領）

▶（C）left（留下）　　　　　　　（D）leaved（不正確的形式）

解析　選項中的動詞原形－過去式－過去分詞分別是：

let-let-let（讓）

lead-led-led（帶領）

leave-left-left（留下）

Q4 Julia _____*C*_____ her teacher when she was about to leave the movie theater.

（茱莉亞在正要離開電影院的時候看到她的老師。）

（A）see　　　　　　　　　　（B）sees

▶（C）saw　　　　　　　　　　（D）seen

解析　動詞 see 的原形－過去式－過去分詞是 see-saw-seen。因為表示時間的子句使用了過去式 was，所以主要子句也要用過去式，saw 是正確答案。

Q5 She _____*B*_____ in love with the man when he came to Taiwan for business last summer.

（去年那個男人來台灣出差的時候，她愛上了他。）

（A）falls　　　　　　　　▶（B）fell

（C）felt　　　　　　　　　　（D）fallen

解析　選項中的動詞原形－過去式－過去分詞分別是：

fall-fell-fallen（掉落）

feel-felt-felt（感覺）

慣用語 fall in love 是「愛上某人」的意思。因為有表示過去的時間副詞 last summer（去年夏天），所以過去式 fell 是正確答案。

Q6 They were late for school because they _____*B*_____ the bus.

（他們上學遲到了，因為他們錯過了巴士。）

（A）miss（錯過（現在式））　　▶（B）missed（錯過（過去式））

（C）take（搭乘（現在式）） 　　（D）took（搭乘（過去式））

▶ **解析** 過去上學遲到的原因應該是錯過巴士，而且也是過去發生的事情，所以 missed 是正確答案。

Q7 Peter usually _____*C*_____ in the library before an exam when he was in school.

（彼得以前在求學的時候，通常會在考試前到圖書館唸書。）

（A）study 　　　　　　　　　（B）studies

▶（C）studied 　　　　　　　　（D）has studied

▶ **解析** 表示時間的 when 子句是過去式，所以主要子句也應該是過去式，studied 是正確答案。這裡使用了頻率副詞 usually（通常），表示這是過去的一種常態。

Q8 His parents _____*B*_____ him to a boarding school when he was only ten.

（他的父母在他只有十歲的時候送他到寄宿學校就讀。）

（A）send 　　　　　　▶（B）sent

（C）bring 　　　　　　　（D）brought

▶ **解析** send 是指把某個人事物送到別的地方，bring 則是指把某個人事物一起帶在身邊，這裡意義比較恰當的動詞是 send。因為表示時間的 when 子句是過去式，所以過去式 sent 是正確答案。

Q9 It is the most beautiful scene I've ever _____*B*_____.

（那是我看過最美的一幕。）

（A）see 　　　　　　▶（B）seen

（C）saw 　　　　　　　（D）seed

▶ **解析** have ever p.p. 表示到目前為止的經驗，是更加強調完成式的說法。see 的動詞原形－過去式－過去分詞是 see-saw-seen。seed 是名詞「種子」。

Q10 I _____*C*_____ to see polar bears, and I finally saw real ones.

（我一直想要看北極熊，而我終於看到真的北極熊了。）

（A）always want   （B）was always wanting

► （C）had always wanted （D）will always want

▶解析 and 連接的第二個子句是過去式，所以第一個子句也應該是表示過去，正確答案是過去完成式 had always wanted，表示「在過去看到北極熊的時間點之前，一直都想看北極熊」。

TYPE 2 | Study | 4 | be 動詞

Q1 Even three-year-olds know that the Earth ___*C*___ round.

（就連三歲小孩都知道地球是圓的。）

（A）becomes   （B）became

► （C）is   （D）was

▶解析 become round 表示「變成圓的」，意思不恰當，所以應該從兩個 be 動詞選項中選擇。因為「地球是圓的」是從過去到未來都不會改變的事實，所以現在式 is 是正確答案。

Q2 Marilyn and her sister ___*A*___ twins. They look just the same.

（瑪莉琳和她的妹妹是雙胞胎。她們看起來一模一樣。）

► （A）are   （B）were

（C）had   （D）have been

▶解析 兩句話所說的是同一件事實，而且第二個句子用的是現在式 look，所以現在式 are 是正確答案。

Q3 It is a lovely day. The sun ___*D*___ and the birds are singing.

（今天是美好的日子。太陽照耀，鳥兒歌唱。）

（A）shine   （B）shines

（C）shone ► （D）is shining

> **解析** 對等連接詞的前後連接相同的文法成分，所以和 are singing 同樣是現在進行式的 is shining 是正確答案。

Q4 She _____*D*_____ a shower when the doorbell rang.

（門鈴響的時候她正在淋浴。）

（A）took　　　　　　　　　（B）takes

（C）has taken　　　　　　▶（D）was taking

> **解析** 表示時間的 when 子句使用過去式，表示過去時間點，所以能表示過去某個時間點正在做什麼的過去進行式 was taking 是正確答案。

Q5 He got hurt _____*C*_____ he was playing football.

（他在打美式足球的時候受傷了。）

（A）so　　　　　　　　　　（B）and

▶（C）while　　　　　　　　（D）that

> **解析** while 表示「在⋯的期間」。so 連接原因和結果，and 則表示並列或順序，兩者都不符合題目的意思。that 子句是名詞子句或形容詞子句（關係子句），也就是整個子句當成一個名詞，或者當成形容詞修飾前面的名詞。

Q6 They _____*D*_____ begin the new work until they finish the current one.

（直到完成目前的工作之前，他們不會開始新的工作。）

（A）will　　　　　　　　　（B）go to

（C）are going to　　　　　▶（D）are not going to

> **解析** 使用從屬連接詞 until 的時候，如果主要子句使用肯定句，表示「做⋯到某個時間點為止」；如果主要子句是否定句，表示「保持不做⋯的狀態到某個時間點為止」。因為 begin（開始）是一次性、非持續性的動詞，不適合用在表示「持續做」的「肯定句 + until」句型裡，所以有否定詞的 are not going to 是正確答案，表示「保持不開始新工作的狀態，直到完成目前的工作為止」。

Q7 When I looked inside, the doctor _____*C*_____ the boy's arm to see whether the bone was broken.

（當我往裡面看的時候，醫師正在觸診男孩的手臂，看看骨頭有沒有斷。）

（A）is feeling　　　　　　　　（B）is going to feel

▶（C）was feeling　　　　　　　（D）will feel

▶解析　表示時間的 When 子句是過去式，所以主要子句也表示過去的事情，過去進行式 was feeling 是正確答案。

Q8 The perfume _____*B*_____ good, but I didn't buy it.

（那香水聞起來很好，但我沒有買。）

（A）will smell　　　　　　　▶（B）smelled

（C）is smelling　　　　　　　（D）was smelling

▶解析　對等連接詞 but 後面是過去式，所以前面也應該表示過去。表示「知覺」的動詞（see, hear, smell, taste, sound）通常不用進行式，所以過去式 smelled 是正確答案。

Q9 I _____*B*_____ a strange sound and woke up suddenly.

（我聽到奇怪的聲音，突然醒了過來。）

（A）hear　　　　　　　　　▶（B）heard

（C）am hearing　　　　　　　（D）was hearing

▶解析　對等連接詞 and 後面是過去式，所以前面也應該表示過去。表示「知覺」的動詞（see, hear, smell, taste, sound）通常不用進行式，所以過去式 heard 是正確答案。

Q10 We all _____*A*_____ Tom plays an important role in our team.

（我們全都認為湯姆在我們的隊伍裡扮演重要的角色。）

▶（A）think　　　　　　　　（B）thought

（C）are thinking　　　　　　（D）were thinking

▶解析　空格後面的部分是現在式，表示現在的事實，所以同樣表示現在情況的 think 是正確答案。如果用現在進行式的話，反而會產生「現在這個片刻正在這樣想，但其他時間並不這麼想」的意義。

Q1 He said, "Debbie _____*B*_____ gone out. Why not come later?"

（他說：「黛比已經出去了。何不稍後再來呢？」）

（A）is   ► （B）has

（C）was   （D）had

▶解析 因為是直接引述某人當時說的話，所以現在完成式 has gone out（已經出去了）是最恰當的答案。過去完成式只會在刻意強調「過去某個時間點之前已經完成了」的時候使用。雖然可以用 be gone 表示「不見了」，但這個用法的 gone 後面不能再加 out。

Q2 "I _____*A*_____ succeed in the examination if I study hard," he thought.

（他想：「如果我努力用功，我考試就能成功。」）

► （A）can   （B）could

（C）have to   （D）had to

▶解析 引號裡面是一個直接引述的句子，而其中的 if 子句是現在式，所以現在式 can 是正確答案。如果用 could 的話，if 子句應該用過去式才對。have to 表示「有義務，不得不，被迫…」的意思。

Q3 James asked the boy how old he _____*B*_____.

（詹姆斯問那個男孩他年紀多大。）

（A）is   ► （B）was

（C）has been   （D）had been

▶解析 這裡間接引述詹姆斯所問的內容，所以和 asked 同樣是過去式的 was 是正確答案。

Q4 The teacher said that if I _____*B*_____ not feel well, I might go home early.

（老師說如果我覺得不舒服，可以早一點回家。）

（A）do　　　　　　　　　► （B）did
（C）may　　　　　　　　 （D）might

▶ 解析　這裡間接引述老師所說的內容，所以和 said 同樣是過去式的 did 是正確答案。從屬連接詞 if 已經表示可能性，不適合再用表示不確定性的助動詞 may 作為假設內容。

問題一致性

時態判斷

分句型結構分析

解答篇

Q5 Tom said that he _____*B*_____ there the next day.

（湯姆說他隔天可以去那裡。）

（A）goes　　　　　　　　► （B）could go
（C）comes　　　　　　　 （D）could come

▶ 解析　這裡間接引述湯姆所說的內容，所以和 said 同樣是過去式的 could go 是正確答案。因為 there 表示「別的地方」，所以動詞會使用 go 而不是 come。

Q6 The manager said that he _____*B*_____ too busy to attend the meeting.

（經理說他太忙了而無法出席會議。）

（A）is　　　　　　　　　► （B）was
（C）was being　　　　　 （D）will be

▶ 解析　這裡間接引述經理所說的內容，所以和 said 同樣是過去式的 was 是正確答案。這裡只是表示單純的情況，所以不需要用進行式來表達。

Q7 The man asked his wife from whom she _____*B*_____ the news.

（那個男人問他的太太是從誰那邊聽到了消息。）

（A）hears　　　　　　　　► （B）heard
（C）has heard　　　　　　 （D）will hear

▶ 解析　這裡間接引述男人所說的內容，所以和 asked 同樣是過去式的 heard 是正確答案。現在完成式 has heard 應該改成過去完成式 had heard 才符合文法。

Q8 Mr. Brown said he _____*D*_____ in Taipei for seven years.

（布朗先生說他已經住在台北七年了。）

（A）lives   （B）lived

（C）has lived   ►（D）had lived

▶解析 這裡間接引述布朗先生所說的內容，主句動詞 said 是過去式，所以過去式 lived 和過去完成式 had lived 是可能的答案。因為後面有表示持續期間的 for seven years（為期七年），所以過去完成式 had lived 是正確答案，表示到過去他說這句話的時間為止，已經住了七年。

Q9 She said that she _____*A*_____ jogging every morning.

（她說她每天上午去慢跑。）

►（A）goes   （B）is

（C）has gone   （D）will go

▶解析 雖然是間接引述句，但因為表示習慣性的行為，所以可以用現在簡單式表達，goes 是正確答案。

Q10 Jimmy asked why an airplane _____*A*_____ fly in the air.

（吉米問為什麼飛機能在空中飛。）

►（A）can   （B）could

（C）will   （D）would

▶解析 雖然是間接引述句，但因為表示永久不變的事實，而且 an airplane 表示「一般的任何一架飛機」，所以應該用現在簡單式表達。從語意來看，表示能力的 can 比表示未來的 will 恰當。

TYPE 3 [Study] 1 代名詞

Q1 Everyone knows Betty. No one doesn't know ___*B*___.

（每個人都認識貝蒂。沒有人不認識她。）

（A）she   ▶（B）her

（C）hers   （D）herself

▶解析

主格	所有格	受格	所有代名詞	反身代名詞
she	her	her	hers	herself

空格要填入動詞 know 的受詞，所以 her 是正確答案。

Q2 Jane said, "Between you and ___*C*___. I don't think he's an honest man."

（珍說：「這是你跟我之間的祕密。我覺得他不是誠實的人。」）

（A）he   （B）him

▶（C）me   （D）them

▶解析 在跟別人說祕密的時候，會說 between you and me，表示這是「只有你和我知道的祕密」，有希望對方不要說出去的意思。

Q3 Sally is a good friend of ___*A*___. We two often have a chat over coffee.

（莎莉是我的一個好朋友。我們兩個經常喝咖啡聊天。）

▶（A）mine   （B）her

（C）hers   （D）ours

▶解析 a good friend of mine 就是 one of my good friends（我的好朋友的其中之一）的意思。第二個句子的主詞是 We two（我們兩個），表示 Sally 和我，所以 mine（我的〔朋友〕）是正確答案。

Q4 No matter where David goes, I always go with ___*B*___.

（不管大衛去哪裡，我總是跟他一起去。）

（A）he   ▶（B）him

（C）himself　　　　　　　　（D）myself

解析 空格是介系詞 with（和…一起）的受詞，所以受格 him 是正確答案。

Q5 The baby is only five months old, and he can't stand by ____*D*____.

（那個嬰兒才五個月大，他不能靠自己站著。）

（A）he　　　　　　　　　　（B）him
（C）his　　　　　　　▶（D）himself

解析 by oneself 是「靠自己」的意思。

Q6 They look at ____*D*____ in the mirror while they're dancing.

（他們在跳舞的時候會看著鏡子裡的自己。）

（A）their　　　　　　　　　（B）theirs
（C）them　　　　　　▶（D）themselves

解析 在鏡子裡看著的人就是自己，主詞和受詞相同，所以反身代名詞 themselves 是正確答案。

Q7 I didn't bring my umbrella, so I had to buy ____*A*____.

（我沒帶自己的傘，所以我不得不買一把。）

▶（A）one　　　　　　　　（B）ones
（C）some　　　　　　　　（D）any

解析 空格裡要表達的意思是 an umbrella（一把雨傘），因為前面已經提到 umbrella，所以用不定代名詞 one 代替。any（任何）會變成「任何可能的雨傘都買」的意思。

Q8 The black cat likes to play, but the white ____*B*____ don't.

（那隻黑貓喜歡玩，但那些白色的不喜歡。）

（A）one　　　　　　　　　　▶（B）ones
（C）other　　　　　　　　　（D）others

解析 空格表示 cats（貓），因為前面已經提到 cat，而且後面的助動詞 do 顯示主詞是複數，所以用複數不定代名詞 ones 代替。代名詞 the other（s）中間不能插入形容詞。

Q9　**My uncle bought his mother a house last month. _____ *C* _____ is five-year-old.**

（我叔叔上個月買了一間房子給他的母親。房子的屋齡是五年。）

　（A）He　　　　　　　　　　　　（B）She

▶（C）It　　　　　　　　　　　　（D）One

　　解析 乍看之下，five-year-old 似乎是指人的年齡，但 My uncle（我的叔叔）和 his mother（他的母親）都不可能只有五歲，所以唯一可能的主詞是「房子」，表示屋齡，正確答案是 It。不定代名詞 One 是用在前面已經提到一個範圍或一種事物，然後要舉出其中一個的情況，但這兩個句子可以確定是在說同一間房子，所以不能用 One。

Q10　**The wet clothes were still in the washing machine, so I had to hang _____ *D* _____ up.**

（當時濕衣服還在洗衣機裡，所以我必須把它們晾起來。）

　（A）it　　　　　　　　　　　　（B）ones

　（C）some　　　　　　　　　▶（D）them

　　解析 空格表示前面提到的 wet clothes，所以表示特定複數名詞的代名詞 them 是正確答案，而不能使用表示非特定對象的不定代名詞（ones, some）。

TYPE 3　Study　2　名詞性質的成分

Q1　**Jamie is fond of _____ *B* _____ basketball. He plays basketball for more than two hours every day.**

（傑米很喜歡打籃球。他每天打籃球超過兩小時。）

　（A）plays　　　　　　　　　▶（B）playing

（C）to play   （D）the play of

▶解析 be fond of doing 是「很喜歡做…」的意思。類似的結構還有 be interested in doing（對於做…有興趣）。

Q2 I like to swim in the morning. ___*C*___ really wakes me up.

（我喜歡晨泳。游泳真的會讓我睡意全消。）

（A）Swim   （B）Swam
►（C）Swimming   （D）Swimmer

▶解析 能表示「游泳」這件事的是動名詞 Swimming。swim 雖然也可以當名詞用，但使用時應該加冠詞，例如 a swim。swimmer 是「游泳者」的意思。

Q3 Daisy's dream is ___*C*___ an astronaut. Therefore, she reads a lot of books on the space.

（黛西的夢想是當太空人。所以她閱讀許多關於太空的書。）

（A）just   （B）likely
►（C）to be   （D）in itself

▶解析 be 動詞 is 後面表示夢想的內容，所以能當名詞使用的不定詞 to be（成為，當）是正確答案。其他三個選項都是副詞／副詞片語，just 表示「只是」，likely 表示「很有可能」，in itself 表示「本質上」，如果用在這個題目裡，意思會變成「夢想＝太空人」，也就是「夢想這件事物是一個太空人」，所以不對。

Q4 To see is ___*D*___. I only believe something when I see it with my own eyes.

（眼見為憑。我只有親眼看到才會相信一件事。）

（A）believe（v. 相信）

（B）belief（n. 信任）

（C）believable（adj. 可信的）

►（D）to believe（to 不定詞 相信）

▶ 解析 句子的主詞是 to 不定詞 to see，這時候補語可以是結構相等的 to believe，表示第一個行為就是第二個行為。to see is to believe（眼見為憑）也是一個慣用的說法。

Q5 It's no use _____*D*_____ over spilt milk. We have to accept it and move on.

（覆水難收。我們必須接受它，然後繼續向前走。）

（A）cry　　　　　　　　　　（B）cries

（C）cried　　　　　　▶（D）crying

▶ 解析 it's no use doing... 表示「做…是沒有用的」。it's no use crying over spilt milk 是一個慣用句，用「對著打翻的牛奶哭泣」比喻「對於無法補救的事實感到難過，是沒有用的」。

Q6 Spending money is much easier than _____*C*_____ it.

（花錢比賺錢容易多了。）

（A）make　　　　　　　　　（B）makes

▶（C）making　　　　　　　（D）to make

▶ 解析 連接詞 than 比較兩個相同的文法結構，因為要比較的是「花錢」和「賺錢」，所以和 Spending 一樣是動名詞的 making 是正確答案。

Q7 Writing English is not as easy as _____*B*_____ it.

（英文寫作不像口說那麼容易。）

（A）speak　　　　　　▶（B）speaking

（C）to speak　　　　　　（D）to speaking

▶ 解析 在 A is as... as B 的句型中，A 和 B 應該是相同的名詞性質成分，所以和 Writing 一樣是動名詞的 speaking 是正確答案。

Q8 I did not know how _____*C*_____ her the truth.

（我當時不知道要怎麼告訴她實情。）

（A）tell　　　　　　　　　（B）telling

▶（C）to tell　　　　　　　（D）told

解析 疑問副詞 when, where, how 後面接 to 不定詞，表示「要在什麼時候做…」、「要在哪裡做…」、「要怎麼做…」，在句子裡可以是主詞、受詞或受詞補語。

Q9 The problem is where _____*C*_____ so much money.

（問題是要去哪裡得到這麼多錢。）

（A）to be （B）will be

▶（C）to get （D）will get

解析 疑問副詞 where 後面接 to 不定詞 to get，表示「要在哪裡得到錢」，在本句是主詞補語。如果用 to be 的話，會變成「要在哪裡成為錢」的意思。

Q10 Smoking will do _____*A*_____ a lot of harm.

（抽菸會對你造成很大的傷害。）

▶（A）you （B）to you

（C）on you （D）for you

解析 動詞後面先接間接受詞，再接直接受詞的時候，間接受詞前面不加介系詞，所以 you 是正確答案。do you harm 就是 do harm to you（傷害你）的意思。

TYPE 3 Study 3 修飾語

Q1 Susie's _____*C*_____ subject is music.

（蘇西最愛的科目是音樂。）

（A）favor（n. 幫忙） （B）flavor（n. 口味）

▶（C）favorite（adj. 最愛的） （D）favorable（adj.有利的）

解析 空格修飾名詞 subject（科目），所以 favorite（最愛的）是正確答案。favorable 是表示「情況很有利」的意思。

Q2 I can't forget how _____*D*_____ she danced.

（我忘不了她跳舞跳得有多棒。）

（Ａ）ugly（adj. 醜的）　　　（Ｂ）friendly（adj. 友善的）

（Ｃ）pretty（adj. 漂亮的）　► （Ｄ）wonderfully（adv. 很好地）

▶ 解析　疑問副詞 how 所引導的子句中，空格修飾動詞 danced（跳舞），所以副詞 wonderfully（很好地）是正確答案。ugly、friendly 是形容詞而不是副詞。pretty 雖然也有副詞的用法，表示「相當，蠻…」，但只能修飾形容詞或副詞。

問一
題性
致

時
態
判
斷

分句
型結
析構

解
答
篇

Q3 Riding a bus is not as ___*C*___ as riding a train.

（搭巴士不如搭火車快。）

（Ａ）late（adj. 晚的）　　　（Ｂ）lately（adv. 最近）

► （Ｃ）fast（adj./adv. 快速）　（Ｄ）soon（adv. 不久）

▶ 解析　動詞 is 是 be 動詞，後面接主詞補語，所以形容詞 fast（快速的）是正確答案。late 是表示「時刻很晚」，而不能表示速度慢的意思。

Q4 My wife drives the car more ___*A*___ than I do.

（我太太比我常開這輛車。）

► （Ａ）often（adv. 經常）　　　（Ｂ）sometimes（adv. 有時候）

（Ｃ）careful（adj. 小心的）　（Ｄ）quick（adj. 動作快的）

▶ 解析　空格修飾動詞 drives（駕駛），所以應該填入副詞。能加上 more 表示程度「比較常…」的 often 是正確答案。sometimes（有時候）不能用比較級或最高級表達。

Q5 Ken can jump ___*C*___ than Kylie does.

（肯能跳得比凱莉高。）

（Ａ）high（adj./adv. 高）　　　（Ｂ）highly（adv. 非常）

► （Ｃ）higher（adj./adv. 比較高）　（Ｄ）highest（adj./adv. 最高）

▶ 解析　表示「高」的副詞是 high，而且後面有表示比較的 than，所以副詞 high 的比較級 higher 是正確答案。另一個副詞 highly（非常），意思和 high 是不一樣的。另外，一般 -ly 形式的副詞，會用 more、the most 表示比較級和最高級，例如 beautifully、more

127

beautifully、the most beautifully。

Q6 Everyone wants to know who will be _____*C*_____ actor of the year.

（每個人都想知道誰會是年度最佳男演員。）

   （A）best   （B）better

► （C）the best   （D）the better

▶解析 因為句子最後提到了範圍 of the year（今年的），所以最高級 the best 是正確答案。注意不要忘了最高級前面的 the。

Q7 Tom is a naughty boy and often makes his parents _____*A*_____.

（湯姆是個調皮的男孩，而且常惹他爸媽生氣。）

► （A）angry（adj. 生氣的）   （B）angrily（adv. 生氣地）

   （C）anger（n. 憤怒）   （D）with anger（帶著怒氣）

▶解析 這裡使用的句型是「make + 受詞 + 受詞補語」，表示「使某人變得…」，所以空格應該填入形容詞而不是副詞，正確答案是 angry（生氣的）。雖然受詞補語也有可能是名詞，但在這裡如果填入 anger 的話，意思會變成「把爸媽變成憤怒這個抽象概念」。

Q8 We got _____*B*_____, so we took a rest.

（我們累了，所以休息了一下。）

   （A）tire（v. 使疲倦）

► （B）tired（adj. 覺得累的）

   （C）tiring（adj. 累人的）

   （D）tiresome（adj. 令人厭倦的）

▶解析 「get + 形容詞」表示「變得…」。從單字的意義來判斷，tired（覺得累的）是最恰當的答案。另外，tire 也可以當成可數名詞，表示「輪胎」。

Q9 If you want to play the guitar _____*C*_____, you have to practice every day.

（如果你想要彈好吉他，你必須每天練習。）

(A) good（adj. 好的） (B) great（adj. 很棒的）

► (C) well（adv. 好地） (D) hard（adv. 努力地）

▶ 解析 空格修飾動詞 play（演奏），應該填入副詞。句子前半表示想要做的事，後半表示為了這個目標而必須做的事，所以副詞 well（好地）是最恰當的答案。

Q10 Don't speak so _____*C*_____. I can't understand what you're saying.

（不要說這麼快。我不懂你在說什麼。）

(A) nice（adj. 好的） (B) hard（adv. 努力地）

► (C) fast（adv. 快地） (D) slow（adj. 慢的）

▶ 解析 空格修飾動詞 speak（說），而可能造成聽不懂的原因是說得太快，所以 fast（快地）是正確答案。

TYPE 3 Study 4 假設句型

Q1 If you don't try your best, you _____*C*_____ what you want.

（如果你不盡全力的話，就不會得到你想要的。）

(A) get (B) are

► (C) will not get (D) are to get

▶ 解析 條件句是「If + 現在簡單式」，表示推測未來可能發生的事，未來式 will not get 是正確答案。現在式條件句的後面，雖然也可以用現在式表示必然發生的情況，但如果填入 get 的話，意思會變成「不盡全力就會得到想要的」，不合邏輯。are to get 使用了「be 動詞 + to 不定詞」的形式，表示預定或可能性，在這裡同樣會變成「不盡全力就會得到想要的」的意思。

Q2 If you _____*B*_____ something, change it. If you can't change it, change yourself.

（如果你不喜歡某件事物，就改變它。如果你不能改變它，就改變自己。）

（A）are like　　　　　　▶（B）don't like

（C）will like　　　　　　（D）haven't liked

解析 條件句是假設可能發生的情況，所以使用現在式，don't like 是正確答案。don't like 的 like 是動詞，表示「喜歡」；are like 的 like 是形容詞，表示「像」。

Q3 If I must choose, I _____*C*_____ die than lie.

（如果我必須選擇的話，我寧願死也不要說謊。）

（A）shall　　　　　　　　（B）had better

▶（C）would rather　　　　（D）have to

解析 would rather... than 是「寧願…也不」的意思，後面接原形動詞。

shall 用在第一人稱時，表示「將會…」。

had better：最好…

have to：必須做…，不得不做…

Q4 In order to pass the exam, I had better _____*A*_____ preparing.

（為了通過考試，我最好開始準備。）

▶（A）start　　　　　　　　（B）starting

（C）to start　　　　　　　（D）not start

解析 had better（最好…）後面接原形動詞。

Q5 If you don't have enough money, you'd better _____*C*_____ a car.

（如果你沒有足夠的錢，最好不要買車。）

（A）buy　　　　　　　　　（B）to buy

▶（C）not buy　　　　　　　（D）not to buy

解析 要表達「最好不要…」的時候，說法是 had better not do...。注意中間不能加 to。

TYPE 3 Study 5 倒裝句型

Q1 He is a great astronaut, _____ B _____ was his father.

（他是個偉大的太空人，以前他父親也是。）

（A）and ►（B）and so

（C）and that （D）as well as

▶️解析 空格前後都是有主詞和動詞的子句，所以要填入連接詞。而因為空格後面的主詞和 be 動詞倒裝，所以有 so 的 and so 是正確答案。

Q2 Donald is my friend, and so _____ B _____. I like both of them.

（唐納是我的朋友，喬也是。我喜歡他們兩個人。）

（A）Joe is ►（B）is Joe

（C）Joe does （D）does Joe

▶️解析 第二句的 both of them 就是第一句的 Donald 和 Joe。空格是省略補語 my friend 的子句，而且前面有 so，所以將主詞和 be 動詞倒裝的 is Joe 是正確答案。

Q3 Wendy didn't lend him money, and _____ D _____ did I.

（溫蒂沒有借他錢，我也沒有。）

（A）so （B）nor

（C）either ►（D）neither

▶️解析 第一個子句是否定句，連接詞是表示語意順接的 and，所以第二個子句應該表示「我也沒有借他錢」。要表達「也不…」的時候，句型是「and neither + 助動詞 + 主詞」。and neither did I lend him money 就等於 and I didn't lend him money, either。選項中的 nor 必須搭配 neither 使用，例如 neither Wendy nor I lent him money（溫蒂和我都沒有借他錢）。

Q4 He can't say no to Mary, and neither _____ D _____.

（他沒辦法對瑪莉說不，我也沒辦法。）

（A）I do　　　　　　　　　　（B）do I

（C）I can　　　　　　　▶（D）can I

▶解析 第一個子句是否定句，連接詞的部分是 and neither，表示前後都是同樣的否定意義。neither 後面的主詞和助動詞要倒裝，所以 can I 是正確答案。

Q5 ___*A*___ have I imagined that I would be able to talk with a foreigner.

（我從來沒想像過自己能跟外國人交談。）

▶（A）Never　　　　　　　　（B）Sometimes

（C）Always　　　　　　　　（D）Often

▶解析 在選項列出的頻率副詞中，只有 Never（從不）帶有否定的意義，在移到句首的時候會使主詞 I 和助動詞 have 發生倒裝。

TYPE 3　Study　6　被動語態

Q1 The class will ___*D*___ by Ms. Lee. She really knows how to deal with young kids.

（這一班將由李老師教導。她真的很懂得怎麼應付小孩。）

（A）teach　　　　　　　　　（B）be teaching

（C）taught　　　　　　▶（D）be taught

▶解析 主詞「班級」是被「老師」所教導的，所以被動態 be taught（被教導）是正確答案。

Q2 Coffee, tea and wine ___*C*___ on the plane.

（飛機上供應咖啡、茶和葡萄酒。）

（A）serve　　　　　　　　　（B）are serving

▶（C）are served　　　　　　（D）be served

▶解析 主詞「咖啡、茶和葡萄酒」是被供應的東西，雖然沒有說由誰

供應，但可想而知應該是空服員，被動態 are served 是正確答案。be served 的 be 動詞應該使用正確的時態，而不能直接使用原形。

問一致題性

時態判斷

分句型結構析

解答篇

Q3 **The morning paper _____*C*_____ over 200,000 people every day.**
（這份早報每天有超過二十萬人閱讀。）
（A）reads （B）is reading
► （C）is read by （D）is about to read
▶解析 主詞「早報」是被閱讀的東西，而空格後面的 over 200,000 people（超過二十萬人）是閱讀者，所以含 by 的被動態 is read by 是正確答案，注意動詞 read 的過去式、過去分詞都寫成 read。另外，is about to read 是「即將閱讀…」的意思。

Q4 **When Janice heard about Margaret's death, she _____*C*_____ and couldn't stop crying.**
（當珍妮絲聽到瑪格莉特過世的消息，她很震驚，而且哭個不停。）
（A）shocked （B）was shocking
► （C）was shocked （D）was shocked by
▶解析 要表示「（因為某事而）感到震驚」的意思時，用 shock 的過去分詞 shocked 表達，用法和形容詞相同。因為空格後面沒有出現行為者（引起震驚的事物，例如 the news〔那個消息〕），所以答案是 was shocked 而不是 was shocked by。shocking 的意思則是「令人震驚的」。

Q5 **English is not only _____*D*_____ in England.**
（英語不只在英格蘭被使用。）
（A）talking （B）speaking
（C）talked ► （D）spoken
▶解析 要表達「某個地方使用某種語言」，和動詞 use（用）比起來，用 speak（說）顯得更自然。因為英語是被說出的事物，所以表示被動的過去分詞 spoken 是正確答案。另外，talk（交談）不能接語言名稱當受詞。

133

Q6 I was very _____*D*_____ when I spilled my drink on the man's shirt.

（當我把飲料打翻到那個男人的襯衫上時，我非常尷尬。）

（A）hurt（受傷的）　　　　　（B）excited（興奮的）

（C）pleased（滿意的）　　► （D）embarrassed（尷尬的）

Q7 Our dog was _____*B*_____ thunder and hid under the bed.

（我們的狗被打雷嚇到，躲在床底下。）

（A）close to（接近⋯的）

► （B）frightened by（被⋯驚嚇的）

（C）finished with（以⋯作為結束的）

（D）made of（由⋯製成的）

Q8 I didn't do well on the exams. I am _____*B*_____ my grades.

（我考試考得不好。我擔心我的成績。）

（A）excited about（對⋯感到興奮的）

► （B）worried about（對⋯感到擔心的）

（C）interested in（對⋯有興趣的）

（D）pleased with（對⋯感到滿意的）

Q9 My parents _____*B*_____ thirty years ago. After all these years, they still love each other very much.

（我爸媽三十年前結婚。這麼多年之後，他們還是很愛彼此。）

（A）were married　　　► （B）got married

（C）had to marry　　　（D）would like to marry

▶ 解析 雖然 were married 和 got married 都是「結婚」的意思，但從句意來看，表示「在那個時間點從未婚變成已婚狀態」的 got married 是最恰當的。were married 則會表現出「過去是已婚的狀態，但現在不是」的含意。had to marry 表示「不得不結婚」，would like to marry 表示「想要結婚」。

Q10 Jake _____*C*_____ for stealing things from the shop.

（杰克因為從店裡偷了東西而被逮捕了。）

（A）arrested ►（B）was arresting

►（C）got arrested （D）was going to arrest

▶解析 因為偷了東西，所以是「被逮捕」而不是「做逮捕的行為」，被動態 got arrested 是正確答案。

TYPE 3 Study 7 形容詞、名詞及副詞子句

Q1 The building in _____*B*_____ the American President works is called White House.

（美國總統辦公的建築物叫「白宮」。）

（A）whom ►（B）which

（C）where （D）that

▶解析 關係詞的先行詞 building（建築物）是事物，而且空格是位置介系詞 in（在⋯裡面）的受詞，所以事物關係代名詞受格 which 是正確答案。關係代名詞 that 不能接在介系詞後面。另外，in which 也可以換成關係副詞 where 來表達。

Q2 Mr. Gates is a mechanic _____*C*_____ you can trust.

（蓋茲先生是你可以信賴的技工。）

（A）which （B）whose

►（C）who （D）for whom

▶解析 關係詞的先行詞 mechanic（技工）是人物，而且關係詞是 trust（相信）的受詞，所以人物關係代名詞受格 who（可代替 whom）是正確答案。動詞 trust 不能搭配介系詞 for 再接受詞，所以不能選擇 for whom。

Q3 He has a horse _____*D*_____ runs faster than any other in the world.

（他有一匹比世界上其他任何馬都跑得快的馬。）

（A）who （B）whom
（C）whose ►（D）that

解析 關係詞的先行詞 horse（馬）是動物，而且關係詞是 runs（跑）的主詞，所以能代替事物關係代名詞主格 which 的 that 是正確答案。

Q4 The boy _____*A*_____ had ran away from home was finally found.

（離家的孩子終於被找到了。）

►（A）that （B）which
（C）whose （D）whom

解析 關係詞的先行詞 boy（男孩）是人物，而且關係詞是 had run（「跑」的過去完成式）的主詞，所以能代替人物關係代名詞主格 who 的 that 是正確答案。

Q5 I understand _____*B*_____ he was too tired to wake up early.

（我了解他太累了而沒辦法早起。）

（A）who ►（B）that
（C）if （D）whether

解析 I understand（我了解）後面所接的全部內容，表示了解的事情，所以引導名詞子句、表示「⋯這件事」的 that 是正確答案。if, whether 都表示「是否⋯」。

Q6 We don't know _____*C*_____ our grandfather will recover from the illness.

（我們不知道祖父會不會從疾病中復原。）

（A）what （B）whose
►（C）whether （D）either

解析 We don't know（我們不知道）後面所接的全部內容，表示知道的事情，所以引導名詞子句、表示不確定性「是否⋯」的 whether 是正確答案。

Q7 _____*C*_____ we were in Sydney, we went to the opera house every month.

（我們在雪梨時，每個月都會上歌劇院。）

（A）If　　　　　　　　　　　（B）Though

► （C）When　　　　　　　　　（D）Whether

▶ **解析**　兩個子句都是過去式，第二個子句表示在雪梨做的事，所以表示時間、提供背景資訊的 When（當…的時候）是最恰當的答案。If（如果…）、Though（雖然）、Whether（不管是否…）在意義上都不適合連接這兩個子句。

Q8 He didn't tell the truth _____*D*_____ he was afraid of being punished.

（他沒有說實話，因為他怕被處罰。）

（A）so　　　　　　　　　　　（B）when

（C）after　　　　　　　► （D）because

▶ **解析**　「怕被處罰」是「沒有說實話」的原因，所以表示原因的連接詞 because（因為…）是正確答案。so（所以…）、when（當…的時候）、after（在…之後）的意義都不適合。

Q9 _____*D*_____ the farmers work from morning till night, they are still poor.

（雖然農夫們從早工作到晚，卻依然貧窮。）

（A）If　　　　　　　　　　　（B）Since

（C）Until　　　　　　　► （D）Although

▶ **解析**　儘管長時間工作，農夫們卻處於貧窮的情況，所以表示和預期相反的連接詞 Although（雖然）是正確答案。If（如果…）、Since（由於…）、Until（直到…）的意義都不適合。

Q10 Sean was surprised that he got better grades _____*C*_____ he had expected.

（尚恩對於自己得到比預期要好的成績感到驚訝。）

（A）as　　　　　　　　　　　（B）to

▶（C）than （D）with

◗ 解析 因為空格前面有比較級 better（比較好的），所以能接比較對象的連接詞 than 是正確答案。than 後面除了接名詞以外，也可以像這裡一樣接子句。

TYPE 3 | Study | 8 不定詞和動名詞

Q1 The child ___D___ crying when he couldn't find his mother.

（那孩子找不到媽媽時，開始哭了起來。）

（A）begins   ▶（B）began

（C）wants   （D）wanted

◗ 解析 表示時間的 when 子句中，助動詞 couldn't 是過去式，所以主要子句也要使用過去式。空格後面接的是動名詞，所以能接動名詞的 begin 的過去式 began 是正確答案。want 後面應該接 to 不定詞。

Q2 Margaret ___A___ exercising so much that she goes to the gym every day.

（瑪格莉特很喜歡運動，所以她每天上健身房。）

▶（A）likes（喜歡）   （B）hates（討厭）

（C）hopes（希望）   （D）prefers（偏好）

◗ 解析 動詞 hope（希望）後面應該接 to 不定詞，而不是動名詞，所以可以先刪去。剩下的三個動詞，後面都可以接 to 不定詞或動名詞。這個句子使用了 so... that...（很⋯以致於⋯）的句型，前後為因果關係，所以 hate（討厭）和句意不符。prefer（偏好）不能用 so much（很⋯）之類表示程度的副詞來修飾，所以 like（喜歡）的第三人稱單數現在式 likes 才是正確答案。

Q3 In winter, Europeans ___A___ sitting in the sun to staying at home.

（冬天的時候，歐洲人比較喜歡坐在陽光下，勝過待在家裡。）

▶（A）prefer（偏好）　　　　　（B）continue（繼續）

（C）remember（記得）　　　　（D）regret（後悔）

▶解析 雖然四個選項後面都能接動名詞，但只有 prefer（偏好）能用 prefer A to B 的句型表示比較，其中的 A 和 B 可以是名詞或動名詞。

Q4 **They continued _____B_____ after a short break.**

（他們在短暫的休息之後繼續跑步。）

（A）run（跑）　　　　　▶（B）running（跑（動名詞））

（C）rest（休息）　　　　（D）resting（休息（動名詞））

▶解析 continue 後面可以接 to 不定詞或動名詞表示「繼續做⋯」。

Q5 **Jason asked his brother _____D_____ making noise.**

（傑森要他的弟弟停止製造噪音。）

（A）don't　　　　　　　　（B）not to

（C）stopping　　　　　　▶（D）to stop

▶解析 ask（要求）的用法是 ask someone to do...，所以 to 不定詞 to stop 是正確答案。雖然也可以用 ask someone not to do...（要求某人不要做⋯）來表達，但因為空格後面接的是動名詞 making，所以不能選擇 not to。

Q6 **Tracy is an easy-going person. She wouldn't _____B_____ sharing a house with someone.**

（崔西是個隨和的人。她不會介意和人共用房屋。）

（A）keep（保持）　　　　　▶（B）mind（介意）

（C）agree（同意）　　　　（D）refuse（拒絕）

▶解析 keep（保持）、mind（介意）後面要接動名詞，agree（同意）、refuse（拒絕）後面則是接 to 不定詞。因為是隨和的人，所以表示「不介意共用房屋」的 mind 是正確答案。

Q7 **Mr. Brown gave up _____B_____ when his first child was born.**

（布朗先生在他第一個孩子出生的時候戒了菸。）

（A）smoke　　　　　　　　► （B）smoking

（C）to smoke　　　　　　　（D）and smoke

解析　give up 雖然是「放棄」的意思，但 give up doing... 也可以表示「戒除習慣」，例如 give up drinking（戒酒）、give up smoking（戒菸）。

Q8　I enjoy _____*A*_____ alone once in a while, but not always.

（我喜歡偶爾獨處，但不要一直獨處。）

► （A）being　　　　　　　　（B）to be

（C）becoming　　　　　　　（D）to become

解析　enjoy（享受）後面接動名詞，表示「喜歡做某事」。enjoy 後面不能接 to 不定詞。

Q9　After playing the online game for four hours, he finally stopped _____*D*_____.

（玩了線上遊戲四個小時之後，他終於停下來去睡覺了。）

（A）going sleeping　　　　　（B）to go sleeping

（C）going to bed　　　► （D）to go to bed

解析　stop doing 表示「停止做…」，而 stop to do 則是「停止目前的行為而去做…」。因為是停止玩線上遊戲而去睡覺，所以 to go to bed 是正確答案。go sleeping 則是錯誤的說法，應該改為 go to sleep 才能表達「去睡覺」的意思。

Q10　My parents are used to _____*B*_____ early.

（我的父母習慣早起。）

（A）get up　　　　　　► （B）getting up

（C）be getting up　　　　　（D）having got up

解析　be used to... 表示「習慣…」，要注意其中的 to 是介系詞，後面應該接名詞或動名詞，所以 getting up 是正確答案。having got up 雖然也將助動詞 have 改為動名詞的形式，但因為是完成式的關係，所以意思會變成「習慣已經早起的狀態」，並不恰當。

Part 2
段落填空

TOPIC 1　家庭

作答說明　Part 2 是段落填空（即所謂「克漏字」），分為 2 個題組，共 8 題，必須選擇最恰當的詞語或句子填入文章段落的空格中。在 8 個題目中，有 2 題是填入整句或長段文字，另外大約有 4 題是詞彙題，2 題是考文法概念。填入整句是新制英檢的新題型，解題重點在於了解整篇文章的內容架構，並且觀察空格前後句的內容，判斷空格中最適合填入的語句。在作答之前，要先試著把答案放進空格的位置，看看是否能自然銜接前後句的內容，才能確定答案。

QUIZ 1

　　For the Chinese New Year holidays, Susan will be going back home to see her parents ___**1**___ the countryside. ___**2**___ it will take one whole day of traveling on the road, Susan is very excited about going back home. She misses her mother's homemade dishes the most because she doesn't have a kitchen in her apartment and always eats out. She is also ___**3**___ getting together with her relatives, for this is the only time of the year when she gets to see them. Celebrating Chinese New Year with them makes Susan feel that ___**4**___.

Q1 _____　（A）at　　　　　（B）in
　　　　　　　（C）on　　　　　（D）from

Q2 _____　（A）Because　　（B）When
　　　　　　　（C）Even though　（D）Before

Q3 _____ （A）getting used to （B）looking forward to
　　　　　　　（C）getting away from （D）holding back from

Q4 _____ （A）she is part of the family
　　　　　　　（B）she wants to have a family
　　　　　　　（C）it's hard to see them again
　　　　　　　（D）it's easier said than done

QUIZ 2

There are five ___1___ in my family: my parents, my brother, me, and our pet, Lucky. Lucky is a cat, and we see her ___2___ an important part of the family. She sleeps on the bed with my brother and has a place at the dinner table, and my mother takes her to the pet salon every week. We also care about her feelings and never force her to do anything. As I see it, ___3___. Sometimes I ___4___ if I were her, I would be happy every day.

☞ pet salon 寵物美容店

Q1 _____ （A）people （B）members
　　　　　　　（C）relatives （D）individuals

Q2 _____ （A）as （B）in
　　　　　　　（C）of （D）with

Q3 _____ （A）there is no other way to happiness
　　　　　　　（B）that is why she is a naughty cat
　　　　　　　（C）there is still a lot we can do for her
　　　　　　　（D）she leads an easier life than we do

Q4 _____ （A）doubt （B）realize
　　　　　　　（C）imagine （D）understand

As the Chinese society becomes more influenced by Western values, young people today are more __**1**__ and therefore do not always listen to their parents. In the old days, however, children would __**2**__. They studied what their parents told them to study, married whom their parents wanted them to marry, and worked __**3**__ their parents told them to work. Some say that even though people in those days did not have individual rights or freedom of choice, society then was more __**4**__ than today. The reason might be that everyone had to think about others in whatever they did, and individual desires were not that strong.

Q1 _____ (A) important   (B) individual

(C) independent   (D) international

Q2 _____ (A) obey their parents in every way

(B) always take care of their parents

(C) have a say in everything

(D) try to listen carefully

Q3 _____ (A) why   (B) who

(C) what   (D) where

Q4 _____ (A) careful   (B) peaceful

(C) precious   (D) generous

TOPIC 2 個人

QUIZ 1

I have always respected doctors because they can help ill people and save them ___**1**___ pain. Everyone, even someone who is rich and famous, ___**2**___, so no one can live well without doctors' help. Therefore, ever since I was a kid, I have wanted to become a doctor and help people get healthy. To make my dream come true, I studied hard and got ___**3**___ to a medical school. There are still a lot of things to do on my way to ___**4**___ a doctor, but I will never give up because it is the most important goal in my life.

☞ medical school 醫學院

Q1 _____ （A）to （B）for
（C）with （D）from

Q2 _____ （A）should have equal rights
（B）cares about those in need
（C）gets sick once in a while
（D）knows the importance of health

Q3 _____ （A）accepted （B）carried
（C）exported （D）introduced

Q4 _____ （A）become （B）becoming
（C）have become （D）having become

QUIZ 2

This summer, Zack __**1**__ alone in Japan for one month. He has the trip planned __**2**__. In his notebook, he wrote down every place to visit and every bus and train to take. __**3**__, Zack will stay at youth hostels, which are cheaper, and he will try to cook his own meals. This is the first time Zack travels in a foreign country, but he is not __**4**__, for his friend Bruce, who goes to Japan very often, told him that Japan is a very safe country for foreign visitors. Zack thinks that he will learn a lot when he travels by himself, and such an experience will be good for his self-development.

☞ youth hostel 青年旅舍

Q1 _____ （A）goes traveling （B）went traveling
（C）has gone traveling （D）is going to travel

Q2 _____ （A）at first （B）by accident
（C）for good （D）in detail

Q3 _____ （A）In order to save money
（B）By planning in this way
（C）Being a first-time traveler
（D）Since he is well-prepared

Q4 _____ （A）confident （B）embarrassed
（C）patient （D）worried

For a service to be successful, it must be able to ___**1**__ individual needs. For example, we all know that more and more people choose to shop online, but only a few online shopping sites grew to become market leaders. One of the secrets behind their success is to know ___**2**__ each customer really wants to buy. By analyzing search and viewing ___**3**__, an online store can know what each customer is interested in, and even show some products that they did not know they would like to buy. In this way, customers will ___**4**__.

☞ analyze 分析

Q1 _____ （A）appreciate （B）compare
（C）explain （D）satisfy

Q2 _____ （A）if （B）that
（C）what （D）whether

Q3 _____ （A）history （B）function
（C）measure （D）operation

Q4 _____ （A）turn away and find something else
（B）know themselves even better
（C）buy more than they have planned to
（D）not buy on other shopping sites

◎TOPIC 3 朋友

QUIZ 1

Anna used to think that good friends should never ___**1**___, but recently she lost her friend Mindy for being too honest. It ___**2**___ when Mindy asked Anna what she thought of her new boyfriend Paul. Anna didn't want to lie, ___**3**___ she told Mindy everything she didn't like about Paul. She even said that Paul feels like a bad guy. Mindy, however, was not happy about what Anna said. She loves Paul too much to listen to anyone who ___**4**___ him. Anna thinks that if she had lied, they would still be friends.

Q1 _____ （A）fight over small things
（B）lie to each other
（C）show their true selves
（D）take things too seriously

Q2 _____ （A）appeared （B）changed
（C）continued （D）happened

Q3 _____ （A）so （B）or
（C）but （D）although

Q4 _____ （A）gets along with （B）gives in to
（C）looks up to （D）speaks ill of

My idea of a good time is getting together with my best friend Sally after work at a local restaurant. We have known each other ___**1**___, so when we have dinner together, we can really relax and talk about everything, no matter how ___**2**___ it may be. I can freely talk about my type of guy or my wildest dream, knowing that she will ___**3**___. Therefore, Sally and I are even ___**4**___ than I am with my family, and she knows some of my secrets that my family do not know.

☞ relax 放鬆

Q1 _____ （A）in ten years   （B）many years ago
                （C）for a long time   （D）when we were young

Q2 _____ （A）serious   （B）common
                （C）personal   （D）difficult

Q3 _____ （A）tell me the truth   （B）take it personally
                （C）just do as I say   （D）accept me as I am

Q4 _____ （A）better   （B）closer
                （C）calmer   （D）friendlier

QUIZ 3

Sometimes, it is your friend that will __**1**__. Someone who seems kind to you can __**2**__ to be your worst enemy. Therefore, you should know better about people around you. If you use your brain and your heart, you can tell who is on your side, and who is just trying to take __**3**__ of you. If you realize that some people you see as friends only care about their own interest, you __**4**__ keep a distance from them, for you never know when they will stab you in the back.

> ☞ observe 觀察
> stab someone in the back 在某人背後捅一刀

Q1 _____ （A）hurt you the most （B）know your enemies
（C）take care of you （D）turn away from you

Q2 _____ （A）turn up （B）turn out
（C）come up （D）come out

Q3 _____ （A）care （B）hold
（C）charge （D）advantage

Q4 _____ （A）had better （B）used to
（C）would like to （D）are able to

TOPIC 4 嗜好

QUIZ 1

In the past, stamp collecting was a popular hobby. Many people collected stamps and dreamed of making money by selling rare items. Today, however, stamps are not worth so much as they __1__, since most people do not send letters anymore. Why should we wait several days for a letter to arrive __2__ we can just send an email? __3__. Besides, young people now have no __4__ with such an old-fashioned hobby. Compared to exciting mobile games, the little pieces of paper do not seem interesting to them.

Q1 _____ （A）are （B）were
（C）will be （D）should be

Q2 _____ （A）when （B）until
（C）except （D）because

Q3 _____ （A）However, emails feel not as important as letters are.
（B）In other words, most people cannot wait so long.
（C）Therefore, it is a waste of time to keep making stamps.
（D）As a result, stamps became far less useful than before.

Q4 _____ （A）problem （B）patience
（C）contact （D）experience

151

_____**1**_____, for their life is more balanced between what they have to do and what they want to do. It is true that work provides us with a sense of purpose and money to support ourselves, but it cannot _____**2**_____ our desire to really be ourselves. _____**3**_____ our true selves, we need to do those things that make us feel great. No matter it is playing basketball or reading novels, a hobby can enrich our life. If life is all about work and no fun, we cannot but feel _____**4**_____ inside.

☞ balanced 平衡的；☞ enrich 使豐富

Q1 _____ （A）People who work longer hours are more successful
　　　　　　 （B）People who have hobbies are usually happier
　　　　　　 （C）Some people know their duties very well
　　　　　　 （D）Some people can find the hobbies they really enjoy

Q2 _____ （A）satisfy　　　　　　（B）explain
　　　　　　 （C）describe　　　　　 （D）appreciate

Q3 _____ （A）Living　　　　　　（B）By living
　　　　　　 （C）To live　　　　　　（D）When we live

Q4 _____ （A）empty　　　　　　（B）missing
　　　　　　 （C）careless　　　　　 （D）independent

Successful businessmen say that the greatest way to make money is to make your hobby a career. Most of us spend a lot of time and money on our hobbies, so why not turn the effort __1__ a business? In that way, you can earn a profit by simply living the way you want, and it is more likely that you will enjoy daily work rather than __2__ about it. __3__, my friend Steve likes to put together computers. He chose to start a computer service company so he can get paid by doing what he loves. If you do not like your job, maybe you should consider __4__.

☞ profit 利潤

Q1 _____ （A）as （B）by
　　　　　　（C）into （D）with

Q2 _____ （A）care （B）dream
　　　　　　（C）think （D）complain

Q3 _____ （A）In fact （B）That is
　　　　　　（C）At first （D）For example

Q4 _____ （A）giving it up （B）trying much harder
　　　　　　（C）creating your own （D）thinking about yourself

家庭

個人

朋友

嗜好

娛樂

旅遊

突發事件

自然

節日

解答篇

TOPIC 5 娛樂

QUIZ 1

Playing online games __1__ an important part of life for teenagers. __2__, but for young people, it is a way to forget their problems and build their self-confidence. __3__, they can make friends with players around the world. In many games, there are missions that require players to complete them __4__ a group and thus provide them with a chance to chat together. When playing such games, you really feel that it is a small world and that you play a role in it.

☞ mission 任務

Q1 _____ （A）becomes （B）will become
（C）has become （D）would have become

Q2 _____ （A）We all have less time to play as we grow up
（B）It does not matter what kind of game they play
（C）We should find the things that are really important for us
（D）Many parents think that playing games is a waste of time

Q3 _____ （A）Even so （B）More importantly
（C）As a result （D）In other words

Q4 _____ （A）as （B）by
（C）for （D）along

QUIZ 2

Oprah Winfrey is one of the most famous and richest people in the world. She ___**1**___ as the host of "The Oprah Winfrey Show". The talk show ran for nearly 25 years and had about 14 million daily viewers in the US, and it was also shown in 149 countries around the world. In the program, Oprah influenced what her audience think and do ___**2**___. Oprah had a ___**3**___ childhood, but she worked hard and achieved success. That is why her words can ___**4**___ people and give them comfort.

☞ viewer 觀看者；☞ comfort 安慰

Q1 _____ （A）knows （B）is known
（C）has known （D）will be known

Q2 _____ （A）from time to time
（B）by talking about it
（C）like a successful person
（D）with her powerful words

Q3 _____ （A）careless （B）difficult
（C）fantastic （D）traditional

Q4 _____ （A）inspire （B）satisfy
（C）surprise （D）celebrate

Many people watch YouTube just to kill time. If you use it __1__, however, it can also be a helpful tool. Besides dramas and music videos, there are actually a lot of material you can __2__ yourself with. No matter you want to learn cooking, painting, or speaking foreign languages, you can find videos that teach you how to do. You can also increase your knowledge __3__ watching channels on topics like history or science. __4__, you can learn about it on YouTube.

Q1 _____ （A）widely （B）wisely
（C）wildly （D）willingly

Q2 _____ （A）behave （B）discover
（C）educate （D）satisfy

Q3 _____ （A）by （B）on
（C）for （D）with

Q4 _____ （A）If you cannot find it
（B）Without going to school
（C）By searching for videos
（D）Whatever you can think of

TOPIC 6 旅遊

QUIZ 1

Joan loves traveling, and she ___**1**___ twenty-four countries so far. She plans to go to even more places, so she works extra hard to earn the money she will need during her trip. The places she has visited include popular destinations, such as Paris and London, ___**2**___ unique places like Greenland and Andorra. With every trip, her English becomes better and better, so she is now ___**3**___ about talking with foreigners. ___**4**___, Joan can learn about different cultures, and it is such experience that makes her feel travel is meaningful.

☞ destination 目的地

Q1 _____ （A）was in （B）went to
（C）has been to （D）has gone to

Q2 _____ （A）as soon as （B）as long as
（C）as well as （D）as far as

Q3 _____ （A）certain （B）confident
（C）curious （D）patient

Q4 _____ （A）Even when she is alone
（B）Because she likes foreigners
（C）By talking with those she meets
（D）Since everyone talks about traveling

If you are looking for the most unique trip, you should consider going to Tibet. Tibet is famous ___**1**___ its traditional culture and wonderful views. The best time to visit Tibet is from April to October, when it is warm and sunny in the day. ___**2**___, even in warmer months, temperatures can drop below 10 degrees Celsius at night. What is more, since Tibet is the highest region on Earth, some may get headaches or ___**3**___ there. Therefore, you should ___**4**___ before going to Tibet, so that you can fully enjoy your experience there.

☞ degree Celsius 攝氏度

Q1 _____ （A）to （B）as
　　　　　　（C）by （D）for

Q2 _____ （A）However （B）Besides
　　　　　　（C）Therefore （D）Naturally

Q3 _____ （A）feel sick （B）fall down
　　　　　　（C）stay away （D）get serious

Q4 _____ （A）make a plan of things to do
　　　　　　（B）prepare your winter clothes
　　　　　　（C）check the weather condition
　　　　　　（D）make sure you are in good health

家庭

個人

朋友

嗜好

娛樂

旅遊

突發事件

自然

節日

解答篇

People today are used to traveling by airplane. We can go to overseas countries fast and easily by flying. Therefore, it is difficult for most of us to imagine how people in the past traveled in a world ___**1**___ airplanes. Before airplanes were invented, ___**2**___. When Christopher Columbus discovered the "New World" in 1492, it took him two months to sail from Spain to America. In 1850s, when gold ___**3**___ in Australia, those who wanted to dig gold would spend about four months just to travel from England to Australia. People in the past were certainly more ___**4**___ than we are!

Q1 _____ （A）beyond （B）through
（C）besides （D）without

Q2 _____ （A）air travel was not as popular as today
（B）ships were the only way to cross the seas
（C）there was no way people could go overseas
（D）some people dreamed about flying in the air

Q3 _____ （A）found （B）was found
（C）could find （D）has been found

Q4 _____ （A）foolish （B）patient
（C）diligent （D）generous

TOPIC 7 突發事件

QUIZ 1

Police have ____**1**____ a man for robbing a convenience store yesterday. The man went into the store and held out a knife at the clerk, asking her to take out money. The clerk gave him all the cash in the cash register, ____**2**____ was about 250 dollars. ____**3**____. However, he drove too fast and hit a tree. The man ____**4**____ get out of the car, so the police were able to catch him easily.

☞ cash register 收銀機

Q1 _____ （A）arrested （B）discovered
（C）embarrassed （D）interviewed

Q2 _____ （A）that （B）which
（C）so （D）for it

Q3 _____ （A）It was a lot of money for the man
（B）The man was proud of his driving skills
（C）After a while, the clerk called the police
（D）The man then ran outside and drove away

Q4 _____ （A）had better （B）would like to
（C）was able to （D）could not but

Smart people keep themselves from ___**1**___ by always being prepared for sudden events. For example, they keep a first-aid kit in the car and at home. Also, they never visit people ___**2**___ do not know very well by themselves. In addition, they always tell their friends or family where they are going and when they will be back. It might seem to be a lot of bother, but it is never wrong to do our best to ___**3**___ accidents. After all, ___**4**___.

☞ first-aid kit 急救箱

Q1 _____ （A）danger （B）failure
　　　　　　 （C）influence （D）protection

Q2 _____ （A）they （B）who
　　　　　　 （C）which （D）that

Q3 _____ （A）avoid （B）consider
　　　　　　 （C）expect （D）face

Q4 _____ （A）to see is to believe
　　　　　　 （B）all is well that ends well
　　　　　　 （C）it is better safe than sorry
　　　　　　 （D）where there is a will, there is a way

Doctors say that although it is a good idea to have a baby sleeping in the same room as parents, they should not ___**1**___ a bed. When parents and their baby sleep in the same bed, the adults may roll on the baby or cover its nose and mouth with heavy blankets ___**2**___. As a result, they may kill their baby ___**3**___ knowing it. Therefore, every parent should ___**4**___ and try not to make such mistakes.

Q1 _____ （A）use （B）need
（C）make （D）share

Q2 _____ （A）by force （B）by chance
（C）by accident （D）by experience

Q3 _____ （A）after （B）while
（C）without （D）besides

Q4 _____ （A）ask their relatives for help
（B）try to keep away from their babies
（C）regret what they have done before
（D）learn about the importance of child safety

TOPIC 8 自然

QUIZ 1

Typhoon Maria is heading west __**1**__ the southern part of Taiwan. Residents __**2**__ to be prepared for strong winds, which are expected to reach speeds of up to 120 kilometers per hour. __**3**__. Therefore, those living in low areas should be __**4**__ of flooding and consider leaving ahead of time. At its current speed, the typhoon is expected to leave Taiwan by noon tomorrow.

☞ flooding 淹水

Q1 _____ （A）above （B）beyond
（C）inside （D）toward

Q2 _____ （A）advise （B）have advised
（C）are advised （D）are advising

Q3 _____ （A）Tree branches could be blown down
（B）There could be light rain and thunder
（C）Heavy rain will also be starting tonight
（D）Many people die in typhoons every year

Q4 _____ （A）afraid （B）careful
（C）certain （D）confident

The summer of 2020 was ___**1**___ hot in some regions in the world. In Siberia, one of the coldest places on Earth, the temperature of a town ___**2**___ Verkhoyansk reached 38 °C. In Taipei, the temperature rose to 38.9 °C, which was a record-high in 124 years ___**3**___ the city's weather station was built in 1896. In fact, according to National Oceanic and Atmospheric Administration of the U.S., the world's land and ocean surface temperature for May 2020 tied with 2016 as the highest in the record. ___**4**___, all the countries should work together to limit greenhouse gas emission. | ☞ greenhouse gas emission 溫室氣體排放

Q1 _____ （A）hardly （B）especially
（C）exactly （D）suddenly

Q2 _____ （A）called （B）calling
（C）to call （D）has called

Q3 _____ （A）because （B）since
（C）until （D）while

Q4 _____ （A）Considering that hot weather is still very rare
（B）While it is possible that the information is false
（C）Since most people prefer to live in warmer places
（D）In order to stop the world from getting even warmer

_____**1**_____. In the past, 46% of the Earth was covered with forests, but in recent centuries, they have been decreasing year by year. Today, half of that 46% is gone, and only one fifth ___**2**___ untouched by human beings. Scientists say that the world's forests decrease ___**3**___ 2.4% every year. Since forests are home to more than half of the world's plants and animals on land, we should do our best to protect our forests and ___**4**___ a better world for future generations.

☞ untouched 未受影響的

Q1 _____ （A）The world's forests are now in danger
（B）A study found new facts about forests
（C）Forests are very important for human beings
（D）The world in the past was better than today

Q2 _____ （A）stops （B）remains
（C）becomes （D）ends up

Q3 _____ （A）by （B）at
（C）to （D）for

Q4 _____ （A）expect （B）give
（C）improve （D）leave

家庭

個人

朋友

嗜好

娛樂

旅遊

突發事件

自然

節日

解答篇

TOPIC 9 節日

QUIZ 1

In America, people celebrate New Year's Eve __1__ parties. They party through the night to __2__ the New Year. At midnight, when the clock strikes twelve, they cheer and kiss their loved ones. At the party, there are also many kinds of foods for the guests to enjoy, such as chips, pizzas, and chicken wings, and some may __3__ eating too much and feeling sick. Therefore, to have a good start into the new year, one should __4__.

☞ instead of 取代⋯

Q1 _____ （A）to have （B）by having
（C）when they have （D）so as to have

Q2 _____ （A）turn to （B）bring in
（C）cheer up （D）deal with

Q3 _____ （A）end up （B）forget about
（C）succeed in （D）apologize for

Q4 _____ （A）go on a diet to get in shape
（B）regret what they have done
（C）plan what to do from day one
（D）focus more on friends than on foods

Do you know that Earth Day is on April 22? It is a day ___**1**___ all of us are invited to take care of our world. On that day, there are events such as music festivals and picnics that aim to ___**2**___. Even though the events are fun themselves, we should know that the meaning of the day is to remind us of environmental problems and ___**3**___ us to do something about them. For example, we can try to use less water or ride a bicycle instead of driving. Saving the Earth starts with all of us, and what we do every day can ___**4**___.

Q1 _____ （A）where （B）on which
　　　　　　（C）in that （D）so that

Q2 _____ （A）be the greatest events on earth
　　　　　　（B）bring the world together as one
　　　　　　（C）take advantage of the environment
　　　　　　（D）bring attention to environmental protection

Q3 _____ （A）allow （B）force
　　　　　　（C）command （D）encourage

Q4 _____ （A）have a say （B）take a chance
　　　　　　（C）break a promise （D）make a difference

家庭

個人

朋友

嗜好

娛樂

旅遊

突發事件

自然

節日

解答篇

In the past, there was a tradition to celebrate New Year on April 1st in some areas of France. In the 16th century, however, the king __**1**__ set the New Year's Day on January 1st. While some __**2**__, others still tried to follow the tradition. __**3**__ a joke on those who were not willing to change, the supporters of the new rule invited them to New Year parties that did not exist and made them the first "April fools". __**4**__ in the 19th century, it became popular in the Western world to pull a trick on others on April 1st.

☞ supporter 支持者

Q1 _____ （A）carefully （B）effectively
（C）generously （D）officially

Q2 _____ （A）did not know the truth yet
（B）never celebrated the New Year
（C）were ready to accept the decision
（D）marked April 1st on their calendars

Q3 _____ （A）To play （B）By playing
（C）Having played （D）When they played

Q4 _____ （A）Yet （B）Later
（C）Likely （D）Especially

ANSWER 段落填空（解答）

TOPIC 1 QUIZ 1

For the Chinese New Year holidays, Susan will be going back home to see her parents ___1___ the countryside. ___2___ it will take one whole day of traveling on the road, Susan is very excited about going back home. She misses her mother's homemade dishes the most because she doesn't have a kitchen in her apartment and always eats out. She is also ___3___ getting together with her relatives, for this is the only time of the year when she gets to see them. Celebrating Chinese New Year with them makes Susan feel that ___4___.

中文翻譯

農曆年假期間，蘇珊會回鄉下老家探望父母。即使會花一整天在路途上，蘇珊還是對於回家感到很興奮。她最想念的是媽媽的家常菜，因為她的公寓沒有廚房，而且她總是外食。她也期待和親戚們相聚，因為她在一年裡只有這個時間能見到他們。和他們一起慶祝農曆新年，讓蘇珊覺得她是這個家庭的一分子。

Q1 ___*B*___
（A）at   ▶（B）in
（C）on   （D）from

解析 像 country（國家）、city（城市）、countryside（鄉間）這種大範圍的空間，適合用介系詞 in 表示「在…」的意思。

Q2 ___*C*___

（A）Because（因為）　　　　　　（B）When（當…時）
► （C）Even though（即使）　　　　（D）Before（在…之前）

▶ 解析　空格後面的兩個子句，前面表示舟車勞頓的辛苦，後面表示期待回家的心情，表達從負面到正面的語氣轉折，所以表讓步的連接詞 Even though 是正確答案。

Q3　　*B*

（A）getting used to（習慣…）
► （B）looking forward to（期待…）
（C）getting away from（擺脫…）
（D）holding back from（退縮而避免…）

▶ 解析　四個選項後面都可以接名詞或動名詞。因為是和親戚見面的唯一機會，所以 looking forward to 是語意上最恰當的答案。

Q4　　*A*

► （A）she is part of the family（她是這個家庭的一分子）
（B）she wants to have a family（她想要有個家庭）
（C）it's hard to see them again（很難再見到他們）
（D）it's easier said than done（說比做來得簡單）

▶ 解析　空格出現在段落的最後，是整段內容的總結，而且延續了上一句的內容。上一句說很期待和難得見面的親戚相聚，所以這一句應該是對於能和他們一起慶祝農曆新年的正面感受，（A）是最恰當的答案。（D）是表達雖然隨口說說很容易，但實踐起來可能並不容易的慣用句。

TOPIC 1 [QUIZ] 2

There are five ___1___ in my family: my parents, my brother, me, and our pet, Lucky. Lucky is a cat, and we see her

___**2**___ an important part of the family. She sleeps on the bed with my brother and has a place at the dinner table, and my mother takes her to the pet salon every week. We also care about her feelings and never force her to do anything. As I see it, ___**3**___. Sometimes I ___**4**___ if I were her, I would be happy every day.

我家有五個成員：我的父母、我的哥哥、我，還有我們的寵物 Lucky。Lucky 是一隻貓，我們把她視為家庭裡很重要的一部分。她跟我哥哥一起睡在床上，在我們晚餐餐桌旁也有個位子，而且我媽媽每個禮拜帶她去寵物美容店。我們也關心她的感受，而且從來不強迫她做任何事。在我看來，她過的生活比我們輕鬆。有時候我會想像，如果我是她的話，我每天都會很快樂。

Q1 ___*B*___
（A）people（人）　　　　　　▶（B）members（成員）
（C）relatives（親戚）　　　　　（D）individuals（個人）
▶**解析** 空格表示家裡有五個什麼，其中包括四個人和一隻貓，所以 members 是最恰當的答案。

Q2 ___*A*___
▶（A）as　　　　　　　　　　（B）in
（C）of　　　　　　　　　　　（D）with
▶**解析** 介系詞 as 有「當作…」的意思，所以 see A as B 就是「把 A 視為 B」的意思。

Q3 ___*D*___
（A）there is no other way to happiness
　　（快樂沒有其他的方法）
（B）that is why she is a naughty cat
　　（那就是她之所以是頑皮的貓的原因）

（C）there is still a lot we can do for her
（還有很多我們可以為她做的）

► （D）she leads an easier life than we do
（她過的生活比我們輕鬆）

解析 空格前面有 As I see it（就我看來），所以空格中的句子是對於前面內容所表達的個人看法，而前面的內容都在說作者的家人對這隻貓有多好。另外，也要注意下一句是表達對於貓咪生活的羨慕。所以，表示「貓的生活很輕鬆」的（D）最能銜接前後文的內容。

Q4　　*C*
（A）doubt（懷疑）
（B）realize（認識到）
► （C）imagine（想像）
（D）understand（了解）

解析 空格後面是假設語氣的句子，表示和現在事實相反的情況。因為作者在想像變成貓之後可能會過著快樂的生活，所以 imagine 是最恰當的答案。

TOPIC 1 QUIZ 3

As the Chinese society becomes more influenced by Western values, young people today are more ___1___ and therefore do not always listen to their parents. In the old days, however, children would ___2___. They studied what their parents told them to study, married whom their parents wanted them to marry, and worked ___3___ their parents told them to work. Some say that even though people in those days did not have individual rights or freedom of choice, society then was

more __4__ than today. The reason might be that everyone had to think about others in whatever they did, and individual desires were not that strong.

中文翻譯

　　隨著華人社會變得更加受到西方價值觀影響，現今的年輕人比較獨立，所以也不會隨時都聽父母的話。然而在以前，孩子會在各方面服從他們的父母。他們會就讀父母叫他們讀的學科，和父母希望他們結婚的對象結婚，並且在父母叫他們工作的地方工作。有些人說，即使當時的人沒有個人的權利或選擇的自由，但那時候的社會比現代來得和平。原因可能是當時每個人做的任何事都必須考慮到其他人，而且個人的欲望也沒有那麼強。

Q1 ___C___

（A）important（重要的）

（B）individual（個別的）

▶（C）independent（獨立的）

（D）international（國際的）

▶解析 空格後面有 and therefore（所以…），所以空格中的形容詞是「不聽父母的話」的原因，independent 是最恰當的答案。

Q2 ___A___

▶（A）obey their parents in every way
　　（在各方面服從他們的父母）

（B）always take care of their parents
　　（總是照顧他們的父母）

（C）have a say in everything（對每件事都有發言的權利）

（D）try to listen carefully（努力仔細聽）

▶解析 空格前面有 In the old days, however（然而在以前…），所以空格的內容是對於以前的描述，而且應該和上個句子關於現代年輕人獨立、不聽父母的話等內容相反。另外，後面的句子也提到以前的小孩在各方面都照父母所說的去做，所以

173

（Ａ）最能衔接前後的內容。（Ｃ）的 have a say 是「有發言權」的意思，也就是可以有自己的意見。（Ｄ）乍看之下似乎是可能的答案，但上一句的 listen to 其實是「聽從」的意思，而 listen carefully 只是「仔細聽內容」而已，並沒有「服從」的意思，所以不對。

Q3　　__*D*__

（Ａ）why　　　　　　　　　（Ｂ）who
（Ｃ）what　　　　　　► （Ｄ）where

▶ 解析　空格所在的動詞片語中，worked（工作）是不及物動詞的用法，所以後面不能接名詞性質的「who + 子句」（…的人）、「what + 子句」（…的事物）、「(the reason) why + 子句」（…的理由）。「where + 子句」則可以當成名詞（…的地方）或副詞（在…的地方），在這裡是副詞的用法，修飾動詞worked。

Q4　　__*B*__

（Ａ）careful（謹慎的）
► （Ｂ）peaceful（和平的）
（Ｃ）precious（珍貴的）
（Ｄ）generous（慷慨的）

▶ 解析　在選項中，careful 和 generous 都是形容人的性格或態度，不能表示非人物主詞 society（社會）的狀態。而後面的句子說到過去的社會之所以如此的理由，可能是因為每個人都考慮到其他人、個人欲望不強，所以 peaceful 是最恰當的答案。

TOPIC 2　QUIZ　1

I have always respected doctors because they can help ill people and save them ___**1**___ pain. Everyone, even someone who is rich and famous, ___**2**___, so no one can live well without doctors' help. Therefore, ever since I was a kid, I have wanted to become a doctor and help people get healthy. To make my dream come true, I studied hard and got ___**3**___ to a medical school. There are still a lot of things to do on my way to ___**4**___ a doctor, but I will never give up because it is the most important goal in my life.

　　我一直以來都很尊敬醫生，因為他們可以幫助生病的人，並且讓他們免於痛苦。每個人，即使是有錢又有名的人，偶爾都會生病，所以沒有人可以不靠醫生的幫助而活得健康。所以，從我還是個小孩的時候，我就想成為醫生並且幫助人們變得健康。為了實現我的夢想，我努力用功並且獲得醫學院的錄取。在我成為醫生的路上還有很多事要做，但我絕對不會放棄，因為這是我人生中最重要的目標。

Q1　　*D*

（A）to　　　　　　　　　　（B）for
（C）with　　　　　　　► （D）from

▶解析　save someone from... 直譯是「把某人從…救出來」，也就是「使某人免於…」的意思。即使不知道這個用法，從「醫師讓人免於痛苦」這個概念來看，也可以推測表示「從…（離開）」的 from 是意義最符合的答案。

Q2　　*C*

（A）should have equal rights（應該有平等的權利）
（B）cares about those in need（關心有需要的人）

175

► (C) gets sick once in a while（偶爾會生病）

（D）knows the importance of health（知道健康的重要性）

▶解析 前面的句子說醫生可以幫助生病的人，而空格所在的句子提到，每個人不管是什麼身分地位，都需要醫生。注意空格後面有連接詞 so（所以…），因此空格中的內容是「需要醫生」的原因。在選項中，（C）能夠呼應上一句的「醫生可以幫助生病的人」，並且能表示每個人都會發生而需要醫生的情況，是最恰當的答案。

Q3 _A_

► （A）accepted（接受）

（B）carried（攜帶，搬運）

（C）exported（出口）

（D）introduced（介紹）

▶解析 每個選項後面都可以接介系詞 to 表示目的地或對象，但只有 accepted 的意義是合適的。be accepted to… 常用在申請入學的情況，表示「被…錄取」。

Q4 _B_

（A）become   ► （B）becoming

（C）have become   （D）having become

▶解析 on the way to… 表示「在往…的路上」，其中的 to 是介系詞，所以後面要接表示目標的名詞或動名詞。這裡不需要用完成式表示「早已成為醫生的狀態」，所以 becoming 是正確答案。

This summer, Zack __1__ alone in Japan for one month. He has the trip planned __2__. In his notebook, he wrote down every place to visit and every bus and train to take. __3__, Zack will stay at youth hostels, which are cheaper, and he will try to cook his own meals. This is the first time Zack travels in a foreign country, but he is not __4__, for his friend Bruce, who goes to Japan very often, told him that Japan is a very safe country for foreign visitors. Zack thinks that he will learn a lot when he travels by himself, and such an experience will be good for his self-development.

中文翻譯

今年夏天，札克會在日本獨自旅行一個月。他把這趟旅行計畫得很詳細。在筆記本裡，他寫下了每個要去的地方，還有他要搭的每班巴士和列車。為了省錢，札克會住在青年旅舍，那裡價錢比較便宜，而他也會試著自己烹煮餐點。這是札克第一次在外國旅行，但他並不擔心，因為他很常去日本的朋友布魯斯告訴他，日本對於外國觀光客而言是非常安全的國家。札克認為他在自己旅行時會學到很多，而這樣的經驗會對他的自我成長有好處。

Q1 __D__

（A）goes traveling　　　　　（B）went traveling

（C）has gone traveling　　►（D）is going to travel

▶解析　雖然句中有表示時間的片語 This summer（今年夏天），但只從這裡無法判斷在日本旅遊是過去還是未來的事。從段落後面的內容，才能得知札克是未來要去日本旅遊。選項中雖然沒有未來式 will go，但用 is going to travel 也可以表示不久的將來要做的事。

Q2   *D*

（A）at first（一開始）

（B）by accident（偶然地）

（C）for good（永久地）

► （D）in detail（詳細地）

▶解析   空格前面的過去分詞 planned 是修飾名詞 the trip，表示「旅遊是被計畫好的」，而空格又修飾 planned。下一個句子說札克把要去的每個地方、要搭的每班車都寫在筆記本裡，顯示他計畫得很詳細，所以 in detail 是正確答案。

Q3   *A*

► （A）In order to save money（為了省錢）

（B）By planning in this way（藉由以這種方式計畫）

（C）Being a first-time traveler（身為第一次旅行的人）

（D）Since he is well-prepared（因為他做了充足的準備）

▶解析   空格後面的內容說，札克會住在便宜的青年旅舍，也會自己烹煮餐點，這些都是省錢的方式，所以表示目的「為了省錢」的（A）是最恰當的答案。

Q4   *D*

（A）confident（有信心的）

（B）embarrassed（尷尬的）

（C）patient（有耐心的）

► （D）worried（擔心的）

▶解析   空格部分和句子的開頭部分用 but 連接，表示雖然是第一次出國旅行，但札克的心態和一般第一次出國旅行的人不同。再加上後面提到朋友說日本很安全，所以用 not worried 表示「不擔心」是最恰當的。

TOPIC 2　QUIZ　3

For a service to be successful, it must be able to ___**1**___ individual needs. For example, we all know that more and more people choose to shop online, but only a few online shopping sites grew to become market leaders. One of the secrets behind their success is to know ___**2**___ each customer really wants to buy. By analyzing search and viewing ___**3**___, an online store can know what each customer is interested in, and even show some products that they did not know they would like to buy. In this way, customers will ___**4**___.

中文翻譯

　　一個服務要成功，就必須能滿足個人的需求。舉例來說，我們都知道越來越多人選擇線上購物，但只有少數線上購物網站成長為市場領先者。它們成功背後的祕密之一是知道每個顧客真正想要買的是什麼。藉由分析搜尋與觀看紀錄，網路商店可以知道每個顧客對什麼有興趣，甚至能顯示顧客不知道自己可能會想買的東西。如此一來，顧客就會購買比原本計畫的更多的東西。

Q1 ___*D*___

（A）appreciate（欣賞）　　　　（B）compare（比較）

（C）explain（解析）　　▶（D）satisfy（滿足）

🔊解析　這段文章主要是敘述購物網站如何透過了解顧客的需求，進而推薦他們可能會想買的物品，所以 satisfy 是最恰當的答案。

Q2 ___*C*___

（A）if　　　　　　　　　　　（B）that

▶（C）what　　　　　　　　　（D）whether

🔊解析　雖然四個選項在文法上都是正確的，但因為後面的句子

179

提到藉由分析搜尋與觀看紀錄來了解每位顧客有興趣的東西，所以用 what 表達「知道顧客想要買的是什麼」是最恰當的。如果在空格填入 that，表示「知道顧客想要買」，而 if 和 whether 則表示「知道顧客是否想要買」。

Q3   *A*

► （A）history（歷史）   （B）function（功能）
（C）measure（措施）   （D）operation（操作）

▶解析   search history 和 viewing history 都是關於網路服務的慣用詞語，表示「搜尋紀錄」和「觀看紀錄」。

Q4   *C*

（A）turn away and find something else
    （轉身離去並且找別的東西）

（B）know themselves even better（更加了解自己）

► （C）buy more than they have planned to
    （購買比原本計畫的更多的東西）

（D）not buy on other shopping sites
    （不在其他購物網站買東西）

▶解析   空格所在的句子中，In this way 是表示上一個句子的全部內容。上一句說到推薦顧客不知道自己可能會想買的東西，表示這些東西可能是顧客有興趣的，只是他們沒有想過而已。所以，顧客有可能在原本計畫要買的東西以外，再多買其他的推薦商品，（C）是最適當的答案。

Anna used to think that good friends should never ____1____, but recently she lost her friend Mindy for being too honest. It ____2____ when Mindy asked Anna what she thought of her new boyfriend Paul. Anna didn't want to lie, ____3____ she told Mindy everything she didn't like about Paul. She even said that Paul feels like a bad guy. Mindy, however, was not happy about what Anna said. She loves Paul too much to listen to anyone who ____4____ him. Anna thinks that if she had lied, they would still be friends.

中文翻譯

　　安娜以前認為好朋友絕對不應該對彼此說謊，但最近她因為太誠實而失去了她的朋友敏蒂。事情發生在敏蒂問安娜對她新男友保羅的想法的時候。安娜不想說謊，所以她告訴敏蒂自己不喜歡保羅的每一點。她甚至說保羅感覺像是壞男人。然而敏蒂對於安娜所說的感到不高興。她太愛保羅了，所以聽不進任何說他壞話的人。安娜認為要是她當時說謊的話，她們或許還會是朋友。

Q1　　___B___

（A）fight over small things（因為小事爭吵）

▶（B）lie to each other（對彼此說謊）

（C）show their true selves（展現真正的自我）

（D）take things too seriously（太認真看待事情）

▶解析　句子前面的 used to 表示「以前總是…」的意思，而空格後面有表示語氣轉折的連接詞 but，所以空格內容表示過去的想法，而且應該和後面的內容是相反的概念。後面說因為太誠實而失去朋友，這也是整篇文章的主題，所以（B）最能和後面的這些內容形成對照。

Q2 _D_

（A）appeared（出現） 　　　　　（B）changed（改變）

（C）continued（持續） 　► （D）happened（發生）

▶ 解析 空格前面的 It 是指上一句說的 she lost her friend... 這件事，所以能表示事情發生的 happened 是正確答案。

Q3 _A_

► （A）so（所以） 　　　　　（B）or（否則）

（C）but（但是） 　　　　　（D）although（雖然）

▶ 解析 空格連接句子前後的內容，前面提到「不想說謊」，後面說「告訴敏蒂自己不喜歡保羅的每一點」，兩者之間是原因與結果的關係，所以 so 是正確答案。

Q4 _D_

（A）gets along with（和…相處融洽）

（B）gives in to（對…讓步）

（C）looks up to（尊敬…）

（D）speaks ill of（說…的壞話）

▶ 解析 這個句子表示上一句「敏蒂對於安娜所說的感到不高興」的理由，所以能夠表示安娜對於保羅表達負面意見的 speaks ill of 是正確答案。

TOPIC 3 QUIZ 2

My idea of a good time is getting together with my best friend Sally after work at a local restaurant. We have known each other ___1___, so when we have dinner together, we can really relax and talk about everything, no matter how ___2___ it may be. I can freely talk about my type of guy or my wildest dream, knowing that she will ___3___. Therefore, Sally and I are even ___4___ than I am with my family, and she knows some of my secrets that my family do not know.

中文翻譯

　　我心目中的好時光，是下班後在本地的一家餐廳和我最好的朋友莎莉聚聚。我們認識彼此已經很久了，所以當我們一起吃晚餐的時候，我們可以真正放鬆並且談論所有事情，不管是多麼私人的事。我可以很自由地談論自己喜歡的男生類型，或者最瘋狂的夢想，因為我知道她會接受真正的我。所以，莎莉和我甚至比我和家人還要親近，而她知道家人所不知道的一些我的祕密。

Q1 ___C___

　（A）in ten years（十年後）

　（B）many years ago（多年前）

▶（C）for a long time（很長一段時間）

　（D）when we were young（當我們年輕的時候）

▶解析　這個題目看起來像是詞彙考題，實際上卻是測試文法概念。因為時態使用現在完成式，表示從過去到現在這段時間保持的狀態，所以要選擇表示期間的（C），而不是表示過去時間點的（B）或（D）。（A）in ten years 通常表示「十年後」的意思，是表達未來時間點的說法。

Q2 ___C___

　（A）serious（嚴肅的）　　　　（B）common（普通的）

▶（C）personal（私人的）　　　（D）difficult（困難的）

▶解析　空格後面的 it 是指前面的 everything，也就是兩人談論的事情。因為下一句說「可以自由談論喜歡的男生類型和最瘋狂的夢想，因為知道她會接受真正的我」，所以這裡應該是要表達談論很私人的話題，personal 是最恰當的答案。

Q3 ___D___

183

（A）tell me the truth（對我說實話）

（B）take it personally（把它當成是針對自己）

（C）just do as I say（就照我說的做）

► （D）accept me as I am（接受真正的我）

▶ 解析　分詞構句 knowing... 的部分是表達理由，因為這個理由，所以作者可以談論喜歡的男生類型和瘋狂的夢想等私人話題。最恰當的答案是（D），字面上的意思就是「照著我現在的樣子接受我」。（B）的 take it personally，意思是認為某人的言行刻意針對自己，而感到不高興。

Q4 ___*B*___

（A）better（比較好的）

► （B）closer（比較親近的）

（C）calmer（比較冷靜的）

（D）friendlier（比較友善的）

▶ 解析　因為後面提到莎莉知道作者家人也不知道的祕密，所以 closer 是正確答案。close 除了表示物理距離上的「接近」以外，也可以表示心理距離上的「親近」。

TOPIC 3　QUIZ　3

　　Sometimes, it is your friend that will ___1___. Someone who seems kind to you can ___2___ to be your worst enemy. Therefore, you should know better about people around you. If you use your brain and your heart, you can tell who is on your side, and who is just trying to take ___3___ of you. If you realize that some people you see as friends only care about their own interest, you ___4___ keep a distance from them, for you never know when they will stab you in the back.

中文翻譯

　　有時候，你的朋友傷你最深。看起來對你親切的人，結果可能變成你最大的敵人。所以，你應該更加了解周遭的人。如果你用你的腦和你的心，你可以分辨誰是站在你這邊，而誰只是試圖利用你。如果你意識到某些你視為朋友的人只關心自己的利益，你最好和他們保持距離，因為你永遠不知道他們什麼時候會在背後捅你一刀。

Q1 　*A*
► （A）hurt you the most（傷你最深）
　（B）know your enemies（知道你的敵人）
　（C）take care of you（照顧你）
　（D）turn away from you（轉過臉不看你）

▶ 解析　這是整個段落的主題句位置。後面的句子說看似親切的人（朋友）可能會變成最大的敵人，後面也提到朋友可能利用你、在背後捅你一刀，所以（A）最能表達這些「朋友」背叛的行為。（B）雖然出現了後面使用的 enemy 這個字，但表達的意義和全文的主旨無關，所以不對。

Q2 　*B*
　（A）turn up（出現）　　　► （B）turn out（結果…）
　（C）come up（出現）　　　　（D）come out（出來）

▶ 解析　前面說某人看起來很親切，後面說他變成最大的敵人，所以能表示「結果變成…」的 turn out 是正確答案，使用時要在後面接 to 不定詞。

Q3 　*D*
　（A）care　　　　　　　　　（B）hold
　（C）charge　　　　　　► （D）advantage
▶ 解析　take care of：照顧…
take hold of：抓住…
take charge of：負責…

take advantage of：利用…

Q4　__*A*__
▶（A）had better（最好…）
　（B）used to（以前總是…）
　（C）would like to（想要…）
　（D）are able to（能夠…）

▶️解析　空格部分表示當發現朋友只關心自己的利益時，要採取的行動，後面又說「因為不知道他們什麼時候會在背後捅你一刀」，所以表示在某個情況下採取特定行動比較好的 had better 是正確答案。

186

家庭
個人
朋友
嗜好
娛樂
旅遊
突發事件
自然
節日
解答篇

In the past, stamp collecting was a popular hobby. Many people collected stamps and dreamed of making money by selling rare items. Today, however, stamps are not worth as much as they __1__, since most people do not send letters anymore. Why should we wait several days for a letter to arrive __2__ we can just send an email? __3__. Besides, young people now have no __4__ with such an old-fashioned hobby. Compared to exciting mobile games, the little pieces of paper do not seem interesting to them.

在過去，集郵是一項很流行的嗜好。許多人收集郵票並夢想可以靠著賣出稀有品項來賺錢。但現在，郵票的價值沒有以前那麼高，因為大部分的人不再寄信了。當我們可以寄電子郵件的時候，為什麼要花個幾天等信送到呢？結果，郵票就遠不如以前那麼實用了。而且，現在的年輕人對於這種老派的嗜好沒有耐性。跟刺激的手機遊戲比起來，這些小小的紙片對他們而言看起來並不有趣。

Q1 __B__
（A）are
▶（B）were
（C）will be
（D）should be

▶解析 文章開頭說以前集郵很流行，而空格所在的句子用 however（然而）表示語氣轉折，而且空格後面用 since（由於）表示理由，提到大部分的人已經不再寄信，所以是要用郵票現在的價值和過去對比，而相對於 as much as（跟…一樣）前面的現在式 are，後面應該用過去式 were 才恰當。

Q2 __A__
▶（A）when（當…的時候）
（B）until（直到…）

187

（C）except（除了…）　　　　　　　　（D）because（因為…）

▶解析　因為空格後面的狀況條件「我們可以寄電子郵件」，所以質疑寄信的必要性，這時候能夠表示所處狀況的 when 是適當的答案。另外，雖然 because 看起來好像是合理的答案，但用在這裡其實會是「因為可以寄電子郵件而花個幾天等信送到」的意思，所以不對。

Q3　*D*

（A）However, emails feel not as important as letters are.（然而，電子郵件感覺沒有信件那麼重要。）

（B）In other words, most people cannot wait so long.（換句話說，大部分的人沒辦法等這麼久。）

（C）Therefore, it is a waste of time to keep making stamps.（所以，繼續製作郵票是浪費時間。）

▶（D）As a result, stamps became far less useful than before.（結果，郵票就遠不如以前那麼實用了。）

▶解析　空格的前面部分提到郵票價值不如以往的理由是大部分的人不再寄信，並且補充說等信送到太花時間，所以（D）能總結以上關於郵票實用價值的內容。

Q4　*B*

（A）problem（問題）

▶（B）patience（耐心）

（C）contact（聯絡）

（D）experience（經驗）

▶解析　後面的句子說，和刺激的手機遊戲比起來，年輕人覺得郵票不有趣，所以 patience 是正確答案。

have no problem with：對於…沒有問題

have no patience with：對於…沒有耐心

have no contact with：和…沒有聯絡

have no experience with：對於…沒有經驗

_____**1**_____, for their life is more balanced between what they have to do and what they want to do. It is true that work provides us with a sense of purpose and money to support ourselves, but it cannot _____**2**_____ our desire to really be ourselves. _____**3**_____ our true selves, we need to do those things that make us feel great. No matter it is playing basketball or reading novels, a hobby can enrich our life. If life is all about work and no fun, we cannot but feel _____**4**_____ inside.

中文翻譯

有嗜好的人通常比較快樂，因為他們的生活在必須做和想做的事情之間比較有所平衡。工作能提供我們目的感以及支持自己的金錢是事實，但工作不能滿足我們真正做自己的渴望。為了活出真實的自己，我們必須做讓我們感覺很棒的事情。不管是打籃球還是讀小說，嗜好都能豐富我們的人生。如果人生只有工作而沒有玩樂，我們心中會不禁感到空虛。

Q1 _A_

（A）People who work longer hours are more successful
（工作時數較長的人比較成功）

►（B）People who have hobbies are usually happier
（有嗜好的人通常比較快樂）

（C）Some people know their duties very well
（有些人很清楚知道自己的義務）

（D）Some people can find the hobbies they really enjoy
（有些人可以找到他們真正喜愛的嗜好）

▶ 解析 這是段落的主題句部分，而整段內容是說明在工作之餘擁有嗜好的重要性。而且，空格後面用 for（因為）表示前句的理由是「他們的生活在必須做和想做的事情之間比較有所平衡」，所以（B）是最適合的答案。

Q2 *A*

► （A）satisfy（滿足）　　　　　（B）explain（說明）
　（C）describe（描述）　　　　　（D）appreciate（欣賞）

▶️解析 句子前半是說明工作對於我們的意義，後半則由表示語氣轉折的連接詞 but（但是）引導，表示和前面相反的內容，另外也要注意下一句是說我們該如何活出真正的自己（也就是從事嗜好活動）。空格表示工作做不到，而嗜好能做到的事，所以 satisfy 是正確答案。

Q3 *C*

　（A）Living　　　　　　　　　（B）By living
► （C）To live　　　　　　　　　（D）When we live

▶️解析 句子後半說明活出真實自我的方法，所以前半部用（C）的 to 不定詞表示目的「為了…」是最恰當的。分詞構句的（A）只能表示理由、時間等等，而不能表示目的。（B）表示方法，（D）表示時間。

Q4 *A*

► （A）empty（空虛的）
　（B）missing（遺失的）
　（C）careless（粗心的）
　（D）independent（獨立的）

▶️解析 因為前面提到「嗜好能豐富我們的人生」，所以如果只有工作而沒有玩樂（嗜好）的話，就會覺得 empty。empty 除了表示物理上的「空」以外，也可以表示心理上的「空虛」。cannot but 是「不禁…，忍不住…」的意思。

家庭

個人

朋友

嗜好

娛樂

旅遊

突發事件

自然

節日

解答篇

Successful businessmen say that the greatest way to make money is to make your hobby a career. Most of us spend a lot of time and money on our hobbies, so why not turn the effort ____**1**____ a business? In that way, you can earn a profit by simply living the way you want, and it is more likely that you will enjoy daily work rather than ____**2**____ about it. ____**3**____, my friend Steve likes to put together computers. He chose to start a computer service company so he can get paid by doing what he loves. If you do not like your job, maybe you should consider ____**4**____.

中文翻譯

成功的企業家說，賺錢最棒的方法是把你的嗜好變成職業。我們大部分的人會花很多時間和金錢在嗜好上，所以為什麼不把這份努力變成一項事業呢？這樣的話，你只要用你想要的方式生活，就能賺到利潤，而且你比較有可能享受每天的工作而不是抱怨。舉例來說，我的朋友史蒂夫喜歡組裝電腦。他選擇成立一家電腦服務公司，好讓他能藉由做自己喜愛的事而獲得收入。如果你不喜歡你的工作，或許你應該考慮創造自己的工作。

Q1　　*C*
　　（A）as　　　　　　　　　　（B）by
▶（C）into　　　　　　　　　（D）with

　▶解析　因為上一句說到「把嗜好變成職業」，所以這裡應該是表達「把（追求嗜好的）努力變成一項事業」，turn A into B 可以表達「把 A 變成 B」的意思。

Q2　　*D*
　　（A）care（關心）　　　　　（B）dream（夢想）
　　（C）think（思考）　　　▶（D）complain（抱怨）

解析 空格前面有 rather than（而不是…），所以空格的內容是和前面的 enjoy daily work（享受每天的工作）形成對比，complain 是最適當的答案。

Q3　*D*

（A）In fact（事實上）

（B）That is（也就是說）

（C）At first（一開始）

► （D）For example（舉例來說）

解析 空格前面說明把嗜好變成工作的好處，後面則開始談到朋友史蒂夫的實際例子，所以表示舉例的 For example 是正確答案。

Q4　*C*

（A）giving it up（放棄）

（B）trying much harder（更努力）

► （C）creating your own（創造你自己的（工作））

（D）thinking about yourself（考慮你自己）

解析 空格部分是整個段落的總結，所以應該考慮整段的內容再選擇答案。因為整段內容都是在談把嗜好變成職業，所以最能表示這個主旨的 creating your own (job) 是正確答案。

家庭

個人

朋友

嗜好

娛樂

旅遊

突發事件

自然

節日

解答篇

Playing online games ___**1**___ an important part of life for teenagers. ___**2**___, but for young people, it is a way to forget their problems and build their self-confidence. ___**3**___, they can make friends with players around the world. In many games, there are missions that require players to complete them ___**4**___ a group and thus provide them with a chance to chat together. When playing such games, you really feel that it is a small world and that you play a role in it.

中文翻譯

對於青少年，玩線上遊戲已經成為人生重要的一部分。許多父母認為玩遊戲是浪費時間，但對年輕人而言，這是忘掉自己的問題以及建立自信的一種方法。更重要的是，他們可以和全世界的玩家交朋友。在許多遊戲中，有需要玩家組團來完成的任務，因此能為他們提供一起聊天的機會。在玩這種遊戲時，你真的會覺得這個世界很小，而你在其中扮演一個角色。

Q1 ___C___
（A）becomes
（B）will become
▶（C）has become
（D）would have become

▶解析 因為「對於青少年，玩線上遊戲成為人生重要的一部分」是已經發生的事實，所以現在完成式 has become 是最恰當的答案。現在簡單式 becomes 表示不分時間、隨時會發生的事實，但「成為人生重要的一部分」所表示的轉變應該是一次性的，而不是一再發生，所以現在簡單式不是合適的答案。would have... 是表示「（過去）本來可能會做（但沒有做）」的意思。

193

Q2 _D_

（A）We all have less time to play as we grow up
（隨著我們長大，我們玩的時間都變少）

（B）It does not matter what kind of game they play
（不管他們玩哪一種遊戲都沒關係）

（C）We should find the things that are really important
for us（我們應該找到對我們而言真正重要的事）

▶（D）Many parents think that playing games is a waste
of time（許多父母認為玩遊戲是浪費時間）

▶解析 空格後面有 but for young people...，並且說明玩線上遊
戲（it）對年輕人的意義，所以空格的內容應該是和年輕人相反的
看法，（D）是最恰當的答案。

Q3 _B_

（A）Even so（即使如此）

▶（B）More importantly（更重要的是）

（C）As a result（結果）

（D）In other words（換句話說）

▶解析 空格前面說線上遊戲可以讓年輕人忘掉自己的問題並建
立自信，空格後面的部分則是在說線上遊戲的交友層面，前後內
容的相關性不強，所以表示讓步的（A）、表示因果關係的
（C）、表示重述內容的（D）都不適合。（B）則是在前面列出
的論點之外，另外列出重要性更高的論點，是最恰當的答案。

Q4 _A_

▶（A）as   （B）by

（C）for   （D）along

▶解析 這裡要表達的是「玩家以團隊的形式來完成任務」，所
以表示「作為…」的介系詞 as 是正確答案。along 是「沿著…」
的意思，必須改成 along with 才能表示「和…一起」。

Oprah Winfrey is one of the most famous and richest people in the world. She ___1___ as the host of "The Oprah Winfrey Show". The talk show ran for nearly 25 years and had about 14 million daily viewers in the US, and it was also shown in 149 countries around the world. In the program, Oprah influenced what her audience think and do ___2___. Oprah had a ___3___ childhood, but she worked hard and achieved success. That is why her words can ___4___ people and give them comfort.

歐普拉‧溫芙蕾是世界最有名、最富有的人之一。她以《歐普拉‧溫芙蕾秀》主持人的身分為人所知。這個脫口秀播出了將近 25 年，在美國有約 1400 萬的每日觀眾，也在全世界 149 個國家播出。在這個節目中，歐普拉用她有力量的話語影響了觀眾的思考與行為。歐普拉的童年很艱困，但她努力而取得了成功。這就是為什麼她的話語能夠激勵人們，並且給他們安慰。

Q1 ___*B*___

（A）knows
▶（B）is known
（C）has known
（D）will be known

解析 空格後面是 as the host of...，表示「作為…的身分」，搭配空格中的動詞 know，表示「以…的身分為人所知」。因為歐普拉是「被人知道」的對象，而且她現在已經廣為人知，所以現在式被動態的 is known 是正確答案。

Q2 ___*D*___

（A）from time to time（偶爾）
（B）by talking about it（藉由談論它）
（C）like a successful person（像個成功人士）

► （D）with her powerful words（用她有力量的話語）

解析 分別套用四個選項的內容，判斷哪個最合適。（A）表示頻率，但歐普拉的節目是每天播出的（前面提到了 daily viewers），所以說「偶爾影響」與事實不符。（B）的代名詞 it 不清楚是指什麼，就算理解成「藉由談論節目來影響觀眾」也不合理。（C）套用在句中的話，意思是「影響觀眾像成功人士一樣（以像是成功人士一樣為前提）想和做的事情」，而不是「影響觀眾變得像成功人士」的意思。（D）說明用所說的話來影響觀眾，是最適合的答案。

Q3　　　*B*

（A）careless（粗心的）

► （B）difficult（艱困的）

（C）fantastic（非常棒的）

（D）traditional（傳統的）

解析 句子的後半部用表示內容轉折的 but（但是）連接，所以相對於後面所說的獲得成功，前面應該是說童年的情況並不好，所以 difficult 是最合適的答案。difficult 除了表示問題、學習內容很難以外，也可以表示處境「艱困」的意思。

Q4　　　*A*

► （A）inspire（激勵）　　　　　（B）satisfy（滿足）

（C）surprise（使驚訝）　　　（D）celebrate（慶祝）

解析 上一句說到歐普拉努力脫離童年時期的困境而獲得成功。因為有這樣的經歷，所以她應該能夠鼓勵別人，inspire 是最合適的答案。

家庭

個人

朋友

嗜好

娛樂

旅遊

突發事件

自然

節日

解答篇

Many people watch YouTube just to kill time. If you use it ___1___, however, it can also be a helpful tool. Besides dramas and music videos, there are actually a lot of material you can ___2___ yourself with. No matter you want to learn cooking, painting, or speaking foreign languages, you can find videos that teach you how to do. You can also increase your knowledge ___3___ watching channels on topics like history or science. ___4___, you can learn about it on YouTube.

中文翻譯

　　許多人看 YouTube 只是為了殺時間。不過,如果你聰明地使用它,它也可以成為有幫助的工具。除了戲劇和 MV 以外,那裡其實有很多你可以用來自學的材料。不管你想要學烹飪、繪畫還是說外語,你都能找到教你怎麼做的影片。你也可以藉由觀看關於歷史或科學之類主題的頻道來增加知識。不管你能想到什麼,都能在 YouTube 上學習。

Q1 ___*B*___

（A）widely（廣泛地）　　　　▶（B）wisely（聰明地）

（C）wildly（狂暴地）　　　　　（D）willingly（願意地）

▶解析　空格所在的句子用 however（然而）和上一句做對比,表示 YouTube 除了用來殺時間以外,也可以是有幫助的工具,所以空格中的副詞是表示與一般不同的使用態度。在選項之中,最能和「殺時間」形成對比的 wisely 是正確答案。

Q2 ___*C*___

（A）behave（守規矩）　　　　　（B）discover（發現）

▶（C）educate（教育）　　　　　（D）satisfy（滿足）

▶解析　這個句子省略了關係代名詞 which,you can... with 的部分修飾先行詞 material。介系詞 with 表示「用（材料）作為工

197

具」，而因為這段文章是表達用 YouTube 來學習，所以 educate 是最合適的答案。educate yourself 字面上是「教育你自己」，也就是「自學」的意思。

Q3 *A*
► （A）by （B）on
（C）for （D）with

▶解析 看關於歷史或科學的頻道，是增加知識的方法，所以表示方法的 by 是正確答案。with 雖然可以表示工具，但不能以後面接動名詞的形式表示方法。

Q4 *D*
（A）If you cannot find it（如果你找不到它）
（B）Without going to school（不上學）
（C）By searching for videos（藉由搜尋影片）
► （D）Whatever you can think of（不管你能想到什麼）

▶解析 空格後面的部分有代名詞 it，而且不能代表上一句裡的複數名詞 channels（頻道），所以空格內容應該要有 it 能夠代表的名詞性成分。選項（D）是複合關係代名詞 whatever 引導的名詞子句，而後面的 it 可以代表這整個名詞子句，表示「不管你能想到什麼東西，都能在 YouTube 上學習那個東西（it）」，所以是正確答案。

TOPIC 6　QUIZ　1

Joan loves traveling, and she ___1___ twenty-four countries so far. She plans to go to even more places, so she works extra hard to earn the money she will need during her trip. The places she has visited include popular destinations, such as Paris and London, ___2___ unique places like Greenland and Andorra. With every trip, her English becomes better and better, so she is now ___3___ about talking with foreigners. ___4___, Joan can learn about different cultures, and it is such experience that makes her feel travel is meaningful.

喬安喜愛旅行，她目前已經去過 24 個國家。她打算去更多地方，所以她格外努力工作來賺取旅行時需要的錢。她拜訪過的地方包括熱門的目的地，像是巴黎和倫敦，以及像格陵蘭和安道爾這樣獨特的地方。隨著每次旅行，她的英語變得越來越好，所以她現在對於和外國人交談很有自信。藉由和她遇見的人交談，喬安可以了解不同的文化，而就是這樣的經驗讓她覺得旅行有意義。

Q1　*C*
（A）was in　　　　　　（B）went to
►（C）has been to　　　（D）has gone to

▶解析　句子最後面的 so far 表示「到目前為止」，所以這個句子是說喬安從過去到現在為止的經驗，應該用現在完成式來表達。在完成式的（C）和（D）之中，has been to 表示「已經去過而且回來了」，has gone to 則是「去了而沒有回來」的意思。

Q2　*C*
（A）as soon as（一…就）

（B）as long as（只要…）

▶（C）as well as（以及…）

（D）as far as（就…而言）

▶解析　空格前面列出熱門的目的地，後面列出獨特的目的地，所以用法類似於連接詞 and 的 as well as 是正確答案。

Q3　*B*

（A）certain（確定的）

▶（B）confident（有信心的）

（C）curious（好奇的）

（D）patient（有耐心的）

▶解析　連接詞 so 連接理由與結果，而前面提到英語越來越好，所以 confident 是最合適的答案。

Q4　*C*

（A）Even when she is alone（即使在她一個人的時候）

（B）Because she likes foreigners（因為她喜歡外國人）

▶（C）By talking with those she meets
　　　（藉由和她遇見的人交談）

（D）Since everyone talks about traveling
　　　（因為每個人都談論旅行）

▶解析　選項（C）延續了上一句「和外國人交談」的內容，而且可以表示後面所說的「了解不同的文化」的方法，是最能連貫前後內容的答案。

TOPIC 6　QUIZ　2

　　If you are looking for the most unique trip, you should consider going to Tibet. Tibet is famous ___1___ its traditional culture and wonderful views. The best time to visit Tibet is from April to October, when it is warm and sunny in the day. ___2___, even in warmer months, temperatures can drop below 10 degrees Celsius at night. What is more, since Tibet is the highest region on Earth, some may get headaches or ___3___ there. Therefore, you should ___4___ before going to Tibet, so that you can fully enjoy your experience there.

如果你在尋找最獨特的旅行，你應該考慮去西藏。西藏以傳統文化和絕佳的景色聞名。拜訪西藏最好的時間是從四月到十月，這時候白天溫暖而晴朗。然而，就算是在比較溫暖的月份，氣溫在晚上也有可能降到低於攝式 10 度。而且，因為西藏是地球上最高的地區，所以有些人在那裡可能會頭痛或者覺得噁心。所以，去西藏之前你應該確定自己身體健康，這樣才能完全享受在那裡的經驗。

Q1 ___D___

（A）to （B）as

（C）by ▶（D）for

▶解析 空格後面的「傳統文化和絕佳的景色」是西藏有名的原因，所以表示原因的介系詞 for 是正確答案。要注意不能使用表示方法、手段的 by。

Q2 ___A___

▶（A）However（然而） （B）Besides（而且）

（C）Therefore（所以） （D）Naturally（自然地）

▶解析 上一句說白天溫暖晴朗，而空格所在的句子則說晚上有可能降到低於 10 度，前後的敘述形成對比，所以表示語氣轉折的連接副詞 However 是正確答案。

Q3 ___A___

▶（A）feel sick（覺得噁心）

（B）fall down（摔倒）

（C）stay away（遠離）

（D）get serious（變得嚴肅）

▶️解析 空格和前面的 get headaches（頭痛）用 or 連接，這裡是列舉在高原地區可能出現的兩種症狀，所以 feel sick 是正確答案，注意這個用法的 sick 不是「生病」的意思，而是指「噁心想吐」。（D）的 serious 在修飾人的時候，是表示「嚴肅」的意思，修飾疾病時才是表示「嚴重」。

Q4 ___*D*___

（A）make a plan of things to do（計畫要做的事）

（B）prepare your winter clothes（準備冬天的衣服）

（C）check the weather condition（查看天氣狀況）

▶（D）make sure you are in good health
（確定自己身體健康）

▶️解析 空格所在的句子用連接副詞 Therefore 開頭，表示上一句是原因，而這一句是結論。上一句說在高原地區可能出現健康上的症狀，所以選項（D）最能呼應上一句的內容。選項（B）、（C）的內容和上上句的天氣說明有關，但在使用連接詞或連接副詞時，應該考慮和距離最近的內容之間的相關性才對。

TOPIC 6 QUIZ 3

People today are used to traveling by airplane. We can go to overseas countries fast and easily by flying. Therefore, it is difficult for most of us to imagine how people in the past traveled in a world ___1___ airplanes. Before airplanes were invented, ___2___. When Christopher Columbus discovered the "New World" in 1492, it took him two months to sail from Spain to America. In 1850s, when gold ___3___ in Australia, those who wanted to dig gold would spend about four months just to travel from England to Australia. People in the past were certainly more ___**4**___ than we are!

中文翻譯

　　現代人習慣了搭飛機旅行。我們可以藉由飛行的方式快速而輕易地前往海外國家。所以，我們大部分的人很難想像過去的人怎麼在沒有飛機的世界旅行。在飛機被發明之前，船是渡海的唯一方式。當克里斯多福‧哥倫布在 1492 年發現「新大陸」時，他花了兩個月的時間從西班牙航行到美洲。在 1850 年代，當黃金在澳洲被發現時，想要挖黃金的人會花大約四個月，就為了從英格蘭旅行到澳洲。過去的人肯定比我們要有耐心！

Q1 *D*
（A）beyond（超越…）　　　　　（B）through（透過…）
（C）besides（除了…還有）　▶（D）without（沒有…）

▶**解析** 空格所在的子句提到過去的人怎麼樣，而下一句的開頭提到「在飛機被發明之前」，所以這裡應該是表達過去沒有飛機，without 是正確答案。

Q2 *B*
（A）air travel was not as popular as today
　　　（航空旅行不如現在流行）
▶（B）ships were the only way to cross the seas
　　　（船是渡海的唯一方式）
（C）there was no way people could go overseas
　　　（人們沒有辦法到國外）
（D）some people dreamed about flying in the air
　　　（有一些人夢想在空中飛行）

▶**解析** 因為下一句提到哥倫布發現新大陸，而且是用 sail（乘船航行）的方式，所以和乘船渡海有關的（B）是意義上和後面的內容最連貫的答案。

Q3   *B*

（A）found   ►（B）was found

（C）could find   （D）has been found

▶ **解析**   黃金是被人發現的東西，所以必須使用 find 的被動態，過去式被動態 was found 是正確答案。（D）是現在完成式，表示現在已經完成的狀態，所以不能用在過去的時間點（in 1850s）。

Q4   *B*

（A）foolish（愚蠢的）

►（B）patient（有耐心的）

（C）diligent（勤奮的）

（D）generous（慷慨的）

▶ **解析**   前面的內容都在說以前的人花很多時間航海，所以相對於現代人能夠搭飛機快速旅行，patient 最適合形容以前的人。因為過去的人沒有其他選擇，並不是因為笨才選擇乘船，所以（A）不是適當的答案。

Police have ___**1**___ a man for robbing a convenience store yesterday. The man went into the store and held out a knife at the clerk, asking her to take out money. The clerk gave him all the cash in the cash register, ___**2**___ was about 250 dollars. ___**3**___. However, he drove too fast and hit a tree. The man ___**4**___ get out of the car, so the police were able to catch him easily.

警方昨天因為一名男子搶劫超商而逮捕了他。這名男子進入店內,並且持刀對著店員,要求她拿出錢。店員給了他收銀機裡的所有錢,大約是 250 美元。然後男子跑了出去並開車逃逸。然而,他開得太快並且撞上一棵樹。男子不得不下車,所以警方能夠很容易地抓到他。

Q1 ___*A*___
► (A) arrested(逮捕)
(B) discovered(發現)
(C) embarrassed(使尷尬)
(D) interviewed(訪談,面試)

▶解析 段落內容提到男子搶劫超商,最後說警方抓到了他,所以 arrested 是最恰當的答案。discovered 雖然看起來也是可能的答案,但句子後面有表示原因的 for,這樣一來意思就變成「因為搶超商的事情而發現了男子」,所以不是合適的答案。

Q2 ___*B*___
(A) that
► (B) which
(C) so
(D) for it

▶解析 空格部分的子句缺少主詞,而且需要和前面的子句連接,所以同時具有代名詞和連接詞功能、能代表前面的 cash 的關

係代名詞 which 是正確答案。for it 雖然文法上沒有錯誤,但表達的意思「因為那大約是 250 美元」在這裡是不恰當的。另外,因為這個關係子句是非限定(補述)用法,所以不能用 that。

Q3 *D*

(A) It was a lot of money for the man
（那對男子而言是一大筆錢）

(B) The man was proud of his driving skills
（男子對自己的開車技術很自豪）

(C) After a while, the clerk called the police
（過了一會兒,店員打電話報警）

► (D) The man then ran outside and drove away
（然後男子跑了出去並開車逃逸）

▶解析 空格裡的句子銜接前面的「店員給了他錢」和後面的「他開得太快並且撞上一棵樹」,所以能補足中間的內容「男子從商店開車逃逸」的(D)是正確答案。

Q4 *D*

(A) had better（最好…）

(B) would like to（想要…）

(C) was able to（能夠…）

► (D) could not but（不得不…）

▶解析 男子本來打算開車逃逸,但因為撞上一棵樹才不得不下車,所以能表示因為情況的關係而別無選擇的 could not but 是正確答案。

TOPIC 7 QUIZ 2

Smart people keep themselves from ____1____ by always being prepared for sudden events. For example, they keep a first-aid kit in the car and at home. Also, they never visit people ___2___ do not know very well by themselves. In addition, they always tell their friends or family where they are going and when they will be back. It might seem to be a lot of bother, but it is never wrong to do our best to ___3___ accidents. After all, ___4___ .

聰明的人會藉由隨時為突發事件做好準備來避免危險。例如，他們會在車上和家裡放急救箱。另外，他們絕對不會自己拜訪不太熟悉的人。還有，他們總是會告訴朋友或家人自己要前往的地方，以及什麼時候會回來。這樣似乎很麻煩，但盡力避免意外是絕對不會錯的。畢竟，確保安全好過事後後悔。

Q1 ___A___

▶（A）danger（危險）　　　（B）failure（失敗）
　（C）influence（影響）　　（D）protection（保護）

▶解析　空格前面的介系詞 from 基本上是「離開…」的意思，而且段落的內容是關於避免意外、確保安全，所以 danger 是最恰當的答案。

Q2 ___A___

▶（A）they　　　　　　　　（B）who
　（C）which　　　　　　　（D）that

▶解析　空格後面的子句 …do not know very well 修飾前面的 people，而且 people 是 know（認識）的對象。當關係代名詞是受格的時候可以省略，而且這裡的關係子句缺少主詞，所以 they 是正確答案（關係子句原本的完整形態是 (who[m]/that) they do not know very well）。因為關係子句缺少主詞，所以關係代名詞 who, which, that 在這裡都會變成 know 的主詞，因此不正確。另外，which 只能用在先行詞是事物的時候。

Q3 _**A**_

► （A）avoid（避免）　　　　　　（B）consider（考慮）

　（C）expect（預期）　　　　　　（D）face（面對）

▶️ 解析 前面提到的都是積極避免意外的方法，而且空格前面有 do our best to（盡我們的力去做…），所以表示採取行動來避免某些事情的 avoid 是最恰當的答案。face 是表示面對已經發生的事，或者已經形成的情況。

Q4 _**C**_

　（A）to see is to believe（眼見為憑）

　（B）all is well that ends well

　　　（只要結果好的話，那就一切都好）

► （C）it is better safe than sorry（確保安全好過事後後悔）

　（D）where there is a will, there is a way（有志者事竟成）

▶️ 解析 這裡要用一句俗語來為整段內容做結尾，所以提醒做好預防措施、確保安全的（C）是正確答案。

TOPIC 7　QUIZ　3

　　Doctors say that although it is a good idea to have a baby sleeping in the same room as parents, they should not __**1**__ a bed. When parents and their baby sleep in the same bed, the adults may roll on the baby or cover its nose and mouth with heavy blankets __**2**__. As a result, they may kill their baby __**3**__ knowing it. Therefore, every parent should __**4**__ and try not to make such mistakes.

中文翻譯

　　醫師說，雖然讓嬰兒和父母睡在同一個房間是個好主意，但他們不應該共用一張床。當父母和他們的嬰兒睡在同一張床的時候，大人可能會意外滾到嬰兒身上，或者讓厚重的棉被蓋住嬰兒的口鼻。結果，他們可能會在沒有察覺的情況下害死嬰兒。所以，每個父母都應該了解兒童安全的重要性，並且努力不要犯這樣的錯誤。

Q1 ＿＿＿ _D_

（A）use（使用）　　　　　　　（B）need（需要）
（C）make（製作）　　▶（D）share（共用）

▶ 解析　因為下一句說明父母和嬰兒睡在同一張床時可能發生的意外，所以能表示「共用一張床」的 share 是正確答案。

Q2 ＿＿＿ _C_

（A）by force（強迫）
（B）by chance（偶然）
▶（C）by accident（意外）
（D）by experience（憑著經驗）

▶ 解析　因為大人並不是故意要滾到嬰兒身上、蓋住嬰兒口鼻的，所以表示意外、不小心的 by accident 是正確答案。by chance 雖然意思和 by accident 相似，但不會用在發生壞事的情況。

Q3 ＿＿＿ _C_

（A）after（在…之後）
（B）while（當…時）
▶（C）without（沒有…）
（D）besides（除了…還有）

▶ 解析　大人不小心滾到嬰兒身上、蓋住嬰兒口鼻，因而害死嬰兒，是在自己不知道做出致命行為的情況下發生的，所以 without 是正確答案。

Q4　　*D*

（A）ask their relatives for help（向他們的親戚求助）

（B）try to keep away from their babies
　　　（努力遠離他們的嬰兒）

（C）regret what they have done before
　　　（後悔他們以前做過的事）

▶（D）learn about the importance of child safety
　　　（了解兒童安全的重要性）

▶ 解析　前面的部分是說明父母和嬰兒同床睡覺的危險性，而空格部分和後面的「努力不要犯這樣的錯誤」是在這樣的前提下採取的行動。在選項中，內容最合理，而且和「努力不要犯這樣的錯誤」最相關的（D）是最合適的答案。

家庭

個人

朋友

嗜好

娛樂

旅遊

突發事件

自然

節日

解答篇

Typhoon Maria is heading west ___**1**___ the southern part of Taiwan. Residents ___**2**___ to be prepared for strong winds, which are expected to reach speeds of up to 120 kilometers per hour. ___**3**___. Therefore, those living in low areas should be ___**4**___ of flooding and consider leaving ahead of time. At its current speed, the typhoon is expected to leave Taiwan by noon tomorrow.

瑪莉亞颱風正朝西往台灣南部行進。建議居民為強風做好準備，風速預計達到最高每小時 120 公里。今晚也將開始下大雨。所以。住在低窪地區的民眾應該小心注意淹水，並且考慮提前離開。以目前的速度，颱風預計在明天中午前離開台灣。

Q1 ___*D*___

（A）above（在…上方）　　　　（B）beyond（越過…）

（C）inside（在…裡面）　　▶（D）toward（向著…）

▶**解析**　因為是表達颱風即將前往的方向，所以表示方向的 toward 是正確答案。

Q2 ___*C*___

（A）advise　　　　　　　　　（B）have advised

▶（C）are advised　　　　　　（D）are advising

▶**解析**　advise（建議）的用法是後面接動名詞，或者接「人物受詞 + to 不定詞」。因為空格和 to 不定詞之間沒有受詞，所以轉換為被動態、將人物受詞變成主詞的 are advised 是正確答案。另外，因為居民是被建議的對象，從意義上也可以判斷要選擇被動態。

Q3 ____C____

（A）Tree branches could be blown down
　　（樹枝可能會被吹落）

（B）There could be light rain and thunder
　　（可能會下小雨並且打雷）

▶（C）Heavy rain will also be starting tonight
　　（今晚也將開始下大雨）

（D）Many people die in typhoons every year
　　（每年有許多人死於颱風）

▶解析　空格後面的句子用連接副詞 Therefore（所以）開頭，所以空格內容是「低窪地區的民眾應該小心注意淹水，並且考慮提前離開」的理由，（C）是最適合的答案。注意（B）的 light rain 是「小雨」的意思，所以不會是造成淹水的原因。

Q4 ____B____

（A）afraid（害怕的）

▶（B）careful（小心的）

（C）certain（確定的）

（D）confident（有信心的）

▶解析　因為這個句子是表達應對颱風的對策，所以能表示小心提防的 careful 是正確答案。

TOPIC 8 QUIZ 2

The summer of 2020 was ___1___ hot in some regions in the world. In Siberia, one of the coldest places on Earth, the temperature of a town ___2___ Verkhoyansk reached 38 °C. In Taipei, the temperature rose to 38.9 °C, which was a record-high in 124 years ___3___ the city's weather station was built in 1896. In fact, according to National Oceanic and Atmospheric Administration of the U.S., the world's land and ocean surface temperature for May 2020 tied with 2016 as the highest in the record. ___4___, all the countries should work together to limit greenhouse gas emission.

中文翻譯

　　2020 年的夏天在世界上的一些地區特別熱。在西伯利亞，地球上最冷的地方之一，一個叫維科揚斯克的城鎮溫度達到 38 ℃。在台北，溫度上升到 38.9 ℃，是自從這個城市的氣象站在 1896 年建立以來的 124 年裡最高的紀錄。事實上，根據美國國家海洋暨大氣總署，2020 年 5 月的世界地表與海洋表面溫度平了 2016 年的最高紀錄。為了阻止世界變得更熱，所有國家應該共同合作限制溫室氣體排放。

Q1　　***B***
　　（A）hardly（幾乎不）　　▶（B）especially（特別）
　　（C）exactly（確切地）　　　（D）suddenly（突然）
　　▶解析　段落中舉出了一些地方突破高溫紀錄的例子，所以 especially 是正確答案。如果用 suddenly 的話，是表示溫度忽然大幅超過一般的水準，但從文章內容無法判斷是否有溫度急遽升高的情形。

Q2　　***A***
　　▶（A）called　　　　　　　　（B）calling
　　　（C）to call　　　　　　　　（D）has called
　　▶解析　空格部分修飾前面的名詞 town，而城鎮是被稱呼的對象，所以表示被動的過去分詞 called 是正確答案。

Q3　　***B***
　　　（A）because（因為）
　　▶（B）since（自從）
　　　（C）until（直到）

（D）while（當⋯的時候，然而）

▶ 解析 空格前面說台北創下 124 年來的最高溫紀錄，而空格所引導的子句提到氣象站在 1896 年建立，也就是 2020 年的 124 年之前，所以表示開始時間點的 since 是正確答案。

Q4 **𝒟**

（A）Considering that hot weather is still very rare
（考慮到炎熱天氣還是很少見）

（B）While it is possible that the information is false
（雖然這項資訊有可能是錯的）

（C）Since most people prefer to live in warmer places
（由於大部分的人偏好住在比較暖的地方）

▶（D）In order to stop the world from getting even warmer
（為了阻止世界變得更熱）

▶ 解析 前面的部分都在說高溫創下新紀錄，而且空格後面提到應該減少溫室氣體排放，所以能表示減少溫室氣體排放理由的（D）是正確答案。

TOPIC 8 QUIZ 3

_____1_____. In the past, 46% of the Earth was covered with forests, but in recent centuries, they have been decreasing year by year. Today, half of that 46% is gone, and only one fifth _____2_____ untouched by human beings. Scientists say that the world's forests decrease _____3_____ 2.4% every year. Since forests are home to more than half of the world's plants and animals on land, we should do our best to protect our forests and _____4_____ a better world for future generations.

　　世界上的森林正面臨危機。在過去，地球的 46% 由森林所覆蓋，但在最近幾世紀，森林一年一年持續減少。如今，那 46% 的一半已經消失，而其中只有五分之一仍然不受人類影響。科學家說世界上的森林每年減少 2.4%。因為森林是世界上超過一半的陸地植物和動物生存的地方，所以我們應該盡力保護我們的森林，並且為未來的世代留下更好的世界。

Q1　　*A*

▶（A）The world's forests are now in danger
（世界上的森林正面臨危機）

（B）A study found new facts about forests
（一項研究發現了關於森林的新事實）

（C）Forests are very important for human beings
（森林對人類而言非常重要）

（D）The world in the past was better than today
（過去的世界比現在來得好）

解析 空格是段落開頭的主題句位置。段落內容主要是關於地球上森林的消失，所以能表達森林面臨消失危機的（A）是正確答案。

Q2　　*B*

（A）stops（停止）

▶（B）remains（維持）

（C）becomes（成為）

（D）ends up（結果變成…）

解析 空格後面是過去分詞形式的形容詞 untouched，表示和原本的狀態一樣、不曾受到影響的意思。空格必須填入後面能接形容詞的連綴動詞，所以可以排除不是連綴動詞的（A）；在剩下的選項中，（C）和（D）都表示狀態的改變，和 untouched 的意義不相容，所以表示狀態不變的 remains 是正確答案。

215

Q3 ___*A*___

► （A）by   （B）at
（C）to   （D）for

▶ 解析 空格後面的 2.4% 是每年減少的幅度，所以表示變化幅度的介系詞 by 是正確答案。如果用介系詞 to 的話，則是表示減少的結果變成多少。

Q4 ___*D*___

（A）expect（預期）   （B）give（給）
（C）improve（改善）   ► （D）leave（留下）

▶ 解析 leave something for someone 表示「為某人留下什麼」，是最適合這個句子的答案。其他選項中，give 的句型是 give something to someone，介系詞 to 不能改成 for；improve 本身已經有「把什麼變得比較好」的意思，如果後面接 a better world（比較好的世界）當受詞的話，反而會讓句子的意思變得很奇怪。

家庭

個人

朋友

嗜好

娛樂

旅遊

突發事件

自然

節日

解答篇

In America, people celebrate New Year's Eve ___**1**___ parties. They party through the night to ___**2**___ the New Year. At midnight, when the clock strikes twelve, they cheer and kiss their loved ones. At the party, there are also many kinds of foods for the guests to enjoy, such as chips, pizzas, and chicken wings, and some may ___**3**___ eating too much and feeling sick. Therefore, to have a good start into the New Year, one should ___**4**___.

中文翻譯

在美國，人們開派對來慶祝跨年夜。他們派對一整晚來迎接新年。在午夜鐘響 12 點的時候，他們會歡呼並親吻心愛的人。在派對上，也會有許多種食物讓賓客享用，例如洋芋片、披薩和雞翅，而有些人最後可能吃太多並且覺得噁心。所以，為了在新年有個好的開始，應該把注意力多放在朋友而不是食物上。

Q1　*B*

（A）to have　　　　　　▶（B）by having
（C）when they have　　（D）so as to have

▶解析　這個段落是說明美國人慶祝跨年夜的方法（也就是開派對），所以表示方法的「by + 動名詞」是正確答案。（A）和（D）都表示目的。

Q2　*B*

（A）turn to（求助於…）　　▶（B）bring in（帶進來）
（C）cheer up（（使）高興起來）　（D）deal with（處理）

▶解析　bring in the New Year 是「迎接新年」的慣用說法，但也可以從字面上「帶進來」理解它的意思。

(Q3)　　 *A*

▶（A）end up（結果…）

（B）forget about（忘記做了…）

（C）succeed in（做…成功）

（D）apologize for（為…道歉）

▶ 解析　空格後面的部分表示參加了派對之後的結果，所以表示結果的 end up 是正確答案，也請注意 end up 後面會接現在分詞（V-ing）。

(Q4)　　 *D*

（A）go on a diet to get in shape（節食以獲得健康）

（B）regret what they have done（後悔自己做的事）

（C）plan what to do from day one
　　（從第一天開始計畫要做的事）

▶（D）focus more on friends than on foods
　　（把注意力多放在朋友而不是食物上）

▶ 解析　空格所在的句子用連接副詞 Therefore（所以）開頭，所以是和上一句相關的結論。上一句提到有些人會在派對上吃得太多而感覺噁心，所以意思表示「多和朋友交流、少吃食物」的（D）是正確答案。（A）雖然也和吃東西有關係，但節制在派對上吃的東西並不等於為了身體而採取的節食，所以不是最適當的答案。

TOPIC 9　QUIZ　2

Do you know that Earth Day is on April 22? It is a day ___1___ all of us are invited to take care of our world. On that day, there are events such as music festivals and picnics that aim to ___2___. Even though the events are fun themselves, we should know that the meaning of the day is to remind us of environmental problems and ____3____ us to do something about them. For example, we can try to use less water or ride a bicycle instead of driving. Saving the Earth starts with all of us, and what we do every day can ____4____.

你知道地球日是在 4 月 22 日嗎？這是我們所有人都被邀請一同照顧我們的世界的日子。在這一天，有音樂節和野餐之類以讓人們關注環境保護為目標的活動。儘管這些活動本身很有趣，但我們應該知道這一天的意義是提醒我們環境的問題，以及鼓勵我們對這些問題做些什麼。舉例來說，我們可以試著用比較少的水，或者騎腳踏車來取代開車。保護地球就從我們所有人開始，而我們每天所做的都能產生影響。

Q1 ____*B*____

（A）where   ►（B）on which

（C）in that   （D）so that

▶ **解析** 空格後面的子句修飾前面的 day，表示這是個什麼樣的日子，所以使用事物關係代名詞 which，並且將表示「在這一天」的介系詞 on 提前的 on which 是正確答案。關係副詞 where 只能用在先行詞是場所的情況。in that 表示「因為」，so that 表示「以便」。

Q2 ____*D*____

（A）be the greatest events on earth
（成為世界上最棒的活動）

（B）bring the world together as one（讓世界團結為一體）

（C）take advantage of the environment（利用環境）

►（D）bring attention to environmental protection
（讓人們關注環境保護）

▶ **解析** 因為整個段落都在談論地球日和環境保護的關係，所以（D）是最恰當的答案。

Q3 __*D*__

（A）allow（容許）　　　　（B）force（強迫）

（C）command（命令）　► （D）encourage（鼓勵）

▶ **解析** 因為地球日是自發性的活動，不能強迫一般大眾做什麼，所以 encourage 是最合適的答案。

Q4 __*D*__

（A）have a say（有發言權）

（B）take a chance（冒險）

（C）break a promise（不守承諾）

► （D）make a difference（產生影響）

▶ **解析** make a difference 是表示做不做某件事，結果會有所不同，也就是有很重要的影響，在這裡是表示每個人在日常生活中採取行動來保護環境的重要性。

TOPIC 9　QUIZ　3

In the past, there was a tradition to celebrate New Year on April 1st in some areas of France. In the 16th century, however, the king ___**1**___ set the New Year's Day on January 1st. While some ___**2**___, others still tried to follow the tradition. ___**3**___ a joke on those who were not willing to change, the supporters of the new rule invited them to New Year parties that did not exist and made them the first "April fools". ___**4**___ in the 19th century, it became popular in the Western world to pull a trick on others on April 1st.

中文翻譯

　　在過去，法國某些地區有在 4 月 1 日慶祝新年的傳統。但在 16 世紀，國王正式將元旦定在 1 月 1 日。雖然有些人準備好要接受這個決定，但其他人還試圖遵循傳統。為了捉弄那些不願意改變的人，新規定的支持者邀請他們去不存在的新年派對，讓他們成為第一批「四月傻瓜」。之後在 19 世紀，西方世界開始流行在 4 月 1 日開玩笑捉弄別人。

Q1 ___*D*___

（A）carefully（小心地）

（B）effectively（有效地）

（C）generously（慷慨地）

▶（D）officially（正式地）

▶解析　因為是國王將元旦定在 1 月 1 日，所以表示「正式，官方」的 officially 是最合適的答案。

Q2 ___*C*___

（A）did not know the truth yet（還不知道事實）

（B）never celebrated the New Year（從來不慶祝新年）

▶（C）were ready to accept the decision
　　　（準備好要接受這個決定）

（D）marked April 1st on their calendars
　　　（在月曆上標註 4 月 1 日）

▶解析　這個句子用連接詞 while（雖然）連結前後兩個子句，而且兩個子句的主詞 some（有些人）、others（其他人）表示不同人的對比，所以前後應該是相反的意思。後面的子句說「其他人還試圖遵循傳統」，所以前面的子句應該是表達「有些人願意放棄傳統、接受新規定」的意思，（C）是最適合的答案。

Q3 ___*A*___

▶（A）To play　　　　　　　　（B）By playing

（C）Having played　　　　　（D）When they played

▶ 解析 句子後面的「邀請他們去不存在的新年派對」是捉弄這些人的方法，所以反過來說，捉弄他們就是這麼做的目的，表示目的的 to 不定詞 To play 是正確答案。（B）表示方法，（C）表示理由，（D）表示時間。

Q4 *B*
（A）Yet（但是）　　　　　　▶（B）Later（後來）
（C）Likely（很有可能）　　　（D）Especially（尤其）

▶ 解析 空格前面都是關於 16 世紀法國的情況，而後面則是關於 19 世紀的歐洲，所以表示時間順序較晚的 Later 是最合適的答案。Likely 雖然看起來也像是合理的答案，但它是用來表示之後發生某件事的可能性，所以不適合用在這裡。

Part 3
閱讀理解

|最|常|考|生|活|情|境|題|型|

TOPIC 1 雙篇文章對照題組

作答說明 雙篇文章對照題組是新制英檢的新題型，每次考試都會出現。題組的其中一篇文章是公告、廣告、時間表、價目表等日常生活中會看到的簡短應用文，另一篇則通常是相關的信件或聊天對話紀錄。雖然感覺比較複雜，但其實只是從舊制的簡單應用文閱讀題加以變化的題型，文章本身的內容是 Part 3 裡面最簡單的，所以絕對不要放棄這個部分。某些題目必須對照兩篇文章的內容才能作答，但解題原則和一般的題目相同：先在文章中找到和題目關鍵字相關的內容，如果不能直接判斷答案的話，就在另一篇文章尋找和一開始找到的內容相關的部分，這時候應該就會看到答案了。

QUIZ 1

Trade in Your Smartphone!

Are you planning to get a new smartphone, but don't know how to deal with your old one? At M-Mobile, you can trade in your old phone and receive a gift card, which can be used when you purchase a new one! We accept any model on the market, but please note that the value of each phone is different. This service is available every day except Sunday, from 9 A.M. to 6 P.M. Please bring your personal ID when you come to our store.

10:13

Hi, Samuel. I am going to buy myself a new smartphone.

Jane

Really? Why? The one you have now still looks new.

Samuel

But it is a 4G phone. To use the 5G network and get higher speed, I'll need a new one.

Jane

I see. Have you found a good data plan?

Samuel

Sure. I did my homework. M-Mobile has several plans that are not expensive. And I can even sell my used phone to them.

Jane

You don't know if you can sell it at a good price, though.

Samuel

That's why I have to go and check it out myself. I plan to go there this afternoon.

Jane

I guess I should come with you, but I'm busy today. How about tomorrow?

Samuel

They don't do trade-in tomorrow. Let's meet the day after tomorrow, OK?

Jane

All right. See you then.

Samuel

雙篇文章
對照題組

信件

人物與
事物介紹

日常與
休閒生活

文化與
娛樂

資訊與
科技

健康與
自然環境

社會現象
討論

解答篇

Q1 _____ **Why does Jane need to get a new smartphone?**

（A）Her phone does not support the faster network.

（B）The one she has now looks pretty old.

（C）The data plan is cheaper when one buys a new phone.

（D）She wants to have a 5G phone like Samuel does.

Q2 _____ **For Jane, what is the advantage of selling her old phone to M-Mobile?**

（A）She can get some cash.

（B）She can get a new smartphone for free.

（C）She can buy a new phone at a lower price.

（D）She can get better service.

Q3 _____ **When will Samuel go to M-Mobile with Jane?**

（A）On Friday

（B）On Saturday

（C）On Sunday

（D）On Monday

QUIZ 2

16:20　Hey, guys. I'm going to bake some chocolate chip cookies tomorrow. Anyone up for joining me? Elsa

 Megan　Count me in! I love baking. What time and where?　16:22

 Emma　Tomorrow? But I have piano lesson every Saturday afternoon.　16:23

雙篇文章
對照題組

信件

人物與
事物介紹

日常與
休閒生活

文化與
娛樂

資訊與
科技

健康與
自然環境

社會現象
討論

解答篇

16:25 Well, come to my house at 9 A.M., then. By the way, I have butter, sugar, flour, and salt, but we still need some items to make cookies. Can you check what we need to prepare and bring the other items? Elsa

16:25 [cookie.jpg]

 Emma
9 A.M. tomorrow is OK with me, and I can bring some eggs. 16:27

 Megan
And I have chocolate chips. It seems we only lack one thing, but don't worry, I'll get it at the supermarket near my place. 16:28

Below is the picture that Elsa sent to her friends.

Preparation time:
20 minutes

Chocolate Chip Cookies

What to prepare:
1 large egg
½ cup butter
¾ cup sugar
1¾ cups flour
1 cup chocolate chips
½ spoon baking soda
½ spoon salt

Q1 _____ **When are they going to make cookies?**
（A）On Saturday morning
（B）On Saturday afternoon

227

（C）On Sunday morning

（D）On Sunday afternoon

Q2 _____ **What will Megan buy at the supermarket?**

（A）Eggs

（B）Chocolate chips

（C）Baking soda

（D）Nothing

Q3 _____ **What is NOT mentioned in the online chat discussion?**

（A）Elsa will teach her friends how to make cookies.

（B）Emma is learning how to play the piano.

（C）Megan loves to make things like bread and cookies.

（D）There is a supermarket close to Megan's house.

QUIZ 3

Summer Camp Activity Leaders
Deer Mountain Day Care, New York

If you love to spend the summer working outside with children, we have an opportunity for you. We are seeking current college students who are patient and good at sports to work as summer camp activity leaders. The summer camps will be held every week, from June 28 to August 20. Summer camp experience is preferred but not required.

To apply:

Please call Mrs. Calin at 877-7780 or mail to calin@deermountaindaycare.com by March 1.

雙篇文章

對照題組

信件

人物與事物介紹

日常與休閒生活

文化與娛樂

資訊與科技

自然環境與健康

社會現象與討論

解答篇

To: Mrs. Calin <calin@deermountaindaycare.com>
From: Reece Smith <reece.smith@ggmail.com>
Date: March 2
Subject: Apply for Activity Leader

Dear Mrs. Calin,

My name is Reece. I am writing to express my interest in the position of activity leader listed on your website.

I am in my second year at the University of Columbia. When I have time, I like swimming and playing basketball. Though I have no experience working in camps, I teach elementary school students math as a part-time job, and I enjoy spending time with them. A friend of mine who has worked with you for two summers told me that activity leaders should take a training course in the middle of June, and I am willing to do that.

Thank you very much for your time. I look forward to hearing from you soon.

Sincerely,
Reece Smith

Q1 _____ **How did Reece get the job information?**

（A）He received it by email from Deer Mountain Day Care.

（B）He knew it from one of his friends.

（C）He read it in a newspaper.

（D）He found it on the Internet.

_____ **What may be the reason that Reece will not be accepted as an activity leader?**

（A）He was too late to apply for the job.

（B）He has no experience as a camp leader.

（C）He has no time to take the training course.

（D）Deer Mountain Day Care does not need math teachers.

Q3 _____ **According to the articles, what do we know about the summer camps?**

（A）Those who work for them need to be trained in advance.

（B）They will be held at Deer Mountain Day Care.

（C）Children will play basketball during the summer camps.

（D）A child who goes to a summer camp will spend two months in it.

QUIZ 4

Star Café Menu	
*Bring your own cup and save NT$ 5!	
Americano (coffee + water)	NT$ 80
Latte (coffee + milk)	NT$ 95
Mocha (coffee + milk + chocolate)	NT$ 100
Green Tea	NT$ 90
Apple Juice	NT$ 120

雙篇文章
對照題組

信件

人物與
事物介紹

日常與
休閒生活

文化與
娛樂

資訊與
科技

健康與
自然環境

社會現象
討論

解答篇

Happy Hour: enjoy a special price every Monday, from 3 P.M. to 5 P.M.!
NT$ 70 for an Americano or Green Tea!

Star Café
Customers' Review

 Paul Carter   April 7

This coffee shop is way better than I expected. Actually, I found the shop because it is near my daughter's school, and I think it is very convenient for my family to visit. The place is comfortable, and people there are friendly and helpful. More importantly, they have some of the best coffee I've had. The milk and chocolate in my coffee were perfect. My wife ordered something different from mine, but she agreed that the milk they use is of good quality. Our daughter had some apple juice, and she seemed to enjoy it. Next time I'd like to order the kind of coffee we haven't tried.

 Mindy Stokes   April 6

I ordered their Americano during the "Happy Hour", and I think it's great value for money, but it's a shame I forgot to bring my own cup. When I order their green tea at the same time next week, I'll remember to bring my own cup to save even more.

Q1 _____ **What does Mr. Carter NOT mention about Star Café?**

（A）Its clerks

（B）Where it is

（C）The taste of its coffee

（D）The style of the building

Q2 _____ What will Mr. Carter order when he visits Star Café next time?

（A）Americano

（B）Latte

（C）Mocha

（D）Green tea

Q3 _____ How much did Ms. Stokes spend for her Americano?

（A）NT$80

（B）NT$75

（C）NT$70

（D）NT$65

QUIZ 5

Japan Railway System Nagoya Station Timetable changes in the coming year					
Train No.	Days	From	To	Leave At	
				This Year	Next Year
17644	Every day	Tokyo	Kyoto	06:50	06:00
22403	Wednesday	Tokyo	Osaka	10:40	10:35
16127	Every day	Shizuoka	Kyoto	13:45	12:25
25738	Every day	Tokyo	Osaka	14:00	13:40

Notice:

Several long-distance trains will leave at different times in the coming year, and the new times will also apply to tickets that are purchased in advance. Therefore, those who are affected can choose to cancel their tickets, and they do not need to pay added fees. Thank you for your understanding.

*Time to cancel tickets at the station: Every day from 8 A.M. to 5 P.M. by December 26

*Cancel tickets online: Go to the "My Ticket" page on japanrailsys.com. You can cancel the affected tickets free of charge on or before December 31.

To: Mark Lee <marklee@ctmail.com>
From: Carrie Masaki <cmasaki@ggmail.com>
Date: December 25
Subject: Change to our travel plan

Hi Mark,

I can't wait to travel with you, and I believe you are also preparing. However, I found that I have to make some change to our travel plan. The train we planned to take in Nagoya will leave at a different time next year, and that will be over half an hour earlier. I'd like to cancel the tickets we booked and choose a later train because I really want to have lunch at a famous restaurant in Nagoya that day, while the new departure time of the train we booked doesn't allow enough time for lunch. Please tell me how you think today, for I want to go to the ticket window myself and ask if they have tickets for later trains.

I look forward to seeing you here in two weeks, and I hope you

雙篇文章對照題組

信件

人物與事物介紹

日常與休閒生活

文化與娛樂

資訊與科技

健康與自然環境

社會現象討論

解答篇

have a good time with your family in Canada before our trip.

Carrie

Q1 _____ **What is the main purpose of Carrie's email?**
（A）To remind Mark to prepare for their trip
（B）To ask Mark's opinion about canceling tickets
（C）To let Mark know which train they are going to take
（D）To say Merry Christmas to Mark's family

Q2 _____ **Which train did Carrie and Mark plan to take?**
（A）Train 17644
（B）Train 22403
（C）Train 16127
（D）Train 25738

Q3 _____ **According to the articles, which of the following is true?**
（A）Carrie is living in Japan.
（B）Carrie and Mark will celebrate New Year's Day in Japan.
（C）Carrie wants to cancel train tickets online.
（D）Carrie will not be able to cancel tickets after tomorrow.

|最|常|考|生|活|情|境|題|型|

雙篇文章
對照題組

信件

人物與
事物介紹

日常與
休閒生活

文化與
娛樂

資訊與
科技

健康與
自然環境

社會現象
討論

解答篇

TOPIC 2 信件

作答說明 Part 3 的四個題組中，除了一個雙篇文章題組之外，其他三個題組都是單篇文章。在三個單篇文章題組中，經常會有一篇文章是信件。

信件有可能是傳統的書信或電子郵件，但實際解題時，兩者沒有什麼差別。考題經常會詢問寫信的目的，而信件的目的通常會在一開始就表明，所以掌握開頭的部分很重要。另外，也要注意寄件者（信件最後出現的名字）和收件者（信件開頭出現的名字）是誰，電子郵件的主旨有時候也是重要的線索。

QUIZ 1

Dear Joanna,

Sorry I haven't written to you for a while. Recently I stay in the library until 9:30 every evening because I have a final exam coming up next week. I feel a lot of stress, but I have to focus on my study. That's why I study in the library rather than in my room. Actually, I had a part-time job, and the pay was not bad, but I found that I had no time to study with that job. I think getting a college degree is the most important thing for me, so I quit the job last month, and I'm glad I made that decision.

I'll get back to you when the school is out. By then we can talk about our trip to the south of Taiwan. I can't wait to go to the sea! Also, I'll remember to bring my sun cream so I don't get burned again.

Sincerely,
Janet

Q1 **What is this letter mainly about?**

（A）Janet's study plan

（B）Janet's recent life

（C）Janet's job

（D）Janet's travel experience

Q2 **Who most likely is Janet?**

（A）A teacher

（B）A student

（C）A library worker

（D）A part-time worker

Q3 **About Janet, which of the following is NOT true?**

（A）She is worried about the tests she is going to take.

（B）She works hard in her studies.

（C）She enjoys working and studying at the same time.

（D）She will have fun at the beach on her trip.

QUIZ 2

To: Hans Peters <hanpeter@kimochimail.com>
From: Sandra Peters <sandrapeters@aonlinemail.com>
Date: August 8
Subject: Thank you!

Dear Uncle Hans and Aunt Bertha,

Thank you for your present for me. Yesterday when I came home

雙篇文章
對照題組

信件

人物與
事物介紹

日常與
休閒生活

文化與
娛樂

資訊與
科技

健康與
自然環境

社會現象
討論

解答篇

from school, Mom said happy birthday to me and showed me a vpackage, saying that it's a gift from you. It was a small package, and I didn't expect it to be something special. When I opened it, however, I couldn't believe my eyes! It was the set of 36 colored pencils that I have always wanted! Mom explained that she told you about my hobby of drawing, and that's why you decided to give me the gift I dream of. I really can't thank you enough.

With the new set of colored pencils, I believe I'll love drawing even more. I plan to draw a picture of you two, so I can give it to you on Uncle Hans' birthday next month. See you then!

Love,
Sandra

Q1 _____ **Why does Sandra write this email to her uncle and aunt?**
（A）To thank them for a birthday gift
（B）To tell them about the kind of gift she wants
（C）To talk about her hobby of drawing
（D）To invite them home next month

Q2 _____ **Which of the following words best describes Sandra's feeling after she opened the package?**
（A）Curious
（B）Nervous
（C）Surprised
（D）Confused

Q3 _____ **According to the email, which of the following is true?**
（A）Sandra's birthday is on August 8.

（B）Sandra did not have any colored pencil before.

（C）Sandra's mother knows what she wants as a gift.

（D）Sandra started to love drawing after receiving the gift.

QUIZ 3

To: Christine Weston <ChristineWeston@cityuniv.edu>
From: Sandy Wong <SandyWong@cityuniv.edu>
Date: December 22
Subject: Re: Christmas Party

Dear Christine,

Thank you for inviting me, but I am sorry that I cannot make it to your Christmas dinner party. I am very busy these days since my parents are coming to America, and I have to show them around. I really wish I could go, as you are such a good cook. I hope I can go to your party sometime soon.

By the way, do you know that Chinese New Year is similar to Christmas in western countries? During Chinese New Year, we also have a week of holidays, and we get together with our relatives—just like you do during Christmas week. However, Chinese New Year is not a holiday in America, which means I cannot go back to Hong Kong then. And that is why my parents come to see me earlier.
After all, thank you for inviting me in the first place!

Best wishes,
Sandy

雙篇文章
對照題組

信件

人物與
事物介紹

日常與
休閒生活

文化與
娛樂

資訊與
科技

健康與
自然環境

社會現象
討論

解答篇

Q1 _____ **What is the purpose of this email?**
   （A）To refuse an invitation
   （B）To accept an invitation
   （C）To introduce Sandy's parents
   （D）To introduce Chinese New Year

Q2 _____ **What is Sandy busy preparing for?**
   （A）A Christmas party
   （B）Chinese New Year
   （C）Hosting her parents
   （D）Returning to Hong Kong

Q3 _____ **Why does Sandy write about Chinese New Year?**
   （A）To make Christine feel closer to her
   （B）To show the difference between cultures
   （C）To explain why her parents are going to see her
   （D）To complain about not having holidays during Chinese New Year

QUIZ 4

Dear Grandma and Grandpa,

Mom says we are going back to Texas and spend summer vacation there, so I am going to see you soon. I remember last winter I had a great time visiting you, and I am so excited about feeding chickens and milking cows again. My friends were so jealous when they saw the pictures of me during my last visit. They kept asking me if I was afraid when I rode the horse. I told them I was a bit scared at first, but since you said practice makes perfect, I kept trying and became familiar with horse riding. This summer I want to have more chances to practice, and I hope to become an expert like Grandpa.

Also, we will take the dog we recently adopted there. He is called "Mylo", and he likes to play with other dogs, so I believe he will make some friends there. I cannot wait to see him running freely with his friends on the open field!

Yours truly,
Henry

Q1 _____ What is the main purpose that Henry writes this letter to his grandparents?
（A）To let them know he is going to visit them
（B）To describe the fun of playing with animals
（C）To thank them for encouraging him to keep trying
（D）To introduce his dog Mylo to them

Q2 _____ Who is Henry's grandfather most likely to be?
（A）A farm owner
（B）A pet shop owner
（C）A zoo keeper
（D）A meat store owner

Q3 _____ According to the letter, which of following is true?
（A）Henry has not tried feeding chickens before.
（B）The pictures Henry showed his friends are all taken by himself.
（C）Henry is now an expert of horse riding.
（D）Henry's grandparents have some dogs.

雙篇文章
對照題組

信件

人物與
事物介紹

日常與
休閒生活

文化與
娛樂

資訊與
科技

健康與
自然環境

社會現象
討論

解答篇

Dear Martha,

I want to share some good news with you. I have been selected to enter the English speech contest! The teacher said I speak really good English. I told him I used to talk in English with a friend from Canada, so my English improved a lot. You know I was talking about you! After you moved back to Canada last year, however, I have much less opportunity to speak English. Not only that, but I also miss when we met at your home and chatted about fashion, boys, and school work on Sunday afternoons. I wish you could live in Taiwan longer, but I understand that your father always wanted to go back to his home country, and that is why you had to leave.

I believe you have already made a lot of friends there, for you are such a nice person, but please remember that you will always be my best friend.

Miss you,
Clair

Q1 _____ **What does Clair want to express in her letter?**
（A）She feels sad that Martha is going back to Canada.
（B）She wants to practice English more often.
（C）She misses Martha very much.
（D）It is easy to make friends with Martha.

Q2 _____ **What might Martha write when she replies to this letter?**
（A）"I am sorry."

(B) "Congratulations!"

(C) "You are welcome!"

(D) "Never mind."

Q3 _____ **According to the letter, which of the following is true?**

(A) Clair won a prize in the speech contest.

(B) Clair and Martha were classmates.

(C) Martha cannot speak Chinese.

(D) Martha's father is from Canada.

雙篇文章
對照題組

信件

人物與
事物介紹

日常與
休閒生活

文化與
娛樂

資訊與
科技

健康與
自然環境

社會現象
討論

解答篇

TOPIC 3　人物與事物介紹

作答說明　Part 3 的四個題組中，通常會有兩個非應用文的單篇文章題組。以下從 TOPIC 3 到 TOPIC 8 的部分，將會把 Part 3 的文章依主題分成六個常見的類型來進行練習。

QUIZ 1

"How dare you!" shouted Greta Thunberg, a teenage girl from Sweden, at the 2019 UN Climate Action Summit in New York. By openly expressing her anger toward governments that fail to protect the Earth, she became known around the world.

At the age of eleven, Thunberg developed an interest in the protection of environment after watching a video about climate change in class. She was shocked that some animals are dying because of human activities that make the Earth warmer every year. She was so sad that she stopped talking, and she was nearly sent to a hospital because she ate very little.

After that, Thunberg gave up school to call for stronger action on climate change, and over one million students joined her and took part in "school strike for climate" in their own countries. It is without doubt that she has made the younger generation more aware of the importance of protecting the environment.

Q1 _____ **What is this article mainly about?**
（A）A person who speaks out about climate change
（B）Some effective ways of stopping climate change

（C）The importance of school education

（D）How to deal with bad feelings and recover

Q2 _____ **What did NOT happen after Thunberg watched the video?**

（A）She became aware of some negative result of human activities.

（B）She stopped speaking like she usually did.

（C）She stopped eating anything.

（D）She stopped going to school.

Q3 _____ **According to this article, what has Thunberg achieved?**

（A）She became a popular person at her school.

（B）She proved that one can learn a lot without going to school.

（C）She took part in making laws that help stop climate change.

（D）She let many students know it is necessary to protect the Earth.

QUIZ 2

Have you ever seen people surfing without waves? With a large power kite, one can fly over water even when there is no wave. Such activity is known as "kiteboarding", one of the most exciting water sports in the world. The idea of kiteboarding first appeared in the 1970s, and with later designs that tried to improve kites and boards, it became easier for people to enjoy the sport. Today, the sport is popular around the world.

To play the sport, you have to practice standing on a surfboard first. And then, you can try controlling a power kite and let the wind pull you through the water. When you have enough skills, you can jump up and show off your moves. Of course, kiteboarding is more dangerous than most water sports, so it would be safer to have a coach who can teach you the basics.

Q1 _____ **What is the main purpose of this article?**
- （A）To introduce the complete history of kiteboarding
- （B）To teach its readers how to be an excellent kiteboarder
- （C）To let its readers have some basic ideas about kiteboarding
- （D）To show that kiteboarding is a dangerous sport

Q2 _____ **According to the article, what do we know about those who can do kiteboarding?**
- （A）They should learn to design boards.
- （B）They can stand on a surfboard.
- （C）They practice flying kites in the park.
- （D）They all learned from their coaches.

Q3 _____ **About kiteboarding, which of the following is true?**
- （A）It is possible to do it without wind.
- （B）It was popular in the 1970s.
- （C）First kites and boards were different from today.
- （D）It requires a boat to pull a board on water.

QUIZ 3

In times of COVID-19, when most people were not free to go to foreign countries, a special tour group going "nowhere" showed up at Taipei Songshan Airport. The event they went for, which was

雙篇文章
對照題組

信件

人物與
事物介紹

日常與
休閒生活

文化與
娛樂

資訊與
科技

健康與
自然環境

社會現象
討論

解答篇

planned by the airport, was called "pretend to go abroad" airport tour. Just like taking an international flight, those who took this tour checked in, got their boarding passes, and even got on the plane. The only difference was that the plane did not take off at all. Even though it was not a real flight, those who took part in were still happy that they got a taste of traveling.

Because of this successful event, some airlines even offered "flights to nowhere". They not only let passengers get on the planes, but they actually let the planes fly before going back to the original airport. These flights were popular, too, and they became an extra source of income for airlines in the difficult times.

☞ pretend 假裝

Q1 _____ **Who invented the "pretend to go abroad" tour?**
（A）An airport
（B）A tour company
（C）Some airlines
（D）Some travel lovers

Q2 _____ **What could the passengers NOT do during the airport tour?**
（A）Get their boarding passes
（B）Board the plane
（C）Fly in the air
（D）Feel like they were traveling

Q3 _____ **Which of the following is the main idea of this article?**
（A）"Pretend to go abroad" tour cannot take the place of real flights.
（B）It is easier to pretend going abroad than really flying to other countries.

（C）Pretending to go abroad was a popular way of experiencing travel.

（D）There are only a few things we can do while pretending to go abroad.

雙篇文章對照題組

信件

人物與事物介紹

日常與休閒生活

文化與娛樂

資訊與科技

健康與自然環境

社會現象討論

解答篇

TOPIC 4 日常與休閒生活

QUIZ 1

A growing number of married couples choose not to have children. Because of long working hours, many of them feel it is impossible to take care of children all the time. They also worry about losing their own freedom after becoming parents. Therefore, more and more couples decide to have pets but not children.

There are some reasons for them to prefer pets over children. Pets can stay home alone when their "parents" go to work or go out with friends, while little children cannot. What is more, some people think that pets always make them happy, while children can make them feel a lot of stress sometimes.

It is interesting to note that, according to a study, married couples without children spend more money on their pets than any other kind of family does. The finding suggests that such couples treat their pets just like their kids. Even without children, they still need someone they can take care of.

Q1 _____ What is NOT a reason that some couples choose to have pets but not children?

(A) They have to spend a lot of time working.

(B) They are afraid that they will not be free to do things they want.

(C) Pets do not always need someone by their side.

(D) Pets will not make troubles like children do.

雙篇文章 對照題組

信件

人物與 事物介紹

日常與 休閒生活

文化與 娛樂

資訊與 科技

健康與 自然環境

社會現象 討論

解答篇

Q2 _____ **According to the article, what can pets do for their owners?**

（A）They can go to work for their owners.

（B）They can give their owners good feelings.

（C）They can take care of their owners' children.

（D）They can help their owners make more money.

Q3 _____ **According to the article, which of the following is true?**

（A）More and more couples are not able to have children.

（B）Most couples want to have pets and children at the same time.

（C）Among all kinds of families, couples without children spend the most on pets.

（D）Those without children do not like to take care of others.

QUIZ 2

Studies show that green plants can improve people's quality of life by making them happy and feel less stress. The reason might be that they make us feel closer to nature. Most of us live in the city and seldom have a chance to go to a forest and enjoy fresh air. However, by adding some plants to our home, we can make the air cleaner and let the touch of leaves calm us down. What is more, a study also points out that people who work in offices with plants are more focused and do their job better.

Besides having positive effects on our mind, house plants are also nice to look at. When decorating your room, just a few plants can add life to a boring space. In fact, plants can also be a key design element of a home. Even though it takes some effort to take care of plants, the advantages are worth the effort.

Q1 _____ **What is this article mainly about?**
　　(A) Some studies on plants
　　(B) Good effects of plants
　　(C) How to take care of plants
　　(D) The importance of nature

Q2 _____ **According to the article, what kind of people might NOT be helped by plants?**
　　(A) Those who feel a lot of stress
　　(B) Those who want to be better at work
　　(C) Those who want to make their home more beautiful
　　(D) Those who want to spend less time maintaining their home

Q3 _____ **According to the article, which of the following is NOT true?**
　　(A) Green plants can create fresh air in a space.
　　(B) Workers in offices with plants pay more attention to their work.
　　(C) The advantages of plants are all about our feelings.
　　(D) Some people see plants as an important part when they design a home.

QUIZ 3

When it comes to winter, we may think of things that make us happy, such as Christmas holidays or skiing. Some people, however, feel sad and sleepy all the time during winter. Such a situation is called "winter blues". It happens because the days in winter are shorter, and there are less time we see the light of sun, which makes us feel brighter. Winter blues are quite common, and they usually do not last long, but a few people may experience it for the whole season.

To beat winter blues, it is important to receive as much light as possible. During the day, try opening the curtains to let natural light in. Even when the sun is hidden behind the clouds, you can still turn on your desk lamp when you work. Doctors also suggest patients to get up early and sit in front of a lamp for thirty minutes every day. As long as we know the cause of winter blues, it is not hard to deal with it.

雙篇文章對照題組

信件

人物與事物介紹

日常與休閒生活

文化與娛樂

資訊與科技

健康與自然環境

社會現象討論

解答篇

Q1 _____ **According to the article, what is the main cause of winter blues?**
（A）Low temperature
（B）Lack of light
（C）Negative way of thinking
（D）Getting up too late

Q2 _____ **Which of the following is NOT a way to treat winter blues?**
（A）Let the light shine through your window
（B）Use a desk lamp at the place where you work
（C）Keep the light on in order to wake up early
（D）Spend some time in the light every morning

Q3 _____ **About winter blues, which of the following is true?**
（A）People who have this problem cannot enjoy skiing.
（B）Only a few people have this problem.
（C）This problem can last for several months.
（D）There is no way to solve this problem.

TOPIC 5 文化與娛樂

QUIZ 1

In early America, it was popular to make a bed cover with pieces of cloth of many colors and shapes. Such bed covers are called "quilts", and they are famous for their colorful patterns. Many women made quilts with friends as a way to spend their free time, and the quilts were nothing but ordinary daily objects.

As time went by, it became cheaper and easier to buy bed covers in stores, so it became rare for people to make quilts. It is lucky, though, that some quilts were passed from parents to children and were not damaged. In the late 1960s, some collectors began collecting these quilts as works of art, and that is when artists began to create quilts as art.

Today, quilt artists use both modern and traditional skills to make their works. Compared to traditional works, quilts today usually have unique designs that reflect an artist's thoughts and experiences, and they are to be appreciated rather than be used.

| ☞ cloth 布 |

Q1 _____ **What is this article mainly about?**

(A) How the meaning of making quilts changed in history

(B) How to decide whether quilts are a kind of art

(C) How to make quilts in the right way

(D) How some collectors saved quilts from disappearing

雙篇文章 對照題組

信件

人物與 事物介紹

日常與 休閒生活

文化與 娛樂

資訊與 科技

健康與 自然環境

社會現象 討論

解答篇

Q2 _____ **What did people in early America think quilts are?**

（A）Works of art

（B）Things to be collected

（C）Tools to express feelings

（D）Objects to be used in daily life

Q3 _____ **How are quilts today different from those in the past?**

（A）They are not made in old ways at all.

（B）They show what an artist thinks about.

（C）They all have similar designs.

（D）Most of them are actually used.

QUIZ 2

When you eat at a restaurant, do you let your camera eat first? In the age of social media, it seems more important to let others know what you are eating than to enjoy its taste. Therefore, people often take photos of their food and share them before feeding themselves.

The rise of food photos have also affected the restaurant industry. Today, a restaurant can suddenly get famous with a widely shared photo of food. Therefore, restaurant owners now pay more attention to the appearance of food. They also improve their lighting so that their food looks better in pictures. Some of them even pay famous social media users to post pictures taken in their restaurants.

Some restaurant owners, however, do not allow their customers to take pictures. They believe a dish should be enjoyed as soon as it is served, or it will get cold and less delicious while the customer is busy taking pictures. They try to remind us that the food itself is more important than the "likes" we get on social media.

Q1 _____ **What does "let your camera eat first" mean?**
（A）Let others know what you eat
（B）Let the camera taste the food first
（C）Take pictures of food before eating
（D）Consider the appearance of food first

Q2 _____ **According to the article, what is the main reason that customers take food photos?**
（A）To get attention from friends
（B）To enjoy the taste more
（C）To make restaurants famous
（D）To practice taking pictures

Q3 _____ **Which of the following is NOT a way for a restaurant to get famous on social media?**
（A）Make its food look beautiful
（B）Use lights that improve the look of food
（C）Hire famous people to post about it
（D）Make its customers eat before taking photos

QUIZ 3

At Golden Horse Awards 2020, Chen Shu-Fang（陳淑芳）won the best leading actress and best supporting actress prizes for two different movies at the age of 81. She was the first one to receive the two prizes at the same time. Before that, however, no one expected she would become a top movie actress.

Chen was born in a rich Taiwanese family in 1939. Because she enjoyed singing and dancing, she made up her mind to be an actress. She has been acting in both movies and TV dramas for over 60 years since she was 19. During her long career, she has had several chances to win a prize at Golden Bell Awards for her appearances in dramas, but she was never picked as a winner. Even so, she still loves acting and tries to do her best every time, and her hard work finally paid off. "As long as you remember me, I will keep acting," said Chen at Golden Horse Awards.

雙篇文章
對照題組

信件

人物與
事物介紹

日常與
休閒生活

文化與
娛樂

資訊與
科技

健康與
自然環境

社會現象
討論

解答篇

Q1 _____ **What is this article mainly about?**
（A）An event
（B）A prize
（C）A movie
（D）A life story

Q2 _____ **Why did Chen Shu-Fang decide to become an actress?**
（A）Her family was rich.
（B）She liked to sing and dance.
（C）She enjoyed seeing movies.
（D）She wanted to get a prize.

Q3 _____ **About Chen Shu-Fang, which of the following is NOT correct?**
（A）She received two prizes at Golden Horse Awards in 2020.
（B）She acts not only in movies but also in TV dramas.
（C）She won several prizes at Golden Bell Awards.
（D）After winning the prizes, she still wants to act.

255

TOPIC 6 資訊與科技

QUIZ 1

When Jawed Karim, one of those who created YouTube, posted the very first YouTube video "Me at the zoo" in 2005, he might not have imagined that making YouTube videos would become a job, or that YouTube would one day take the place of traditional television. Today, YouTube is one of the media that influence young people the most.

Being a YouTuber is now the most popular career choice for children. According to a study in UK, about 75% of people under 18 have thought about being a YouTuber. Even though some YouTubers do earn a lot, money is not the main reason that young people take them as role models. According to the study, the top reason they want to make YouTube videos is that they need a place to create things freely, and the second reason is that they want to be famous and influence many people. Therefore, we can say it is the need to express themselves that led to the rise of young YouTubers.

Q1 _____ **What did Jawed Karim do in 2005?**
（A）He started the YouTube Web site.
（B）He posted the first video about YouTube.
（C）He made a living by making videos.
（D）He changed the way people watch TV.

Q2 _____ **What is the most important reason that young people want to be YouTubers?**
（A）They want to make a lot of money.

(B) They want to create things the way they want.

(C) They want to become famous.

(D) They want to influence many people.

Q3 _____ **According to the article, which of the following is true about YouTube?**

(A) It is not as important as traditional television.

(B) It can affect the way young people think or do.

(C) 75% of its users are children under 18.

(D) Most people can earn a lot of money on it.

QUIZ 2

It is fun to share your life experience online, but it would be dangerous if you share too much personal information, as some may take advantage of it and cause troubles in real life. For example, they can try signing in to your bank account with your information and steal your money. Therefore, it is better not to give out information such as your phone number, home address, and the place you work at. You should also check if your photos show such information before posting them.

Also, you should be careful who you trust online. People you meet online are actually strangers in real life, so you should not easily let them know your personal information while chatting. Even if you decide to meet a friend in person, you should meet in a public place and not tell them your phone number—you can send messages online! With safety in mind, you can protect yourself.

Q1 _____ **What is this article mainly about?**

(A) How to be safe on the Internet

(B) How to be smart when meeting friends

(C) How to tell who is a bad guy

雙篇文章
對照題組

信件

人物與
事物介紹

日常與
休閒生活

文化與
娛樂

資訊與
科技

健康與
自然環境

社會現象
討論

解答篇

（D）The bad results of giving out personal information

Q2 _____ **What is NOT a kind of information this article tells us not to share?**

（A）Where you have visited

（B）Where you live

（C）Your cell phone number

（D）The name of your company

Q3 _____ **Which of the following is a way to keep your personal information safe?**

（A）Avoid opening a bank account online

（B）Post your information in the form of photos

（C）Try to meet an online friend in person

（D）Not to contact an online friend on the phone

QUIZ 3

In the past, people have imagined that one day they would be able to see their friends far away and talk with them, and it would be possible to watch any movie they want anytime, anywhere. Today, we know that these have already come true, thanks to smartphones and 4G networks. And then, after about ten years since 4G service started, 5G arrived. It is the next generation of 4G, and it promises faster speed. At first, many people thought 4G was fast enough, so 5G seemed like a waste of money for them. However, the faster speed of 5G means we can do more with it.

For example, fans can now watch a live concert on their phone without worrying about Internet speed, and they can even select which part of the stage to see. It is also possible to see a doctor on the phone, as high-quality real-time video can let patients be seen clearly and help doctors make correct decisions. With 5G, we can imagine more.

Q1 _____ **What is this article mainly about?**

（A）The way people imagine

（B）Faster cell phone network

（C）Enjoying videos on the phone

（D）How 5G can help doctors

Q2 _____ **What did many people think about 5G at first?**

（A）They did not think they needed it.

（B）They did not think it is as good as 4G.

（C）They did not think it is fast enough.

（D）They thought it was worth the money.

Q3 _____ **Which of the following is not a thing we can do with 5G?**

（A）Talk with friends and see them at the same time

（B）Watch any movie no matter where we are

（C）See different parts of the stage while watching a live concert

（D）Getting treated by talking on the phone

雙篇文章
對照題組

信件

人物與
事物介紹

日常與
休閒生活

文化與
娛樂

資訊與
科技

健康與
自然環境

社會現象
討論

解答篇

TOPIC 7 健康與自然環境

QUIZ 1

What you eat can affect how you sleep. In a recent study, scientists found that a diet rich in sugar can negatively affect sleep quality. According to the study, those who eat a lot of white bread or donuts fall asleep quickly, but they wake up more often at night. On the other hand, eating more vegetables and fish seems to help people get a good night's sleep.

Surprisingly, sleep quality also have something to do with our food choices. In another study, scientists found that those who sleep less eat more snacks and fast food than others. However, after sleeping well for several nights, they become less interested in this kind of food.

From the two different studies, we know that sleep and diet can affect each other. Therefore, to improve our health, we should pay attention to our sleep and diet at the same time.

Q1 _____ **What is the main idea of this article?**

（A）Bad food choices are bad for your sleep.

（B）People who sleep well eat well.

（C）Diet and sleep affect each other.

（D）There are many advantages of sleeping well.

Q2 _____ **According to this article, what will happen if someone sleeps well for several nights?**

（A）He or she will fall asleep quickly.

（B）He or she will eat more fish.

（C）He or she will eat less fast food.

（D）He or she will pay more attention to health.

Q3 ＿＿＿＿＿ **For whom is this article written?**

（A）Sleep scientists

（B）People who give advice on eating

（C）Fast food restaurant owners

（D）Those who care about their health

QUIZ 2

Not many people notice that the fashion industry is polluting the Earth. For example, fashion uses one-tenth of water used in all industries. A lot of water is used while making clothes, and after being used, the water is not clean anymore. When the dirty water goes back to the river, it can kill animals living in it. As fast fashion encourages people to buy more clothes, the problem of water pollution also gets more serious.

To solve the problem, it is important for us not to buy too many clothes. Ask yourself before buying new clothes: Do I really need them? Are there similar items in my closet? Thinking about these questions, you may realize that you already have enough. Also, there must be something in your closet that you almost never wear, proving that you have bought more than you need. By buying less clothes and keeping them longer, we can help reduce water pollution caused by the fashion industry.

☞ reduce 減少

Q1 ＿＿＿＿＿ **What is true about the fashion industry?**

（A）Among all industries, it uses the most water.

（B）It pollutes water in the river.

（C）It throws clothes in the river.

（D）Only fast fashion is to blame for pollution.

雙篇文章 對照題組

信件

人物與 事物介紹

日常與 休閒生活

文化與 娛樂

資訊與 科技

健康與 自然環境

社會現象 討論

解答篇

Q2 _____ **Which of the following is NOT a sign that you have enough clothes?**

（A）You do not think you really need new ones.

（B）You already have something that looks like the item you want.

（C）You have something that you seldom wear.

（D）You keep an item for a very long time.

Q3 _____ **What does this article encourage its readers to do?**

（A）Tell other people about water pollution

（B）Say no to fashion industry

（C）Not to buy new clothes at all

（D）Cut pollution by buying less clothes

QUIZ **3**

Onions are good for our health in many ways. For example, they can improve sleep, make skin brighter, help avoid cancer, etc. Even with these advantages, however, most of us do not like to cut onions, as they can make us cry when we cut them.

Some scientists think that the reason onions make us cry is to protect themselves. An onion is in fact a part of the plant that grows under the ground, and it is the energy store of the plant. If an onion is left under the ground over winter, it will grow again in spring. Since it is an important part of the plant, scientists say the chemicals in it that make our eyes tear actually serve to protect it from attacks.

To have an easier time cutting onions, you can put them in a refrigerator for half an hour before cutting. When you cut onions, remember to open your window and finish cutting as quickly as you can. By doing so, the kitchen will not be filled with the chemicals that bring tears to your eyes.

Q1 _____ **What is this article mainly about?**

（A）The advantages of eating onions

（B）The reason that onions make us cry

（C）The parts of an onion plant

（D）The ways to cook with onions

Q2 _____ **Why is an onion an important part of the plant?**

（A）It makes people cry.

（B）It grows under the ground.

（C）It can provide energy for the plant.

（D）It cannot be seen on the ground.

Q3 _____ **Which of the following is NOT a way to cut onions without crying?**

（A）Make yourself easy while cutting

（B）Put onions in a fridge before cutting

（C）Keep your window open

（D）Finish cutting within a short time

雙篇文章對照題組

信件

人物與事物介紹

日常與休閒生活

文化與娛樂

資訊與科技

健康與自然環境

社會現象討論

解答篇

TOPIC 8 社會現象討論

QUIZ 1

In the past, not many restaurants deliver food to their customers, for they would need to hire extra workers to do so. Today, restaurants just need to sign contracts with third-party services such as Foodpanda and Uber Eats, and the service providers will take care of everything related to delivering food. By becoming a "partner" of such services, a restaurant can also be seen in their apps and take orders from customers who live far away.

The rise of food delivery services has also changed customers' habits. According to a recent study, there are about a million people in Taiwan who use these services at least once a week. Most people say they use the services when they want to save time or when the weather is bad. Some people also say they enjoy the experience of choosing from all kinds of restaurants listed in the apps. In short, food delivery services has become convenient tools for both restaurants and customers.

Q1 _____ **What is this article mainly about?**
（A）Food delivery services
（B）Restaurants that deliver food
（C）Customers' habits
（D）A recent study

Q2 _____ **What is NOT a reason that restaurants sign contracts with a food delivery service?**
（A）They can save hiring costs.

（B）They want to handle everything.

（C）They can let more people know them.

（D）People far away can order from them.

Q3 _____ **Which of the following is NOT a reason that people use food delivery services?**

（A）They eat out at least once a week.

（B）They do not have enough time.

（C）They do not want to go out in bad weather.

（D）There are many different choices on the apps.

QUIZ 2

Parents usually think that playing video games is bad for their children. It is true that children will forget about their homework or stay up late if they spend too much time playing video games, but it is also true that games have some good effects. For example, some studies found that video game players have better memory and attention, which can in turn help them learn better. Therefore, if parents want their children to do better at school, maybe they should consider allowing some time for video games.

Some may worry that video game players have less time to develop their social skills. However, many online games actually require players to play in teams. In order to reach their goals, they have to learn how to work together. Some players even make friends with teammates they often play with. In this way, not only do online games help develop social skills, but they have also become an important part of social life.

Q1 _____ **What is this article mainly about?**

（A）The bad results of playing games

（B）The positive effects of playing games

雙篇文章
對照題組

信件

人物與
事物介紹

日常與
休閒生活

文化與
娛樂

資訊與
科技

健康與
自然環境

社會現象
討論

解答篇

(C) The social value of video games

(D) The purpose of making video games

Q2 _____ **According to this article, what is a reason that video game players learn better?**

(A) Video games make them stay up late.

(B) Video games make them remember things better.

(C) Video games make them work in teams.

(D) Video games contain some learning materials.

Q3 _____ **According to this article, what is true about the social side of online games?**

(A) All online games ask their players to play in teams.

(B) Players will know how to work with others in online games.

(C) Online game players have worse social skills.

(D) Online games can take the place of social activity in real life.

QUIZ 3

Recently, I was shocked by a story shared by a friend of mine. Her relative John tried several jobs after finishing university, but he has never been in a job for over three months. He is not happy with any of the jobs, so he stopped trying and stays at home every day doing nothing.

Such people are known as NEETs (Not in Education, Employment, or Training), and there are more and more of them in developed countries. For example, there are over 700,000 NEETs between 15 and 39 years of age in Japan. Without income, most of them are supported by their parents or relatives. In the UK, however, most NEETs live in low-income families and thus need more help from the government.

The main reason NEETs do not work is that they cannot find jobs that suit them. Therefore, governments should provide necessary training and help them discover more career choices so that their young years are not wasted.

雙篇文章對照題組

信件

人物與事物介紹

日常與休閒生活

文化與娛樂

資訊與科技

健康與自然環境

社會現象討論

解答篇

Q1 _____ **Why did John become a NEET?**
   （A）He does not have a university degree.
   （B）He has never been in a job.
   （C）He has not tried to find a job.
   （D）He cannot find a job he is satisfied with.

Q2 _____ **According to this article, what is the difference between NEETs in Japan and in the UK?**
   （A）NEETs in the UK live in poorer families.
   （B）NEETs in Japan are younger in age.
   （C）NEETs are not helped by the government in Japan.
   （D）There are less NEETs in the UK.

Q3 _____ **According to this article, what should governments do for NEETs?**
   （A）Help NEETs find jobs that suit them
   （B）Offer jobs that do not need training
   （C）Choose jobs for NEETs
   （D）Tell NEETs that they are wasting their time

267

 ANSWER 閱讀理解（解答）

TOPIC 1 QUIZ 1

Trade in Your Smartphone!

Are you planning to get a new smartphone, but don't know how to deal with your old one? At M-Mobile, you can trade in your old phone and receive a gift card, which can be used when you purchase a new one! We accept any model on the market, but please note that the value of each phone is different. This service is available every day except Sunday, from 9 A.M. to 6 P.M. Please bring your personal ID when you come to our store.

單字解釋：

trade in 用舊的東西作為折抵　　smartphone（n.）智慧型手機

model（n.）款式，型號　　available（adj.）可得的

personal ID 個人身分證

 中文翻譯

用你的智慧型手機折抵購物！

您打算買一支新的智慧型手機，卻不知道怎麼處理舊的手機嗎？在 M-Mobile，您可以用舊手機換取在購買新手機時可以使用的禮券！我們接受市場上的任何型號，但請注意每支手機的價值不同。這項服務除了週日以外每天上午 9 點至下午 6 點提供。來店時請攜帶您的個人身分證。

雙篇文章
對照題組

信件

人物與
事物介紹

日常與
休閒生活

文化與
娛樂

資訊與
科技

健康與
自然環境

社會現象
討論

解答篇

Jane: Hi, Samuel. I am going to buy myself a new smartphone.

Samuel: Really? Why? The one you have now still looks new.

Jane: But it is a 4G phone. To use the 5G network and get higher speed, I'll need a new one.

Samuel: I see. Have you found a good data plan?

Jane: Sure. I did my homework. M-Mobile has several plans that are not expensive. And I can even sell my used phone to them.

Samuel: You don't know if you can sell it at a good price, though.

Jane: That's why I have to go and check it out myself. I plan to go there this afternoon.

Samuel: I guess I should come with you, but I'm busy today. How about tomorrow?

Jane: They don't do trade-in tomorrow. Let's meet the day after tomorrow, OK?

Samuel: All right. See you then.

單字解釋：

network（n.）網路　　　　　data plan 行動數據方案

珍：嗨，山繆。我打算給自己買一支新的智慧型手機。

山繆：真的嗎？為什麼？妳現在的那一支看起來還很新。

珍：但這是 4G 手機。為了使用 5G 網路並且得到更高的速度，我需要新的。

山繆：我明白了。妳找到好的行動數據方案了嗎？

珍：當然。我做了功課。M-Mobile 有幾個不貴的方案。我甚至可以把我用過的手機賣給他們。

山繆：但妳不知道能不能用好的價錢賣出去。

　珍：所以我才得自己去了解一下。我打算今天下午過去。

山繆：我想我應該跟你一起去，但我今天很忙。明天怎麼樣？

　珍：他們明天不做舊機折抵。我們後天見吧，好嗎？

山繆：好。到時候見。

Q1　　_A_

Why does Jane need to get a new smartphone?

（為什麼珍需要買新的智慧型手機？）

▶（A）Her phone does not support the faster network.
　　　（她的手機不支援比較快的網路。）

　（B）The one she has now looks pretty old.
　　　（她現在的手機看起來很舊。）

　（C）The data plan is cheaper when one buys a new phone.
　　　（如果買新手機的話，行動數據方案會比較便宜。）

　（D）She wants to have a 5G phone like Samuel does.
　　　（她想要有 5G 手機，就像山繆一樣。）

🔊解析　在聊天紀錄中，山繆說「Why?」詢問買新手機的理由，珍回答「it is a 4G phone. To use the 5G network and get higher speed, I'll need a new one.」，表示她的手機是 4G 手機，需要新的手機才能使用 5G 網路並獲得更高的速度，所以（A）是正確答案。山繆提到珍的手機「still looks new」（看起來還很新），所以（B）不對。（C）、（D）在文章中沒有提到。

Q2　　_C_

For Jane, what is the advantage of selling her old phone to M-Mobile?

（對於珍而言，把她的舊手機賣給 M-Mobile 的優點是什麼？）

　（A）She can get some cash.
　　　（她可以得到一些現金。）

　（B）She can get a new smartphone for free.
　　　（她可以免費得到新的智慧型手機。）

雙篇文章

對照題組

信件

人物與
事物介紹

日常與
休閒生活

文化與
娛樂

資訊與
科技

健康與
自然環境

社會現象
討論

解答篇

►（C）She can buy a new phone at a lower price.

（她可以用比較低的價格買新的手機。）

（D）She can get better service.

（她可以得到比較好的服務。）

▶解析　廣告中提到「you can trade in your old phone and receive a gift card, which can be used when you purchase a new one」，表示可以用舊手機折抵換禮券，而禮券在買新手機的時候可以使用，所以（C）是正確答案。廣告中並沒有提到可以獲得現金或免費手機，所以（A）、（B）不對。（D）在文章中沒有提到。

Q3　*D*

When will Samuel go to M-Mobile with Jane?

（山繆什麼時候會和珍一起去 M-Mobile？）

（A）On Friday（星期五）

（B）On Saturday（星期六）

（C）On Sunday（星期日）

►（D）On Monday（星期一）

▶解析　在聊天紀錄的結尾部分，珍本來說自己今天要去 M-Mobile，但山繆提議陪珍一起去，於是兩人開始約定要去的日子。山繆說今天很忙，問明天可不可以，而珍則回答「They don't do trade-in tomorrow.」（他們明天不做舊機折抵），提議後天見面，並且獲得了山繆的同意。但因為不知道後天是星期幾，所以還需要參考廣告的內容。廣告提到「This service is available every day except Sunday」，表示星期日不做舊機折抵，所以兩人所說的「後天」是不提供服務的星期日的隔天，也就是星期一，（D）是正確答案。

> **Elsa:** Hey, guys. I'm going to bake some chocolate chip cookies tomorrow. Anyone up for joining me?
>
> **Megan:** Count me in! I love baking. What time and where?
>
> **Emma:** Tomorrow? But I have piano lesson every Saturday afternoon.
>
> **Elsa:** Well, come to my house at 9 A.M., then. By the way, I have butter, sugar, flour, and salt, but we still need some items to make cookies. Can you check what we need to prepare and bring the other items?
>
> **Emma:** 9 A.M. tomorrow is OK with me, and I can bring some eggs.
>
> **Megan:** And I have chocolate chips. It seems we only lack one thing, but don't worry, I'll get it at the supermarket near my place.

單字解釋：

chocolate chip（通常做成小圓錐或半圓粒狀的）巧克力豆

count in 把某人算進去，讓某人加入

艾莎：嘿，大家。我明天要烤一些巧克力豆餅乾。有人要和我一起嗎？

梅根：算我一份！我愛烘焙。幾點，在哪裡？

艾瑪：明天？但是我每週六下午有鋼琴課。

艾莎：嗯，那就上午 9 點來我家吧。對了，我有奶油、糖、麵粉和鹽，但我們還需要一些東西來做餅乾。你們可以看看我們需要準備什麼，並且把其他東西帶來嗎？

艾瑪：明天上午 9 點我可以，我也能帶一些雞蛋。

梅根：我有巧克力豆。看起來我們只缺一樣東西，但不要擔心，我會在我家附近的超市買。

Chocolate Chip Cookies

Preparation time:

20 minutes

What to prepare:

1 large egg

½ cup butter

¾ cup sugar

1¾ cups flour

1 cup chocolate chips

½ spoon baking soda

½ spoon salt

單字解釋：

baking soda 小蘇打

<hr />

巧克力豆餅乾

準備（製作）時間：

20 分鐘

要準備什麼：

1 個大的雞蛋

½ 杯奶油

¾ 杯糖

1¾ 杯麵粉

1 杯巧克力豆

½ 匙小蘇打

<hr />

雙篇文章對照題組

信件

人物與事物介紹

日常與休閒生活

文化與娛樂

資訊與科技

健康與自然環境

社會現象討論

解答篇

½ 匙鹽

Q1 ___*A*___

When are they going to make cookies?

（他們什麼時候要做餅乾？）

▶（A）On Saturday morning（星期六上午）

　（B）On Saturday afternoon（星期六下午）

　（C）On Sunday morning（星期日上午）

　（D）On Sunday afternoon（星期日下午）

▶ 解析　在聊天內容的開頭，艾莎說明天要做餅乾，並且邀請大家一起做。之後艾瑪回應「Tomorrow? But I have piano lesson every Saturday afternoon.」，表示因為每週六下午有鋼琴課的關係，所以可能有困難，從這裡也可以知道明天是星期六。之後艾莎回應「come to my house at 9 A.M., then」，將時間定在星期六上午 9 點，而艾瑪說「9 A.M. tomorrow is OK with me」，同意在這個時候去艾瑪家做餅乾。所以，正確答案是（A）。

Q2 ___*C*___

What will Megan buy at the supermarket?

（梅根會在超市買什麼？）

　（A）Eggs（蛋）

　（B）Chocolate chips（巧克力豆）

▶（C）Baking soda（小蘇打）

　（D）Nothing（什麼也不買）

▶ 解析　艾莎在聊天的中間說自己有奶油、糖、麵粉和鹽，並且請大家看看她傳的圖片，把其他的材料帶到她家。之後艾瑪說她會帶雞蛋，而梅根說她有巧克力豆。對照食譜的內容，可以得知三個人都沒有的東西是小蘇打，而且梅根說會在超市買大家還缺少的東西，所以（C）是正確答案。

Q3 ___*A*___

What is NOT mentioned in the online chat discussion?

（網路聊天討論中沒有提到什麼？）

▶（A）Elsa will teach her friends how to make cookies.
（艾莎會教她的朋友如何做餅乾。）

（B）Emma is learning how to play the piano.
（艾瑪正在學怎麼彈鋼琴。）

（C）Megan loves to make things like bread and cookies.
（梅根很愛做麵包和餅乾之類的東西。）

（D）There is a supermarket close to Megan's house.
（梅根的家附近有一家超市。）

▶解析　對於詢問「（沒有）提到什麼」的題目，必須在文章中找出和各個選項相關的內容，才能判斷答案。和（B）相關的部分是艾瑪所說的「I have piano lesson every Saturday afternoon」，和（C）相關的部分是梅根所說的「I love baking」（baking 是指烘焙麵包、蛋糕、餅乾之類的東西），和（D）相關的部分是梅根所說的「the supermarket near my place」（my place 是指梅根的家）。至於選項（A），雖然是艾莎邀請朋友一起做餅乾，但不見得是要教朋友做，也有可能是大家一邊研究食譜一邊做，從文章內容無法得知是哪種情況，所以（A）是正確答案。

TOPIC 1 　QUIZ　3

Summer Camp Activity Leaders
Deer Mountain Day Care, New York

If you love to spend the summer working outside with children, we have an opportunity for you. We are seeking current college students who are patient and good at sports to work as summer camp activity leaders. The summer

雙篇文章對照題組

信件

人物與事物介紹

日常與休閒生活

文化與娛樂

資訊與科技

健康與自然環境

社會現象討論

解答篇

camps will be held every week, from June 28 to August 20. Summer camp experience is preferred but not required.

To apply:

Please call Mrs. Calin at 877-7780 or mail to calin@deermountaindaycare.com by March 1.

單字解釋：

summer camp 夏令營	day care （日間）托兒所
opportunity （n.）機會	current （adj.）目前的
seek （v.）尋找	prefer （v.）偏好
require （v.）要求具備	

夏令營活動領隊
鹿山托兒所，紐約

如果您喜歡和小孩一起在戶外度過夏天的工作，我們有個機會要給您。我們正在尋找有耐心並且擅長運動的在學大學生擔任夏令營活動領隊。這系列夏令營將會在 6 月 28 日到 8 月 20 日之間每週舉行。有夏令營經驗優先，但並非必要條件。

申請方式：

請在 3 月 1 日前致電 877-7780 找卡林女士，或者寄信至 calin@deermountaindaycare.com。

To: Mrs. Calin <calin@deermountaindaycare.com>
From: Reece Smith <reece.smith@ggmail.com>
Date: March 2
Subject: Apply for Activity Leader

Dear Mrs. Calin,

My name is Reece. I am writing to express my interest in the position of activity leader listed on your website.

I am in my second year at the University of Columbia. When I have time, I like swimming and playing basketball. Though I have no experience working in camps, I teach elementary school students math as a part-time job, and I enjoy spending time with them. A friend of mine who has worked with you for two summers told me that activity leaders should take a training course in the middle of June, and I am willing to do that.

Thank you very much for your time. I look forward to hearing from you soon.

Sincerely,
Reece Smith

雙篇文章
對照題組

信件

事物介紹
人物與

休閒生活
日常與

娛樂
文化與

科技
資訊與

自然環境
健康與

討論
社會現象

解答篇

單字解釋：

apply（v.）申請，應徵   position（n.）職位

list（v.）列出   part-time job 兼職工作

look forward to 期待

收件者：卡林女士 <calin@deermountaindaycare.com>

寄件者：里斯・史密斯 <reece.smith@ggmail.com>

日期：3 月 2 日

主旨：應徵活動領隊

277

親愛的卡琳女士：

我叫里斯。我寫這封信是要表達對於貴機構網站上列出的活動領隊職位的興趣。

我現在在哥倫比亞大學就讀二年級。有空的時候，我喜歡游泳和打籃球。雖然我沒有在營隊工作的經驗，但我教小學生數學當作兼職工作，而且我很喜歡和他們共度時光。我一個曾經為貴機構工作過兩個夏天的朋友告訴我，活動領隊應該在六月中上訓練課程，我很願意做這件事。

非常感謝您（讀這封信）的寶貴時間。期待很快收到您的回信。

誠摯地
里斯・史密斯

Q1 _____ _D_

How did Reece get the job information?

（里斯是怎麼獲得工作訊息的？）

（A）He received it by email from Deer Mountain Day Care.

   （他收到了鹿山托兒所寄的電子郵件。）

（B）He knew it from one of his friends.

   （他從一位朋友那邊知道的。）

（C）He read it in a newspaper.（他在報紙上讀到的。）

▶（D）He found it on the Internet.（他在網路上找到的。）

▶解析　因為題目問的是里斯得知這項工作的方式，所以要從里斯所寫的電子郵件尋找答案。在電子郵件中，里斯提到「the position of activity leader listed on your website」（貴機構網站上列出的活動領隊職位），可知他是在托兒所的網站上得知這項工作的，所以（D）是正確答案。

Q2 _____ _A_

What may be the reason that Reece will not be accepted

雙篇文章
對照題組

信件

人物與
事物介紹

日常與
休閒生活

文化與
娛樂

資訊與
科技

健康與
自然環境

社會現象
討論

解答篇

as an activity leader?

（里斯不會被接受擔任活動領隊的原因可能是什麼？）

▶（A）He was too late to apply for the job.

（他太晚應徵這份工作了。）

（B）He has no experience as a camp leader.

（他沒有擔任營隊領隊的經驗。）

（C）He has no time to take the training course.

（他沒有時間上訓練課程。）

（D）Deer Mountain Day Care does not need math teachers.

（鹿山托兒所不需要數學老師。）

▶ 解析 徵人廣告的最後提到「To apply: Please call Mrs. Calin... or mail to... by March 1」，表示要在 3 月 1 日之前打電話或寄郵件應徵，而里斯的電子郵件顯示寄件日期是 3 月 2 日，已經太晚了，所以（A）是正確答案，請記得「by + 日期」是表示截止日期的意思。徵人廣告提到的「Summer camp experience is preferred but not required」是表示偏好有夏令營經驗的人，但並不要求必須有這項經驗，所以（B）不會是里斯被拒絕的理由。

Q3 ___*A*___

According to the articles, what do we know about the summer camps?

（根據這兩篇文章，我們可以知道關於夏令營的什麼事情？）

▶（A）Those who work for them need to be trained in advance.

（為夏令營工作的人需要事先接受訓練。）

（B）They will be held at Deer Mountain Day Care.

（夏令營會在鹿山托兒所舉行。）

（C）Children will play basketball during the summer camps.

（孩子們會在夏令營期間打籃球。）

（D）A child who goes to a summer camp will spend two months in it.（去夏令營的小孩會花 2 個月在裡面。）

▶ 解析 必須逐一對照和每個選項相關的內容，才能判斷答案。和（A）相關的部分是電子郵件中的「A friend... told me that activity leaders should take a training course in the middle of June」，表示活動領隊應該在六月中上訓練課程，而且徵人廣告顯示夏令營是從 6 月 28 日開始，所以（A）是正確答案。（B）和（C）在文章中沒有提到。和（D）相關的部分是徵人廣告中的「The summer camps will be held every week, from June 28 to August 20」，雖然是要在 2 個月的期間中舉辦夏令營沒錯，但請注意是「每週舉辦」，所以每週的夏令營屬於不同的梯次，並不是一場夏令營連續進行 2 個月，所以（D）是錯的。

TOPIC 1 QUIZ 4

Star Café Menu *Bring your own cup and save NT$ 5!	
Americano (coffee + water)	NT$ 80
Latte (coffee + milk)	NT$ 95
Mocha (coffee + milk + chocolate)	NT$ 100
Green Tea	NT$ 90
Apple Juice	NT$ 120
Happy Hour: enjoy a special price every Monday, from 3 P.M. to 5 P.M.! NT$ 70 for an Americano or Green Tea!	

星咖啡菜單

*攜帶您自己的杯子並節省新台幣 5 元！

美式咖啡（咖啡＋水）	新台幣 80 元
拿鐵咖啡（咖啡＋牛奶）	新台幣 95 元
摩卡咖啡（咖啡＋牛奶＋巧克力）	新台幣 100 元

雙篇文章 對照題組

信件

人物與 事物介紹

日常與 休閒生活

文化與 娛樂

資訊與 科技

健康與 自然環境

社會現象 討論

解答篇

綠茶　　　　　　　　　　　　　　　　　新台幣 90 元
蘋果汁　　　　　　　　　　　　　　　　新台幣 120 元

快樂時段：每週一下午 3 點至 5 點享受特價！
美式咖啡或綠茶新台幣 70 元！

Star Café
Customers' Review

 Paul Carter　　　　　　　　　　　　　April 7

This coffee shop is way better than I expected. Actually, I found the shop because it is near my daughter's school, and I think it is very convenient for my family to visit. The place is comfortable, and people there are friendly and helpful. More importantly, they have some of the best coffee I've had. The milk and chocolate in my coffee were perfect. My wife ordered something different from mine, but she agreed that the milk they use is of good quality. Our daughter had some apple juice, and she seemed to enjoy it. Next time I'd like to order the kind of coffee we haven't tried.

 Mindy Stokes　　　　　　　　　　　　April 6

I ordered their Americano during the "Happy Hour", and I think it's great value for money, but it's a shame I forgot to bring my own cup. When I order their green tea at the same time next week, I'll remember to bring my own cup to save even more.

單字解釋：

convenient（adj.）便利的　　comfortable（adj.）舒適的

helpful（adj.）樂於幫忙的　　be great value for money 很划算
it's a shame 很可惜

星咖啡
顧客評論

保羅‧卡特　　　　　　　　　　　　　　　　　　　　4 月 7 日
這間咖啡店比我預期的要好很多。事實上，我找到這家店是因為它離我女兒
的學校很近，我認為我的家庭拜訪這裡很方便。這個地方很舒適，那裡的人
也很友善而且樂於幫忙。更重要的是，他們有我喝過最好的一些咖啡。我咖
啡裡的牛奶和巧克力很完美。我太太點了和我不一樣的東西，但她同意他們
使用的牛奶品質很好。我們的女兒喝了些蘋果汁，她看起來很喜歡。下次我
想要點我們沒喝過的咖啡。

敏蒂‧斯托克斯　　　　　　　　　　　　　　　　　　4 月 6 日
我在「快樂時段」點了他們的美式咖啡，我認為很划算，但很可惜我忘了帶
自己的杯子。下禮拜我在同樣的時間點他們的綠茶的時候，我會記得帶自己
的杯子來節省更多。

Q1　　　D

What does Mr. Carter NOT mention about Star Café?
（關於星咖啡，卡特先生沒有提到什麼？）
（A）Its clerks（店員）
（B）Where it is（所在的地方）
（C）The taste of its coffee（咖啡的味道）
▶（D）The style of the building（建築物的風格）

🅳 解析　在卡特先生的評論中，和（A）相關的部分是「people
there are friendly and helpful」，和（B）相關的部分是「it is
near my daughter's school」，和（C）相關的部分是「The milk
and chocolate in my coffee were perfect.」。（D）在文章中沒有
提到，所以是正確答案。

雙篇文章 對照題組

信件

人物與 事物介紹

日常與 休閒生活

文化與 娛樂

資訊與 科技

健康與 自然環境

社會現象 討論

解答篇

Q2 _____A_____

What will Mr. Carter order when he visits Star Café next time?

（卡特先生下次拜訪星咖啡的時候會點什麼？）

▶（A）Americano（美式咖啡）

（B）Latte（拿鐵咖啡）

（C）Mocha（摩卡咖啡）

（D）Green tea（綠茶）

▶**解析** 在卡特先生的評論中，提到了「milk and chocolate in my coffee」，對照菜單可知卡特先生點了摩卡咖啡；下一句說他的太太點了別的，但同意牛奶品質很好，所以她點的是另一種有牛奶的咖啡，也就是拿鐵咖啡。評論最後說「Next time I'd like to order the kind of coffee we haven't tried」，表示下次想點他們沒試過的另一種咖啡，所以（A）是正確答案。

Q3 _____C_____

How much did Ms. Stokes spend for her Americano?

（斯托克斯小姐花了多少錢買美式咖啡？）

（A）NT$80（新台幣 80 元）

（B）NT$75（新台幣 75 元）

▶（C）NT$70（新台幣 70 元）

（D）NT$65（新台幣 65 元）

▶**解析** 斯托克斯小姐說自己在「快樂時段」買了美式咖啡，但忘了帶自己的杯子，對照菜單可知這個時候美式咖啡的特價是新台幣 70 元，所以（C）是正確答案。請注意她並沒有獲得自己攜帶杯子的 5 元折扣。

Japan Railway System
Nagoya Station
Timetable changes in the coming year

Train No.	Days	From	To	Leave At	
				This Year	Next Year
17644	Every day	Tokyo	Kyoto	06:50	06:00
22403	Wednesday	Tokyo	Osaka	10:40	10:35
16127	Every day	Shizuoka	Kyoto	13:45	12:25
25738	Every day	Tokyo	Osaka	14:00	13:40

Notice:

Several long-distance trains will leave at different times in the coming year, and the new times will also apply to tickets that are purchased in advance. Therefore, those who are affected can choose to cancel their tickets, and they do not need to pay added fees. Thank you for your understanding.

*Time to cancel tickets at the station: Every day from 8 A.M. to 5 P.M. by December 26

*Cancel tickets online: Go to the "My Ticket" page on japanrailsys.com. You can cancel the affected tickets free of charge on or before December 31.

單字解釋：

railway（n.）鐵路 timetable（n.）時間表
leave（v.）離開，出發 apply to 適用於
purchase（v.）購買 in advance 事前，預先
cancel（v.）取消

日本鐵路系統
名古屋車站
明年的時間表變更

列車編號	星期	起點站	終點站	出發時間	
				今年	明年
17664	每天	東京	京都	06:50	06:00
22403	星期三	東京	大阪	10:40	10:35
16127	每天	靜岡	京都	13:45	12:25
25738	每天	東京	大阪	14:00	13:40

通知：

　　幾班長程列車明年將在不同的時間出發，新的時間也將適用於預先購買的車票。所以，受到影響的人可以選擇取消車票，不需要付額外的費用。感謝您的諒解。

*在車站取消車票的時間：每天上午 8 點到下午 5 點，到 12 月 26 日為止
*線上取消車票：上 japanrailsys.com 的「我的車票」頁面。您可以在 12 月 31 日或之前免費取消受到影響的車票。

To: Mark Lee <marklee@ctmail.com>
From: Carrie Masaki <cmasaki@ggmail.com>
Date: December 25
Subject: Change to our travel plan

Hi Mark,

I can't wait to travel with you, and I believe you are also preparing. However, I found that I have to make some

雙篇文章
對照題組

信件

人物與
事物介紹

日常與
休閒生活

文化與
娛樂

資訊與
科技

健康與
自然環境

社會現象
討論

解答篇

change to our travel plan. The train we planned to take in Nagoya will leave at a different time next year, and that will be over half an hour earlier. I'd like to cancel the tickets we booked and choose a later train because I really want to have lunch at a famous restaurant in Nagoya that day, while the new departure time of the train we booked doesn't allow enough time for lunch. Please tell me how you think today, for I want to go to the ticket window myself and ask if they have tickets for later trains.

I look forward to seeing you here in two weeks, and I hope you have a good time with your family in Canada before our trip.

Carrie

單字解釋：

half（adj.）一半的 allow（v.）容許

收件者：馬克・李 <marklee@ctmail.com>
寄件者：凱莉・正木 <cmasaki@ggmail.com>
日期：12 月 25 日
主旨：對我們旅遊計畫的變更

嗨，馬克：

我等不及要和你一起旅行了，我相信你也正在準備。不過，我發現我必須對我們的旅遊計畫做點改變。我們本來打算在名古屋搭的列車，明年會在不同的時間出發，時間會早超過半小時。我想要取消我們訂的票，並且選擇比較晚的列車，因為我那天真的很想在名古屋一家有名的餐廳吃午餐，而我們訂的列車新的出發時間沒辦法容許有足夠的時間吃午餐。請在今天告訴我你的

想法，因為我想要親自去售票窗口，並且問他們有沒有時間比較晚的列車車票。

我很期待兩週後在這裡看到你，我也希望你在我們的旅行之前和你在加拿大的家人過得愉快。

凱莉

雙篇文章
對照題組

信件

人物與
事物介紹

日常與
休閒生活

文化與
娛樂

資訊與
科技

健康與
自然環境

社會現象
討論

解答篇

Q1 _____ *B*

What is the main purpose of Carrie's email?

（凱莉的電子郵件主要的目的是什麼？）

（A）To remind Mark to prepare for their trip

（為了提醒馬克為他們的旅行做準備）

▶（B）To ask Mark's opinion about canceling tickets

（為了詢問馬克對於取消車票的意見）

（C）To let Mark know which train they are going to take

（為了讓馬克知道他們要搭哪班列車）

（D）To say Merry Christmas to Mark's family

（為了向馬克的家人說聖誕快樂）

▶ 解析 首先看到電子郵件的主旨是「Change to our travel plan」（對我們旅遊計畫的變更），內容大部分在說因為明年列車時間變更的關係，所以想要取消車票並且選擇比較晚的列車，並且要求馬克「Please tell me how you think today」（請在今天告訴我你的想法），所以（B）是正確答案。

Q2 _____ *C*

Which train did Carrie and Mark plan to take?

（凱莉和馬克本來預計搭哪班列車？）

（A）Train 17644（列車 17644）

（B）Train 22403（列車 22403）

▶（C）Train 16127（列車 16127）

（D）Train 25738（列車 25738）

287

▶ 解析　在電子郵件中，凱莉提到「that will be over half an hour earlier」，表示新的出發時間比原本早超過半小時，後面又提到「the new departure time... doesn't allow enough time for lunch」，表示變成新的時間之後，就沒有足夠的時間在名古屋吃午餐。對照公告中的表格，可知時間提早超過半小時，而且接近中午的 16127 是他們本來要搭的車，所以（C）是正確答案。

Q3　　*A*

According to the articles, which of the following is true?
（根據這兩篇文章，以下哪一項是正確的？）

▶（A）Carrie is living in Japan.（凱莉現在住在日本。）

　（B）Carrie and Mark will celebrate New Year's Day in Japan.
　　　（凱莉和馬克會在日本慶祝元旦。）

　（C）Carrie wants to cancel train tickets online.
　　　（凱莉想要在網路上取消列車車票。）

　（D）Carrie will not be able to cancel tickets after tomorrow.
　　　（凱莉在明天之後將無法取消車票。）

▶ 解析　必須逐一對照文章中和選項相關的內容，才能判斷答案，同時也要注意凱莉寄信的日期是 12 月 25 日。和（A）相關的部分是電子郵件中的「I want to go to the ticket window myself」（我想要親自去售票窗口），而且寄信的日期就是車站退票截止日期的前一天，再加上最後一段提到 seeing you here，顯示凱莉人應該在日本，所以（A）是正確答案。和（B）相關的部分是電子郵件中的「I look forward to seeing you here in two weeks, and I hope you have a good time with your family in Canada before our trip.」，顯示未來兩週馬克會在加拿大，所以他元旦不會在日本。和（C）相關的部分是電子郵件中的「I want to go to the ticket window myself」，不符合選項內容。和（D）相關的部分是公告最後的部分，提到 12 月 26 日截止車站退票，12 月 31 日截止網路退票，所以即使過了明天還是能在網路退票，不符合選項內容。

雙篇文章
對照題組

信件

人物與
事物介紹

日常與
休閒生活

文化與
娛樂

資訊與
科技

健康與
自然環境

社會現象
討論

解答篇

Dear Joanna,

Sorry I haven't written to you for a while. Recently I stay in the library until 9:30 every evening because I have a final exam coming up next week. I feel a lot of stress, but I have to focus on my study. That's why I study in the library rather than in my room. Actually, I had a part-time job, and the pay was not bad, but I found that I had no time to study with that job. I think getting a college degree is the most important thing for me, so I quit the job last month, and I'm glad I made that decision.

I'll get back to you when the school is out. By then we can talk about our trip to the south of Taiwan. I can't wait to go to the sea! Also, I'll remember to bring my sun cream so I don't get burned again.

Sincerely,
Janet

單字解釋：

library（n.）圖書館　　　　final exam 期末考

stress（n.）壓力　　　　　focus（v.）專注

part-time job 兼職工作　　college degree 大學學位

quit a job 辭職　　　　　get back to 之後再寫信給某人

school is out 學期結束

親愛的喬安娜：

　　抱歉我有一陣子沒寫信給妳了。最近我每天晚上在圖書館待到 9:30，因為我下星期有期末考。我覺得壓力很大，但我必學專注在學習上。這就是我在圖書館而不是在房間裡讀書的原因。事實上，我以前有兼職工作，而且薪水不差，但我發覺自己有那份工作就沒時間讀書。我認為取得大學學位對我而言是最重要的事，所以我上個月離職了，我很高興自己做了這個決定。

　　學期結束之後，我會再寫信給妳。到時候我們可以談談去台灣南部的旅行。我等不及要去海邊了！還有，我也會記得帶我的防曬霜，好讓我不會再被曬傷。

誠摯地
珍娜

Q1 ___*B*___

What is this letter mainly about?

（這封信主要是關於什麼？）

（A）Janet's study plan（珍娜的讀書計畫）

► （B）Janet's recent life（珍娜最近的生活）

（C）Janet's job（珍娜的工作）

（D）Janet's travel experience（珍娜的旅遊經驗）

　▶ 解析　信件的開頭提到「Recently, I...」，交代了最近為了準備考試而在圖書館讀書的情況，之後又提到「I quit the job last month」，表示上個月辭掉了兼職工作，所以（B）是正確答案。其他選項都不能概括描述第一段的主要內容。

Q2 ___*B*___

Who most likely is Janet?

（珍娜最有可能是什麼人？）

（A）A teacher（老師）

雙篇文章

對照題組

信件

人物與事物介紹

日常與休閒生活

文化與娛樂

資訊與科技

健康與自然環境

社會現象討論

解答篇

► （B）A student（學生）

（C）A library worker（圖書館員工）

（D）A part-time worker（兼職員工）

▶ 解析 從信件中的 I have a final exam（我有期末考）、I have to focus on my study（我必須專注在學習上）、getting a college degree is the most important thing for me（取得大學學位對我而言是最重要的事）等內容，可以確定珍娜是學生，所以（B）是正確答案。雖然內容提到她做過兼職工作，但因為問句是現在式，所以（D）不對。

Q3 _____ C _____

About Janet, which of the following is NOT true?

（關於珍娜，以下何者不正確？）

（A）She is worried about the tests she is going to take.

（她對於自己要考的試感到擔心。）

（B）She works hard in her studies.（她很努力學習。）

► （C）She enjoys working and studying at the same time.

（她很享受同時工作和學習。）

（D）She will have fun at the beach on her trip.

（她旅行時會在海邊玩耍。）

▶ 解析 必須對照和每個選項相關的內容，才能判斷答案。和（A）相關的部分是「I have a final exam coming up next week. I feel a lot of stress」，表示因為考試而壓力很大，符合選項敘述。和（B）相關的部分是「I stay in the library until 9:30 every evening」和「I study in the library」，表示每天晚上在圖書館讀書，符合選項敘述。和（C）相關的部分是「I found that I had no time to study with that job」，表示有工作就很難同時學習，不符合選項敘述，所以（C）是正確答案。和（D）相關的部分是「I can't wait to go to the sea」，表示會去海邊，符合選項敘述。

To: Hans Peters <hanpeter@kimochimail.com>
From: Sandra Peters <sandrapeters@aonlinemail.com>
Date: August 8
Subject: Thank you!

Dear Uncle Hans and Aunt Bertha,

Thank you for your present for me. Yesterday when I came home from school, Mom said happy birthday to me and showed me a package, saying that it's a gift from you. It was a small package, and I didn't expect it to be something special. When I opened it, however, I couldn't believe my eyes! It was the set of 36 colored pencils that I have always wanted! Mom explained that she told you about my hobby of drawing, and that's why you decided to give me the gift I dream of. I really can't thank you enough.

With the new set of colored pencils, I believe I'll love drawing even more. I plan to draw a picture of you two, so I can give it to you on Uncle Hans' birthday next month. See you then!

Love,
Sandra

單字解釋：

present（n.）禮物　　　　　package（n.）包裹

gift（n.）禮物	colored pencil 色鉛筆
hobby（n.）嗜好	draw（v.）畫畫

收件者：漢斯・彼得斯 <hanpeter@kimochimail.com>
寄件者：珊卓・彼得斯 <sandrapeters@aonlinemail.com>
日期：8月8日
主旨：謝謝！

親愛的漢斯叔叔和貝莎阿姨：

謝謝你們送給我的禮物。昨天我放學回到家的時候，媽媽對我說生日快樂，並且給我看一個包裹，說是你們送的禮物。那是個小包裹，我並不期待那會是什麼特別的東西。但當我打開的時候，我不敢相信自己的眼睛！是我一直想要的 36 色鉛筆組！媽媽解釋說，她把我畫畫的嗜好告訴了你們，而那就是你們決定送我夢想禮物的原因。我真的感激不盡。

有了新一套的色鉛筆，我相信我會更愛畫畫。我打算畫你們兩個的圖畫，這樣下個月漢斯叔叔生日的時候我就可以送給你們。到時候見！

愛你們
珊卓

Q1 _A_

Why does Sandra write this email to her uncle and aunt?
（珊卓為什麼寫這封電子郵件給她的叔叔和阿姨？）

▶ （A）To thank them for a birthday gift
（為了感謝他們的生日禮物）

（B）To tell them about the kind of gift she wants
（為了告訴他們自己想要的禮物種類）

（C）To talk about her hobby of drawing
（為了談論她畫畫的嗜好）

（D）To invite them home next month

雙篇文章 對照題組

信件

人物與 事物介紹

日常與 休閒生活

文化與 娛樂

資訊與 科技

健康與 自然環境

社會現象 討論

解答篇

中文翻譯

（為了邀請他們下個月到家裡來）

解析 信件主旨就提到「Thank you」，內文第一句也說「Thank you for your present for me」，而從後面的內容可以得知叔叔和阿姨送了珊卓生日禮物，所以（A）是正確答案。信件最後雖然提到下個月見面，但不知道會在哪裡見面，所以不能選（D）。

Q2 ___*C*___

Which of the following words best describes Sandra's feeling after she opened the package?

（以下哪個單字最能描述珊卓打開包裹之後的感覺？）

（A）Curious（好奇的）

（B）Nervous（緊張的）

► （C）Surprised（驚訝的）

（D）Confused（困惑的）

解析 「When I opened it, however, I couldn't believe my eyes!」的部分顯示，禮物的內容讓珊卓不敢相信自己所看到的，後面也提到這正好是珊卓一直想要的東西，所以（C）是正確答案。

Q3 ___*C*___

According to the email, which of the following is true?

（根據電子郵件，以下何者正確？）

（A）Sandra's birthday is on August 8.

（珊卓的生日在 8 月 8 日。）

（B）Sandra did not have any colored pencil before.

（珊卓以前完全沒有色鉛筆。）

► （C）Sandra's mother knows what she wants as a gift.

（珊卓的媽媽知道她想要什麼當作生日禮物。）

（D）Sandra started to love drawing after receiving the gift.

（珊卓在收到禮物之後開始喜歡畫畫。）

解析 必須對照和每個選項相關的內容，才能判斷答案。和

雙篇文章

對照題組

信件

人物與
事物介紹

日常與
休閒生活

文化與
娛樂

資訊與
科技

健康與
自然環境

社會現象
討論

解答篇

（A）相關的部分是寄件日期「August 8」和「Yesterday... Mom said happy birthday to me」，所以珊卓的生日是 8 月 7 日才對。至於選項（B），雖然文中提到收到想要的 36 色鉛筆，但無法依此判斷以前是不是沒有色鉛筆。和（C）相關的部分是「she [Mom] told you about my hobby of drawing, and that's why you decided to give me the gift I dream of.」，表示媽媽跟叔叔、阿姨說珊卓的嗜好是畫畫，也使得他們送出珊卓夢想的禮物，從這裡可以推斷媽媽知道珊卓夢想的禮物是什麼，並且告訴了叔叔和阿姨，所以（C）是正確答案。和（D）相關的部分是「I'll love drawing even more」，表示以前喜歡畫畫，未來會更喜歡，而不是以前沒喜歡過畫畫的意思，不符合選項敘述。

TOPIC 2 QUIZ 3

To: Christine Weston <ChristineWeston@cityuniv.edu>
From: Sandy Wong <SandyWong@cityuniv.edu>
Date: December 22
Subject: Re: Christmas Party

Dear Christine,

Thank you for inviting me, but I am sorry that I cannot make it to your Christmas dinner party. I am very busy these days since my parents are coming to America, and I have to show them around. I really wish I could go, as you are such a good cook. I hope I can go to your party sometime soon.

By the way, do you know that Chinese New Year is similar

to Christmas in western countries? During Chinese New Year, we also have a week of holidays, and we get together with our relatives—just like you do during Christmas week. However, Chinese New Year is not a holiday in America, which means I cannot go back to Hong Kong then. And that is why my parents come to see me earlier.

After all, thank you for inviting me in the first place!

Best wishes,
Sandy

單字解釋：
make it to 能夠參加
show someone around 帶某人四處遊覽
western countries 西方國家　　　　**relative**（n.）親戚

收件者：克莉斯汀・威斯頓 <ChristineWeston@cityuniv.edu>
寄件者：珊蒂・王 <SandyWong@cityuniv.edu>
日期：12 月 22 日
主旨：回覆：耶誕派對

親愛的克莉斯汀：

謝謝妳邀請我，但很抱歉我沒辦法參加妳的耶誕晚餐派對。我這陣子很忙，因為我爸媽要來美國，而我必須帶他們四處遊覽。我真的很希望自己能去派對，因為妳是很好的廚師。希望我不久之後可以參加妳的派對。

對了，妳知道華人的新年就類似西方國家的耶誕節嗎？在新年期間，我們也有一週的假日，而我們會和我們的親戚相聚——就像你們在耶誕節週所做的一樣。不過，華人的新年在美國不是假日，這意味著我不能在那時候回香

雙篇文章 對照題組

信件

人物與 事物介紹

日常與 休閒生活

文化與 娛樂

資訊與 科技

健康與 自然環境

社會現象 討論

解答篇

港。這就是我爸媽要早一點來看我的原因。

不管怎樣，還是感謝妳一開始邀請了我！

祝福妳
珊蒂

Q1 _A_

What is the purpose of this email?

（這封電子郵件的目的是什麼？）

► （A）To refuse an invitation（拒絕邀請）
（B）To accept an invitation（接受邀請）
（C）To introduce Sandy's parents（介紹珊蒂的父母）
（D）To introduce Chinese New Year（介紹華人的新年）

▶️**解析** 開頭的「Thank you for inviting me, but I am sorry that I cannot make it to your Christmas dinner party.」就表明了寫信的目的，是要表達自己沒辦法參加耶誕派對，所以（A）是正確答案。第一段後面出現的「I really wish I could go」，請注意 wish 後面接過去式是表達和現在事實相反，也就是「雖然很希望去，但我不能去」，而不是會去派對的意思。

Q2 _C_

What is Sandy busy preparing for?

（珊蒂現在忙著準備什麼？）

（A）A Christmas party（耶誕派對）
（B）Chinese New Year（華人新年）
► （C）Hosting her parents（接待爸媽）
（D）Returning to Hong Kong（回香港）

▶️**解析** 提到 busy 的句子是第一段的「I am very busy these days, since my parents are coming to America, and I have to show them around」，表示忙碌的原因是爸媽要來美國，所以（C）是正確答案。host 當動詞時，是「主人接待客人」的意

思。

Q3　　_C_

Why does Sandy write about Chinese New Year?

（為什麼珊蒂寫到關於華人新年的事情？）

（A）To make Christine feel closer to her

（為了讓克莉斯汀感覺和她更親近）

（B）To show the difference between cultures

（為了顯示文化之間的不同）

►（C）To explain why her parents are going to see her

（為了說明她父母要去見她的理由）

（D）To complain about not having holidays during Chinese New Year（為了抱怨華人新年沒有放假）

🔘**解析**　第二段介紹華人新年和耶誕節的相似處，包括會和家人團聚之後，提到華人新年在美國不是假日，所以那個時候不能回香港，而最後結論是「And that is why my parents come to see me earlier.」，表示因為不能在華人新年團聚，所以爸媽選擇早一點去美國和珊蒂見面。所以，之所以提到華人新年，最終是為了要解釋（C）這一點。

TOPIC 2　QUIZ　4

Dear Grandma and Grandpa,

　　Mom says we are going back to Texas and spend summer vacation there, so I am going to see you soon. I remember last winter I had a great time visiting you, and I am so excited about feeding chickens and milking cows again. My friends were so jealous when they saw the pictures of me during my last visit. They kept asking me if I

雙篇文章
對照題組

信件

人物與
事物介紹

日常與
休閒生活

文化與
娛樂

資訊與
科技

健康與
自然環境

社會現象
討論

解答篇

was afraid when I rode the horse. I told them I was a bit scared at first, but since you said practice makes perfect, I kept trying and became familiar with horse riding. This summer I want to have more chances to practice, and I hope to become an expert like Grandpa.

Also, we will take the dog we recently adopted there. He is called "Mylo", and he likes to play with other dogs, so I believe he will make some friends there. I cannot wait to see him running freely with his friends on the open field!

Yours truly,
Henry

單字解釋：

feed（v.）餵   milk（v.）擠奶
jealous（adj.）嫉妒的，羨慕的   practice makes perfect 熟能生巧
familiar（adj.）熟悉的   expert（n.）專家
adopt（v.）領養

親愛的爺爺奶奶：

　　媽媽說我們要回德州過暑假，所以我很快就會見到你們了。我記得上個冬天拜訪你們的時候過得很愉快，我也對於再去餵雞、擠牛奶感到很興奮。我的朋友們看到我上次拜訪的照片時很羨慕。他們一直問我騎馬的時候是不是很害怕。我告訴他們自己一開始有點怕，但因為你們說熟能生巧，所以我持續嘗試，而變得熟悉騎馬了。今年夏天我想要有更多機會練習，也希望成為像爺爺一樣的專家。

　　還有，我們會帶最近領養的狗過去。他叫「麥羅」，他喜歡和其他狗一起玩，所以我相信他會在那裡交到一些朋友。我等不及要看他和朋友一起在開闊的原野自由奔跑了！

你真誠的

亨利

Q1 ___*A*___

What is the main purpose that Henry writes this letter to his grandparents?

（亨利寫這封信給祖父母的主要目的是什麼？）

► （A）To let them know he is going to visit them

（為了讓他們知道他要去拜訪他們）

（B）To describe the fun of playing with animals

（為了描述和動物一起玩耍的樂趣）

（C）To thank them for encouraging him to keep trying

（為了感謝他們鼓勵他持續嘗試）

（D）To introduce his dog Mylo to them

（為了介紹他的狗麥羅給他們）

▶ 解析 信件的主要目的往往會寫在開頭的第一句，而這封信的第一句是告知要回德州過暑假，所以很快會見到祖父母，由此可知（A）是正確答案。

Q2 ___*A*___

Who is Henry's grandfather most likely to be?

（亨利的爺爺最有可能是什麼人？）

► （A）A farm owner（農場主人）

（B）A pet shop owner（寵物店店主）

（C）A zoo keeper（動物園飼養員）

（D）A meat store owner（肉店店主）

▶ 解析 從亨利可以在祖父母那邊餵雞、擠牛奶、騎馬、讓狗在原野奔跑這些線索來看，祖父母應該有一座農場，所以（A）是正確答案。

Q3 ___*D*___

According to the letter, which of following is true?

300

（根據這封信，以下何者正確？）

（A）Henry has not tried feeding chickens before.
（亨利以前沒有試過餵雞。）

（B）The pictures Henry showed his friends are all taken by himself.（亨利給朋友看的照片都是他自己拍的。）

（C）Henry is now an expert of horse riding.
（亨利現在是騎馬的專家了。）

► （D）Henry's grandparents have some dogs.
（亨利的祖父母有一些狗。）

▶ 解析 必須對照文章中和每個選項相關的內容，才能判斷答案。和（A）相關的部分是「feeding chickens… again」，既然是再次餵雞，就表示以前曾經餵過，所以不符合選項的敘述。（B）在文中沒有提到，也請注意文中的「pictures of me」是指「畫面上有我的照片」，而不是指「我拍的照片」。和（C）相關的部分是「I hope to become an expert」，因為是想要成為專家，所以現在還不是專家，不符合選項敘述。和（D）相關的部分是「he likes to play with other dogs, so I believe he will make some friends there」，這裡的 friends 是指其他的狗，由此可知亨利的祖父母那邊有一些狗，所以（D）是正確答案。

TOPIC 2 QUIZ 5

雙篇文章
對照題組

信件

人物與
事物介紹

日常與
休閒生活

文化與
娛樂

資訊與
科技

健康與
自然環境

社會現象
討論

解答篇

Dear Martha,

I want to share some good news with you. I have been selected to enter the English speech contest! The teacher said I speak really good English. I told him I used to talk in English with a friend from Canada, so my English improved a lot. You know I was talking about you! After you moved back to Canada last year, however, I have much less opportunity to speak English. Not only that, but I also miss when we met at your home and chatted about fashion, boys, and school work on Sunday afternoons. I wish you could live in Taiwan longer, but I understand that your father always wanted to go back to his home country, and that is why you had to leave.

I believe you have already made a lot of friends there, for you are such a nice person, but please remember that you will always be my best friend.

Miss you,
Clair

單字解釋：

select（v.）選擇　　　　　　enter a contest 參加比賽
improve（v.）改善　　　　　　opportunity（n.）機會
chat（v.）聊天　　　　　　　home country 母國

親愛的瑪莎：

　　我想跟妳分享一個好消息。我被選上參加英語演講比賽了！老師說我英語說得很好。我告訴他自己以往會和來自加拿大的朋友用英語交談，所以我的英語進步了很多。妳知道我說的是妳！但在妳去年搬回加拿大之後，我說英語的機會就少了很多。不僅如此，我也想念我們每個禮拜日下午在妳家見面聊時尚、男孩子和學業的時候。我很希望妳能住在台灣久一點，但我了解妳爸爸一直想回到母國，而那就是妳必須離開的原因。

　　我相信妳已經在那裡交了許多朋友，因為妳是很好的人，但請記得妳永遠會是我最好的朋友。

想念妳

克萊兒

雙篇文章對照題組

信件

人物與事物介紹

日常與休閒生活

文化與娛樂

資訊與科技

健康與自然環境

社會現象討論

解答篇

Q1 _____C_____

What does Clair want to express in her letter?

（克萊兒在信中想要表達什麼？）

（A）She feels sad that Martha is going back to Canada.

（她對於瑪莎將要回加拿大感到難過。）

（B）She wants to practice English more often.

（她想要更常練習英語。）

▶（C）She misses Martha very much.（她非常想念瑪莎。）

（D）It is easy to make friends with Martha.

（和瑪莎交朋友很容易。）

解析 第一段中間提到「I... miss when we...」，表示很想念以前和瑪莎在一起的時候，後面又說很希望瑪莎能住在台灣久一點，這些內容都表達了對瑪莎的想念，所以（C）是正確答案。請注意文章內容說瑪莎去年已經搬回加拿大，所以說瑪莎「將要回加拿大」的選項（A）是錯的。

Q2 _____B_____

What might Martha write when she replies to this letter?

（瑪莎回覆這封信的時候，可能會寫什麼？）

（A）"I am sorry."（我很抱歉。）

▶（B）"Congratulations!"（恭喜！）

（C）"You are welcome!"（不客氣！）

（D）"Never mind."（那就算了。）

解析 因為克萊兒在信件開頭提到自己獲選參加英語演講比賽，所以（B）是瑪莎可能回覆的內容。瑪莎回到加拿大並不是犯了什麼錯，所以不太可能使用表示道歉的「I am sorry」。如果要回應克萊兒想念她的心情，應該會說「I miss you so much, too」。

303

Q3 ___*D*___

According to the letter, which of the following is true?

（根據這封信，以下何者正確？）

（A）Clair won a prize in the speech contest.

（克萊兒在演講比賽得了獎。）

（B）Clair and Martha were classmates.

（克萊兒和瑪莎曾經是同班同學。）

（C）Martha cannot speak Chinese.（瑪莎不會說中文。）

►（D）Martha's father is from Canada.

（瑪莎的爸爸來自加拿大。）

▶ 解析　必須對照文章中和每個選項相關的內容，才能判斷答案。（A）、（B）、（C）在文章中沒有提到。和（D）相關的部分是「you moved back to Canada」和「your father always wanted to go back to his home country, and that is why you had to leave」，從這兩個部分可以推斷克萊兒的爸爸是加拿大人，所以（D）是正確答案。

"How dare you!" shouted Greta Thunberg, a teenage girl from Sweden, at the 2019 UN Climate Action Summit in New York. By openly expressing her anger toward governments that fail to protect the Earth, she became known around the world.

At the age of eleven, Thunberg developed an interest in the protection of environment after watching a video about climate change in class. She was shocked that some animals are dying because of human activities that make the Earth warmer every year. She was so sad that she stopped talking, and she was nearly sent to a hospital because she ate very little.

After that, Thunberg gave up school to call for stronger action on climate change, and over one million students joined her and took part in "school strike for climate" in their own countries. It is without doubt that she has made the younger generation more aware of the importance of protecting the environment.

單字解釋：

shout（v.）呼喊　　　　　　express（v.）表達
anger（n.）憤怒　　　　　　government（n.）政府
protection（n.）保護　　　　environment（n.）環境
climate change 氣候變遷　　shocked（adj.）感到震驚的
call for 呼籲　　　　　　　strike（n.）罷工，罷課
generation（n.）世代　　　　aware（adj.）意識到的
importance（n.）重要性

雙篇文章對照題組
信件
人物與事物介紹
日常與休閒生活
文化與娛樂
資訊與科技
健康與自然環境
社會現象討論
解答篇

中文翻譯

　　「你們竟敢這樣！」在 2019 年紐約的聯合國氣候行動峰會上，來自丹麥的少女格蕾塔·通貝里喊叫道。藉著對於無法保護地球的各國政府公開表達她的憤怒，她變成全世界知名的人物。

　　11 歲時，通貝里在課堂上看了關於氣候變遷的影片之後，發展出對於環境保護的興趣。對於一些動物因為讓地球每年越來越暖的人類活動而逐漸死亡，她感到很震驚。她因為難過而停止說話，也因為吃得非常少而差點被送進醫院。

　　在那之後，通貝里為了呼籲對氣候變遷採取更強烈的行動而輟學，而超過一百萬名學生加入她的行列，在各自的國家參加了「為氣候罷課」的活動。毫無疑問，她使得年輕世代更加意識到保護環境的重要性。

Q1 ___*A*___

What is this article mainly about?
（這篇文章主要是關於什麼？）

▶（A）A person who speaks out about climate change
　　　（一個對於氣候變遷坦率說出意見的人）

（B）Some effective ways of stopping climate change
　　　（阻止氣候變遷的一些有效方法）

（C）The importance of school education
　　　（學校教育的重要性）

（D）How to deal with bad feelings and recover
　　　（如何處理壞情緒並且恢復過來）

▶ 解析　整篇文章都在介紹格蕾塔·通貝里這個人，第一段也提到她對於無法保護地球的各國政府公開表達憤怒，所以（A）是正確答案。

Q2 ___*C*___

What did NOT happen after Thunberg watched the video?
（通貝里看了影片之後，沒有發生什麼事？）

（A）She became aware of some negative result of human

雙篇文章
對照題組

信件

人物與
事物介紹

日常與
休閒生活

文化與
娛樂

資訊與
科技

健康與
自然環境

社會現象
討論

解答篇

activities.（她意識到人類活動的某種負面結果。）

（B）She stopped speaking like she usually did.

（她停止像以前一樣說話。）

▶（C）She stopped eating anything.（她不再吃任何東西。）

（D）She stopped going to school.（她不再上學。）

▶️解析　選項（A）對應「She was shocked...」之後的內容，選項（B）對應「she stopped talking」，選項（D）對應「Thunberg gave up school」。文中提到的「she ate very little」是指她吃得非常少，而不是不吃任何東西，所以不符合文章內容的（C）是正確答案。

Q3 ___*D*___

According to this article, what has Thunberg achieved?

（根據這篇文章，通貝里達成了什麼事？）

（A）She became a popular person at her school.

（她在學校裡成為受歡迎的人物。）

（B）She proved that one can learn a lot without going to school.（她證明不上學也能學到很多事情。）

（C）She took part in making laws that help stop climate change.（她參與了幫助阻止氣候變遷的法律制定。）

▶（D）She let many students know it is necessary to protect the Earth.（她讓許多學生知道保護地球是必要的。）

▶️解析　文章的最後提到「she has made the younger generation more aware of the importance of protecting the environment」，表示她讓年輕人更認知到保護環境的重要性，所以（D）是正確答案。

TOPIC 3 QUIZ 2

Have you ever seen people surfing without waves? With

a large power kite, one can fly over water even when there is no wave. Such activity is known as "kiteboarding", one of the most exciting water sports in the world. The idea of kiteboarding first appeared in the 1970s, and with later designs that tried to improve kites and boards, it became easier for people to enjoy the sport. Today, the sport is popular around the world.

To play the sport, you have to practice standing on a surfboard first. And then, you can try controlling a power kite and let the wind pull you through the water. When you have enough skills, you can jump up and show off your moves. Of course, kiteboarding is more dangerous than most water sports, so it would be safer to have a coach who can teach you the basics.

單字解釋：

surf（v.）衝浪 　　　　　power kite（形狀像飛行傘的）動力風箏
*kiteboarding（n.）風箏衝浪　design（n.）設計
improve（v.）改善　　　　*surfboard（n.）衝浪板
coach（n.）教練

你看過有人在沒有浪的情況下衝浪嗎？靠著大型的動力風箏，人可以在沒有浪的情況下在水上飛躍。這種活動稱為「風箏衝浪」，是世界上最刺激的水上運動之一。風箏衝浪的想法一開始出現在 1970 年代，而靠著之後試圖改良風箏與板子的設計，使得人們能更容易享受這種運動。現在，這種運動在全世界都很流行。

要玩這種運動，你必須先練習站在衝浪板上。然後，你可以試著控制動力風箏，讓風拉著你在水上行進。當你有足夠的技術時，你可以往上跳並炫耀你的動作。當然，動力風箏比大部分的水上運動危險，所以有能夠教你基礎的教練會比較安全。

Q1 ＿＿*C*＿＿

What is the main purpose of this article?

（這篇文章的主要目的是什麼？）

（A）To introduce the complete history of kiteboarding

（為了介紹風箏衝浪的完整歷史）

（B）To teach its readers how to be an excellent kiteboarder

（為了教讀者如何成為優秀的風箏衝浪玩家）

►（C）To let its readers have some basic ideas about kiteboarding （為了讓讀者對於風箏衝浪有些基本的概念）

（D）To show that kiteboarding is a dangerous sport

（為了顯示風箏衝浪是一項危險的運動）

▶解析 文章中稍微提到了風箏衝浪的歷史和學習方式，但都不是很詳細的介紹，所以（C）是最恰當的答案。

Q2 ___*B*___

According to the article, what do we know about those who can do kiteboarding?

（根據這篇文章，我們對於能夠風箏衝浪的人知道些什麼？）

（A）They should learn to design boards.

（他們應該要學習設計板子。）

►（B）They can stand on a surfboard.

（他們可以站在衝浪板上。）

（C）They practice flying kites in the park.

（他們在公園練習放風箏。）

（D）They all learned from their coaches.

（他們都是向教練學習。）

▶解析 第二段的開頭提到「To play the sport, you have to practice standing on a surfboard first」，表示學風箏衝浪的人都要先練習站在衝浪板上，可見能風箏衝浪的人應該都能站在衝浪板上，所以（B）是正確答案。

Q3 ___*C*___

About kiteboarding, which of the following is true?

雙篇文章
對照題組

信件

人物與事物介紹

日常與休閒生活

文化與娛樂

資訊與科技

健康與自然環境

社會現象討論

解答篇

（關於風箏衝浪，以下何者正確？）

（A）It is possible to do it without wind.

（可以在沒有風的情況下進行。）

（B）It was popular in the 1970s.（在 1970 年代很流行。）

▶（C）First kites and boards were different from today.

（一開始的風箏跟板子和現在不一樣。）

（D）It requires a boat to pull a board on water.

（需要船在水上拉動板子。）

🅓 解析 必須對照文中和各選項相關的內容，才能判斷答案。（A）、（B）在文中沒有提到。和（C）相關的部分是「later designs that tried to improve kites and boards」，表示後來有一些設計改善了風箏和板子，可見過去的風箏跟板子和現在不一樣，所以（C）是正確答案。和（D）相關的部分是「you can try controlling a power kite and let the wind pull you through the water」，表示是藉由控制動力風箏，讓風拉著人前進，而沒有提到用船拉板子，所以不符合選項內容。

TOPIC 3 QUIZ 3

In times of COVID-19, when most people were not free to go to foreign countries, a special tour group going "nowhere" showed up at Taipei Songshan Airport. The event they went for, which was planned by the airport, was called "pretend to go abroad" airport tour. Just like taking an international flight, those who took this tour checked in, got their boarding passes, and even got on the plane. The only difference was that the plane did not take off at all. Even though it was not a real flight, those who took part in were still happy that they got a taste of traveling.

Because of this successful event, some airlines even

offered "flights to nowhere". They not only let passengers get on the planes, but they actually let the planes fly before going back to the original airport. These flights were popular, too, and they became an extra source of income for airlines in the difficult times.

單字解釋：

*COVID-19（n.）2019年冠狀病毒疾病
international flight 國際航班
take off 起飛
airline（n.）航空公司
income（n.）收入

tour group 旅行團
boarding pass 登機證
get a taste of 體驗到
source（n.）來源

　　在2019年冠狀病毒疾病流行，大部分的人無法自由出國的時期，有個「不去任何地方」的特別旅行團出現在台北松山機場。他們要去的這場由機場規劃的活動，叫做「偽出國」機場體驗旅遊。就像搭乘國際航班一樣，參加這次旅遊的人會辦理報到手續、取得登機證，甚至搭上飛機。唯一的不同是飛機並沒有起飛。儘管這不是一趟真正的飛行，但參加的人還是很高興能體驗旅遊的感覺。

　　因為這場成功的活動，一些航空公司甚至提供「不去任何地方的航班」。他們不僅讓乘客搭上飛機，還實際讓飛機飛行，再回到原來的機場。這些航班也很受歡迎，也成為航空公司在艱困時期的額外收入來源。

Q1 ___A___

Who invented the "pretend to go abroad" tour?

（是誰發明了「偽出國」旅行？）

▶（A）An airport（一座機場）

（B）A tour company（一家旅行社）

（C）Some airlines（一些航空公司）

（D）Some travel lovers（一些旅遊愛好者）

解析　「The event... was planned by the airport」的部分顯

雙篇文章
對照題組
信件
人物與
事物介紹
日常與
休閒生活
文化與
娛樂
資訊與
科技
健康與
自然環境
社會現象
討論
解答篇

示，是機場規劃了這個活動，所以（A）是正確答案。航空公司的活動是後來才推出，所以不能說是「發明」。

Q2 _C_

What could the passengers NOT do during the airport tour?

（在機場旅遊活動中，乘客不能做什麼？）

（A）Get their boarding passes（取得登機證）

（B）Board the plane（搭上飛機）

▶（C）Fly in the air（在空中飛行）

（D）Feel like they were traveling（感覺像在旅行）

解析 第一段後半提到「got their boarding passes」、「got on the plane」、「they got a taste of traveling」，分別對應（A）、（B）、（D）。關於（C）的部分是「the plane did not take off at all」，表示飛機沒有起飛，所以（C）是正確答案。

Q3 _C_

Which of the following is the main idea of this article?

（這篇文章的中心思想是什麼？）

（A）"Pretend to go abroad" tour cannot take the place of real flights.（「偽出國」旅遊不能取代真正的航班。）

（B）It is easier to pretend going abroad than really flying to other countries.（假裝出國比真正飛到其他國家容易。）

▶（C）Pretending to go abroad was a popular way of experiencing travel.

（假裝出國曾經是一種受歡迎的體驗旅遊方式。）

（D）There are only a few things we can do while pretending to go abroad.

（在假裝出國的時候，我們只有很少的事情可以做。）

解析 雖然四個選項看起來都是事實，但因為題目問的是文章要表達的想法，所以必須掌握文章內容才能作答。文章中分別介紹了機場體驗旅遊和不飛到任何目的地的航班，並且給予「those who took part in were still happy that they got a taste of traveling」、「These flights were popular」、「they became an extra source of income」等正面的結論，所以提到這類行程受歡迎的（C）是正確答案。文中並沒有比較假裝出國和真正出國的容易程度，所以不能選（B）。

雙篇文章
對照題組

信件

人物與
事物介紹

日常與
休閒生活

文化與
娛樂

資訊與
科技

健康與
自然環境

社會現象
討論

解答篇

A growing number of married couples choose not to have children. Because of long working hours, many of them feel it is impossible to take care of children all the time. They also worry about losing their own freedom after becoming parents. Therefore, more and more couples decide to have pets but not children.

There are some reasons for them to prefer pets over children. Pets can stay home alone when their "parents" go to work or go out with friends, while little children cannot. What is more, some people think that pets always make them happy, while children can make them feel a lot of stress sometimes.

It is interesting to note that, according to a study, married couples without children spend more money on their pets than any other kind of family does. The finding suggests that such couples treat their pets just like their kids. Even without children, they still need someone they can take care of.

單字解釋：

a growing number of 越來越多的	married couple 已婚夫婦
working hour 工作時間	freedom（n.）自由
prefer A over B 偏好 A 勝過 B	stress（n.）壓力
note（v.）注意	finding（n.）研究結果
suggest（v.）暗示	treat（v.）對待

　　有越來越多已婚夫婦選擇不生小孩。因為很長的工作時間，在他們之中有許多人覺得不可能隨時照顧小孩。他們也擔心在成為父母之後失去自己的自由。所以，越來越多伴侶決定養寵物而不是小孩。

　　他們偏好寵物勝過小孩有一些理由。寵物可以在「爸媽」（指主人）上

班或者和朋友外出時獨自待在家裡，而年紀小的小孩不行。而且，有些人覺得寵物總是讓他們快樂，而小孩有時候會讓他們感受到很大的壓力。

有趣的是，根據一項研究，沒有小孩的已婚夫婦在寵物身上花的錢比其他類型的家庭都要多。這個研究結果暗示這類伴侶對待寵物就像自己的小孩一樣。就算沒有小孩，他們還是需要可以照顧的對象。

雙篇文章
對照題組

信件

人物與
事物介紹

日常與
休閒生活

文化與
娛樂

資訊與
科技

健康與
自然環境

社會現象
討論

解答篇

Q1 ___*D*___

What is NOT a reason that some couples choose to have pets but not children?

（何者不是某些伴侶選擇養寵物而不是小孩的原因？）

（A）They have to spend a lot of time working.

（他們必須花很多時間工作。）

（B）They are afraid that they will not be free to do things they want.（他們害怕不能自由做想做的事。）

（C）Pets do not always need someone by their side.

（寵物並不是隨時都需要有人在身邊。）

▶（D）Pets will not make troubles like children do.

（寵物不會像小孩一樣製造麻煩。）

▶解析 必須對照和每個選項相關的內容，才能判斷答案。和（A）相關的部分是「long working hours」，和（B）相關的部分是「They also worry about losing their own freedom」，和（C）相關的部分是「Pets can stay home alone」。選項（D）在文章中沒有提到，所以（D）是正確答案。

Q2 ___*B*___

According to the article, what can pets do for their owners?

（根據這篇文章，寵物可以為主人做什麼？）

（A）They can go to work for their owners.

（他們可以為主人去上班。）

▶（B）They can give their owners good feelings.

（他們可以讓主人感覺很好。）

（ C ）They can take care of their owners' children.
（他們可以照顧主人的孩子。）

（ D ）They can help their owners make more money.
（他們可以幫主人賺更多錢。）

▶ 解析　第二段提到「pets... make them happy」，所以意思相近的（B）是正確答案。其他選項在文章裡都沒有提到。

Q3　　*C*

According to the article, which of the following is true?
（根據這篇文章，以下何者正確？）

（ A ）More and more couples are not able to have children.
（越來越多伴侶無法生小孩。）

（ B ）Most couples want to have pets and children at the same time.（大部分伴侶想要同時有寵物和小孩。）

►（ C ）Among all kinds of families, couples without children spend the most on pets.（在所有類型的家庭中，沒有小孩的伴侶花在寵物身上的錢最多。）

（ D ）Those without children do not like to take care of others.
（沒有小孩的人不喜歡照顧別人。）

▶ 解析　選項（A）、（B）、（D）在文章中沒有提到。和選項（C）相關的部分是第三段的「married couples without children spend more money on their pets than any other kind of family does」，表示沒有小孩的伴侶花在寵物身上的錢比其他任何類型的家庭都要多，也就是他們花的錢最多的意思，所以（C）是正確答案。另外也請注意選項（A）的 are not able to have children 是「無法生育小孩」的意思，而不能用來表達「因為情況不允許而選擇不生」。

雙篇文章對照題組

信件

人物與事物介紹

日常與休閒生活

文化與娛樂

資訊與科技

健康與自然環境

社會現象討論

解答篇

Studies show that green plants can improve people's quality of life by making them happy and feel less stress. The reason might be that they make us feel closer to nature. Most of us live in the city and seldom have a chance to go to a forest and enjoy fresh air. However, by adding some plants to our home, we can make the air cleaner and let the touch of leaves calm us down. What is more, a study also points out that people who work in offices with plants are more focused and do their job better.

Besides having positive effects on our mind, house plants are also nice to look at. When decorating your room, just a few plants can add life to a boring space. In fact, plants can also be a key design element of a home. Even though it takes some effort to take care of plants, the advantages are worth the effort.

單字解釋：

improve（v.）改善　　　　quality（n.）品質
calm down 使平靜下來　　point out 指出
focused（adj.）專注的　　positive（adj.）正面的
decorate（v.）裝飾，裝潢　key（adj.）重要的
element（n.）元素　　　　advantage（n.）優點

　　研究顯示，綠色植物能讓人快樂並感受較少的壓力，而藉此改善人們的生活品質。原因可能是綠色植物讓我們感覺比較接近自然。我們大部分的人都生活在城市，很少有機會去森林享受新鮮空氣。不過，藉由在家中增加一些植物，我們可以讓空氣變得比較清潔，並且讓葉子的觸感將我們的心平靜下來。另外，一項研究也指出，在有植物的辦公室工作的人比較專注，工作

表現也比較好。

　　除了對我們的心智有正面影響以外，家中的植物看起來（視覺上）也很棒。在裝飾你的房間時，只要少許植物就能為無聊的空間增添生氣。事實上，植物也可以是家中的重要設計元素。儘管照顧植物需要一些努力，但植物的優點是值得這份努力的。

Q1 ___*B*___

What is this article mainly about?

（這篇文章主要是關於什麼？）

（A）Some studies on plants（一些關於植物的研究）

► （B）Good effects of plants（植物的良好影響）

（C）How to take care of plants（如何照顧植物）

（D）The importance of nature（自然的重要性）

▶**解析**　文章的第一段談論植物在心理上產生的正面影響，第二段則是植物美化居家的功能，所以能概括文章內容的（B）是正確答案。因為第二段和研究結果無關，所以不能選（A）。

Q2 ___*D*___

According to the article, what kind of people might NOT be helped by plants?

（根據這篇文章，哪一種人可能不會受到植物的幫助？）

（A）Those who feel a lot of stress（感覺壓力很大的人）

（B）Those who want to be better at work
　　（想在工作上表現更好的人）

（C）Those who want to make their home more beautiful
　　（想讓自己的家更美的人）

► （D）Those who want to spend less time maintaining their
　　home（想少花一點時間維護自己的家的人）

▶**解析**　文章中的「making them... feel less stress」、「people who work in offices with plants... do their job better」、「just a few plants can add life to a boring space」分別對應選項（A）、（B）、（C）。和選項（D）相關的部分是「it takes some effort

318

to take care of plants」，表示照顧植物需要花些工夫，也就是會讓人多花一點時間來維護居家環境，所以（D）是正確答案。

雙篇文章
對照題組

信件

人物與
事物介紹

日常與
休閒生活

文化與
娛樂

資訊與
科技

健康與
自然環境

社會現象
討論

解答篇

Q3　　__C__

According to the article, which of the following is NOT true?

（根據這篇文章，以下何者不正確？）

（A）Green plants can create fresh air in a space.
（綠色植物可以在空間中製造新鮮空氣。）

（B）Workers in offices with plants pay more attention to their work.（在有植物的辦公室中工作的人，會花比較多注意力在工作上。）

► （C）The advantages of plants are all about our feelings.
（植物的好處全都和我們的情感相關。）

（D）Some people see plants as an important part when they design a home.
（有些人在設計住家時把植物看成重要的一部分。）

▶ 解析　文章中的「make the air cleaner」、「people who work in offices with plants are more focused and do their job better」、「plants can also be a key design element of a home」分別對應選項（A）、（B）、（D）。和選項（C）相關的部分是「Besides having positive effects on our mind, house plants are also nice to look at」，表示除了心智方面的好處以外，植物還有視覺上好看的優點，後面還提到了植物在居家設計方面的重要性，這些並不是全都部和情感相關，所以（C）是正確答案。

TOPIC 4 QUIZ 3

When it comes to winter, we may think of things that

make us happy, such as Christmas holidays or skiing. Some people, however, feel sad and sleepy all the time during winter. Such a situation is called "winter blues". It happens because the days in winter are shorter, and there are less time we see the light of sun, which makes us feel brighter. Winter blues are quite common, and they usually do not last long, but a few people may experience it for the whole season.

To beat winter blues, it is important to receive as much light as possible. During the day, try opening the curtains to let natural light in. Even when the sun is hidden behind the clouds, you can still turn on your desk lamp when you work. Doctors also suggest patients to get up early and sit in front of a lamp for thirty minutes every day. As long as we know the cause of winter blues, it is not hard to deal with it.

單字解釋：

when it comes to 說到…	sleepy（adj.）想睡覺的
bright（adj.）明亮的，明朗的	common（adj.）常見的
experience（v.）經歷	beat（v.）打敗
curtain（n.）窗簾	desk lamp 檯燈
patient（n.）患者	cause（n.）起因
deal with 處理	

說到冬天，我們可能會想到讓我們快樂的事，像是聖誕假日或者滑雪。不過，有些人在冬天總是覺得悲傷、想睡覺。這樣的情況稱為「冬季憂鬱症」。它發生的原因是冬天的白天比較短，我們看到太陽光的時間比較少，而太陽光會讓我們感覺比較開朗。冬季憂鬱症很常見，持續的時間通常不長，但少數人可能整個季節都會經歷冬季憂鬱症。

要克服冬季憂鬱症，儘可能多接收到光是很重要的。在白天的時候，試著把窗簾打開，讓自然光進來。即使是太陽藏在雲背後的時候，還是可以在你工作時打開檯燈。醫師也建議患者每天早起並且坐在燈前面 30 分鐘。只要我們知道冬季憂鬱症的成因，就不難處理了。

雙篇文章
對照題組

信件

人物與
事物介紹

日常與
休閒生活

文化與
娛樂

資訊與
科技

健康與
自然環境

社會現象
討論

解答篇

Q1   *B*

According to the article, what is the main cause of winter blues?

（根據這篇文章，冬季憂鬱症的主要成因是什麼？）

（A）Low temperature（低溫）

► （B）Lack of light（缺少光線）

（C）Negative way of thinking（負面的思考方式）

（D）Getting up too late（太晚起床）

▶ 解析　第一段的「It happens because the days in winter are shorter, and there are less time we see the light of sun」提到，冬季憂鬱症的原因是冬季白天比較短，而我們看到太陽光的時間比較少，所以（B）是正確答案。

Q2   *C*

Which of the following is NOT a way to treat winter blues?

（以下何者不是治療冬季憂鬱症的方式？）

（A）Let the light shine through your window
（讓光透過窗戶照進來）

（B）Use a desk lamp at the place where you work
（在工作的地方使用檯燈）

► （C）Keep the light on in order to wake up early
（讓燈一直開著，好讓自己早點醒來）

（D）Spend some time in the light every morning
（每天早上花一些時間在有光的地方）

▶ 解析　以「To beat winter blues」開頭的第二段，列出了一些克服冬季憂鬱症的方法，其中「opening the curtains to let natural light in」、「turn on your desk lamp when you work」、「get up early and sit in front of a lamp for thirty minutes every day」分別對應選項（A）、（B）、（D）。至於選項（C），雖然文中提到早起，但沒有提到要為了早起而「keep the light on」（讓燈一

直開著），所以（C）是正確答案。

Q3 **_C_**

About winter blues, which of the following is true?

（關於冬季憂鬱症，何者正確？）

（A）People who have this problem cannot enjoy skiing.

（有這個問題的人不能享受滑雪。）

（B）Only a few people have this problem.

（只有少數人有這個問題。）

►（C）This problem can last for several months.

（這個問題可以持續幾個月。）

（D）There is no way to solve this problem.

（這個問題沒有解決的方法。）

▶解析 （A）在文章中沒有提到。和（B）相關的部分是「Winter blues are quite common」，表示很常見，和選項敘述相反。和（C）相關的部分是「a few people may experience it for the whole season」，表示少數人可能整個季節都會有這個問題，符合選項敘述，所以（C）是正確答案。和（D）相關的部分是「it is not hard to deal with it」，表示這個問題不難處理，和選項敘述相反。

雙篇文章
對照題組

信件

人物與
事物介紹

日常與
休閒生活

文化與
娛樂

資訊與
科技

健康與
自然環境

社會現象
討論

解答篇

In early America, it was popular to make a bed cover with pieces of cloth of many colors and shapes. Such bed covers are called "quilts", and they are famous for their colorful patterns. Many women made quilts with friends as a way to spend their free time, and the quilts were nothing but ordinary daily objects.

As time went by, it became cheaper and easier to buy bed covers in stores, so it became rare for people to make quilts. It is lucky, though, that some quilts were passed from parents to children and were not damaged. In the late 1960s, some collectors began collecting these quilts as works of art, and that is when artists began to create quilts as art.

Today, quilt artists use both modern and traditional skills to make their works. Compared to traditional works, quilts today usually have unique designs that reflect an artist's thoughts and experiences, and they are to be appreciated rather than be used.

單字解釋：

bed cover 床罩　　　　　　　　 *quilt（n.）拼布縫製的被子
pattern（n.）花樣　　　　　　　 ordinary（adj.）平凡的
as time went by 隨著時間過去　　 rare（adj.）少見的
collector（n.）收藏者　　　　　　 modern（adj.）現代的
traditional（adj.）傳統的　　　　 unique（adj.）獨特的
reflect（v.）反映　　　　　　　　 thought（n.）想法
appreciate（v.）欣賞

　　在早期的美國，很流行用許多顏色與形狀的布塊製作床罩。這種床罩稱為「拼布」，它們以色彩繽紛的花樣聞名。許多女性會和朋友一起做拼布作為度過空閒時間的方式，而拼布當時就只是平凡的日常物品。

　　隨著時間過去，在店裡買床罩變得更便宜也更簡單，所以人們就變得很少做拼布。但幸運的是，有些拼布從父母傳給了小孩而沒有受損。在 1960 年代晚期，一些收藏家開始收集這些拼布當成藝術品，這時候藝術家也開始製作拼布作為藝術。

　　現在，拼布藝術家會用現代和傳統的技法來製作作品。和傳統作品相比，現在的拼布通常有反映藝術家想法與經驗的獨特設計，而它們是用來欣賞而不是拿來使用的。

Q1 ___*A*___

What is this article mainly about?

（這篇文章主要是關於什麼？）

▶（A）How the meaning of making quilts changed in history
　　　（製作拼布的意義在歷史上如何改變）

（B）How to decide whether quilts are a kind of art
　　　（如何決定拼布是不是一種藝術）

（C）How to make quilts in the right way
　　　（如何用正確的方法做拼布）

（D）How some collectors saved quilts from disappearing
　　　（一些收藏家如何拯救拼布免於消失）

▶ 解析　三段內容分別是拼布的起源、拼布的式微與獲得收藏家重視、現代拼布的意義，所以能夠概括這些內容的（A）是正確答案。

Q2 ___*D*___

What did people in early America think quilts are?

（早期美國的人認為拼布是什麼？）

（A）Works of art（藝術品）

（B）Things to be collected（收藏品）

（C）Tools to express feelings（表達情感的工具）

► （D）Objects to be used in daily life（日常生活中使用的物品）

▶️解析 關於早期美國的敘述在「In early America」開頭的第一段，這一段的最後提到「the quilts were nothing but ordinary daily objects」，表示當時拼布只是平凡的日常物品，所以（D）是正確答案。

Q3 ___*B*___

How are quilts today different from those in the past?

（現代的拼布和過去有什麼不一樣？）

（A）They are not made in old ways at all.

（完全不用舊的方式製作。）

► （B）They show what an artist thinks about.

（展現藝術家的想法。）

（C）They all have similar designs.（全都有類似的設計。）

（D）Most of them are actually used.（大部分是實際使用的。）

▶️解析 關於現代拼布的敘述在「Today」開頭的第三段，其中「use both modern and traditional skills」、「have unique designs」、「they are to be appreciated rather than be used」不符合選項（A）、（C）、（D）的敘述。關於選項（B）的部分是「Compared to traditional works, quilts today usually have unique designs that reflect an artist's thoughts and experiences」，表示和傳統的作品比起來，現代的拼布具有反映藝術家想法與經驗的獨特設計，所以（B）是正確答案。

TOPIC 5 QUIZ 2

When you eat at a restaurant, do you let your camera eat first? In the age of social media, it seems more important to let

對照題組 雙篇文章

信件

事物介紹 人物與

休閒生活 日常與

娛樂 文化與

科技 資訊與

自然環境 健康與

討論 社會現象

解答篇

others know what you are eating than to enjoy its taste. Therefore, people often take photos of their food and share them before feeding themselves.

The rise of food photos have also affected the restaurant industry. Today, a restaurant can suddenly get famous with a widely shared photo of food. Therefore, restaurant owners now pay more attention to the appearance of food. They also improve their lighting so that their food looks better in pictures. Some of them even pay famous social media users to post pictures taken in their restaurants.

Some restaurant owners, however, do not allow their customers to take pictures. They believe a dish should be enjoyed as soon as it is served, or it will get cold and less delicious while the customer is busy taking pictures. They try to remind us that the food itself is more important than the "likes" we get on social media.

單字解釋：

camera（n.）相機　　　　　　age（n.）時代

social media 社群媒體　　　　　feed（v.）餵

rise（n.）興起　　　　　　　　industry（n.）產業

pay attention to 注意　　　　　appearance（n.）外觀

lighting（n.）照明　　　　　　dish（n.）菜餚

serve（v.）上（菜）

當你在餐廳吃東西時，你會讓相機先吃嗎？在社群媒體的時代，讓別人知道你在吃什麼，似乎比享受食物的味道重要。所以，人們經常會在餵飽自己之前先拍食物的照片並且分享（照片）。

食物照片的興起也影響了餐廳業。現在，一間餐廳可能因為一張受到廣為分享的照片而突然變得有名。所以，餐廳老闆現在會更注意食物的外觀。他們也會改善照明，好讓他們的食物在照片裡看起來更好。有些餐廳老闆甚

至會付錢請有名的社群媒體使用者發表在他們餐廳裡拍的照片。

不過，有些餐廳老闆不允許顧客拍照。他們認為一道菜應該在上菜的時候馬上享用，不然它會在顧客忙著拍照的時候變冷而變得比較不美味。他們試圖提醒我們，食物本身比我們在社群媒體上得到的「讚」來得重要。

雙篇文章

對照題組

信件

人物與事物介紹

日常與休閒生活

文化與娛樂

資訊與科技

健康與自然環境

社會現象討論

解答篇

Q1 _C_

What does "let your camera eat first" mean?

（「讓相機先吃」是什麼意思？）

（A）Let others know what you eat（讓其他人知道你吃什麼）

（B）Let the camera taste the food first（讓相機先品嚐食物）

▶（C）Take pictures of food before eating
（在吃東西前拍食物的照片）

（D）Consider the appearance of food first
（先考慮食物的外觀）

▶解析 在「let your camera eat first」後面，「people often take photos of their food and share them before feeding themselves」解釋了這個表達方式的意思，就是在吃東西之前先拍照，所以（C）是正確答案。

Q2 _A_

According to the article, what is the main reason that customers take food photos?

（根據這篇文章，顧客拍食物照片的主要原因是什麼？）

▶（A）To get attention from friends（為了獲得朋友的關注）

（B）To enjoy the taste more（為了更加享受味道）

（C）To make restaurants famous（為了讓餐廳出名）

（D）To practice taking pictures（為了練習拍照）

▶解析 在第一段做出「所以人們經常會在吃東西之前拍照片並分享」的結論之前，「it seems more important to let others know what you are eating than to enjoy its taste」的部分提供了理由，也就是讓朋友知道自己吃的東西似乎很重要，所以（A）是正確答案。

Q3 ___*D*___

Which of the following is NOT a way for a restaurant to get famous on social media?

（以下何者不是餐廳在社群媒體上出名的方式？）

（A）Make its food look beautiful（讓食物看起來很美）

（B）Use lights that improve the look of food
（使用能改善食物外表的燈光）

（C）Hire famous people to post about it
（聘請名人來發表關於它的內容）

► （D）Make its customers eat before taking photos
（讓顧客在拍照前先吃）

▶ 解析　第二段說明了餐廳老闆透過照片讓餐廳出名的方式，其中「pay more attention to the appearance of food」、「improve their lighting so that their food looks better」、「pay famous social media users to post pictures taken in their restaurants」分別對應（A）、（B）、（C）。（D）在文章中沒有提到，所以（D）是正確答案。

TOPIC 5 QUIZ 3

At Golden Horse Awards 2020, Chen Shu-Fang(陳淑芳) won the best leading actress and best supporting actress prizes for two different movies at the age of 81. She was the first one to receive the two prizes at the same time. Before that, however, no one expected she would become a top movie actress.

Chen was born in a rich Taiwanese family in 1939. Because she enjoyed singing and dancing, she made up her mind to be an actress. She has been acting in both movies and

雙篇文章對照題組

信件

人物與事物介紹

日常生活與休閒生活

文化與娛樂

資訊與科技

健康與自然環境

社會現象討論

解答篇

TV dramas for over 60 years since she was 19. During her long career, she has had several chances to win a prize at Golden Bell Awards for her appearances in dramas, but she was never picked as a winner. Even so, she still loves acting and tries to do her best every time, and her hard work finally paid off. "As long as you remember me, I will keep acting," said Chen at Golden Horse Awards.

單字解釋：

leading actress 女主角   supporting actress 女配角

make up one's mind 下定決心 career（n.）職業，生涯

pick（v.）挑選

  在 2020 年的金馬獎上，陳淑芳以 81 歲的年齡，靠著兩部不同的電影贏得了最佳女主角和女配角獎。她是第一位同時獲得這兩個獎項的人。然而在這之前，沒有人預期她會成為一線電影演員。

  陳淑芳 1939 年出生在富有的台灣家庭。因為她喜歡唱歌跳舞，所以她下定決心要成為演員。她從 19 歲開始，在電影和電視劇演了超過 60 年的戲。在她長長的職業生涯中，她曾經有幾次因為戲劇演出而在金鐘獎得獎的機會，但從來沒有獲選為得獎者。儘管如此，她還是喜愛演戲，而且每次都努力做到最好，而她的努力最後終於有了回報。她在金馬獎上說：「只要你們記得我，我就會演下去。」

Q1 __*D*__

What is this article mainly about?

（這篇文章主要是關於什麼？）

（A）An event（一場活動）

（B）A prize（一個獎項）

（C）A movie（一部電影）

▶（D）A life story（一段人生經歷）

▶ 解析 文章內容是介紹演員陳淑芳，但選項中並沒有「An

actress」（一位女演員），而是改用「A life story」（一個人的生平事跡等等）來表達。

Q2 ___*B*___

Why did Chen Shu-Fang decide to become an actress?

（陳淑芳為什麼決定成為演員？）

（A）Her family was rich.（她的家庭很富有。）

▶（B）She liked to sing and dance.（她喜歡唱歌跳舞。）

（C）She enjoyed seeing movies.（她喜歡看電影。）

（D）She wanted to get a prize.（她想要得獎。）

▶ 解析 文中「she made up her mind to be an actress」的部分提到她下定決心成為演員，前面表示原因的 Because 子句就是答案：「Because she enjoyed singing and dancing」（因為她喜歡唱歌跳舞），所以（B）是正確答案。

Q3 ___*C*___

About Chen Shu-Fang, which of the following is NOT correct?

（關於陳淑芳，以下何者不正確？）

（A）She received two prizes at Golden Horse Awards in 2020.（她 2020 年在金馬獎獲得了兩個獎項。）

（B）She acts not only in movies but also in TV dramas.
（她不止在電影，也在電視劇演出。）

▶（C）She won several prizes at Golden Bell Awards.
（她在金鐘獎得了幾個獎。）

（D）After winning the prizes, she still wants to act.
（得獎之後，她還是想要演戲。）

▶ 解析 文中的「At Golden Horse Awards 2020, Chen Shu-Fang won the best leading actress and best supporting actress prizes」、「She has been acting in both movies and TV dramas」、「I will keep acting」分別對應選項（A）、（B）、（D）。和選項（C）相關的部分是「she has had several chances to win a prize at Golden Bell Awards… but she was never picked as a winner.」，表示雖然有幾次機會在金鐘獎得獎，但從來沒獲選為得獎者，不符合選項敘述，所以（C）是正確答案。

雙篇文章
對照題組

信件

人物與
事物介紹

日常與
休閒生活

文化與
娛樂

資訊與
科技

健康與
自然環境

社會現象
討論

解答篇

When Jawed Karim, one of those who created YouTube, posted the very first YouTube video "Me at the zoo" in 2005, he might not have imagined that making YouTube videos would become a job, or that YouTube would one day take the place of traditional television. Today, YouTube is one of the media that influence young people the most.

Being a YouTuber is now the most popular career choice for children. According to a study in UK, about 75% of people under 18 have thought about being a YouTuber. Even though some YouTubers do earn a lot, money is not the main reason that young people take them as role models. According to the study, the top reason they want to make YouTube videos is that they need a place to create things freely, and the second reason is that they want to be famous and influence many people. Therefore, we can say it is the need to express themselves that led to the rise of young YouTubers.

單字解釋：

post（v.）發表　　　　　　　imagine（v.）想像

media（n.）媒體　　　　　　　influence（v.）影響

role model 榜樣　　　　　　　lead to 導致，造成

　　當 YouTube 創始人之一的賈德‧卡林姆在 2005 年發表第一支 YouTube 影片「我在動物園」時，他可能沒想像過製作 YouTube 影片會成為一種工作，或者 YouTube 有一天會取代傳統電視。現在，YouTube 是影響年輕人最深的媒體之一。

　　當 YouTuber 是現在最受小孩歡迎的職業選擇。根據在英國的一項研究，大約 75% 的未滿 18 歲孩子曾經想過成為 YouTuber。儘管有些

YouTuber 的確賺很多錢，但錢並不是年輕人把他們當成榜樣的主要原因。根據這項研究，他們想要製作 YouTube 影片的第一大原因是需要自由創作的地方，而第二名的原因是想變得有名並影響許多人。所以，我們可以說是表達自我的需求導致了年輕 YouTuber 的興起。

Q1 ___*A*___

What did Jawed Karim do in 2005?

（賈德・卡林姆在 2005 年做了什麼？）

► （A）He started the YouTube Web site.

（他開設了 YouTube 網站。）

（B）He posted the first video about YouTube.

（他發表了第一支關於 YouTube 的影片。）

（C）He made a living by making videos.

（他靠著製作影片謀生。）

（D）He changed the way people watch TV.

（他改變了人們看電視的方式。）

▶ 解析 在第一段，Jawed Karim 後面的「one of those who created YouTube」說明了他是 YouTube 創辦人之一，所以（A）是正確答案。注意（B）是陷阱選項，因為他是發表了第一支 YouTube 的影片，而不是第一支「關於」YouTube 的影片。

Q2 ___*B*___

What is the most important reason that young people want to be YouTubers?

（年輕人想要當 YouTuber，最重要的原因是什麼？）

（A）They want to make a lot of money.

（他們想要賺很多錢。）

► （B）They want to create things the way they want.

（他們想要用自己的方式創作。）

（C）They want to become famous.（他們想要變得有名。）

（D）They want to influence many people.

（他們想要影響許多人。）

雙篇文章 對照題組

信件

人物與 事物介紹

日常與 休閒生活

文化與 娛樂

資訊與 科技

健康與 自然環境

社會現象 討論

解答篇

▶解析 在第二段，「the top reason they want to make YouTube videos is that they need a place to create things freely」的部分提到他們想製作 YouTube 影片的主要原因，是需要自由創作的地方，所以（B）是正確答案。

Q3   *B*

According to the article, which of the following is true about YouTube?

（根據這篇文章，關於 YouTube，以下何者正確？）

（A）It is not as important as traditional television.

（它不如傳統電視重要。）

▶（B）It can affect the way young people think or do.

（它可以影響年輕人的想法或行為。）

（C）75% of its users are children under 18.

（75% 的使用者是未滿 18 歲的孩子。）

（D）Most people can earn a lot of money on it.

（大部分的人可以在上面賺很多錢。）

▶解析 （A）和（C）在文章中沒有提到。和（B）相關的部分是「YouTube is one of the media that influence young people the most」，表示它是對年輕人影響力最大的媒體之一，符合選項敘述，所以（B）是正確答案。和（D）相關的部分是「some YouTubers do earn a lot」，表示有些 YouTuber 賺很多錢，但並不是「大部分」都賺很多錢，不符合選項敘述。

TOPIC 6 **QUIZ** 2

It is fun to share your life experience online, but it would be dangerous if you share too much personal information, as some may take advantage of it and cause troubles in real life. For example, they can try signing in to your bank account with

雙篇文章 對照題組

信件

人物與 事物介紹

休閒生活 日常與

文化與 娛樂

資訊與 科技

健康與 自然環境

社會現象 討論

解答篇

your information and steal your money. Therefore, it is better not to give out information such as your phone number, home address, and the place you work at. You should also check if your photos show such information before posting them.

Also, you should be careful who you trust online. People you meet online are actually strangers in real life, so you should not easily let them know your personal information while chatting. Even if you decide to meet a friend in person, you should meet in a public place and not tell them your phone number—you can send messages online! With safety in mind, you can protect yourself.

單字解釋：

personal information 個人資料
sign in 登入
stranger（n.）陌生人
message（n.）訊息

take advantage of 利用
*account（n.）帳戶
public（adj.）公共的

在網路上分享你的生活經驗很有趣，但如果分享太多個人資料會很危險，因為有些人可能利用這些資料，並且造成實際生活上的麻煩。舉例來說，他們可以試著用你的資料登入銀行帳戶並且偷走你的錢。所以，最好不要洩露你的電話號碼、自家地址和工作地點之類的資訊。在發布照片之前，也應該檢查照片是否顯示這類資訊。

另外，你也應該小心在網路上該相信誰。你在網路上遇到的人，其實是實際生活中的陌生人，所以你應該不要在聊天時輕易讓他們知道你的個人資料。就算你決定當面和朋友見面，也應該在公共場所見面，而且不要告知你的電話號碼——你可以在網路上傳訊息！只要把安全放在心上，你就能保護自己。

Q1 ___A___

What is this article mainly about?

（這篇文章主要是關於什麼？）

► （A）How to be safe on the Internet（如何在網路上保持安全）

（B）How to be smart when meeting friends
（如何聰明地和朋友見面）

（C）How to tell who is a bad guy（如何分辨誰是壞人）

（D）The bad results of giving out personal information
（洩露個人資訊的不良後果）

▶ 解析　這篇文章主要是說不要在網路上洩露個人資料，但是並沒有這個選項，所以最接近的（A）是正確答案。（B）和（D）雖然都有提到，但都只是文章中的一部分，而不能概括整篇文章的內容。

Q2　_____A_____

What is NOT a kind of information this article tells us not to share?

（何者不是這篇文章叫我們不要分享的資訊？）

► （A）Where you have visited（你去過的地方）

（B）Where you live（你住的地方）

（C）Your cell phone number（你的手機號碼）

（D）The name of your company（你公司的名稱）

▶ 解析　「it is better not to give out information such as your phone number, home address, and the place you work at」的部分提醒我們，最好不要洩露電話號碼、自家地址和工作的地方，對應選項（C）、（B）、（D），所以沒有提到的（A）是正確答案。

Q3　_____D_____

Which of the following is a way to keep your personal information safe?

（以下何者是保持你個人資料安全的方法？）

（A）Avoid opening a bank account online
（避免在網路上開銀行帳戶）

（B）Post your information in the form of photos

（用照片的形式發表個人資訊）

（C）Try to meet an online friend in person

（試著當面和網路上的朋友見面）

► （D）Not to contact an online friend on the phone

（不要用電話聯絡網路上的朋友）

▶ 解析 第二段「you should... not tell them your phone number—you can send messages online」的部分提到，不要把自己的電話號碼告訴網友，而可以在網路上傳訊息，所以不用電話聯絡是避免洩露電話號碼的方法，（D）是正確答案。雖然文章中提到和網友見面，但這不是保持個人資料安全的方法，所以不能選（C）。

TOPIC 6 QUIZ 3

In the past, people have imagined that one day they would be able to see their friends far away and talk with them, and it would be possible to watch any movie they want anytime, anywhere. Today, we know that these have already come true, thanks to smartphones and 4G networks. And then, after about ten years since 4G service started, 5G arrived. It is the next generation of 4G, and it promises faster speed. At first, many people thought 4G was fast enough, so 5G seemed like a waste of money for them. However, the faster speed of 5G means we can do more with it.

For example, fans can now watch a live concert on their phone without worrying about Internet speed, and they can even select which part of the stage to see. It is also possible to see a doctor on the phone, as high-quality real-time video can let patients be seen clearly and help doctors make correct decisions. With 5G, we can imagine more.

單字解釋：

come true 變成真的

promise（v.）承諾

*concert（n.）音樂會，演唱會

stage（n.）舞台

generation（n.）世代

live（adj.）現場演出的

select（v.）選擇

patient（n.）患者

在過去，人們曾經想像有一天能夠看到遠方的朋友並且和他們交談，也有可能隨時隨地看任何想要看的電影。現在，我們知道這些已經實現了，多虧有了智慧型手機和 4G 網路。然後，在 4G 服務開始大約十年後，5G 來了。它是 4G 的下一代，並且承諾提供更快的速度。一開始，許多人認為 4G 夠快了，所以 5G 對他們而言似乎是浪費錢。不過，5G 更快的速度意味著我們能用它做更多事。

舉例來說，歌迷現在可以在手機上觀看現場演唱會，而不用擔心網路速度，甚至可以選擇要看舞台的哪個部分。在手機上看醫生也是有可能的，因為高品質即時影像可以讓患者被清楚看見，並且幫助醫師做出正確的決定。有了 5G，我們可以想像更多。

Q1 ___B___

What is this article mainly about?

（這篇文章主要是關於什麼？）

（A）The way people imagine（人們想像的方式）

► （B）Faster cell phone network（比較快的行動電話網路）

（C）Enjoying videos on the phone（在手機上享受影片）

（D）How 5G can help doctors（5G 能怎樣幫助醫師）

▶解析　文章先提到智慧型手機和 4G 網路讓想像變成現實，然後介紹速度比較快的 5G 讓我們能夠做什麼，所以（B）是正確答案。（C）和（D）都只是文章的部分內容，不能概括全部。

Q2 ___A___

What did many people think about 5G at first?

（許多人一開始對 5G 的想法是什麼？）

► （A）They did not think they needed it.

（他們不覺得自己需要它。）

（B）They did not think it is as good as 4G.

（他們不認為它有 4G 那麼好。）

（C）They did not think it is fast enough.

（他們不認為它夠快。）

（D）They thought it was worth the money.

（他們認為它值得那個價錢。）

▶ 解析　第一段的「At first, many people thought 4G was fast enough, so 5G seemed like a waste of money for them.」說明了許多人一開始對 5G 的態度，是認為 4G 已經夠快了，5G 浪費錢，所以選項（A）是最符合的答案。

Q3 　　　*D*　　　

Which of the following is not a thing we can do with 5G?

（以下何者不是我們可以用 5G 做的事？）

（A）Talk with friends and see them at the same time

（和朋友交談的同時看見他們）

（B）Watch any movie no matter where we are

（不管我們在哪裡都能看任何電影）

（C）See different parts of the stage while watching a live concert（看現場演唱會時看見舞台的不同部分）

► （D）Getting treated by talking on the phone

（藉由講電話來獲得治療）

▶ 解析　這一題要注意的是，因為 5G 速度比 4G 快，所以用 4G 可以做的事，在 5G 上也做得到。文中「see their friends far away and talk with them」、「watch any movie they want anytime, anywhere」、「fans can now watch a live concert… and they can even select which part of the stage to see」分別對

應選項（A）、（B）、（C）。雖然文中也提到可以在電話上看病，但選項（D）的 treat 指的是實際用藥物或親身接觸的手法治療疾病，在電話上是做不到的，所以（D）是正確答案。

雙篇文章
對照題組

信件

事物介紹
人物與

休閒生活
日常與

娛樂
文化與

科技
資訊與

自然環境
健康與

討論
社會現象

解答篇

What you eat can affect how you sleep. In a recent study, scientists found that a diet rich in sugar can negatively affect sleep quality. According to the study, those who eat a lot of white bread or donuts fall asleep quickly, but they wake up more often at night. On the other hand, eating more vegetables and fish seems to help people get a good night's sleep.

Surprisingly, sleep quality also have something to do with our food choices. In another study, scientists found that those who sleep less eat more snacks and fast food than others. However, after sleeping well for several nights, they become less interested in this kind of food.

From the two different studies, we know that sleep and diet can affect each other. Therefore, to improve our health, we should pay attention to our sleep and diet at the same time.

單字解釋：

scientist（n.）科學家   diet（n.）飲食

sugar（n.）糖   negatively（adv.）負面地

surprisingly（adv.）意外地

have something to do with 和…有些關係

　　你所吃的東西會影響你的睡眠品質。在最近的一項研究中，科學家發現富含糖分的飲食可能負面影響睡眠品質。根據這項研究，吃許多白麵包或甜甜圈的人會很快睡著，但他們在晚上比較常醒來。另一方面，吃比較多的蔬菜和魚似乎能幫助人們睡個好覺。

　　令人意外的是，睡眠品質也和我們的食物選擇有些關係。在另一項研究中，科學家發現睡得比較少的人會比其他人吃更多零食和速食。不過，在好好睡了幾晚之後，他們就變得對這種食物比較沒興趣。

從這兩項不同的研究，我們得知睡眠和飲食可以互相影響。所以，為了改善健康，我們應該同時注意自己的睡眠和飲食。

Q1 _C_

What is the main idea of this article?

（這篇文章的主要概念是什麼？）

（A）Bad food choices are bad for your sleep.

　　（不好的食物選擇對你的睡眠不好。）

（B）People who sleep well eat well.（睡得好的人就吃得好。）

▶（C）Diet and sleep affect each other.

　　（飲食和睡眠會互相影響。）

（D）There are many advantages of sleeping well.

　　（睡好覺有許多好處。）

▶ **解析** 文章的三段內容分別是飲食影響睡眠、睡眠影響飲食，以及對於兩者互相影響的總結，所以只有（C）才能概括整篇文章的內容。

Q2 _C_

According to this article, what will happen if someone sleeps well for several nights?

（根據這篇文章，如果有人好好睡了幾晚，會發生什麼事？）

（A）He or she will fall asleep quickly.（會很快睡著。）

（B）He or she will eat more fish.（會吃比較多魚。）

▶（C）He or she will eat less fast food.（會吃比較少速食。）

（D）He or she will pay more attention to health.

　　（會更注意健康。）

▶ **解析** 第二段的「after sleeping well for several nights, they become less interested in this kind of food」提到好好睡上幾晚的效果，其中 this kind of food 是指上一句的 snacks and fast food，所以（C）是正確答案。

Q3 _D_

For whom is this article written?

（這篇文章是寫給誰看的？）

（A）Sleep scientists（睡眠科學家）

（B）People who give advice on eating

（提供飲食方面建議的人）

（C）Fast food restaurant owners（速食餐廳老闆）

► （D）Those who care about their health（關心健康的人）

解析 這篇文章的內容是介紹關於睡眠與飲食的研究，最後的結論「to improve our health, we should...」提醒讀者為了健康而注重睡眠與飲食，所以（D）是這篇文章的主要對象。

TOPIC 7 QUIZ 2

Not many people notice that the fashion industry is polluting the Earth. For example, fashion uses one tenth of water used in all industries. A lot of water is used while making clothes, and after being used, the water is not clean anymore. When the dirty water goes back to the river, it can kill animals living in it. As fast fashion encourages people to buy more clothes, the problem of water pollution also gets more serious.

To solve the problem, it is important for us not to buy too many clothes. Ask yourself before buying new clothes: Do I really need them? Are there similar items in my closet? Thinking about these questions, you may realize that you already have enough. Also, there must be something in your closet that you almost never wear, proving that you have bought more than you need. By buying less clothes and keeping them longer, we can help reduce water pollution caused by the fashion industry.

雙篇文章　對照題組

信件

人物與　事物介紹

日常與　休閒生活

文化與　娛樂

資訊與　科技

健康與　自然環境

社會現象　討論

解答篇

單字解釋：

fashion industry 時尚業　　　industry（n.）產業
encourage（v.）鼓勵　　　　　solve（v.）解決
similar（adj.）類似的　　　　　closet（n.）衣櫃
prove（v.）證明

　　並沒有很多人注意到時尚產業正在污染地球。舉例來說，時尚業使用所有產業用水的十分之一。製造衣服時會使用許多水，而在使用過後，這些水就不再乾淨了。當污水回到河川時，可能會殺死生活在其中的動物。隨著快時尚鼓勵人們買更多衣服，水污染的問題也變得更嚴重。

　　為了解決這個問題，我們不要買太多衣服是很重要的。在買新衣服之前問自己：我真的需要嗎？我的衣櫃裡有沒有類似的東西？思考這些問題，你可能會了解到自己已經擁有夠多了。還有，你的衣櫃裡一定有幾乎從來不穿的東西，證明你已經買了超過你所需要的。藉由購買比較少的衣服，以及持有衣服比較長的時間，我們可以幫忙減少時尚業造成的水污染。

Q1　　*B*

What is true about the fashion industry?

（關於時尚產業，何者正確？）

（A）Among all industries, it uses the most water.

　　　（在所有產業中，它使用最多水。）

▶（B）It pollutes water in the river.

　　　（它污染河川中的水。）

（C）It throws clothes in the river.

　　　（它把衣服丟到河裡。）

（D）Only fast fashion is to blame for pollution.

　　　（只有快時尚是應該怪罪的污染原因。）

▶ 解析　和（A）相關的部分是「fashion uses one-tenth of water used in all industries」，表示時尚產業用水佔所有產業十分之一，但無法得知是否使用最多。和（B）相關的部分是「When the dirty water goes back to the river, it can kill animals living in

344

it」，表示當污水回到河川，會殺死河中的生物，所以（B）是正確答案。（C）在文章中沒有提到。和（D）相關的部分是「As fast fashion encourages people to buy more clothes, the problem of water pollution also gets more serious.」，表示快時尚讓水污染更嚴重，但並不代表在快時尚出現之前就沒有污染問題。

雙篇文章
對照題組

信件

人物與事物介紹

日常與休閒生活

文化與娛樂

資訊與科技

健康與自然環境

社會現象討論

解答篇

Q2　　*D*

Which of the following is NOT a sign that you have enough clothes?

（以下何者不是你已經擁有足夠衣物的徵兆？）

（A）You do not think you really need new ones.
（你不覺得自己真的需要新衣服。）

（B）You already have something that looks like the item you want.（你已經有了看起來像是想要的衣服的東西。）

（C）You have something that you seldom wear.
（你有自己幾乎不穿的東西。）

► （D）You keep an item for a very long time.
（你持有一件衣服非常久。）

解析 第二段提到，思考「Do I really need them? Are there similar items in my closet?」這兩個問題，可能會讓我們發現自己已經有足夠的衣服，兩者分別對應（A）和（B）。後面提到「there must be something in your closet that you almost never wear」是你買了超過自己所需的證據，對應選項（C）。（D）並不是已經擁有足夠衣服的證據，所以（D）是正確答案。

Q3　　*D*

What does this article encourage its readers to do?

（這篇文章鼓勵讀者做什麼？）

（A）Tell other people about water pollution
（跟別人說關於水污染的事）

（B）Say no to fashion industry（向時尚業說不）

（C）Not to buy new clothes at all（完全不要買新衣服）

345

► （D）Cut pollution by buying less clothes
（藉由買比較少的衣服來減少污染）

▶ 解析 在文章最後的結論部分，作者提到「By buying less clothes... we can help reduce water pollution」，呼籲讀者藉由購買比較少的衣服來減少水污染，所以（D）是正確答案。

TOPIC 7 QUIZ 3

Onions are good for our health in many ways. For example, they can improve sleep, make skin brighter, help avoid cancer, etc. Even with these advantages, however, most of us do not like to cut onions, as they can make us cry when we cut them.

Some scientists think that the reason onions make us cry is to protect themselves. An onion is in fact a part of the plant that grows under the ground, and it is the energy store of the plant. If an onion is left under the ground over winter, it will grow again in spring. Since it is an important part of the plant, scientists say the chemicals in it that make our eyes tear actually serve to protect it from attacks.

To have an easier time cutting onions, you can put them in a refrigerator for half an hour before cutting. When you cut onions, remember to open your window and finish cutting as quickly as you can. By doing so, the kitchen will not be filled with the chemicals that bring tears to your eyes.

單字解釋：

onion（n.）洋蔥   protect（v.）保護
ground（n.）地面   store（n.）儲存
chemical（n.）化學物質   tear（v.）流眼淚

refrigerator（n.）冰箱

雙篇文章對照題組

信件

人物與事物介紹

日常與休閒生活

文化與娛樂

資訊與科技

健康與自然環境

社會現象討論

解答篇

　　洋蔥在許多方面對我們的健康有益。舉例來說，洋蔥可以改善睡眠、美白肌膚、幫助預防癌症等等。不過，儘管有這些好處，我們大部分的人還是不喜歡切洋蔥，因為洋蔥會在我們切的時候讓我們哭。

　　有些科學家認為，洋蔥讓我們哭的原因是為了保護自己。洋蔥事實上是這種植物在地下生長的一部分，而它是這種植物的能量儲藏處。如果洋蔥被留在地下度過冬天，它會在春天再次生長。因為它是這種植物重要的一部分，所以科學家說，洋蔥中讓我們流眼淚的化學物質其實是用來保護它免於攻擊。

　　為了在切洋蔥的時候輕鬆一點，你可以在切之前把它們放進冰箱半小時。在切洋蔥的時候，記得打開窗戶，並且儘快切完。這樣做，廚房就不會充滿讓我們眼睛流淚的化學物質了。

Q1 ___*B*___

What is this article mainly about?

（這篇文章主要是關於什麼？）

（A）The advantages of eating onions（吃洋蔥的好處）

▶（B）The reason that onions make us cry
　　　（洋蔥讓我們哭的原因）

（C）The parts of an onion plant（洋蔥植物的部位）

（D）The ways to cook with onions（用洋蔥烹飪的方法）

▶解析　要注意偶爾也有文章第一句並不是全文主題的情況。雖然本文第一句提到洋蔥對健康有益，但後面的內容都和洋蔥讓人流淚有關，所以（B）才是正確答案。

Q2 ___*C*___

Why is an onion an important part of the plant?

（為什麼洋蔥是這種植物重要的部分？）

（A）It makes people cry.（它會讓人哭。）

（B）It grows under the ground.（它生長在地下。）

▶（C）It can provide energy for the plant.
（它可以為植物提供能量。）

（D）It cannot be seen on the ground.（它從地面上看不到。）

▶**解析**　雖然四個選項都是事實，但文中「Since it is an important part of the plant」（因為它是這種植物重要的一部分）前面的內容才是表明重要性的關鍵。「it is the energy store of the plant. If an onion is left under the ground over winter, it will grow again in spring」的部分提到，它是這種植物的能量儲藏處，而「過冬之後會再生長」這一點也顯示它儲藏能量的功能，所以（C）是正確答案。

Q3　_A_

Which of the following is NOT a way to cut onions without crying?
（以下何者不是切洋蔥不流淚的方法？）

▶（A）Make yourself easy while cutting
（在切的時候讓自己從容自在）

（B）Put onions in a fridge before cutting
（在切之前把洋蔥放進冰箱）

（C）Keep your window open（讓窗戶開著）

（D）Finish cutting within a short time（在很短的時間內切完）

▶**解析**　最後一段用「To have an easier time cutting onions」開頭，表示接下來要介紹讓切洋蔥比較輕鬆，也就是不會流淚的方法，「put them in a refrigerator… before cutting」、「open your window」、「finish cutting as quickly as you can」分別對應選項（B）、（C）、（D）。（A）在文章中沒有提到，所以（A）是正確答案。

TOPIC 8 QUIZ 1

雙篇文章
對照題組

信件

人物與
事物介紹

日常與
休閒生活

文化與
娛樂

資訊與
科技

健康與
自然環境

社會現象
討論

解答篇

In the past, not many restaurants deliver food to their customers, for they would need to hire extra workers to do so. Today, restaurants just need to sign contracts with third-party services such as Foodpanda and Uber Eats, and the service providers will take care of everything related to delivering food. By becoming a "partner" of such services, a restaurant can also be seen in their apps and take orders from customers who live far away.

The rise of food delivery services has also changed customers' habits. According to a recent study, there are about a million people in Taiwan who use these services at least once a week. Most people say they use the services when they want to save time or when the weather is bad. Some people also say they enjoy the experience of choosing from all kinds of restaurants listed in the apps. In short, food delivery services has become convenient tools for both restaurants and customers.

單字解釋：

deliver（v.）配送　　　　　sign a contract 簽約

third-party 第三方的　　　　*provider（n.）提供者

take an order 接受訂單　　　list（v.）列出

中文翻譯

　　過去，並沒有很多餐廳外送食物給顧客，因為他們會需要雇用額外的員工來做這件事。現在，餐廳只需要和 Foodpanda、Uber Eats 之類的第三方服務簽約，這些服務提供者就會處理和外送食物相關的一切。藉由成為這類服務的「合作夥伴」，餐廳也可以在他們的 app 上被看到，並且接受住在遠方的顧客所下的訂單。

食物外送服務的興起也改變了顧客的習慣。根據一項最近的研究，台灣有大約一百萬人每週至少使用這些服務一次。大部分的人說，他們在想要省時間或者天氣不好的時候使用這些服務。有些人也說他們喜歡從 app 列出的各種餐廳中挑選的體驗。簡而言之，食物外送服務對於餐廳和顧客而言都成為了方便的工具。

Q1 ___*A*___

What is this article mainly about?

（這篇文章主要是關於什麼？）

▶（A）Food delivery services（食物外送服務）

（B）Restaurants that deliver food（外送食物的餐廳）

（C）Customers' habits（顧客的習慣）

（D）A recent study（一項最近的研究）

▶解析 文章第一段說明食物外送服務對餐廳的好處，第二段則是顧客使用食物外送服務的理由，所以（A）是整篇文章的主題。

Q2 ___*B*___

What is NOT a reason that restaurants sign contracts with a food delivery service?

（何者不是餐廳和食物外送服務簽約的理由？）

（A）They can save hiring costs.（它們可以節省雇用的成本。）

▶（B）They want to handle everything.

（它們想要處理每件事。）

（C）They can let more people know them.

（它們可以讓更多人知道它們。）

（D）People far away can order from them.

（在遠方的人可以向他們訂購。）

▶解析 在第一段，「they would need to hire extra workers to do so」表示以前餐廳需要雇用額外員工來外送，後面則提到只要和食物外送服務簽約，對方就會處理所有和外送有關的事，當然也會包括雇用外送人員，所以（A）符合文章內容。第一段最後的「be seen in their apps」和「take orders from customers who

live far away」分別對應選項（C）和（D）。「the service
providers will take care of everything」的部分是說外送服務會處
理一切，而不是餐廳會處理，所以（B）是正確答案。

Q3 _*A*_

**Which of the following is NOT a reason that people use
food delivery services?**

（以下何者不是人們使用食物外送服務的理由？）

▶（A）They eat out at least once a week.
  （他們每週至少外食一次。）

（B）They do not have enough time.（他們沒有足夠的時間。）

（C）They do not want to go out in bad weather.
  （他們不想在壞天氣時出門。）

（D）There are many different choices on the apps.
  （app 上有許多不同選擇。）

▶️解析 第二段提到人們使用外送服務的理由，「they want to
save time」、「the weather is bad」、「they enjoy the
experience of choosing from all kinds of restaurants listed in the
apps」分別對應選項（B）、（C）、（D）。（A）在文中沒有
提到，所以（A）是正確答案。

TOPIC 8　QUIZ　2

Parents usually think that playing video games is bad for
their children. It is true that children will forget about their
homework or stay up late if they spend too much time playing
video games, but it is also true that games have some good
effects. For example, some studies found that video game
players have better memory and attention, which can in turn
help them learn better. Therefore, if parents want their children

雙篇文章
對照題組

信件

人物與
事物介紹

日常與
休閒生活

文化與
娛樂

資訊與
科技

健康與
自然環境

社會現象
討論

解答篇

to do better at school, maybe they should consider allowing some time for video games.

Some may worry that video game players have less time to develop their social skills. However, many online games actually require players to play in teams. In order to reach their goals, they have to learn how to work together. Some players even make friends with teammates they often play with. In this way, not only do online games help develop social skills, but they have also become an important part of social life.

單字解釋：

video game 電玩遊戲　　　　memory（n.）記憶，記憶力

attention（n.）注意，注意力　social skills 社交技能

team（n.）隊伍

　　父母通常認為玩電玩遊戲對孩子不好。的確，如果孩子花太多時間玩電玩遊戲的話，他們會忘記自己的作業或者熬夜，但遊戲有一些好的影響也是事實。舉例來說，一些研究發現玩電玩遊戲的人有比較好的記憶力和注意力，而這能夠幫助他們學習得更好。所以，如果父母想要他們的孩子在學校表現得比較好，或許應該考慮容許一些電玩遊戲的時間。

　　有些人可能擔心玩電玩遊戲的人比較少有時間發展社交技能。不過，許多線上遊戲其實要求玩家組隊遊玩。為了達到目標，他們必須學習如何共同合作。有些玩家甚至和經常一起玩的隊友交朋友。因此，線上遊戲不但有助於發展社交技能，還成為了社會生活重要的一部分。

Q1 ___ *B*___

What is this article mainly about?

（這篇文章主要是關於什麼？）

（A）The bad results of playing games（玩遊戲的不良後果）

▶（B）The positive effects of playing games

　　　（玩遊戲的正面影響）

雙篇文章
對照題組

信件

人物與
事物介紹

日常與
休閒生活

文化與
娛樂

資訊與
科技

健康與
自然環境

社會現象
討論

解答篇

（C）The social value of video games（電玩遊戲的社會價值）

（D）The purpose of making video games
（製作電玩遊戲的目的）

▶️解析　文章的兩段內容分別是玩遊戲能提升學習能力，以及玩遊戲有助於發展社交技能，所以（B）是正確答案。雖然也提到了玩遊戲的壞處，但只是稍微談到而已，所以不能選（A）。

Q2　___*B*___

According to this article, what is a reason that video game players learn better?

（根據這篇文章，何者是玩電玩遊戲的人學習得比較好的理由？）

（A）Video games make them stay up late.
（電玩遊戲讓他們熬夜。）

▶（B）Video games make them remember things better.
（電玩遊戲讓他們把事情記得更清楚。）

（C）Video games make them work in teams.
（電玩遊戲讓他們團隊合作。）

（D）Video games contain some learning materials.
（電玩遊戲中含有一些學習材料。）

▶️解析　「video game players have better memory and attention, which can in turn help them learn better」的部分說明了電玩遊戲有助於學習的原因，其中的 in turn 是表示某件事的結果造成另一個結果，而 which 是指前面的 better memory and attention。所以，是因為遊戲玩家有比較好的記憶力和注意力，使他們學習得比較好，所以（B）是正確答案。

Q3　___*B*___

According to this article, what is true about the social side of online games?

（根據這篇文章，關於線上遊戲的社交方面，何者正確？）

（A）All online games ask their players to play in teams.
（所有線上遊戲都要求玩家組隊遊玩。）

▶（B）Players will know how to work with others in online games.（玩家在線上遊戲中會知道如何和其他人合作。）

（C）Online game players have worse social skills.

（線上遊戲玩家的社交技能比較差。）

（D）Online games can take the place of social activity in real life.（線上遊戲可以取代實際生活中的社交活動。）

▶解析 和（A）有關的部分是「many online games actually require players to play in teams」，但 many（很多）並不是 all（全部）的意思。和（B）有關的部分是「they have to learn how to work together」，符合選項敘述，所以（B）是正確答案。（C）在文中沒有提到。和（D）相關的部分是「they have also become an important part of social life」，表示線上遊戲成為社交生活的一部分，但這並不表示線上遊戲就是社交生活的全部。

TOPIC 8　QUIZ　3

Recently, I was shocked by a story shared by a friend of mine. Her relative John tried several jobs after finishing university, but he has never been in a job for over three months. He is not happy with any of the jobs, so he stopped trying and stays at home every day doing nothing.

Such people are known as NEETs (Not in Education, Employment, or Training), and there are more and more of them in developed countries. For example, there are over 700,000 NEETs between 15 and 39 years of age in Japan. Without income, most of them are supported by their parents or relatives. In the UK, however, most NEETs live in low-income families and thus need more help from the government.

The main reason NEETs do not work is that they cannot

find jobs that suit them. Therefore, governments should provide necessary training and help them discover more career choice, so that their young years are not wasted.

單字解釋：

university（n.）大學

*NEET (Not in Education, Employment, or Training) 尼特族（不是在接受教育、沒有職業，也不是正在接受職業訓練的人）

developed country 已開發國家　　income（n.）收入

suit（v.）適合　　　　　　　　discover（v.）發現

最近，我因為一位朋友分享的故事而感到震驚。她的親戚約翰在大學畢業後嘗試過幾份工作，但他從來沒有在一份工作中待超過三個月。他對這些工作都不滿意，所以他不再嘗試，並且每天待在家裡什麼也不做。

這種人被稱為尼特族（不是在接受教育、沒有職業，也不是正在接受職業訓練的人），這種人在已開發國家越來越多。舉例來說，日本有超過 70 萬名 15 至 39 歲的尼特族。因為沒有收入，所以他們大部分是靠父母或親戚支援。但在英國，大部分的尼特族生活在低收入家庭，所以需要更多來自政府的幫助。

尼特族不工作的主要原因是他們無法找到適合他們的工作。所以，政府應該提供必要的訓練，並且幫助他們發現更多職業選擇，好讓他們的年輕歲月不會被浪費。

Q1　*D*

Why did John become a NEET?

（為什麼約翰變成了尼特族？）

（A）He does not have a university degree.

（他沒有大學學位。）

（B）He has never been in a job.（他從來沒有工作過。）

（C）He has not tried to find a job.（他沒有試過尋找工作。）

►（D）He cannot find a job he is satisfied with.

（他找不到自己滿意的工作。）

▶ 解析 關於約翰的內容在第一段，其中「He is not happy with any of the jobs, so he stopped trying and...」的部分提到他成為尼特族（不再嘗試找工作而待在家裡）的原因，是他對於做過的工作都不滿意，所以（D）是正確答案。（A）、（B）、（C）都不符合文章中的敘述。

Q2 ___*A*___

According to this article, what is the difference between NEETs in Japan and in the UK?

（根據這篇文章，日本和英國的尼特族有什麼不同？）

▶（A）NEETs in the UK live in poorer families.

（英國的尼特族生活在比較窮的家庭。）

（B）NEETs in Japan are younger in age.

（日本的尼特族比較年輕。）

（C）NEETs are not helped by the government in Japan.

（日本的尼特族沒有受到政府幫助。）

（D）There are less NEETs in the UK.

（英國的尼特族比較少。）

▶ 解析 第二段「In the UK, however, most NEETs live in low-income families」的部分，however（然而）是表示和前面日本尼特族敘述形成對比，而這一句說英國大部分尼特族生活在低收入家庭，所以可以推斷日本的低收入家庭尼特族不像英國那麼多，因此（A）是正確答案。

Q3 ___*A*___

According to this article, what should governments do for NEETs?

（根據這篇文章，政府應該為尼特族做什麼？）

▶（A）Help NEETs find jobs that suit them

（幫助尼特族找到適合他們的工作）

（B）Offer jobs that do not need training

（提供不需要訓練的工作）

（C）Choose jobs for NEETs（為尼特族選擇工作）

（D）Tell NEETs that they are wasting their time
（告訴尼特族他們在浪費時間）

▶ 解析 　第三段「governments should...」的部分只提到政府應該提供訓練、幫助尼特族發現更多職業選擇，不過這些都是在回應上一句的「they cannot find jobs that suit them」（他們找不到適合他們的工作），也就是幫助他們找到適合的工作的方法，所以（A）是正確答案。

雙篇文章

對照題組

信件

人物與事物介紹

日常與休閒生活

文化與娛樂

資訊與科技

健康與自然環境

社會現象討論

解答篇

英檢初級閱讀
實戰完整模擬試題

閱讀能力測驗

本測驗分三部分，全部都是單選題，共 30 題，作答時間 35 分鐘。

第一部份：詞彙

共 10 題，每個題目裡有一個空格。請從四個選項中選出一個最適合題意的字或詞作答。

1. My mother brings her cell phone close to her eyes to read the _____.
   A. manners
   B. messages
   C. measures
   D. meanings

2. If it is too hot inside, you can open the window to let the wind blow _____ the room.
   A. through
   B. against
   C. down
   D. out of

3. Surfing in Kenting was a _____ experience. It was very exciting.
   A. horrible
   B. terrible
   C. peaceful
   D. terrific

4. His store is losing money every day. I guess he has no talent for _____.
   A. business
   B. education
   C. experience
   D. influence

5. You should _____ your notebook computer when the power is low.
   A. judge
   B. charge
   C. supply
   D. provide

6. Everyone says it is a famous restaurant, but I have never _____ it.
   A. heard of
   B. listened to
   C. spoken of
   D. come up with

7. Sandy does not want to gain _____, so she eats only vegetables for dinner.
   A. growth
   B. weight
   C. increase
   D. range

8. Students can learn at a _____ by taking online courses.
   A. moment
   B. loss
   C. distance
   D. point

9. Tom will forget to bring his wallet if you do not _____ him.
   A. remember
   B. remind
   C. recover
   D. realize

10. Many people have died or gotten hurt _____ drunk driving accidents.

    A. out of

    B. because of

    C. along with

    D. away from

第二部份：段落填空

    共 8 題，包括二個段落，每個段落各含四個空格。每格均有四個選項，請依照文意選出最合適的答案。

Questions 11-14

In order to save our Mother Earth, many people _____(11)_____ live in a way that is better for the environment. Some cut the use of water, paper, and plastic, while others take the bus or metro instead of driving their own cars. Also, there are efforts to make the public know the _____(12)_____ of protecting the environment and join the cause. In addition to individual efforts, some companies develop new products _____(13)_____ can help protect this planet. For example, there are now cars that run on electricity and thus can reduce the use of oil. _____(14)_____, many believe we should not just care about prices, but also make better choices for the Earth.

> ☞ instead of 取代

11. A. are not able to

    B. are willing to

    C. are nervous to

    D. are allowed to

12. A. regret

    B. danger

    C. solution

    D. importance

13. A. who

    B. that

    C. whose

    D. what

14. A. Although governments let people live well

    B. Because governments made laws

    C. Though people have to pay more for them

    D. If people have a better planet

Questions 15-18

A recent study shows that the longer teenagers stay online every day, the more likely they ___(15)___. When asked about why they spend many hours online, some teenagers said they want to see what their friends do every day, and they feel connected by doing so. However, seeing how other people enjoy their life on social media can also make them feel their own lives are not good enough. ___(16)___ the Internet can be bad for our mental health. ___(17)___, experts encourage teenagers to spend some time doing activities other than using their smartphones. Parents should also keep an eye on what their children do and ___(18)___ their time online.

☞ mental 精神方面的

15. A. feel down
    B. get bored
    C. behave themselves
    D. become responsible

16. A. This is because
    B. This can happen when
    C. This does not mean that
    D. This is one of the reasons that

17. A. However
    B. Therefore
    C. In addition
    D. For example

18. A. limit
    B. spend
    C. respect
    D. treasure

第三部份：閱讀理解

共 12 題，包括 4 個題組，每個題組含 1 至 2 篇短文，與數個相關的四選一的選擇題。請由試題冊上的選項中選出最適合的答案。

Questions 19-21

 8:39 P.M.

I've sent you some plans for our summer trip. What do you think?

Mike

I like the idea of taking a ship and riding a bicycle, but the cost is a bit high for me.

Simon

How about we go for the cheapest one, then?

Mike

I'm afraid my younger brother will get bored. He likes to play outside, and he is not interested in art or history.

Simon

Well, maybe the train trip will do. Actually, my uncle in Hualien have some bikes. We can borrow from him and ride to the beach.

Mike

Great! I think we three will all enjoy the trip. Also, we can now think about what to do in the other places.

Simon

Summer Trip		
Plan A	**Plan B**	**Plan C**
- 7 days - Travel around Taiwan by train - Stay in relatives' houses in Taichung, Tainan, Kaohsiung, and Hualien - NT$ 5000 each person	- 5 days - Take a bus to Keelung, then go to Penghu by ship - Go to several islands of Penghu by bicycle - Stay at Lanshi Hotel - NT$ 10000 each person	- 4 days - Visit museums in Taipei by metro and bus - Visit famous night markets - Stay at a rented house - NT$ 4000 each person

19. Which plan of summer trip have Mike and Simon selected?

    A. Plan A

    B. Plan B

    C. Plan C

    D. They have not decided yet.

20. What does Simon **NOT** like about the plan to go to Penghu?

    A. It requires taking a ship.

    B. It is boring to go outside.

    C. The hotel is not good.

    D. It is too expensive.

21. Who will go on the summer trip?

    A. Mike and Simon

    B. Mike, Simon, and Mike's uncle

    C. Mike, Simon, and Simon's brother

    D. Mike, Simon, Mike's uncle, and Simon's brother

To: Jane Jang <jane1999@hitmail.com>
From: Tiffany Young <youngone89@ggmail.com>
Subject: Asking for some advice

Dear Jane,

Do you remember me? We first met at Haley's party last month. It was a pleasure talking with you. I am writing to you because I just got a wonderful opportunity to be an international student at SFU in Canada. Since you have studied in Vancouver for two years, I would like to ask you some questions.

First, what kind of clothes should I pack? I have prepared scarves, gloves, and two heavy coats for Canada's winter. Do you think that will be enough? Is there anything else I should prepare?

Second, what should I do to work part-time in Canada? I heard the cost of living in Canada is quite high, so I want to make some money myself. How can I find a job like you did? What do I have to prepare in advance?

I am sorry for asking you so many questions, but I really want to hear your experience. I look forward to hearing from you.

Thank you,
Tiffany

22. Why did Tiffany write to Jane?

    A. She wants to invite Jane to Canada.

    B. She wants to ask Jane a favor.

    C. She wants to know how to apply for schools.

    D. She is planning a visit to Jane's place.

23. What is Tiffany preparing for?

    A. A job interview in Canada

    B. A winter fashion show in Canada

    C. A business trip to Canada

    D. A new campus life in Canada

24. Which of the following is true about Tiffany and Jane?

    A. They have known each other for years.

    B. They have never seen each other.

    C. They are new friends.

    D. They are relatives.

Questions 25-27

In 2020, due to the spreading of COVID-19, face masks became a necessary item for everyone in the world. Since COVID-19 spreads when a person with the virus coughs, sneezes, or talks, governments began to ask their people to wear masks in public places.

There is actually a long history of wearing face masks. In 13th-century China, for example, servants covered their mouths and noses with silk scarves when they served food to their masters. It was believed that by wearing silk scarves, the breath of servants would not affect the smell and taste of food.

In the 19th century, it was proved that face masks can prevent people from some diseases. In 1899, a French doctor sewed a piece of cloth on the upper part of his clothes, so he could use it to cover his nose and mouth when he needed to. Little by little, face masks became the form we are familiar with today, and it became easier to wear them or take them off.

25. What is the purpose of this article?
    A. To advise people to wear face masks
    B. To prove the effect of face masks
    C. To describe the history of face masks
    D. To show how to make face masks

26. Why did people start wearing face masks in 2020?
    A. They had the duty to wear masks.
    B. They wore masks for fun.
    C. Face masks were popular fashion items then.
    D. Wearing masks made them more comfortable.

27. According to this article, which of the following is **NOT** true?
    A. Face masks can help to control the spread of COVID-19.
    B. In 13th-century China, servants wear silk scarves to protect themselves from getting sick.
    C. In the 19th century, people began to know that face masks are effective.
    D. Face masks today are easier to use than those in the past.

Questions 28-30

In the past, many sports fans enjoyed attending games, but new data show that more and more people prefer to watch games from home. According to a recent study, 59% of Americans would rather watch games on TV than see it in person. Among people over the age of 35, there are 65% of them who prefer to stay at home.

Why do they choose not to go in person to cheer for their favorite teams? According to the study, 57% of Americans complain that food and drinks at stadiums are too expensive. On top of that, ticket prices are quite high, and stadium parking can cost as much as game tickets. Even though it is possible to go by subway, many still find it not as convenient as driving. Since it can take several hundred dollars for a family to attend a game at a stadium, many would rather have a game-watching party at home.

☞ stadium 體育場

28. According to this article, what is the main reason that many Americans choose not to watch a game at a stadium?

    A. They want to save the time of going to a stadium.

    B. They think that food and drinks at stadiums do not taste good.

    C. They do not want to spend too much money.

    D. They prefer to get together with friends at home.

29. Which of the following does **NOT** make it expensive to attend a game?

    A. Buying food and drinks at a stadium

    B. Buying tickets

    C. Stadium parking

    D. Going by subway

30. What can we learn from this article?

    A. Most Americans are not interested in sports.

    B. It is more exciting to watch a game with friends.

    C. It is worth spending time and money on sports teams.

    D. More than half Americans prefer to watch a game at home.

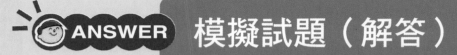

1. My mother brings her cell phone close to her eyes to read the
    ___**B**___.

    （我媽媽把手機拿近眼睛來閱讀訊息。）

    A. manners（禮貌）

    ►B. messages（訊息）

    C. measures（措施）

    D. meanings（意義）

    ▶解析 會呈現在手機螢幕上的是 messages（訊息）。另外，題目提
    到「把手機拿近眼睛」，強調用眼睛看清楚的意思，所以不能選擇用頭
    腦理解而得到的 meanings（意義）。

2. If it is too hot inside, you can open the window to let the wind blow
    ___**A**___ the room.

    （如果裡面太熱的話，你可以打開窗戶，讓風吹過房間。）

    ►A. through（穿過…）

    B. against（逆著…）

    C. down（往下）

    D. out of（從…出去）

    ▶解析 因為要表示為室內散熱的意思，所以能表示風吹進室內又流出
    的 through（穿過）是正確答案。

3. Surfing in Kenting was a ___**D**___ experience. It was very
    exciting.

    （在墾丁衝浪是很棒的經驗。那非常刺激。）

    A. horrible（可怕的）

    B. terrible（糟糕的）

    C. peaceful（平靜的）

    ►D. terrific（很棒的）

解析 第二句的 exciting（刺激的）是正面的形容詞，所以對於這次經驗表示正面意見的 terrific（很棒的）是正確答案。peaceful（平靜的）雖然也是正面的形容詞，但意思和 exciting 互相矛盾。

4. His store is losing money every day. I guess he has no talent for _____*A*_____.

    （他的商店每天都在虧錢。我猜他沒有做生意的天分。）

    ►A. business（商業，生意）

    B. education（教育）

    C. experience（經驗）

    D. influence（影響）

    解析 have no talent for 表示「對…沒有天分」。因為第一個句子說的是經營商店虧錢，所以能表示經商的 business 是正確答案。

5. You should _____*B*_____ your notebook computer when the power is low.

    （你應該在快沒電的時候為你的筆記型電腦充電。）

    A. judge（判斷）

    ►B. charge（充電）

    C. supply（供應）

    D. provide（提供）

    解析 power is low 表示「電量很低」的意思，所以 charge（充電）是正確答案。supply 和 provide 都表示「把筆記型電腦提供出去」的意思。

6. Everyone says it is a famous restaurant, but I have never _____*A*_____ it.

    （每個人都說那是一間有名的餐廳，但我從來沒聽說過。）

    ►A. heard of（聽說）

    B. listened to（聆聽）

    C. spoken of（談到）

    D. come up with（想出）

⏵解析 but 表示語氣轉折，所以相對於前半句說的「那間餐廳很有名」，後半句是表達自己並不知道那間餐廳很有名，所以 heard of（聽說）是正確答案。listen to 是「集中注意力去聽某個對象」的意思。

7. Sandy does not want to gain _____*B*_____, so she eats only vegetables for dinner.
（珊蒂不想要增加體重，所以她晚餐只吃蔬菜。）

   A. growth（成長）

   ▶B. weight（體重）

   C. increase（增加）

   D. range（範圍）

   ⏵解析 gain weight 是表示「體重增加」的固定說法，也是晚餐只吃蔬菜所能避免的事。

8. Students can learn at a _____*C*_____ by taking online courses.
（學生們可以藉由修線上課程進行遠距學習。）

   A. moment（片刻）

   B. loss（失去）

   ▶C. distance（距離）

   D. point（點）

   ⏵解析 at a distance 是指「隔著一段距離」，也可以表示「遠距⋯」的意思。

   at a moment：在某個片刻

   at a loss：不知所措

   at a point：在某個點上

9. Tom will forget to bring his wallet if you do not _____*B*_____ him.
（如果你不提醒他的話，湯姆會忘記帶他的皮夾。）

   A. remember（記得）

   ▶B. remind（提醒）

   C. recover（恢復）

   D. realize（意識到）

▶ 解析　題意是「如果不對他做什麼的話，他就會忘記」，所以表示讓人記起來的 remind（提醒）是正確答案。

10.　Many people have died or gotten hurt _____*B*_____ drunk driving accidents.
（許多人因為酒駕事故而死亡或受傷。）
A. out of（出自於）
▶B. because of（因為）
C. along with（和…一起）
D. away from（離開）

▶ 解析　酒駕事故是死亡和受傷的原因，所以表示原因的 because of（因為）是正確答案。out of 在字典裡雖然也有「因為」的解釋，但後面其實只能接心理上的原因，表示某人做某事的理由，例如 out of fear（出於恐懼）、out of love（出自於愛）等等。along with 從中文字面上來看似乎是可能的答案，實際上卻是「許多人和酒駕事故一起死亡或受傷」→「人和意外事故都死亡或受傷了」的意思。

Questions 11-14

In order to save our Mother Earth, many people __(11)__ live in a way that is better for the environment. Some cut the use of water, paper, and plastic, while others take the bus or metro instead of driving their own cars. Also, there are efforts to make the public know the __(12)__ of protecting the environment and join the cause. In addition to individual efforts, some companies develop new products __(13)__ can help protect this planet. For example, there are now cars that run on electricity and thus can reduce the use of oil. __(14)__, many believe we should not just care about prices, but also make better choices for the Earth.

為了拯救地球母親，許多人願意以對環境比較好的方式生活。有些人減少水、紙張和塑膠的使用，其他人則搭乘公車或捷運來取代開自己的車。另外，也有一些讓大眾知道保護環境重要性並且響應這個目標的努力。除了個人的努力以外，也有一些公司開發能幫助保護這個星球的新產品。舉例來說，現在有靠電力運行，因而能減少石油使用的汽車。雖然人們必須為這些產品付更多錢，但許多人相信我們應該不要只在乎價格，也要為地球做出更好的選擇。

11. ___*B*___

A. are not able to（沒有能力做…）

▶B. are willing to（願意做…）

C. are nervous to（對於做…感到緊張）

D. are allowed to（被允許做…）

▶解析　空格所在的句子提到用對環境更好的方式生活，下一句則是說明具體的方式，而且是現在的事實（現在式）。所以，能表達許多人力行環保是一件事實的 are willing to（願意做…）是正確答案。從事環保的行為並不需要別人允許，所以不能選 are allowed to。

12. ___*D*___

A. regret（後悔）

B. danger（危險）

C. solution（解決方法）

▶D. importance（重要性）

▶解析　句子後半提到要讓大眾能 join the cause（一起加入保護環境的目標），所以讓大眾知道保護環境的 importance（重要性）是達到這個目標的方法。solution 是指「問題」的解決方法，而「保護環境」這件事並不是一個問題，所以 solution 不是正確答案。

13. ___*B*___

A. who

► B. that

C. whose

D. what

🔘 解析　空格引導的關係子句修飾前面的 products（產品），而且空格是 can help 的主詞，所以要填入主格關係代名詞。因為 products 是物品，所以人事物都通用的關係代名詞 that 是正確答案。

14.　　　*C*

A. Although governments let people live well（雖然政府讓人民過好日子）

B. Because governments made laws（因為政府制定了法律）

► C. Though people have to pay more for them
　　（雖然人們必須為這些產品付更多錢）

D. If people have a better planet（如果人們有一個比較好的星球）

🔘 解析　空格後面提到，許多人相信我們應該不要只在乎價格，也要為地球做出更好的選擇，這裡說的價格、做出更好的選擇都和前面提到的環保產品有關。在選項中，能延續關於環保產品的話題，並且和後面的「不要只在乎價格」形成對比的 C. 是最合適的答案。

Questions 15-18

A recent study shows that the longer teenagers stay online every day, the more likely they ___(15)___. When asked about why they spend many hours online, some teenagers said they want to see what their friends do every day, and they feel connected by doing so. However, seeing how other people enjoy their life on social media can also make them feel their own lives are not good enough. ___(16)___ the Internet can be bad for our mental health. ___(17)___, experts encourage teenagers to spend some time doing activities other than using their smartphones. Parents should also keep an eye on what their children do and ___(18)___ their time online.

中
文
翻
譯

　　最近的一項研究顯示，青少年每天在網路上待得越久，越有可能感覺心情低落。當被問到為什麼花許多時間在網路上時，有些青少年說他們想要看朋友每天做什麼，而這樣做讓他們感覺和人有所連結。不過，在社群媒體上看到別人如何享受生活，可能也會讓他們感覺自己的生活不夠好。這是網路可能對我們的精神健康有害的原因之一。所以，專家鼓勵青少年花一些時間做使用智慧型手機以外的活動。父母也應該留意他們的孩子做什麼，並且限制他們在網路上的時間。

15. ___*A*___

▶A. feel down（感覺心情低落）

B. get bored（感覺無聊）

C. behave themselves（守規矩）

D. become responsible（變得負責任）

▶解析　文章後面的內容提到，在網路上看到別人的生活，會讓人感覺自己的生活不夠好，而可能對精神健康有害，所以能表達這種情況的 feel down（感覺心情低落）是正確答案。

16. ___*D*___

A. This is because（這是因為）

B. This can happen when（這可能在⋯的時候發生）

C. This does not mean that（這並不意味著）

▶D. This is one of the reasons that（這是⋯的原因之一）

▶解析　上一句提到，在網路上看到別人的生活，會讓人感覺自己的生活不夠好，而空格所在的句子提到網路可能對精神健康有害。前者是後者的原因，所以能表達這個關係的 D. 是正確答案。

17. ___*B*___

A. However（然而）

▶B. Therefore（所以）

C. In addition（另外）

D. For example（舉例來說）

▶️解析　上一句提到網路可能對精神健康有害，而空格所在的句子說專
家鼓勵青少年做使用智慧型手機以外的活動，兩者之間有因果關係，所
以連接副詞 Therefore（所以）是正確答案。

18. ___*A*___

▶A. limit（限制）

B. spend（花費）

C. respect（尊重）

D. treasure（珍惜）

▶️解析　因為長時間上網可能對精神健康有害，所以 limit（限制）孩子
在網路上的時間是最合理的答案。

Questions 19-21

> **Mike:** I've sent you some plans for our summer trip. What do you think?
>
> **Simon:** I like the idea of taking a ship and riding a bicycle, but the cost is a bit high for me.
>
> **Mike:** How about we go for the cheapest one, then?
>
> **Simon:** I'm afraid my younger brother will get bored. He likes to play outside, and he is not interested in art or history.
>
> **Mike:** Well, maybe the train trip will do. Actually, my uncle in Hualien have some bikes. We can borrow from him and ride to the beach.
>
> **Simon:** Great! I think we three will all enjoy the trip. Also, we can now think about what to do in the other places.

中文翻譯

麥克：我把我們夏天旅行的一些計畫寄給你了。你覺得怎樣？

賽門：我喜歡搭船和騎腳踏車的主意，但費用對我來說有點高。

麥克：那麼，我們選最便宜的怎麼樣？

賽門：我怕我的弟弟會覺得無聊。他喜歡在外面玩，而且他對藝術或歷史沒

有興趣。

麥克：嗯，或許火車旅行行得通。事實上，我在花蓮的叔叔有一些腳踏車。我們可以跟他借，然後騎到海邊。

賽門：太好了！我想我們三個人都會很享受這次旅行。還有，我們現在可以思考在其他也方要做什麼了。

Summer Trip		
Plan A	**Plan B**	**Plan C**
- 7 days - Travel around Taiwan by train - Stay in relatives' houses in Taichung, Tainan, Kaohsiung, and Hualien - NT$ 5000 each person	- 5 days - Take a bus to Keelung, then go to Penghu by ship - Go to several islands of Penghu by bicycle - Stay at Lanshi Hotel - NT$ 10000 each person	- 4 days - Visit museums in Taipei by metro and bus - Visit famous night markets - Stay at a rented house - NT$ 4000 each person

夏季旅行		
計畫 A	**計畫 B**	**計畫 C**
- 7 天 - 搭火車環島 - 留宿台中、台南、高雄和花蓮親戚的家 - 每人 5000 元	- 5 天 - 搭巴士到基隆，然後搭船到澎湖 - 騎腳踏車到澎湖的幾座島嶼 - 住宿在蘭詩飯店 - 每人 10000 元	- 4 天 - 搭捷運和巴士拜訪台北的博物館 - 拜訪有名的夜市 - 住宿在出租屋 - 每人 4000 元

19. ___*A*___

Which plan of summer trip have Mike and Simon selected?

（麥克和賽門選了哪個夏季旅行的計畫？）

▶A. Plan A（計畫 A）

B. Plan B（計畫 B）

C. Plan C（計畫 C）

D. They have not decided yet.（他們還沒有決定。）

▶️**解析** 在對話的最後，麥克說「或許火車旅行行得通」，並且提到跟花蓮的叔叔借腳踏車，而賽門說「太好了」表示同意。對照表格內容，符合麥克所說內容的 Plan A 是正確答案。

20. ___*D*___

What does Simon **NOT** like about the plan to go to Penghu?

（關於去澎湖的計畫，賽門不喜歡哪一點？）

A. It requires taking a ship.（需要搭船。）

B. It is boring to go outside.（去戶外很無聊。）

C. The hotel is not good.（飯店不好。）

▶D. It is too expensive.（太貴了。）

▶️**解析** 在對話的一開始，賽門所說的「我喜歡搭船和騎腳踏車的主意，但費用對我來說有點高」是關於澎湖旅行（計畫 B）的意見，因為只有澎湖旅行的計畫提到要搭船。因為賽門說費用對他來說有點高，所以選項 D. 是他不喜歡這個計畫的地方。

21. ___*C*___

Who will go on the summer trip?

（誰會去夏季旅行？）

A. Mike and Simon（麥克和賽門）

B. Mike, Simon, and Mike's uncle（麥克、賽門和麥克的叔叔）

▶C. Mike, Simon, and Simon's brother（麥克、賽門和賽門的弟弟）

D. Mike, Simon, Mike's uncle, and Simon's brother

（麥克、賽門、麥克的叔叔和賽門的弟弟）

▶️ 解析 在對話中，賽門提到「我怕我的弟弟會覺得無聊」，最後的 I think we three will all enjoy the trip（我想我們三個人都會很享受這次旅行）也表明了是三個人去旅行，所以 C. 是正確答案。

Questions 22-24

To: Jane Jang <jane1999@hitmail.com>
From: Tiffany Young <youngone89@ggmail.com>
Subject: Asking for some advice

Dear Jane,

Do you remember me? We first met at Haley's party last month. It was a pleasure talking with you. I am writing to you because I just got a wonderful opportunity to be an international student at SFU in Canada. Since you have studied in Vancouver for two years, I would like to ask you some questions.

First, what kind of clothes should I pack? I have prepared scarves, gloves, and two heavy coats for Canada's winter. Do you think that will be enough? Is there anything else I should prepare?

Second, what should I do to work part-time in Canada? I heard the cost of living in Canada is quite high, so I want to make some money myself. How can I find a job like you did? What do I have to prepare in advance?

I am sorry for asking you so many questions, but I really want to hear your experience. I look forward to hearing from you.

Thank you,
Tiffany

收件者：珍・張 <jane1999@hitmail.com>
寄件者：蒂芬妮・楊 <youngone89@ggmail.com>
主旨：尋求一些建議

親愛的珍：

你記得我嗎？我們上個月在海莉的派對上第一次見面。我很高興能和妳談話。我寫這封信給妳，是因為我剛獲得一個很棒的機會，可以成為加拿大SFU 的國際學生。因為妳在溫哥華留學過兩年，所以我想要問妳一些問題。

首先，我應該打包什麼樣的衣服？我為加拿大的冬天準備了圍巾、手套和兩件厚重的大衣。妳覺得這樣夠嗎？還有什麼我應該準備的嗎？

第二，要在加拿大兼職工作，我應該做什麼？我聽說加拿大的生活費很高，所以我想要自己賺一些錢。我要怎樣才能像妳一樣找到工作呢？我必須事先準備什麼？

很抱歉問妳這麼多問題，但我真的很想聽聽妳的經驗。我期待收到妳的回信。

謝謝
蒂芬妮

22. __*B*__

Why did Tiffany write to Jane?
（蒂芬妮為什麼寫信給珍？）

A. She wants to invite Jane to Canada.（她想邀請珍去加拿大。）

▶B. She wants to ask Jane a favor.（她想請珍幫個忙。）

C. She wants to know how to apply for schools.
（她想知道怎麼申請學校。）

D. She is planning a visit to Jane's place.（她正在計畫拜訪珍的家。）

▶**解析** 在信件的第一段，蒂芬妮表明自己寫信是因為獲得了成為國際學生的機會，並且想要問有留學經驗的珍一些問題，所以用 ask a favor（請求幫忙）來表達寫信目的的選項 B. 是正確答案。

---

23. ___*D*___

What is Tiffany preparing for?

（蒂芬妮正在準備什麼？）

A. A job interview in Canada（在加拿大的工作面試）

B. A winter fashion show in Canada（在加拿大的冬季時裝秀）

C. A business trip to Canada（到加拿大的出差）

▶D. A new campus life in Canada（在加拿大新的校園生活）

▶**解析** 蒂芬妮是為了成為國際學生做準備，所以選項 D. 是正確答案。這裡用 campus life（校園生活）來表達 school life 的意思。

---

24. ___*C*___

Which of the following is true about Tiffany and Jane?

（關於蒂芬妮和珍，以下何者正確？）

A. They have known each other for years.（他們認識彼此很多年。）

B. They have never seen each other.（他們從來沒有見過彼此。）

▶C. They are new friends.（他們是新認識的朋友。）

D. They are relatives.（他們是親戚。）

▶**解析** 在信件的開頭，蒂芬妮提到「我們上個月在海莉的派對上第一次見面」，所以選項 C. 是正確答案。

Questions 25-27

In 2020, due to the spreading of COVID-19, face masks became a necessary item for everyone in the world. Since COVID-19 spreads when a person with the virus coughs, sneezes, or talks, governments began to ask their people to wear masks in public places.

There is actually a long history of wearing face masks. In 13th-century China, for example, servants covered their mouths and noses with silk scarves when they served food to their masters. It was believed that by wearing silk scarves, the breath of servants would not affect the smell and taste of food.

In the 19th century, it was proved that face masks can prevent people from some diseases. In 1899, a French doctor sewed a piece of cloth on the upper part of his clothes, so he could use it to cover his nose and mouth when he needed to. Little by little, face masks became the form we are familiar with today, and it became easier to wear them or take them off.

在 2020 年，由於 COVID-19（2019 年冠狀病毒）的擴散，口罩成為了世界上每個人都必須要有的物品。由於 COVID-19 會在帶有病毒的人咳嗽、打噴嚏或說話時散播，所以各國政府開始要求人民在公共場所戴口罩。

戴口罩其實有很長的歷史。例如在 13 世紀的中國，僕人在端上食物給主人時會用絲巾遮住口鼻。當時相信藉由戴上絲巾，僕人的呼吸不會影響食物的氣味和味道。

在 19 世紀，口罩被證明能預防人們得到一些疾病。在 1899 年，一位法國醫師將一塊布縫在他衣服上面的部分，好讓他在需要時能用它來蓋住自己的口鼻。漸漸地，口罩成為我們現在熟悉的形式，戴口罩和脫口罩也變得比較簡單了。

25. ___*C*___

What is the purpose of this article?

（這篇文章的目的是什麼？）

A. To advise people to wear face masks（建議人們戴口罩）

B. To prove the effect of face masks（證明口罩的效果）

►C. To describe the history of face masks（描述口罩的歷史）

D. To show how to make face masks（展示如何製作口罩）

▶️ 解析　第一段談到 COVID-19 讓每個人都需要口罩，之後的內容都在說明歷史上的口罩形式，所以選項 C. 是正確答案。

383

26.   *A*

Why did people start wearing face masks in 2020?

（在 2020 年，人們為什麼開始戴口罩？）

►A. They had the duty to wear masks.（他們有義務戴口罩。）

B. They wore masks for fun.（他們為了好玩而戴口罩。）

C. Face masks were popular fashion items then.

（口罩在那時候是受歡迎的時尚物品。）

D. Wearing masks made them more comfortable.

（戴口罩讓他們感覺比較自在。）

▶解析　第一段提到，為了避免 COVID-19 擴散，各國政府開始要求人民在公共場所戴口罩，所以用 duty（義務）表達不得不戴口罩的選項 A. 是正確答案。選項 D. 中的 comfortable 是表示心理上覺得「自在」的意思。

27.   *B*

According to this article, which of the following is **NOT** true?

（根據這篇文章，以下何者不正確？）

A. Face masks can help to control the spread of COVID-19.

（口罩可以幫助控制 COVID-19 的散播。）

►B. In 13th-century China, servants wear silk scarves to protect themselves from getting sick.

（在 13 世紀的中國，僕人戴上絲巾來保護自己免於生病。）

C. In the 19th century, people began to know that face masks are effective.

（在 19 世紀，人們開始知道口罩是有效的。）

D. Face masks today are easier to use than those in the past.

（現在的口罩比以前來得容易使用。）

▶解析　在文章中，「Since COVID-19 spreads when..., governments began to ask their people to wear masks in public places.」、「In the 19th century, it was proved that face masks can prevent people from some diseases」、「face masks became the form we are familiar with today, and it became easier to wear them or take them off」分別

對應選項 A.、C.、D.。關於 B. 的部分是「It was believed that by wearing silk scarves, the breath of servants would not affect the smell and taste of food」，表示戴絲巾是為了不影響食物的氣味和味道，而不是防止僕人生病，所以選項 B. 是正確答案。

Questions 28-30

In the past, many sports fans enjoyed attending games, but new data show that more and more people prefer to watch games from home. According to a recent study, 59% of Americans would rather watch games on TV than see it in person. Among people over the age of 35, there are 65% of them who prefer to stay at home.

Why do they choose not to go in person to cheer for their favorite teams? According to the study, 57% of Americans complain that food and drinks at stadiums are too expensive. On top of that, ticket prices are quite high, and stadium parking can cost as much as game tickets. Even though it is possible to go by subway, many still find it not as convenient as driving. Since it can take several hundred dollars for a family to attend a game at a stadium, many would rather have a game-watching party at home.

在過去，許多運動迷喜歡到場看比賽，但新的數據顯示越來越多人偏好在家看比賽。根據一項最近的研究，59% 的美國人寧願在電視上看比賽，而不是親自去看。在超過 35 歲的人群中，有 65% 偏好留在家裡。

為什麼他們選擇不要親自去為他們最愛的隊伍加油呢？根據這項研究，57% 的美國人抱怨體育場的食物和飲料太貴了。除此之外，門票價格很高，而在體育場停車的花費可能會和比賽門票一樣多。儘管可以搭地鐵去，許多人還是覺得不如開車方便。因為一個家庭要到體育場看比賽可能會花費數百美元，所以很多人寧願在家舉行觀賽派對。

28.　　　*C*　　

According to this article, what is the main reason that many Americans choose not to watch a game at a stadium?

（根據這篇文章，許多美國人選擇不在體育場看比賽的主要原因是什麼？）

A. They want to save the time of going to a stadium.

（他們想要節省去體育場的時間。）

B. They think that food and drinks at stadiums do not taste good.

（他們認為體育場的食物和飲料不美味。）

►C. They do not want to spend too much money.

（他們不想要花太多錢。）

D. They prefer to get together with friends at home.

（他們偏好在家和朋友聚會。）

▶解析 第二段的開頭先問「為什麼他們選擇不要親自去為他們最愛的隊伍加油呢？」，然後說明其中的理由是各種花費很貴，所以選項 C. 是正確答案。

29. ____**D**____

Which of the following does **NOT** make it expensive to attend a game?

（以下何者不會使到場觀看比賽變得很貴？）

A. Buying food and drinks at a stadium（在體育場買食物和飲料）

B. Buying tickets（買門票）

C. Stadium parking（在體育場停車）

►D. Going by subway（搭地下鐵去）

▶解析 關於觀看比賽的昂貴費用，第二段提到「food and drinks at stadiums are too expensive」、「ticket prices are quite high」、「stadium parking can cost as much as game tickets」，分別對應選項 A.、B.、C.。文中沒有提到搭地下鐵很貴，所以選項 D. 是正確答案。

30. ____**D**____

What can we learn from this article?

（我們可以從這篇文章得知什麼？）

A. Most Americans are not interested in sports.

（大部分的美國人對體育活動沒有興趣。）

B. It is more exciting to watch a game with friends.
（和朋友一起看比賽比較刺激。）

C. It is worth spending time and money on sports teams.
（花時間和錢在體育隊伍上是值得的。）

▶D. More than half Americans prefer to watch a game at home.
（超過一半的美國人偏好在家觀看比賽。）

▶解析　選項 A.、B.、C. 在文中沒有提到。和選項 D. 相關的部分是第一段的「59% of Americans would rather watch games on TV than see it in person」，表示有 59% 的美國人寧願在電視上看比賽，而不是親自去看，符合選項敘述，所以 D. 是正確答案。

台灣廣廈 國際出版集團
Taiwan Mansion International Group

國家圖書館出版品預行編目（CIP）資料

新制全民英檢初級閱讀測驗必考題型 / 國際語言中心委員會，
許秀芬著. -- 初版. -- 新北市：國際學村, 2021.04
　面；　公分
ISBN 978-986-454-150-8（平裝）
1. 英語 2. 讀本

805.1892　　　　　　　　　　　　　110002009

國際學村

NEW GEPT 新制全民英檢初級閱讀測驗必考題型

作　　　者／國際語言中心委員會、　編輯中心編輯長／伍峻宏・編輯／賴敬宗
　　　　　　　許秀芬　　　　　　　　封面設計／何偉凱・內頁排版／菩薩蠻
　　　　　　　　　　　　　　　　　　製版・印刷・裝訂／東豪・紘億・秉成

行企研發中心總監／陳冠蒨　　　　　媒體公關組／陳柔彣
　　　　　　　　　　　　　　　　　　綜合業務組／何欣穎

發　行　人／江媛珍
法 律 顧 問／第一國際法律事務所 余淑杏律師・北辰著作權事務所 蕭雄淋律師
出　　　版／國際學村
發　　　行／台灣廣廈有聲圖書有限公司
　　　　　　　地址：新北市235中和區中山路二段359巷7號2樓
　　　　　　　電話：（886）2-2225-5777・傳真：（886）2-2225-8052

代理印務・全球總經銷／知遠文化事業有限公司
　　　　　　　地址：新北市222深坑區北深路三段155巷25號5樓
　　　　　　　電話：（886）2-2664-8800・傳真：（886）2-2664-8801
郵 政 劃 撥／劃撥帳號：18836722
　　　　　　　劃撥戶名：知遠文化事業有限公司（※單次購書金額未滿1000元需另付郵資70元。）

■ 出版日期：2021年3月　　　　ISBN：978-986-454-150-8
　　　　　　　2024年4月5刷　　　版權所有，未經同意不得重製、轉載、翻印。